THE
GOOD
FATHER

THE
GOOD
FATHER

NOAH HAWLEY

HODDER &
STOUGHTON

First published in Great Britain in 2012 by Hodder & Stoughton
An Hachette UK company

1

Copyright © Noah Hawley 2012

The right of Noah Hawley to be identified as the Author
of the Work has been asserted by him in accordance with the
Copyright, Designs and Patents Act 1988.

Grateful acknowledgment is made to King, Holmes, Paterno & Berliner, LLP
on behalf of Cinderful Music for permission to reprint an excerpt from *Today*,
lyrics and music by Billy Corgan. Published by Cinderful Music.

A CIP catalogue record for this title is
available from the British Library

Hardback ISBN 978 1 444 73036 4
Trade Paperback ISBN 978 1 444 73037 1

Printed and bound by CPI Group (UK) Ltd, Croydon, CR0 4YY

Hodder & Stoughton policy is to use papers that are natural, renewable
and recyclable products and made from wood grown in sustainable forests.
The logging and manufacturing processes are expected to conform to the
environmental regulations of the country of origin.

Hodder & Stoughton Ltd
338 Euston Road
London NW1 3BH

www.hodder.co.uk

For Kyle and Guinevere, proof that life is good

He bought the gun in Long Beach, at a pawnshop called Lucky's. It was a Trojan 9-mm. This is from the police report. The trigger mechanism was rusty so he replaced it, using a kit he bought on the Internet. It was May. He was still living in Sacramento, a squinty kid with chapped lips who spent his days reading about famous murders at the public library. Before that he'd lived in Texas, Montana, and Iowa. Nowhere for more than four months. Sometimes he slept in his car. There was a journey he was taking. Each mile brought him closer to an end.

The Trojan was one of three guns he'd purchased in the months leading up to the event. He kept them in the trunk of his car, an old yellow Honda the police would later find in a parking lot near the Staples Center in downtown Los Angeles. The odometer read 210,000 miles. He had done a lot of driving in the fifteen months since he'd left college. Sometimes he took odd jobs for cash: day labor, fast food, construction. He stayed off the grid. Everybody said the same thing: he was quiet, kept to himself, a little intense. This was later, after the multipronged investigations, the illustrated timelines documenting his journey, the painstaking reconstruction of each leg. Now there are bar graphs, books in progress. But in the early hours after the event, nobody knew anything. Who was this young man? Where had he come from? They say nature abhors a vacuum, but CNN hates it more. Seconds after the first shot, journalists were scrambling for context, rewinding the tape, analyzing angles and trajectories. Within hours they had a name, pictures. A young man, bright-eyed and milky-skinned, frowning into the sun. Nothing as damning as Lee Harvey Oswald brandishing his rifle, but

viewed through the lens of what had happened, the photos seemed pro-
phetic somehow, like Hitler's baby pictures. A feral glint in the eye. And
yet what could you see for sure? It was only a photo after all. The closer
you got, the grainier it became.

Like any event that can be called historic there is a mystery to the
details that remains impenetrable. Flashes of light. An echo unexplained. Even now, months later, there are holes, days that can't be
accounted for, in some cases whole weeks. We know he did volunteer
work in Austin, Texas, in August, the year before the event. Organizers
remember him as a bright kid, hardworking. Ten months later he was
working as a roofer in Los Angeles, fingernails black with tar, a skinny
man perched on sweltering shale, breathing the smoky air.

He'd been on the road for more than a year at that point. A rubber
hobo losing himself in the great American absence. Somewhere along
the way he changed his name. He started calling himself Carter Allen
Cash. He liked the sound of it, the feel on his tongue. His given name
was Daniel Allen. He was twenty years old. As a boy he had never been
attracted to the mindless aggression of men. He did not collect toy guns
or turn everything he touched into a weapon. He saved birds that had
fallen from their nests. He shared. And yet there he was in two-lane
Texas, test-firing automatics on a narrow gun range with cigarette butts
on the floor.

On clear May nights he would sit on motel-room floors and polish
his thoughts. He would handle the bullets, opening the box and letting
them crackle in his hand. He was a human arrow racing toward an
inevitability. The TV news showed images of politicians making stump
speeches in small-town diners and dusty midwestern farmhouses. It
was an election year, voters and candidates, pundits and money rushing
toward a great democratic surge. Primary season was almost over. Par-
tisan conventions loomed. Sitting on his motel-room floor, Carter Allen
Cash fantasized casting his vote with a bullet.

When he was seven he lived for the swing. He would pump his feet
and point his heels toward the sky, yelling *more, more*. He was a vora-
cious child, unstoppable, and so alive it made everyone around him
seem sickly and still. At night he would lie in a tangled heap on his bed,
clothes half on, his brow knit, fists clenched, like a twister that had run
out of air. Who was this boy and how did he become a man in a motel

room fondling bullets? What made him ditch his comfortable life and embrace an act of barbarity? I have read the reports. I have watched the footage, but the answer continues to elude me. More than anything I want to know.

I am his father, you see.

He is my son.

One

HOME

Thursday night was pizza night in the Allen household. My last appointment of the day was scheduled for eleven a.m., and at three o'clock I would ride the train home to Westport, thumbing through patient charts and returning phone calls. I liked to watch the city recede, the brick buildings of the Bronx falling away on the side of the tracks. Trees sprang up slowly, sunlight bursting forth in triumph, like cheers at the end of a long, oppressive regime. The canyon became a valley. The valley became a field. Riding the train I felt myself expand, as if I had escaped a fate I thought inevitable. It was odd to me, having grown up in New York City, a child of concrete and asphalt. But over the decades I had found the right angles and constant siren blare to be crushing. So ten years earlier I had moved my family to Westport, Connecticut, where we became a suburban family with suburban family hopes and dreams.

I was a rheumatologist—the chief of rheumatology at Columbia Presbyterian Hospital in Manhattan. It was a specialty that most people didn't recognize, concerned they'd guess with the watery eyes and phlegmy cough of a bad pollen allergy. But in truth, rheumatology is a subspecialty of internal medicine and pediatrics. The term "rheumatology" originates from the Greek word *rheuma*, meaning "that which flows as a river or stream" and the suffix -*ology*, meaning "the study of." Rheumatologists mainly deal with clinical problems involving joints, soft tissues, and allied conditions of connective tissues. We are often the doctor of last resort when patients develop mysterious symptoms involving most of the body's systems: nervous, respiratory, circulatory.

The rheumatologist is called to consult when a diagnosis remains elusive.

I was a diagnostician by trade, a medical detective, analyzing symptoms and test results, looking for the most pernicious diseases and intangible traumas. After eighteen years I still found the work fascinating and often took it to bed with me, mulling patient histories in the slippery moments before sleep, looking for patterns in the grain.

June 16 was a sunny day, not too hot but with the threat of New York summer in the air. You could smell the first wisp of humidity rising off the macadam. Soon any breeze would feel like the hot breath of a stranger. Soon you would be able to reach up and smudge car exhaust across the sky like oil paint. But for now there was just the threat, a slight smother, a trickle in the armpits.

I was late getting home that night. Afternoon rounds had taken longer than expected, and I didn't step off the train until close to six. I walked the nine blocks to our house through rows of manicured lawns. American flags hung from mailboxes. White picket fences, at once welcoming and prohibitive, ran beside me like the sprockets of a bicycle wheel, half seen from the corner of my eye. A sense of motion, of one thing being ticked off, then another. It was a town of affluence, and I was one of its citizens, a medical expert, a lecturing professor at Columbia.

I had become an MD in the era before the HMO, before the nickel-and-diming of doctors, and I had done well for myself. The money afforded certain freedoms and luxuries. A four-bedroom house, a few acres of hilly land with a weeping willow and a faded white hammock that swung lazily in the breeze. On these early evenings when the weather was warm I walked through the suburban quiet with a sense of peace, a feeling of accomplishment, not smug or petty but deep-seated and human. It was the triumph of a marathoner after a race, the jubilation of a soldier after a long war is over. A challenge had been faced and overcome, and you were better, wiser for the facing.

Fran was already working the dough when I walked in the door, rolling it out against the marble countertop. The twins were grating cheese and scattering toppings. Fran was my second wife, a tall redhead, with the slow curves of a lazy river. Turning forty had changed the quality of her beauty from the athletic glow of a volleyball player to a languid voluptuousness. Contemplative and sure-footed, Fran was a woman who thought things through, who took a long-term approach to problems. These were not qualities my first wife shared, prone as she was to impulse and the full roller coaster of emotion. But I like to think that one of my better qualities is that I learn from my mistakes. And that, when I asked Fran to marry me, it was because we were—for lack of a more romantic word—compatible in the truest sense of the word.

Fran was a virtual assistant, which meant she worked from home, helping people she'd never met schedule appointments and make flight reservations. Instead of earrings, Fran wore a Bluetooth earpiece, which she put in when she awoke and didn't remove until just before bed. This meant she spent large portions of every day conducting what appeared to be a long conversation with herself.

The twins, Alex and Wally, were ten that year. They were fraternal and not in any way similar. Wally had a harelip and a slight air of menace about him, like a boy who is just waiting for you to turn your back. In truth, he was the sweeter of the two, the more innocent. A miscoded gene had given him a cleft palate, and though surgery had mostly corrected it, there was still a quality to his face that seemed off-kilter, imprecise, vulnerable. His twin, Alex, fair-haired, comparatively angelic looking, had gotten into some trouble recently for fighting. It was a familiar problem for him, starting in the sandbox era as a willingness to battle anyone who made fun of his brother. But over the years, that instinct to protect had evolved into an irresistible need to champion the underdog—fat kids, nerds, kids with braces. A few months back—after being called to the principal's office for the third time that semester—Fran and I took Alex to lunch and explained to him that while we approved of his instinct to protect the meek, he would have to find less physical ways to do so.

"If you want these bullies to learn a lesson," I said, "you have to teach them something. And I guarantee, violence never taught anybody anything."

Alex had always had a quick wit and a sharp tongue. I suggested he sign up for debate classes, where he could learn to beat his opponents with words.

He shrugged, but I could tell he liked the idea. And over the next few months, Alex became the top debater in his class. Now he turned every request to eat his vegetables or help with the chores into an Aristotelian voir dire.

I had no one to blame but myself.

This was our nuclear family. A father, a mother, and two sons. Daniel, the son from my first marriage, had lived with us for a year during his sullen teens, but had departed as impulsively as he'd arrived, waking me one morning before dawn to ask if I could drive him to the airport. His mother and I had split when he was seven, and he had stayed with her on the West Coast when I had come east.

Three years after his brief stay with us, Danny, eighteen, had started college. But he dropped out after less than a year, climbing into his car and heading west. Later, he would say that he just wanted to "see the country." He didn't tell us he'd left. Instead, I sent a card to his dorm, and it came back unopened, with a stamp OCCUPANT NO LONGER AT THIS ADDRESS. This had been his way since childhood. Danny was a boy who never stayed where you left him, who popped up in unexpected places at unexpected times. Now he called infrequently; sent e-mails from Internet cafés in the flat states of the Midwest. The occasional postcard scrawled in a moment of summer nostalgia. But always at his convenience, not mine.

The last time I saw him was in Arizona. I'd flown in for a medical conference. Daniel was passing through on his way north. I bought him breakfast in a hipster coffee shop near my hotel. His hair was long and he ate his pancakes without pause, his fork moving from plate to mouth like a steam shovel.

He told me he'd been doing a lot of camping in the Southwest. During the day he hiked. At night he read by flashlight. He seemed happy. When you're young there is no more romantic conceit than freedom— the boundless certainty that you can go anywhere, do anything. And though it still bothered me that he had dropped out of college six months earlier, knowing him as I did, I can't say I was surprised.

Daniel had grown up traveling. He was a teenage gypsy, shuttled between Connecticut and California, living partly with me and partly with his mother. Children of joint custody are, by nature of the divorce settlement, independent. All those Christmases spent in airports, all those summer vacations shuffling back and forth between mom and dad. Unaccompanied minors, crisscrossing the nation. Daniel seemed to survive it without major trauma, but I still worried, the way any parent does. Not enough to keep me up at night, but enough to add a layer of doubt to each day, a nagging sense of loss, like something important had been misplaced. And yet he had always been self-sufficient, and he was a smart, likable kid, so I convinced myself that wherever he went, he was fine.

Last fall, sitting across from each other in that Arizona coffee shop, Daniel teased me about my coat and tie. It was Saturday, and he said he didn't see the point.

"It's a medical conference," I told him. "I have a professional reputation to uphold."

He laughed at the thought of it. To him all these grown men and women acting and dressing in a manner that society deemed "professional" was ridiculous.

When we parted I tried to give him five hundred dollars, but he wouldn't take it. He said he was doing good, working odd jobs here and there. He said it would feel strange carrying that much money around with him.

"It'd throw off the balance, you know?"

The hug he gave me when we parted was full-bodied and long. His hair smelled unwashed, the sweet musk of the hobo. I asked him if he was sure about the money. He just smiled. I watched him walk away with a deep feeling of impotence. He was my son and I had lost control of him, if I'd ever really had it. I was a bystander now, an observer, watching his life from the sidelines.

When he reached the corner, Daniel turned and waved. I waved back. Then he stepped into the street and I lost him in the crowd. I hadn't seen him since.

Now, in the kitchen of our Connecticut home, Fran came over and kissed me on the mouth. Her hands were covered in flour and she held them up the way I had held mine up a few hours ago walking into the ICU.

"Alex got in another fight," she said.

"It wasn't a fight," Alex corrected her. "A fight is where you hit someone and they hit back. This was more like a mugging."

"Mr. Smart Ass has been suspended for three days," she told me.

"I plan on being furious," I told them. "After I have a drink." I took a beer from the fridge. Fran had returned to the pizza stone.

"We figured pepperoni and mushroom tonight," she said.

"Far be it from me," I told her.

Apropos of nothing Fran said, "Yes, the seven-fifteen flight to Tucson."

Tucson? Then I noticed the blue light.

"Yes, he'll need a car."

I started to speak, but she held up a finger.

"That sounds great. Will you e-mail me the itinerary? Thank you." The blue light went off. The finger came down.

"What can I do?" I said.

"Set the table. And I'll need you to take it out in ten minutes. That oven still scares me."

The TV was on in the corner, playing *Jeopardy!* It was another ritual in our house, this watching of game shows. Fran thought it was good for the kids to compete with contestants on TV. I had never understood why. But every night around seven our house became a cacophony of barked non sequiturs.

"James Garfield," said Wally.

"Madison," corrected Fran.

"In the form of a question," said Alex.

"Who is James Garfield?" said Wally.

"Madison," said Fran.

"Who is James Madison?"

I had gotten used to the nightly confusion, looked forward to it. Families are defined by their routines. The pickups and drop-offs. The soccer games and debate clubs, doctors' appointments and field trips. Every night you eat and clean. You check to make sure homework is done. You turn off the lights and lock the doors. On Thursdays you drag the Toters to the curb. Friday mornings you bring them in. After a few years, even the arguments are the same, as if you are living out the same day over and over. There is comfort in this, even as it drives you mad. As a virtual assistant, Fran was militant about order. We were her family, but also her ground force. She sent us e-mails and text messages almost hourly, updating calendar events in real time. *The dentist appointment has been rescheduled. Glee club has been replaced by ice-skating.* Armies are less regimented. Twice a week in the Allen household we synchronized our watches like a special-ops team tasked with blowing up a bridge. The occasional annoyance this raised in me was tempered by love. To have married once and failed is to realize who you are in some deep and unromanticized way. The veneer of personal embarrassment about your weaknesses and idiosyncrasies is lifted, and you are then free to marry the person who best complements the real you, not the idealized version of you that lives in your head.

This is what led me to Fran after eight years of marriage to Ellen Shapiro. Though I had long thought of myself as a spontaneous and open person, I realized after my marriage to Ellen fell apart that I was, in fact, a creature of rigidity and repetition. I cannot stand living with uncertainty and forgetfulness. The bright-eyed, hippie ditziness that seemed charming in Ellen at first glance quickly became infuriating. Similarly, all the qualities that made me a good doctor—my meticulousness, my love of redundancy, the long hours I worked—proved to be qualities that Ellen found oppressive and dull. We took to fighting at every opportunity. It wasn't so much what I did or what she did. It was who we were. And the disappointment we voiced to each other was disappointment in ourselves for making such poor choices. This is the learning process. And though our marriage produced Daniel, it was a union best dissolved before any real damage was done.

I took a glass from the cabinet, poured the remainder of my beer into it. I was thinking about the patient who had kept me late at the hospital today, Alice Kramer. She had presented herself to me two weeks earlier complaining of leg pain. It felt like her legs were on fire, she said. The pain had started three months ago. A few weeks later she'd developed a cough. At first it was dry, but soon it became bloody. She had been a marathon runner, but now even a short walk exhausted her.

I was not the first doctor she'd seen. There had been an internist, a neurologist, and a pulmonologist. But a valid diagnosis remained elusive, and despite their best efforts, the weakness and shortness of breath had persisted.

Other than the cough she seemed healthy. Her lungs sounded clear. She had some mild weakness in her right hip, but her joints, skin, and muscle were all normal. The symptoms she presented with suggested that her illness involved the nervous and pulmonary systems. This was unusual. Could it be Sjögren's syndrome? This was a disease where the body's immune system mistakenly attacks its fluid-producing glands. Except patients with Sjögren's usually complain of eye pain and dry mouth, and she had neither of these.

Or maybe it was scleroderma, which is caused by an overproduction of collagen. The condition causes a thickening of the skin and can affect other organs of the body. I ordered blood tests. While I waited for them to return I went back over the patient's medical files. As the doctor of last resort it is the rheumatologist's job to reexamine every detail with fresh eyes. I reviewed her CAT scans and MRIs. On the chest CT, I saw faint cloudy patches on both lungs. By themselves they didn't mean anything. It was the context in which I read them that gave them meaning. Looking at Alice's film, another piece of the puzzle fell into place.

I'd ordered a lung biopsy. The pathology report showed evidence of inflammation. When the tissue came back I sat with the pathologist and reviewed the slides under a double-headed microscope. And there I saw the pivotal clue: a granuloma, a cell formation made up of groups of cells up to one hundred times the size of normal cells. They are found in the lungs only in a few diseases. The most common are sarcoidosis and tuberculosis. And since the patient showed no symptoms of tuberculosis, I was certain she suffered from sarcoid, a chronic disease characterized by tissue inflammation.

This afternoon when I told her I had a diagnosis, Alice had started crying. It had been months since the onset of her symptoms. She had been to dozens of doctors, many of whom had said her disease was all in her head. But it was my job to believe the patients who came to see me, to take pieces that didn't seem to match and solve the puzzle.

On TV, the game show was interrupted by a newscaster. Banner headlines. Crisis colors. None of us noticed at first. We were deep in the ritual of pizza. The dough was rolled. The cheese and sauce applied. Children were scolded for an overly liberal application of toppings.

"I'm no structural engineer," I told them, "but nothing round can hold up under that kind of weight."

Wally told us about what he'd learned that day. Frederick Douglass was a freed slave. George Washington Carver invented the peanut.

"I don't think he invented it," Fran told him.

"Discovered it?"

"I think you need to go back over your notes," I told him, finishing my beer and getting another.

Fran was the first to notice. She turned to the television and instead of toothy hosts and eager guests found shaky camera footage of some kind of rally.

"What's this?" she said.

We turned to look. On-screen were images of a political event in Los Angeles. We saw pictures of a crowd. Red, white, and blue banners hung on the walls. A presidential candidate stood onstage making a speech. The words were lost in the commercial mute of the TV. It is something the kids do when the ads come on, cutting the volume, letting the hucksters pantomime their sales pitches to the walls. As we watched the politician flinched, staggered back. Behind him two Secret Service agents pulled their weapons.

"Volume," said Fran.

"Where's the remote?" I asked, searching around.

It took precious seconds to find the remote, then many more to locate the mute button. All the while the children yelled at me to push this button or that one. When we finally got the volume working we heard the newscaster saying, ". . . reports of at least two shots fired by an unknown gunman. Seagram has been taken to a nearby hospital. No report yet as to the extent of his injuries."

On-screen the footage played again. The candidate onstage, the sound of shots fired from the crowd. This time the frames played slower, the camera pushing in.

"We are trying to find a better angle," the newscaster said.

I turned the channel. CNN had it. So did ABC and NBC.

"To repeat, thirty minutes ago Jay Seagram, a Democratic senator from Montana and the presidential front-runner, was shot by an unknown gunman."

Back on CNN we found a female reporter standing in front of a hospital. Wind whipped her hair sideways. She spoke with one hand on top of her head.

"Ted, we're hearing that Senator Seagram is in surgery. He suffered at least two gunshot wounds, one to the chest and one to the neck. No word yet as to his prognosis."

This is how it happens. There is nothing and then, suddenly, something. A family is making dinner, talking, laughing, and then the outside world muscles in.

Fran sent the kids into the living room. They were too young for this. She was upset. She had gone to Seagram's rally the last time he came to town. She had even gone so far as to stuff envelopes for him one weekend last month. He was young and handsome and spoke with authority. She had come to believe he was what she called "the real deal."

"Who would do such a thing?" she said.

As a doctor I knew that Seagram was in for a long night. Reporters said that the first bullet had punctured a lung and the second had severed the carotid artery. Paramedics had gotten him to the hospital quickly, but those injuries would cause extensive blood loss. The loss of blood would depress his circulation, hindering his already compromised breathing. It would take a skilled surgeon to fix the damage in time.

We ate pizza in separate rooms, everyone glued to their TVs. Fran sat at the kitchen table, typing on her laptop, scouring the Web for the latest rumors. In the living room the kids watched Disney pirates seeking adventure on the high seas, the whimsy of the score offsetting our hawkish watching of the news. Every few minutes I would wander in and make sure they were okay. This is what you do when crisis strikes, check on the people you love.

On TV a witness said, "I was watching and then, suddenly, blam blam blam."

Three shots? The news anchors had mentioned only two.

"Two hours," said Fran. "But you'll have to connect through Dallas." She was sitting at her computer trying to do two different things at once. Her Bluetooth earpiece was glowing. On her computer screen I could see the airline's website side by side with a real-time political blog.

"Turn on MSNBC," Fran told me, looking up from the computer monitor. I changed the channel. We arrived in time to see the event filmed from a new angle. Camcorder quality, shot from the far right of the stage.

"The footage you are about to see," said the anchor, "is quite graphic, and may be disturbing to younger viewers."

I checked to make sure the kids were in the living room. On-screen the camcorder zoomed in on Seagram's face as he spoke. The audio was shaky, homemade. This time the sound of the first shot made us jump. It sounded like the gunman was standing right next to the camera.

Onstage the senator stumbled, blood spurting from his chest. The cameraman turned, and for a split second we saw the gun elevated above the crowd. The gunman was wearing a white button-down shirt. His face was blurred by motion and chaos. People were screaming in the background, running. As we watched, the gunman turned and started pushing his way toward the door. A Secret Service agent jumped into the crowd, trying to reach him.

"Who does he look like?" said Fran. "An actor, maybe. Do you ever get that? That feeling that you've seen people before? Is it that they remind you of someone? Or maybe just déjà vu."

The camera swung wildly. Spectators grabbed the gunman. Agents and police reached him. They were lost to the camera.

I got closer to the TV, but rather than make things clearer it made them harder to identify.

"We are getting word," said the anchor, "that police have identified the gunman."

The doorbell rang.

Fran and I looked at each other. I reviewed in my head all the disasters of my life. The death of my father, a car crash in high school that required three separate surgeries, the demise of my first marriage, the deaths of every patient I had ever lost. I weighed them against one another. It was a warm spring night, and I was a man who had found contentment in life, happiness. A lucky man, who had come to expect good things. I wiped my hands on my napkin and moved toward the hall.

There were two men in suits at the door, several others on the lawn. I saw a series of SUVs parked at the curb, blue-and-red lights flashing silently.

"Paul Allen," said one of the men. He was tall, a white man with an impossibly close shave. There was a plastic-coated wire winding from his collar to his left ear. The man next to him was black, broad shouldered. He may have been a linebacker in a former life.

"I'm Agent Moyers," said the white man. "This is Agent Green. We're with the Secret Service. We need you to come with us."

The image I was seeing didn't make sense. The words he spoke.

"I'm sorry," I said. "Are you sure you have the right house?"

Fran crept up behind me and stood wide-eyed in the foyer. She had taken the Bluetooth from her ear. The orchestral narrative of Captain Jack Sparrow reached us from the living room.

"They're saying it's Daniel," said Fran. "The TV. They're saying he did it."

I looked at the Secret Service agents. They were affectless, steel-eyed.

"Mr. Allen," said Moyers, "we need you to come with us."

I felt like a boxer who had taken an uppercut he never even saw.

"Let me get my coat," I said.

I walked back into the kitchen, each step taken as if through water. I thought about the beers I'd had, the train ride home. I thought about the fences and the lawns and the neighbors I had known for years. How would they look at me now?

On television I saw a photo of my son. This is the speed of the world. Before you can even think, an action has occurred. It had been less than an hour since the shooting. Where had they gotten a photograph? It was one I didn't recognize. Daniel stood on a wide lawn in a sweatshirt and jeans. He was squinting against the sunlight, one hand raised to shield his eyes. He looked about eighteen. A college photo maybe. I remembered the day I dropped him off at Vassar, a skinny kid with all his belongings in a footlocker. A boy who had tried to grow a mustache at fourteen but ended up with only a few whiskers on each side of his mouth like a cat.

What have you done? I thought. But even as I thought it I didn't know if the question was meant for Daniel or for me.

I rode alone in the backseat of the SUV. The new-car smell fed my underlying nausea. Ahead of us was a lead car. A third SUV tailed close behind. We drove fast, sirens on, lights flashing. Agent Moyers and Agent Green sat in front. Moyers was driving. They said nothing for the first few minutes as we hauled ass through residential streets, taking the bumps at full speed, the SUV bucking like a horse.

I pictured Daniel the last time I'd seen him, the long hair, the bear hug, the final wave, and the feeling I'd had—like a man who is watching a movie he doesn't understand. Why did I let go? I should have dragged him to my hotel. I should have forced him to come home with me. A shower, a hair cut, a good meal. To be surrounded by family, people who love you, isn't that the deepest human need? Instead I'd watched him disappear.

"Is my son okay?" I wanted to know.

They didn't respond. I watched the houses of my neighbors recede in the fading light, lit warmly from inside. Families in their dens, feet up, listening to music, watching TV. Had they seen Daniel's picture yet? Had they made the connection?

"My son," I said. "Is he okay?"

"Your son has a bullet in his leg," said Agent Moyers.

"Which leg? Did it hit the femoral artery? Please. I'm a doctor."

Green turned in the passenger seat. I could see the earbud in his ear. It was colored to match the flesh of a white man. I wondered if this bothered him, that the world did not believe technological advances needed to be made available to people of his race.

"When Secret Service agents hear shots," said Green, "we stand up tall to try to make ourselves bigger targets."

The words didn't make sense to me, and for a moment I wasn't even sure he was speaking English.

"We attempt to draw fire away from our protectee," he continued. "If you watch the tape again, you'll see that this is what the agents were doing in Los Angeles. They ran *toward* the gunfire."

"Unfortunately," said Moyers, "your son was a good shot."

"Please," I said. "There must be some mistake."

Green turned away.

"We have been told to take you to a secure facility for questioning," he said. "This is the extent of our involvement."

"He's my son."

"Dr. Allen, your son killed the next president of the United States."

The words flared around me. I heard a steady droning sound, blood rushing in my ears.

"He's dead?" I asked.

Green looked out the passenger window, the blue-and-red lights of the lead car strobing cold, hot, cold, hot.

"We're taking you to a secure facility," he repeated.

"My family."

"Your family is safe," said Moyers. "Agents have been assigned to your house. In situations like these people are upset. They act without thinking."

"Situations like what?"

"Assassinations. Elections are about hope."

We were on the highway now, the blare of sirens drowning out the growl of the engine. The speedometer read 106 miles per hour.

"I'm sorry," I said, "did you just say elections are about hope?"

He didn't answer. I closed my eyes, took a deep breath. From my years in emergency medicine I knew that in order to think clearly in hectic circumstances, I needed to slow things down. Approach the problem in stages. As a scientist I had to stay clear, to put the facts together. I couldn't afford to get emotional. Emotions cloud the mind. They make you careless. I tried to review the facts. My son was in Los Angeles. He'd been arrested at a political rally and accused of shooting a senator. There was videotape, but none so far that showed his face. The gunman had fired two shots, maybe three, and then disappeared into the crowd. It was possible the police had made a mistake. That they'd captured the wrong man.

Racing down the highway I thought about the congresswoman in Phoenix. The one who'd been shot outside a supermarket. What was her name? Giffords? A sunny day in January. Card tables have been set up. *Come meet your representative.* A crowd builds. The congresswoman steps out into the sun, smiles and waves. She shakes hands with her constituents, and then a pale, moon-faced man steps up beside her and opens fire with a semiautomatic pistol, one bullet passing through the congresswoman's head at point-blank range. Six were killed. Thirteen injured by a Glock 9-mm that held more than thirty bullets.

I thought of the mug shot. Jared Loughner, twenty-two years old. It was everywhere in the weeks after the shooting. An eerie grin on the suspect's puffy face, like a fat kid who just won first prize at the state fair. There was something chilling about the image. The yellow glare of the camera flash giving his skin the jaundiced hue of an old bruise. His nearly bald head read unnatural, cancerous, misshapen. And on his face, an unblinking stare, one eye darkened by shadow, hovering over a Joker's grin. From the photo alone you could tell. This was not a sane person. He was a madman, a droog from *A Clockwork Orange.*

I tried to see my son in that way—a deranged assassin with a maniacal scheme—but my brain literally refused to make the connection. Danny was a normal kid from a normal home. Okay. The product of divorce, but isn't that considered normal these days? Fifty percent of all marriages end in divorce, and you don't see all those kids growing up to be lone gunmen. No. This was a mistake. And I would put it right.

"Listen," I said. "I demand that my son get medical attention immediately."

"With all due respect, sir," said Green, "fuck you and your son."

Those were the last words we spoke until we arrived at the secure facility.

Twenty-eight minutes later we pulled up outside a nondescript office tower in Stamford, Connecticut. A guard with a machine gun waved us through a gate. We came to a fast stop beside a rear entrance. Armed agents climbed out of all three SUVs, slamming doors with a sound like gunshots. The night was warm. The air smelled like French fries, the aroma wafting from a fast-food restaurant on the other side of the highway. Entering the lobby, we passed men in suits carrying assault rifles. We rode the elevator in silence, six men watching the LED numbers rise. Arriving on the fifth floor, I saw a mechanized hub, men and women in suits manning telephones, hunched over keyboards, navigating online chatter, collating data. There was an air of controlled panic. Men walked quickly, ties flapping. Women on cell phones hustled down hallways, carrying urgent faxes.

The agents steered me down the hall. Passing a conference room I saw a white board pasted with details of my son's life; all the information federal agents could draw together in two hours. The story of my family as cataloged by banks and federal databases. How surreal to see them there. Dates and events that, when we lived them, we called our lives, but to these men now, putting together the pieces, were just facts, data collected forensically. Anniversaries to be studied; decisions we had made, the places we had lived, the people we had known.

I saw pictures of Daniel, an arrest report, the black whorl of fingerprints. There were stills of the video images taken from the auditorium. Later I'd learn that this was how they'd identified him. Fingerprints had yielded a name, a recent arrest for vagrancy, an alias. A timeline had been started: my son's birthday, the dates of his schooling. There were yearbook photos, copied and enlarged. I saw all this in the time it took to walk ten feet.

From the command center I heard somebody say, "I don't care who her father is. Nobody leaves the hall without a thorough screening."

I was led into a windowless room and told to wait. There was synthetic tan carpeting on the floor and a sink hanging on the far wall. It was a strange thing to see in an office. A sink. *Was this where confessions were beaten out of men?* I wondered. It seemed silly to put carpet in a room that might see blood.

Sitting there I tried to assemble what I knew about the kinds of young men who took shots at public figures. Hinckley, Chapman, Oswald. The details of their crimes were fuzzy in my mind. Loughner was the clearest, being the most recent. I'd been as shocked as everyone else by the violence, had read the articles and watched the endless coverage. A twenty-two-year-old high-school dropout with a 9-mm bullet tattooed on his right shoulder, a burgeoning crackpot who railed against our currency. This was not my Danny. Loughner was a kid who once showed up at his high school so drunk they had to take him to the emergency room. A kid who wrote on Facebook that his favorite books were *Mein Kampf* and *The Communist Manifesto*. As a teenager he made people nervous by smiling when there wasn't anything to smile about. He was an angry young man who tried to enlist in the army but failed the drug test.

Sitting there I tried to find similarities between Loughner and my son. Did the kids at Vassar think Danny was creepy? Did my son make strange outbursts in the middle of class or verbally threaten the teachers who critiqued his schoolwork? If he did, I had never heard anything about it. I had visited the school several times, had met the dean. Danny's grades were average, his attendance adequate. Everything I knew told me that Danny was a normal student, hardly an overachiever but not a nut case.

Loughner, on the other hand, had been expelled from community college and told he wouldn't be welcomed back until he presented certification from a mental health professional that said he was not a threat. At twenty-two, the signs of mental illness were clear. He was evolving from a troubled teen into a full-blown paranoid schizophrenic.

Danny was a quiet kid, a little withdrawn, but no one had ever suggested he was mentally ill. The newspapers said that when Loughner walked into his local bank, tellers would put their fingers on the alarm button. He struck people as creepy, menacing. Loughner believed women should not hold positions of power. He told the tattoo artist who drew the bullet on his shoulder that he dreamed fourteen to fifteen hours a day. He said he could control his dreams.

That was not my son.

The night before he opened fire on the crowd at a political rally, Loughner took pictures of himself in a bright red G-string holding a Glock. When the cabdriver dropped him off at the supermarket the next morning, Loughner asked if he could shake the man's hand. And then he pulled a gun and began killing people.

This was not my boy.

Sitting in the cold fluorescent glow, I found myself getting angry. I was not intimidated by the authority of this place. I had faced death in all its forms. As a doctor I was used to being in control. The decisions I made saved lives. I would not be bullied by government bureaucrats. If Daniel had been shot, he must be treated. He was an American citizen. He had rights. I wished I had thought to call Murray Berman, my lawyer. Daniel should have representation immediately. I took out my cell phone, started to dial. The door opened. Moyers and Green entered accompanied by an older man in a gray suit. His gapped teeth were yellow from years of smoking.

"Mr. Allen, my name is Clyde Davidson. I'm the assistant director of the Secret Service. I am here to talk to you about your son."

"It's *Doctor* Allen."

"Of course. Dr. Allen."

"I'm told my son has been shot. I want to go on record saying I will not answer a single question until I'm certain he's receiving treatment."

Davidson sat, adjusting the crease of his trousers. He was a heavyset man with short white hair. At his age he should have thought about getting more exercise, losing weight. He should also quit smoking immediately. The human heart starts to congest after fifty. Arteries clog. The risk of stroke increases dramatically, the threat of cardiac arrest.

"Dr. Allen, a lot has happened very quickly. I think we both need to take a deep breath."

I studied him as if he were a resident fresh out of medical school.

"People say *shot in the leg*," I said, "like it's nothing. But a bullet literally crushes the tissue it hits. A high enough caliber can shatter the femur. A low-caliber bullet can ricochet off the bone and slice up into the bowel and abdomen."

Davidson looked at Moyers. Moyers nodded, spoke into his wrist. Davidson opened his hands in front of him in a gesture meant to be magnanimous.

"Your son will be treated immediately," he said.

"I want to speak to his doctor."

Davidson sat back, crossed his legs. "Dr. Allen, let me explain something to you. I can have the president on the phone in fifteen seconds. This is the level of my authority. When I say something will be done, it is being done as we speak."

I thought about this.

"There's no way Daniel did this," I said.

"We have video and still photographs. He was caught with a gun. Ballistics and fingerprint tests are outstanding, but rest assured, your son has been positively identified."

"He needs a lawyer."

"He's twenty years old. If he wants a lawyer he must ask for one himself."

I sat back, rubbed my temples. It was beginning to dawn on me that I was not in control here, that, in fact, I never had been. Control was an illusion, a luxury of the mind. If they were right, I had created a life, and that life had taken another life. The low-lying nausea I had felt for the last hour became a wave of sickness. I gritted my teeth against it.

"Have you ever heard your son use the name *Carter Allen Cash*?" Davidson asked.

"No. Who is that?"

"It's an alias your son has been using for the last six months. We still don't have all the details, but it appears he registered at motels in both Dallas, Texas, and Sacramento, California, using that name."

Carter Allen Cash. It sounded like a country singer.

"We call him Daniel or Danny," I said.

"When was the last time you spoke with your son?"

"I don't know, three weeks ago, maybe. He was on the road. I bought him a cell phone last Christmas, but he lost it."

"You and his mother are divorced. Is that correct?"

I rubbed my eyes.

"We separated when Danny was seven."

"He went to Vassar College."

"For a while. He dropped out last spring without telling us."

"Would you say you were close to your son, Dr. Allen?"

I checked his tone for traces of sarcasm but found none. For a moment I saw myself through his eyes: an absent father who had not seen his son in months, had not spoken to him in weeks. A man who was too busy building his résumé to be a father.

"Agent Moyers said the senator died of his wounds," I said.

"About thirty minutes ago. The first bullet punctured his aorta as well as his lung. Dr. Harden did everything he could."

"I know Dr. Harden. He's a good surgeon."

"Not good enough," said Moyers. Davidson silenced him with a look.

I thought about what Seagram's insides would have looked like. A bullet enters the human body like a sledgehammer. Once punctured, the chest cavity filled quickly with blood, compressing the lungs, suffocating its victim. And if, at the same time, his heart were also compromised, Seagram never had a chance.

"His wife," I said.

"Rode with him in the ambulance. His two children are at home in Montana."

Two children; Neal, ten, and Nora, thirteen. I had seen pictures of them on the news. They would grow up now without a father, children who slept with photographs of the dead under their pillows.

"What's going to happen to my son?" I asked.

"That depends," said Davidson. "Officially your son is a terrorist."

"He's what?"

"Political assassination by definition is an act of terror. This gives the federal government great leeway in terms of punishment and prosecution."

He paused, letting me process this. *When does a criminal act become an act of terrorism?* I wondered.

"You should know," I said, "that the publisher of *The New York Times* is a patient of mine."

If Davidson was impressed by this, it didn't show.

"If we choose," he said, "we can have your son classified as an enemy combatant. He can be tried in a military court. We can control his access to legal counsel. He could be held, if not indefinitely, then at least for several years without a hearing."

"I won't let you do that."

"It's sweet," said Davidson, "that you think you could stop us."

We stared at each other.

"Luckily for you," he said, "this administration needs a victory. Too many terror-cell prosecutions without positive outcomes. Not enough evidence, groups arrested before a crime was committed. Conspiracy to commit what? Here we have witnesses. We have video. There is a smoking gun and a dead senator. This is our slam dunk."

Looking at him, I caught my first glimpse of the scope of this event. A presidential candidate was dead. Danny was accused of his murder. In a split second my son had become public property. A tool to be used for political gain, an effigy to be burned. He was no longer a child to most people, no longer even human. If I didn't act quickly, my boy would become a slave to history.

"My point," said Davidson, "is don't worry about Daniel. Or should I call him Carter? It is in our best interest to keep him safe and well."

Slow down, I thought. *Stay cool.*

"The last time I checked," I said, "in this country a man is innocent until proven guilty."

Davidson shrugged.

"There are questions we're trying to answer," he said. "Who were your son's friends? Why did he go to Texas? Why Sacramento? Was he meeting his handler? We need to know whether your son was working as part of a team."

"I don't know," I said. "The last time he called me he said he was in Seattle."

"As far as we know," said Davidson, "your son has never been to Seattle."

By the door, Moyers put his finger to his ear, came over, and whispered something to Davidson.

"Interesting," said Davidson, "it seems your son volunteered for the Seagram campaign in Austin, Texas. Did you know that?"

I didn't. I knew nothing about my son, apparently.

Moyers whispered something else to Davidson. He stood.

"Excuse me," he said.

They left me alone. My jaw was tight. I had sweated through the armpits of my shirt. There was a metallic taste in my mouth. I could hear the nasal hum of the fluorescents overhead, mixed with the dim buzz of chatter from the war room outside. I tried to picture my son holed up in some interrogation room, a crude tourniquet around his leg. He would be answering questions to the barrel of a gun, surrounded by angry men with bruised knuckles. If I thought about it too long I felt faint. Had it really been three weeks since we'd last spoke? Worse, it may have been five. There was an ache in my side. Is it possible my Danny had shot a senator?

In medicine, when grave errors are made, hospitals hold a morbidity and mortality conference. At Columbia these meetings were held on Thursday afternoons at five. Attendance was mandatory. There, all the botched cases were presented. An emergency tracheotomy. An accidental overdose of pain medication. We reviewed the patient's symptoms, the chronology of events. We weighed the choices that surgeons and residents made. We looked not to assign blame but to learn from our mistakes. This was the only way we could improve. As doctors we knew it was only a matter of time before each one of us made a fatal mistake. It was the nature of our business. Thousands of patients treated in the course of a career, thousands of life-or-death decisions. How could you possibly get them all right? The M&M conferences were considered privileged under the law. Nothing said there could be used in a court of law. How could we punish others for crimes we ourselves commit every day? This was why only the grossest negligence was ever punished at hospitals. We took our failures as an opportunity to learn.

Sitting in that room I allowed a shred of doubt to sneak through my resolve. What if he'd done it? What if they were right, and my child was a murderer? Why would he do such a terrible thing? Was it political? Was he sick? Or was it my fault? His mother's? Had we broken him, ruined his childhood in some deep and profound way? There were too many questions, too many miserable combinations. As quickly as the door opened, I slammed it shut.

Slow down, I thought. *Think it through*. There weren't enough facts yet to make a diagnosis. I needed to see Daniel. I needed to review the evidence. Until I could see the whole case, all I knew for sure was that my son was in the crowd, and now he was in custody. I would get to the bottom of it. I was the man who took nothing for granted, who showed no bias, who didn't let his emotions get in the way. Until the authorities showed me undeniable proof my son was guilty, I would remain objective. I would collect the facts and form a studied conclusion. This was the case I'd been training for my entire life.

It would be months before I knew the whole story.

There is a quality some politicians have. A grandeur. They seem to fill whatever space they're in. People have said this about Jack Kennedy. They have said it about Ronald Reagan and Bill Clinton. These men (and they are usually men) bring an intensity and focus to every interaction, no matter how mundane. Friends of mine who have met Clinton remark that they have never spoken to anyone who hung on their every word the way he did, who focused with such totality on what was, to be fair, a slight encounter, brief and inconsequential. His attention overwhelmed them, flustered them, put them at the center of a miraculous universe, if only for a second. It left them wanting more.

Jay Seagram was a character like this. He had been a federal prosecutor before entering politics, a crusader who believed that all crime should be punished, whether committed by an individual or a corporation. The child of a single mother, he grew up poor. He won his first Senate seat when he was only thirty-four. He was six foot one and handsome. He had the smile and he had the voice, that Baptist pulpit swell. From years of jury trials he understood that his delivery was just as important as his message. In his six years in the Senate, he'd risen to the top of the Democratic leadership. He was always quick with a joke, a man who relaxed the people around him. In a room full of empty smiles his was a stare of substance. And in January 20__ when he announced his candidacy for the presidency it was as if a switch had been flipped all over the country, like all the lights on a city straightaway turning green at once.

There was buzz. There was hope.

Many people around the nation, Democrat and Republican alike, felt that our country had lost its way. They believed that the administration was filled with liars. In the last few years, political discourse had turned snarky and barbarous. We were a nation of enemies, vengeful and disenfranchised. Into this climate of distrust, Seagram emerged, a character without guile. A candidate who said what he meant, who fought his battles in the open.

Voters looked at Seagram and saw a man who had married his high-school sweetheart, Rachel, a sensible brunette with kind eyes who now chaired the Red Cross. There was love in their eyes when they looked at each other. Photos in the newspaper invariably showed them absently holding hands or stealing a kiss. But theirs was a family that had survived tragedy. Their first child, Nathan, had drowned at the age of six, falling through thin ice during a family vacation in Vermont. Afterward, Seagram had taken to his bed for three weeks. He didn't bathe. He didn't shave. He wouldn't eat. When he emerged from his grief, he had decided to run for public office. As he described it, he felt a powerful need to give something back.

In the Senate he became known as the "charity" senator. The bills he sponsored were primarily dedicated to eradicating poverty at home and abroad. He said he would not rest until he had ended childhood starvation in the inner cities. But he was still a prosecutor at heart, and as a result he was not soft on crime or the threat of foreign aggression. He had voted time and again to expand funding for the military, but always insisted on tacking on a provision that earmarked funds and services for veterans. He believed in planning for the future, not just addressing the woes of the present.

Personally, I'd been on the fence about Seagram. It worried me to have a litigator in the White House. As a doctor, I believed that the glut of malpractice lawsuits over the last two decades was the real reason health care had become so expensive in this country. Afraid of being sued, doctors performed unnecessary tests and procedures. We let patients dictate their treatment, hoping to keep our insurance premiums low. I was also concerned that Seagram would raise taxes once he came to power. He had never used the words, but in the spring of 20__, the American economy was still struggling, and Seagram went on TV calling on Americans to "take responsibility," which had always been code for accepting a greater financial burden.

I'd be lying, though, if I said the man's rhetoric and demeanor hadn't appealed to me. In a sea of milquetoast candidates, Seagram had the spark of greatness, the charisma of a political giant. And I, too, was hungry for some kind of reform.

As the election season deepened, there was little doubt that Seagram would be the Democratic nominee. He had swept the Iowa caucus and the New Hampshire primary, had won handily on Super Tuesday. He was a candidate that liberals and moderates—Democratic and Republican, young and old—could feel good about. And so it was he flew into Los Angeles on the morning of June 16 to take meetings with campaign donors and deliver a speech before an audience of college students on the UCLA campus.

His wife came with him. She slept on the flight, her head in his lap. Their two children were home in Helena. It was a school day. Seagram would speak to them via Internet camera moments before going onstage. Later an aide, who was in the room, would describe the scene to a packed congressional hearing. The senator's children were boisterous, joking. His daughter, Nora, told Daddy he looked tired. His son Neal read him a sonnet he'd written for class.

He said, *Dad, hey Dad. A cow and a squirrel are eating ice cream. The cow says, Like it? I made it myself. The squirrel says, I don't even want to know how you got the nuts in there.*

Seagram laughed. He said he would be home in the morning, and they would go to the park. *I love you very much*, he told them.

At three fifteen, after an introduction from a celebrated Hollywood actor, Seagram took the stage to a standing ovation.

He was forty-six years old.

My watch read 9:45 p.m. I had been sitting alone for almost thirty minutes. I took out my cell phone, dialed. Murray answered on the second ring.

"Murray, it's Paul."

"My God," he said. "The news."

"Listen, I need you to call someone in L.A. Danny needs a lawyer."

"It doesn't make sense," said Murray. "There are so many Republicans to shoot. Why this guy?"

Murray had represented me on two medical malpractice lawsuits. His firm drafted my will and handled my real estate dealings. He was fifty-one, silver-haired, recently divorced. Now he wore mock turtlenecks and boots with his suits. He drove a Porsche. He chased girls young enough to be his daughter.

"He needs a lawyer," I said. "He's been shot. I'm not convinced they're treating him."

"I'll make some calls, but a thing like this—"

"The Secret Service came to my house. I'm in an office tower in Stamford. They put me in a room with a sink. What do you think it means?"

"Don't say another word. I'm getting in the car. My coat is already on."

"I don't know the address. It's somewhere near Green Street."

"I have a guy I can call. I'll be there in forty-five minutes."

"I'm going to call Alverson," I said.

There was a pause as he thought about this.

"If I were him, I wouldn't go anywhere near this. Call Ken Sunshine. You're going to need a publicist."

"No."

"Bubby, listen to me. Your son just shot the most popular man in America."

"He's innocent."

"In court, but not in the press. Right now he's the forest they can burn. There are going to be reporters following you around for months, maybe years. Press conferences. They're going to blame you for everything. You need counsel. And if Danny's going to get out of this without getting a lethal injection, we'll need a sympathetic jury."

I thought about this. Months of news vans camped out on the lawn, of cops asking questions, of death threats and hate mail. It was overwhelming.

"Get him a lawyer," I said.

I hung up, dialed the house. Fran answered on the second ring.

"Paul," she said. "Are you okay?"

"I'm fine. How are the kids?"

"They're upstairs peeking through the blinds. There are reporters from Spain on the lawn."

"Spain?"

"From everywhere, CNN, NBC, the BBC. There are so many lights on it looks like nine a.m. outside."

"Stay indoors. Don't say anything. I called Murray. He's on his way."

"The TV is saying Danny was shot by a police officer. They showed blood on the carpet in the auditorium."

"He was shot in the leg. I'm working on it."

I could hear fear in her breathing. We had been together for twelve years. I knew every inch of her.

"Ellen called," she said. "Your first wife."

"I know who Ellen is."

"She wants you to call her."

"Not now. I have to deal with this."

"People have been calling the house."

"People we know?"

"Some. Some we don't. They don't have very nice things to say."

"Don't answer the phone. I'll send you a text on your cell when I know something."

"I love you."

"I love you, too."

I hung up. In the address book on my phone I found the number for Dean Alverson. Dean had been a patient of mine for close to a decade. He suffered from rheumatoid arthritis. His wife and Fran had become friends and we saw them socially from time to time.

Dean had been undersecretary of state under Bill Clinton. He was retired now after a long and distinguished diplomatic career, but if anyone could help me reach my son it was him.

He answered on the first ring.

"Paul," he said, "I can't talk to you."

"He's my son, Dean. I need to know if he's okay."

"He shot a presidential candidate. I assure you, he is being taken care of."

Not good enough. Every minute that passed took Daniel farther away into some deep dark bureaucratic labyrinth.

"I need more than that," I said. "They're calling him a terrorist. He needs a lawyer. He needs a fair chance. There's no way he did this thing. My son was a liberal Democrat. He belonged to Greenpeace. For Christ's sake, he worked for the guy in Texas. Does a kid like that shoot a Jay Seagram?"

There was silence for so long I worried we'd been disconnected.

"Stay by the phone," Alverson told me, and hung up.

Jay Seagram wasn't the first politician to be killed on a warm June evening in Los Angeles. On June 5, 1968, Robert Kennedy was gunned down in the kitchen of the Ambassador Hotel. It was a few minutes after midnight. He had just won the California primary, and his future as president of the United States seemed assured. Onstage he said, "So thanks to all of you, and it's on to Chicago, and let's win there." Leaving the stage, Kennedy was led through a nearby pantry and into the ballroom's kitchen. A small, dark-haired man stepped in front of him and said, "Kennedy, you son of a bitch." He fired a .22-caliber pistol repeatedly. Kennedy was shot three times: twice in the torso, once in the head.

His attacker was wrestled to the ground by bystanders that included the football player Roosevelt Grier and the writer George Plimpton. Plimpton would later recall that the young man had "enormous, peaceful eyes."

At Good Samaritan Hospital, Kennedy received blood transfusions. Doctors performed an emergency tracheotomy, then operated on his brain to remove as much of the bullet as possible.

He died twenty-four hours later.

In custody, Kennedy's assassin refused to give his name. "I wish to remain incognito," he said. He talked about the stock market and asked philosophical questions about the nature of justice. The suspect was described as "dark-skinned" and "curly-haired." Some said he was Filipino, others Mexican or Cuban. He was later identified by his brother Adel after a still photograph was shown on television. Kennedy's killer was named Sirhan Sirhan. He was a Palestinian immigrant, born in

Jerusalem. The fifth son of nine children, Sirhan had immigrated to America at the age of twelve. He was a self-professed anti-Semite and a hater of Israel. He had attended John Muir High School and Pasadena City College. For a short time he had worked at a racetrack in Santa Anita and at a local Pasadena health-food store.

After he was identified, police went to his residence, where they found a detailed notebook containing incriminating statements. In a journal entry dated May 18, 1968, Sirhan wrote:

> My determination to eliminate R.F.K. is becoming more and more of an unshakable obsession . . . R.F.K. must die . . . R.F.K. must be killed . . . Robert F. Kennedy must be assassinated before 5 June 68.

Having been raised with a hatred of Israel, his beliefs about the Jews had become increasingly paranoid in the months leading up to the assassination. "The Jews are behind the scenes wherever you go," he said. He confessed that he was not "psychotic . . . except when it comes to the Jews."

Sirhan's father was a domineering man who had been physically abusive. In 1957, a year after he brought his family to America, he abandoned them and went back to Jordan. Sirhan was thirteen. He never saw his father again.

After the assassination, friends said that Sirhan Sirhan had often expressed admiration for Adolf Hitler and his "solution" to the Jewish problem.

Ten years after his father left, on June 5, 1967, Israel and Egypt went to war. Jordan, which had signed a mutual defense treaty with Egypt, attacked Israel from the east. Six days later Israel had gained control of the Sinai peninsula, Gaza Strip, West Bank, and Golan Heights. Egypt and Jordan had lost a war they had no right losing.

That fall Sirhan, unemployed, spent most of his time at the Pasadena public library reading extensively about the Six-Day War. He read the *B'nai B'rith Messenger* so he could keep track of what he called "Zionist intentions." His anger was like an animal he raised in his bedroom, feeding it, nurturing it, helping it grow.

On May 26, 1968, Robert Kennedy made a speech at a Jewish temple in Portland, Oregon, supporting the sale of advanced fighter planes to Israel. One week later, on June 4, 1968, Sirhan saw an advertisement announcing a march down Wilshire Boulevard to commemorate the first anniversary of Israel's victory in the Six-Day War. It was a "big sign, for some kind of fund, or something . . . a fire started burning in me . . . I thought the Zionists or Jews or whoever it was were trying to rub it in that they had beat hell out of the Arabs."

At his trial Sirhan said "that brought me back to the six days in June of the previous year . . . I was completely pissed off at American justice at the time . . . I had the same emotionalism, the same feelings, the fire started burning inside me . . . at seeing how these Zionists, these Jews, these Israelis . . . were trying to rub in the fact that they had beaten the hell out of the Arabs the year before . . . when I saw that ad, I was off to go down and see what these sons of bitches were up to."

After extensive interviews with Sirhan, psychiatrist Dr. George Y. Abe described his political thoughts as irrational. Sirhan, he said, had "paranoid-inclined ideations, particularly in the political sphere, but there is no evidence of outright delusions or hallucinations."

Defense psychiatrists claimed Sirhan suffered from paranoid schizophrenia and was in a dissociative state at the time of the assassination. The prosecution argued that Sirhan's repeated written exclamations that "R.F.K. must die" showed premeditation and planning.

At trial, Sirhan testified that his feelings toward Robert Kennedy turned to hate when he saw television reports of RFK participating in an Israeli Independence Day celebration. Asked by his lawyer, Grant Cooper, if anyone had put it in his mind that Robert Kennedy was a "bad person," Sirhan said, "No, no, this is all mine . . . I couldn't believe it. I would rather die . . . rather than live with it . . . I have the shock of it . . . the humility and all this talk about the Jews being victorious . . ."

In April 1968, two months before the assassination, Sirhan spoke of his hatred for RFK to an African American garbage worker he'd befriended. Alvin Clark testified under oath at the trial about Sirhan's desire to shoot Kennedy.

According to Clark, Sirhan said he'd heard a radio broadcast in which "the announcer said Robert Kennedy was at some Jewish Club or Zionist Club in Beverly Hills." Kennedy had said, "We are committed to Israel's survival. We are committed to defying any attempt to destroy Israel, whatever the source. And we cannot and must not let that commitment waver." Sirhan left the room putting his hands on his ears and almost weeping.

According to one of his lawyers, after the broadcast Sirhan "was disturbed that both his mother and his brothers did not see Senator Kennedy as the same destructive and malevolent and dangerous person as Sirhan perceived him to be; and I gather that he and his family . . . had some arguments about this."

On June 5, 1968, exactly one year after the Six-Year War broke out, Sirhan Sirhan went to the Ambassador Hotel. He waited in the kitchen for Kennedy's speech to end. And then, as Kennedy made his way through the pantry, Sirhan took an Iver Johnson eight-shot .22-caliber pistol out of his pocket, stepped in front of him, and fired.

These are the facts. And yet if Sirhan Sirhan was standing in front of Kennedy, how did he shoot him three times in the back?

Murray arrived at ten thirty. I heard him yelling in the hall. After a few minutes the door opened and Moyers escorted him in.

"Get your coat," he told me.

We rode the elevator in silence. When I tried to speak, Murray put his finger to his lips.

The temperature had dropped a few degrees, enough for me to shiver as I crossed the parking lot to his car.

"There's a myth," said Murray, "that Secret Service agents take a blood oath where they swear to lay down their lives to protect our president. In truth, there's no such oath."

We climbed into his Porsche. I buckled the racing harness.

"With your car I always feel like I'm climbing into a fighter plane," I told him.

He put the car in gear, pulled out of the gate, throwing a middle finger at the guards.

"Here's the latest," he said. "I talked to the Department of Justice. They sent me to Homeland Security. I called Homeland Security and they said, 'Call the Secret Service,' so I called a guy I know at the FBI. He says they're holding Danny at a facility in downtown Los Angeles. He has been treated by a paramedic but has not been to a hospital. As far as my guy knows, the bullet is still in his leg."

"He could lose the leg, Murray."

"Calm down. Then I called another guy I know at CBS and leaked the story that the Secret Service is denying Danny treatment. They're going to run it on the eleven o'clock news."

Looking down I noticed a red stain on my shirt. Had I cut myself somehow? But then I remembered the pizza, Fran and I hunched over in front of the TV, eating. It felt like two hundred years ago.

"My buddy also said they have still photographs of Danny pulling the trigger," said Murray. "No way it wasn't him. For what it's worth."

I couldn't believe it. This was a boy who'd cried over the death of a neighbor's cat. Until I saw the picture myself, I refused to believe he'd been anything more than an innocent bystander.

"Somebody set him up," I said.

Murray raised his eyebrows as if to say, *I'm sure you're right.* But I could tell he didn't believe it.

As a clinician I asked myself, what did this photograph show? My son with a gun, or my son *firing* a gun? They were two very different things. He was a boy in a crowd. An assassin fires at the stage. There is a struggle with spectators. My son gets caught in the middle. He ends up with the gun. Is it likely? No. But it is possible, and in my business it is the unlikely that shows itself time after time to be true.

Two years ago I'd had a patient who came into the hospital complaining of chest pains. Tests showed an inflammation of the pericarditis. He complained of weakness and loss of appetite. His CBC and ESR were elevated, as was his blood pressure. The resident who saw him diagnosed classic heart disease and called in a cardiologist. For two weeks they treated him as a heart patient, and his condition got progressively worse. After noticing signs of livedo reticularis on his arms and legs, the original doctor called me in.

We reviewed the symptoms together. Then I spoke with the patient. He told me that a few months earlier he had contracted hepatitis B. When his kidney function test came back with a BUN greater than forty milligrams per deciliter I knew that the problem wasn't his heart. The patient suffered from polyarteritis nodosa, which is a disease of unknown cause in which immune cells attack a patient's arteries. We treated him with prednisone and cyclophosphamide, and he began to improve immediately.

Every doctor who saw him swore the problem was his heart. But in medicine you have to look past the easy assumptions. The facts can be misleading. There is a tendency to recognize only the symptoms that add up to the diagnosis in your head, but it is the symptom that doesn't fit you should be following.

We drove north on I-95. My cell rang. I answered. It was Dean.

"You're booked on a flight from JFK to LAX. It leaves in an hour. Can you make it?"

I looked at Murray.

"JFK," I said.

Murray swerved across three lanes of traffic, took the exit at fifty, blew a stop sign, made a U-turn, and merged back onto the highway going the opposite direction. My heart was somewhere in my armpit.

"They've taken Danny to Cedars-Sinai Hospital," said Dean. "In the morning they'll move him to a federal penitentiary, and then it will take weeks to see him. I have assurances that if you arrive before then you will be allowed to see him."

"Thank you, Dean."

"Keep my name out of this," he said. "I've spent my life serving the Democratic Party. The last thing I need is the press to get hold of this."

"I'll take it to my grave," I said.

"Well," said Dean, "maybe not to the grave. None of us should carry anything that far."

We made JFK with fifteen minutes to spare. Dropping me off, Murray said he would drive straight to my house. He told me he would protect my family as if they were his own. In his eyes I could see him calculating the billable hours. To reach the terminal we had to pass through three security checkpoints. Murray was told to pop the trunk, not once but twice. One of the officers explained that Homeland Security had raised the threat level from yellow to red.

"'Cause that kid shot the senator," he said.

That kid. Already the story was taking hold. It had a hero and a villain. How long before my son's life was beyond saving?

Inside, the terminal was a chaotic, bubbling cauldron of madness. A bug-eyed hysteria had gripped the crowd. Armed guards and soldiers were everywhere. Modern air travel had already become a metaphor for the refugee experience. Tonight there was an added sense of desperation to our flight. We, the nation's travelers, were Africans chased into the desert by drought, Albanians running toward tent cities, hounded by the deafening whumpa of bombs. We were herded together clutching our things, menaced by men with guns. We stripped off our clothes, passed through scanners, our every possession analyzed, our bodies wanded by humorless men in uniform, watched over by soldiers and bomb-sniffing dogs. We showed our travel documents, our IDs, praying our names had not made it onto some kind of list.

As the father of the country's most notorious gunman, I knew it was just a matter of time before I was recognized, before men in white shirts with automatic weapons pulled me aside and escorted me into the dark bowels of the machine. But bureaucracies are notorious for their slowness, their incoherence. And so, though I waited to be pulled aside, I passed through every checkpoint with little more than a second look. In fact, it would be weeks before my name made it onto any kind of watch list, a fact that would serve as both a relief and a caution for all the implications it carried about our government's true ability to keep us safe.

I flew to L.A. nonstop, the 747 punching its way through the jet stream. Dean had booked me a first-class ticket. There were warm nuts and a pillow for my neck. I tried to sleep, but my head was too busy with thoughts of my son. Being on an airplane brought back memories I had long tried to suppress. Memories of fear and grief. Memories of panic and guilt. Daniel had almost died on an airplane when he was eight. It was on a flight to Los Angeles from New York. It was the first year of my divorce from his mother, and he had visited me for Christmas. As usual he flew alone, entrusted to the care of busy flight attendants. At the airport he had been paired with another child, a young girl, also traveling between divorced parents for the holidays. Jenny Winger. Jenny had turned eleven one month earlier. The kids sat together in the middle of the plane, Daniel in the window seat, Jenny by the aisle.

I had often wondered what these flights were like for my son. I suppose I had romanticized them in my mind: picturing a young boy on his own, enjoying an adventure. Though separation had been difficult, I liked to think that I was helping my son become a world traveler, that as a result of his parents' divorce he would reach his teens mature beyond his years. When other parents criticized me for shipping him off, I would point out how much more self-sufficient my son was becoming than their coddled brood. And wasn't that what we, as parents, were supposed to do? Prepare our children as best we could to function on their own in the outside world?

This particular flight was early in our divorce. Possibly even Daniel's third solo trip. If he had ever been scared by these airport adventures, he had not shared it with me. It was a night flight, leaving New York around six. The skies were clear over JFK, but storms had been gathering over the Midwest for days, pounding the region with heavy rain, sleet, and snow. I took Daniel to the airport in a cab, paying the driver to wait. I walked Daniel through security and all the way to his gate, where a flight attendant checked us in. I told her that my son was flying alone, that I wanted to make sure he got to Los Angeles in one piece. The flight attendant pointed to Jenny, who sat alone, watching the flashing lights of the tarmac through the large plate-glass window. The flight attendant said children often traveled better in pairs. She winked at Danny. Maybe he'd even end up with a girlfriend.

I was single myself back then, a divorced man with a conflicted hunger for women, and I have to admit that I studied the stewardess's profile when she turned. I noted the tightness of her skirt, the multiple piercings in one ear—which indicated a rebellious streak, a slight hint of sexual anarchy. She was young and busty and blond. She laughed easily. I mentioned I was a doctor, and that my son was going to visit my *ex*-wife. The attendant told me she would take extra-special care of Daniel. She gave his shoulder a squeeze.

On the plane Daniel had a Sprite and some animal crackers. He had a backpack stuffed with clothes, games, comic books. Anything I could think of that might keep him occupied for the long flight. The movie on the flight was *Titanic*, an odd choice for a mode of transportation fueled by prayer and the suspension of disbelief. It was over Ohio that the turbulence hit, a great sudden jerk, like the plane had dropped off a ledge. After the first jolt the captain put on the FASTEN SEAT BELT sign and instructed flight attendants to take their seats. He tried to find a smoother altitude. A second jolt hit the plane, then a third. The fourth jolt opened several overhead compartments, loosing luggage. Drinks spilled. A passenger was struck in the head by a woman's laptop. This was when the first scream rang out.

Outside the windows, passengers could see lightning strikes. Rain buffeted the wings and fuselage. My son sat alone in a plane full of strangers. The lights flickered and went out. The plane's electrical system had shut down. In the cockpit warning sirens came on. The plane started an uncontrolled descent, a free fall. What must that feel like? To fall from the sky? The terrifying, weightless plunge. The violence of speed. An airplane without propulsion tumbles like a mountain through space. In the main cabin, the screams multiplied. People began to shout and beg.

In the cockpit, the captain fought to bring the plane out of its dive. He knew he had seconds to correct the situation before the plane and all aboard were lost. His first officer had frozen. Without electrics, the captain knew he would never keep the plane in the air. His only chance was to turn everything off and restart the engines, hoping that this would reset the electrics. It was an insane risk. Once off, the engines might not restart. The ground was, at most, seven to ten minutes away. But the captain was out of options. Every second that passed they lost more and more altitude, descending into the heart of the storm. So the captain barked orders to his crew. He said a little prayer, and then he reached over and turned off the plane.

In the main cabin my son sat gripping his armrests. He was eight years old. For his last birthday we'd had cake from Carvel and played racing games at the arcade. The icing from the cake stained his lips blue, like a corpse, turning him into a tiny, pale-faced zombie. Danny thought it was funny and I agreed. I was used to the look of death. I wasn't superstitious about it. I knew the difference between a living child with sugar-blue lips and a corpse.

For his birthday, Daniel had gotten a skateboard from his mother, a science kit from me. He seemed happy. He appeared untroubled by the fact that his mother and father couldn't stand each other. That they needed to put three thousand miles between them in order to have a civilized conversation on the phone. He went to bed that night with sticky fingers, still in his clothes, long after his bedtime. He was happy, he said. But was that true? Or had he already begun to tell me what I wanted to hear?

Now, twenty-five thousand feet above Ohio and dropping, my son clung to the armrests of a dead airplane, falling like a ball of paper tossed into a garbage can. In the cockpit, the captain counted to fifteen, then flipped the switches to restart the engines. For a brief moment nothing happened. His prayers went unanswered. The crew and passengers were all dead. Then the port engine roared to life, followed by starboard. The electrical system flickered, once, twice, and came back on. He had power. The captain and first officer, working together, pulled the plane out of its dive. The world stabilized. The screaming in the main cabin slowly stopped, and cheers of disbelief rang out.

Did my son cheer? Did he feel relief? Did he cry? A small child all alone in the face of death. Did he vomit or urinate in his pants? I saw the story on the news later that night, a plane that had lost power over the

Midwest. Heart in my throat, I called his mother, who said that Daniel seemed fine. The plane had landed on time, and when she asked him how the flight was he said, "Long." I sat up all night crying, consumed by thoughts of my only son dying. My poor boy. No one should have to face that kind of fear alone.

I thought of him now, handcuffed to some hospital bed, a bullet in his leg, arrested for a crime he could not have committed. Was this fear worse? Did the perspective of age make the fear of death greater? In this respect, maybe, the child has the advantage over the man. And yet what father wouldn't want to protect his son from all fear, to hide from him the truth about death? After that flight, I had vowed never to send him off alone again.

In the months that followed, we tried to get Daniel to talk about what happened, his feelings. But he was never interested. The most he ever admitted was that it had been "scary" when the plane went into a dive, but that he had stayed busy trying to keep Jenny from "freaking out too bad." How heroic he had seemed to me at that moment, a boy who stayed calm under pressure, who thought of others first. I was proud of him, and felt in some ways rewarded for having raised such a strong, unflappable child.

But now, sitting in first class, flying into the unknown, I wondered if something else might have happened on that cross-country flight. Something tectonic. In the face of certain death had my son come face-to-face with the notion of abandonment? Had he, as the plane fell, understood in some deep-seated way that he was on his own in this life, that his parents, who were supposed to protect him from the dangers of the world, had instead thrown him into the void? Did something in this eight-year-old boy harden at that moment, something that was still meant to be soft and hopeful? Was a worldview born of that event, one that separated my son from the only people in the world he was supposed to feel close to? Was this why he had dropped out of school and taken to the road? Was this why he never called, never wrote? Was that the moment I had lost him?

And if it was, how could I have been too blind to see it?

It was three a.m. when I landed at LAX. The smut of car exhaust greeted me as I exited the terminal. Outside the airport I hailed a cab and gave the address to the driver. We rode in silence through city streets awash in yellow gloom. I had done my residency here in the eighties, at Saint John's Health Center in Santa Monica. It's where I met Ellen, at a party thrown by a fellow resident. She was the green-eyed girl on the balcony, smoking a joint. I was the second-year resident who'd been up for thirty-six hours straight. I still wore my scrubs.

"No one told me it was a costume party," she said.

"No," I said. "I'm a doctor."

She had the body of a girl who knows how to get into trouble.

"I bet you practice saying that in the mirror," she said.

She offered me the joint. I shook my head.

"Well, I'm not a doctor," she said, "but I am a hypochondriac."

"A match made in heaven," I told her.

Ellen was a photographer who worked in a clothing store. She had grown up in a communal-housing complex in Berkeley, eating flaxseed and carob, and celebrating martyrs of the Workers Party, until her father, Bertrand, left her mother, Molly, for the Hennessy sisters, proving once and for all that "free love" was just another way for men to follow their pricks.

Ellen ended up living with her newly single mother in a condo in Glendale. She was nine. They ate Crunch bars for breakfast and watched daytime TV in marathon sessions of disillusioned sloth. Ellen's mother showed little interest in finding work or encouraging her daughter's education. At least twice a week she invented reasons to keep Ellen home from school because she didn't want to be alone.

Believing herself to be an artist and a spiritualist in the same vein as Gertrude Stein, Molly encouraged her daughter's artistic side. But the lessons she taught were of whimsy, not hard work, and as a result Ellen never developed the kind of doggedness and perseverance that artists need to make it in the modern world. Without discipline, Ellen became the kind of person who waits endlessly for the right mood to strike, who battles a constant sense of failure and irrelevance. She was a dreamer, not a doer, and though that quality was attractive to me at first, I quickly came to find it maddening.

During my residency I lived in a cottage by the beach. On the rare mornings when I was home I would run on the sand, letting the waves break against my ankles. Ellen moved in after two months. She said it was the only way she'd ever see me. I used to stumble home asleep with my eyes open. Ellen would run me a bath, get me a drink, and pour me into bed. It seemed to suit her, this sensual nurturing. But the feeling didn't last. She spent too much time by herself, haunted by the ghost of a depressed mother. As an only child her feelings of loneliness were pathological. If she hadn't gotten pregnant, I doubt we would have lasted a year.

My taxi pulled up in front of Cedars-Sinai Hospital at 4:15 a.m. I had spent the flight picturing this moment. Danny was upstairs, scared, wounded. Between us was the titanic weight of the federal government and our own reluctant history. Would he be happy to see me? Relieved? Or would he view this as just another incidence of his father arriving too late? Whatever the failures of the past, I would fix them now. My son was going to survive this. He was going to thrive. There are times when all men have to pick up a banner and charge into battle. This was mine. The more my son became a villain to others, the more he would become a cause to me. His vindication would be my grail.

I paused outside the hospital to straighten my rumpled suit. As a doctor I knew that family members were often brushed off by medical personnel, trivialized. Given the high profile of the case it seemed best to enter the situation as Paul Allen, doctor, instead of Paul Allen, worried father.

Inside the lobby a young man in a blue suit stood up. He put a photograph in his pocket.

"Dr. Allen," he said. "I'm David Tolan from State. Our friend sent me."

I nodded, shook his hand. Dean was a good man. I felt bad that he'd risked so much for me. My hands were trembling. Now that I was here I had no idea what I would say to my son. I had talked to hundreds of patients in dozens of hospitals. I always knew just what to say, even if it was to pass on a death sentence. But this? What could I say that would possibly matter?

"Is he okay?"

"I'll let the doctor tell you," said Tolan, "but they got the bullet out and he seems to be resting comfortably. Or as comfortably as you can rest when you're handcuffed to a bed."

We rode the elevator alone.

"I have cleared your visit with the Secret Service," said Tolan. "They are doing this as a courtesy to State. You will have ten minutes with your son. No longer. Anything he says that illuminates the crime we would ask you to share with us, but I won't be surprised if you don't. The one condition of your visit is that you keep it secret. If you tell the press that we let you see your son, we will deny it."

I nodded.

"I want to tell the senator's wife how sorry I am," I said.

"She won't take your call. After today, don't be surprised if no one will. Your name is now mud."

My mind was racing. What would Danny look like? What would he say? I considered the phrase *your name is mud*. I knew that it came from Dr. Samuel Mudd, the Civil War–era surgeon who set John Wilkes Booth's broken leg after he assassinated Abraham Lincoln. For helping Booth, Mudd was tried as an accomplice and jailed. His name became a symbol of disgrace, disgust.

As we rode in silence I realized I was still trying to press the wrinkles out of my suit. I wished I had a tie. I had gone to prep school, where we were taught that our appearance was our calling card. *If I had a tie*, I thought, *I could handle anything*.

"Dr. Allen," said Tolan just before the elevator doors opened, "no offense. But if your son did this I hope he gets the chair."

The north tower's fifth floor had been emptied of patients. Danny had the whole wing to himself. I saw Secret Service agents standing at the nurses' station, manning the exits. There were several Los Angeles police officers mingled with nurses and doctors, and men in suits I assumed to be Secret Service or FBI. I pulled my jacket tighter to cover the stain on my shirt, feeling small in that moment, outnumbered and outmatched.

"I'd like to see my son's chart," I said.

Tolan spoke to one of the Secret Service agents. He told me to raise my arms. I was patted down and then wanded. I handed over my cell phone and pager, my wallet and keys, belt and shoelaces. They didn't want me passing anything to my son he might use to harm himself or escape. When they were done, Tolan approached accompanied by an older man in a white lab coat.

"This is Dr. Coppola," he said.

I offered my hand. Coppola thought for a moment before shaking it.

"I read your article on fibromyalgia last year," he told me.

I nodded. He handed me Danny's chart.

"Your son presented with a bullet wound to the left thigh. The bullet was lodged next to the femur, close to his femoral artery. He also had multiple contusions to his face and arms, obtained I assume from the police's efforts to subdue him."

I felt anger, but I let it go.

"Bleeding?" I asked.

"Minimal," said Dr. Coppola. "I was able to remove the bullet and sew up the wound using only a local. We'll watch him for infection, but in my opinion he should be walking around in a few days."

I felt relief. And then panic. With his physical condition taken care of, the worries became less practical.

"Who shot him?" I wanted to know.

"We don't know for sure," said Tolan. "No law enforcement officer on the scene reports firing their weapon. The early reports we're hearing is that in the struggle, Danny's gun went off and the bullet struck him in the leg."

Danny's gun. The words sounded ridiculous. My son hated guns. He hated hunters. He had been a vegetarian for two years in high school.

"So you're saying he shot himself," I said.

"Right now that's our theory."

Convenient, I thought.

"Has he asked for a lawyer?" I said.

"As far as I know," said Tolan, "your son hasn't said a word since his arrest."

I looked at their faces. I could see it in their eyes. They all thought he had done it. He was a monster, and I, as his father, was at best a sad, pathetic man, and at worst a parent guilty of almost criminal negligence. Monsters don't just become monsters, after all. They are forged in a laboratory of abuse and neglect. And who else is to blame but the parents? Even Tolan, who had shown the most sympathy, was careful not to stand too close.

"I want to see him," I said.

Tolan spoke to a Secret Service agent. And then, at 4:37 on the morning of June 17, I was taken to see my son.

The day after Robert Kennedy was killed, conspiracy theories about his murder started to bubble up like toxic oil from the ground. His brother Jack had been shot four years earlier and allegations had been flying for months about multiple shooters, railroad hoboes, and Cuban hit squads. Just two months before the RFK shooting, Martin Luther King Jr. had been assassinated by a sniper with a Remington Gamemaster 760 as he stood on the balcony of a Memphis motel. James Earl Ray had been captured, but no one was convinced he had acted alone.

It was in this climate that the news of RFK's assassination emerged. Even though he had been killed in a crowded kitchen with dozens of witnesses, even though the event, though not filmed, had been captured on audiotape, no one could believe that this solitary, diminutive Arab had killed America's golden boy. Kennedy was a figure of controversy, after all. He had waged a long and public war with J. Edgar Hoover, the notorious head of the FBI. He had spent his years as U.S. attorney general under his brother's presidency prosecuting the Italian Mafia. He was a marked man. He had enemies. This much was clear.

Questions arose quickly. The gun taken off Sirhan Sirhan was capable of firing eight shots, but some witnesses swore there were at least ten shots fired. Then there was the location of the wounds. Kennedy had been shot twice in the back, at a spot just under his right shoulder blade. Both shots originated from a low angle, the bullets traveling upward. The third wound was to the back of the head, the bullet entering just under his right ear and penetrating up through his brain. Witnesses all put Sirhan Sirhan in front of Kennedy. How then had he managed to shoot him in the back?

Then there was "the girl in the polka-dot dress." Several witnesses had claimed to see her and a man exiting the hotel moments after Kennedy was shot. Sandra Serrano, a campaign worker who was sitting on a fire escape outside the Ambassador Hotel, recalls a girl in a polka-dot dress running out of the hotel yelling, "We shot him!" Serrano said the girl was with two men.

Vincent DiPierro, a waiter at the Ambassador Hotel, recalls seeing a girl in a polka-dot dress next to Sirhan Sirhan prior to the shooting.

Melvin S. Hall, a cabdriver, claimed to have picked up a girl and two men outside the hotel moments after the shooting.

Booker Griffin, a campaign organizer, described seeing a tall man and a girl in the kitchen prior to the shooting.

The list goes on. What does it mean? In medicine we are taught to create a differential diagnosis, a laundry list of possible causes for the symptoms with which the patient presents. We are taught to organize a patient's history: his chief complaint, associated symptoms, past medical history, relevant social data, past and current therapies. These criteria help us diagnose illness, but every symptom a patient presents with is not necessarily connected to his underlying illness. Sometimes they are peripheral. The doctor's job is to review all the data and determine which symptoms are relevant and which are irrelevant.

A kitchen full of people, men and women alike. A girl in a polka-dot dress. She leaves the hotel with two men. Witnesses hear her yell, "We shot him!" But it's possible that instead she said, "They shot him!"

Dr. Thomas Noguchi, the Los Angeles coroner, examined Kennedy just hours after the shooting. He removed one intact bullet and several fragments from Kennedy's body. Three forensic pathologists from the Armed Forces Institute of Pathology and two city coroners witnessed the autopsy. In his report, Noguchi wrote that the shot that killed RFK "had entered through the mastoid bone, an inch behind the right ear and had traveled upward to sever the branches of the superior cerebral artery." The largest fragment of that bullet lodged in the brain stem.

A second shot entered through Kennedy's armpit and exited through his upper chest at a fifty-nine-degree angle. The coroner wrote that Kennedy's arm must have been raised at the time.

A third shot penetrated one and a half inches below the previous one. It came to rest in Kennedy's neck near the sixth cervical. This is the bullet that was found intact.

A fourth bullet hole was found in Kennedy's jacket.

The shot that killed Kennedy—the one that entered the back of his neck, fragmenting upon impact and lodging in his brain stem—was fired so close that it left thick powder burns on the skin. Noguchi estimated that the shot was fired at a range no more distant than one and a half inches. But Sirhan Sirhan stood at least a foot and a half in front of Kennedy.

Eight shots fired. Three hit Kennedy. The gunman stands in front of him. He is shot in the back. How is this possible? Perhaps the first shot missed him and he turned to escape. The subsequent shots hit him in the back. What is the symptom? What is the disease?

Conspiracy theorists are quick to mention Thane Eugene Cesar, who was hired at the last minute to be Kennedy's bodyguard. He was a man in a uniform with a gun holstered at his side, reported to have been leading Kennedy by his right arm at the time of the shooting. He is known to have owned a .22-caliber pistol. Was he carrying it the night of the assassination? Did he draw this pistol after Sirhan started shooting and shoot Kennedy from below three times? If this is the case, then who was Cesar really working for?

The case against Cesar is pure speculation, and he, of course, denies having any involvement in Kennedy's death. But the coincidences are provocative, and start the gears of an analytical mind spinning.

A patient presents with a seizure disorder. His blood pressure is low. He has been having headaches recently, and his right foot is swollen. As a doctor you must decide: Are these all symptoms of the condition causing the seizure? What if you learn the patient has gout? This explains the swelling but not the seizures. Discount the swelling, reexamine the remaining symptoms. The key to a successful diagnosis is to find the pattern in a sea of camouflaging factors.

A girl in a polka-dot dress. A security guard hired at the last minute. An eight-shot pistol. An audiotape that seems to have recorded at least ten shots. What is relevant? What is irrelevant? To make the proper diagnosis you must put aside your own prejudices. You do not, after all, fit the symptoms to the condition. You fit the condition to the symptoms. Your own beliefs are not an issue. Your ego. It is a question of science. Of fact.

This is how I was trained to think. To diagnose an illness, a doctor creates a clinical decision tree. Arrows branch from the patient's major symptom to his other symptoms, his lab results, and family history. Is there a fever or not? Have other family members suffered similar symptoms? Ultimately following the branches to the end should result in the correct diagnosis and the proper therapy. In reality flesh-and-blood decision making relies on pattern recognition. With enough experience a doctor learns to recognize diseases. He relies on instincts. From the moment a patient walks in, the doctor is already considering a diagnosis, and then as questions are answered and test results received, that diagnosis is refined. These types of doctoring shortcuts are called "heuristics."

But shortcuts can be dangerous. This is why diagnostics is such a tricky game. If you are too literal, you might not make the imaginative leap needed to find the underlying disease. But if you are too intuitive, you might discount important criteria.

A patient presents with a deadly illness. It is a determined and canny hider. Undiagnosed, the patient will die. He has already been hospitalized. His health is failing. As a specialist, I must review the data—blood tests, X-rays, MRIs. There will be dead ends, scientific misdirects. New symptoms will appear making old diagnoses instantly impossible. As his doctor I cannot give up. The harder the disease is to diagnose, the harder I must work, the more creative I must become.

This is how a good doctor becomes great.

This is how I will discover the truth of what happened.

Danny was handcuffed to the bed. This was the first thing I noticed. The cuffs slid along the metal rails of the bed with the sound of a shower curtain being drawn. Open, closed. Open, closed. He was sitting up, his eyes raised to the ceiling-mounted television. His face was bruised. There were scratches on his cheek, and the skin around his left eye was starting to darken. The white button-down shirt he wore was torn and speckled with blood. He was watching the Weather Channel, as if it possibly mattered what the weather was anywhere in the world. As if he was a regular Joe who wanted to check his morning commute. But Danny's outdoor days were over. Soon he would be a creature of small rooms, of cold, unforgiving surfaces—metal and concrete—spaces that were easy to clean, to squeegee free of blood and shit and piss. The only weather he experienced would be internal—great storms of remorse or anger moving across his central plains.

There was a Secret Service agent sitting by the bed. When David Tolan led me into the room, the agent stood.

"Ten minutes," he said, walking past us.

I stepped into the room. Tolan, remaining in the hall, closed the door behind me. For the first time in months I was alone with my son.

My mouth was dry. I thought of Danny's birth. Six pounds, ten ounces, big blue eyes. I pushed this away. They were cheap thoughts, easy tears. Now was not the time for heartbreak. This was a rescue mission.

"I'm trying to get you a lawyer," I said.

He didn't say anything. On TV a perky weatherman with a spray-on tan told us what the week held in store for Cincinnati and the surrounding region.

"I'm going to see your mother after I leave here," I said. The blinds were closed, the fluorescents flattening every shadow. I had stood in a thousand hospital rooms talking to a thousand patients. But this time I didn't know what to do with my hands.

He shifted on the bed, the cuffs rattling against metal rails.

"This is the only channel I could find where they weren't showing it over and over," he said.

I nodded. *It. Showing it.* As if the thing he was accused of doing was an inconvenience ruining his prime-time viewing experience.

"A public event," I said. "Hundreds of students with cameras, reporters, cameramen from local and national media outlets. There will be new footage for months, photographs."

On TV the weatherman said, "High winds in the Plains states, possible funnel clouds."

"Do you think you could get me another blanket?" he said.

I tried to meet his eyes, to find some connection, but he kept his eyes glued to the screen, as if somehow the weather held the key to understanding his predicament.

In a closet I found a thin cotton throw. I put it over him. I didn't know what to say. There wasn't language to address a tragedy of this size. It was an event so big as to block out the sun. New words needed inventing, new idioms and phrases. And yet I should just ask him. Straight-out. He would tell me the truth, wouldn't he? I was his father. But I couldn't. Part of me didn't want to know.

"Have you eaten anything?" I asked.

He shook his head. I went to the sink and washed my hands thoroughly. I dried them on a paper towel, then crossed to him and checked the bandage on his leg. It was something concrete to do. An act of medical routine I hoped would ground me, take the race out of my heartbeat.

"The wound looks good," I told him. "Just a few stitches. You might not even have a scar."

He smiled without teeth.

"That's too bad," he said. "I'll probably need a few scars where I'm going. Scars and a sock full of pennies."

He was a skinny kid, average height, handsome. What did convicts in prison movies call the pretty ones? A chicken.

"They told me you spent some time in Austin," I said.

"I went all over," he said after a moment. "The mountains, the desert. It really is an amazing country."

You loved the landscape so you shot a politician, I wanted to say. But I didn't. There was no room for sarcasm in this place. Besides, he was innocent. I would will it to be true.

"Danny," I said.

"It's Carter now," he said.

"I don't know that person," I said. "But I know Daniel Allen. I know my son. I know he's not a man who could do a thing like this. Shoot someone. I know that. I know it. Just tell me what happened. A man stands next to you. He pulls a gun. He fires a few shots. You wrestle the gun away from him just as the cameras turn. Things like that happen all the time."

Did they? Even as I said it, it sounded crazy. We lived in a world of instant images. A shot was fired and the gunman was captured on film. Where was the room for error?

We shared a moment of silence. Tomorrow would be a hot day in Oklahoma and parts of the Southwest. Rainstorms were expected in Portland, Oregon.

"I don't want to talk about it," he said.

"What does that mean?" I said. "You have been arrested for the murder of a senator. He was going to be president. Now is the time to talk about it, to bang the table and shout you didn't do it."

He watched the weatherman.

"I'm tired," he said.

I sat carefully on the edge of the bed. Between us I felt the weight of so much history. I was the father who had divorced his mother when he was seven. I was the absent dad, the one who had missed birthday phone calls, who had forgotten to send presents. I was the weekend dad, the summer-vacation dad. I was the hypocrite who said *Don't do drugs*, who told him not to get too serious about the girls of his youth, to play the field before he got married. I was the kind of dad you talk about in therapy. What did he owe me? Why should I expect a straight answer?

"We don't have time," I said. "Ten minutes. You heard him. Give me something. Something I can tell your mother. Something I can tell the kids. Say you didn't do this and I will fight to my dying breath to get you off."

He turned to look at me. His left eye was half shut. There were flecks of dried blood under his nose.

"What if I did do it?" he said. "Would you still fight?"

I heard the words, but my brain was slow to distinguish them. *What if I did do it?* It was as if he had asked *What if the sun were made of ice? Or What if rain fell up instead of down?* Was such a thing possible—a universe in which my son could commit murder?

No. It seemed clear that this was a test. He was testing the unconditional nature of my love, looking to affirm once and for all that I was his father, constant, unyielding. We had been close once and had lost touch, and he was testing me to see if I was still his father.

"Yes," I said, "of course. You're my son."

He thought about this. I could see from his face that he wasn't sure he believed me. Then he laid his head back against the pillow and closed his eyes.

"I'm tired," he said again.

I tried to take his hand, but he jerked it away from me.

"I'm sorry," I said.

He didn't speak. I reached out to touch his face.

"I'm sorry," I repeated.

The door opened. Tolan stood there with two Secret Service agents. Their expressions said it all. It was time. I thought about fighting, about grabbing my son and refusing to let go. *Send me to prison,* I thought. *Let me take his place. I will do the time. It's my fault.*

I looked at Danny. His eyes were open and he was staring at the agents in their suits, handguns holstered at their sides. Then he looked at me, and shrugged.

"Too late," he said.

I met Ellen at a diner in Malibu. She had told me on the phone not to come to her house. She said camera crews were set up on her lawn. She would sneak out the back, climb a neighbor's fence, and slip down through the canyon. It was eight o'clock in the morning. I sat in a booth near the back, watching surfers bob on the ocean. I couldn't get Danny's face out of my mind. On the table in front of me were the day's papers. *The New York Times* had dedicated most of the front page to the story. The banner headline read SEAGRAM ASSASSINATED. GUNMAN WOUNDED, IN CUSTODY.

I scoured the article looking for incongruities, details that didn't add up. I wrote down the names of the witnesses who were quoted. Jane Chapman, eighteen, said she was standing behind a man in a white button-down shirt who fired three shots at the stage, then turned and ran. She didn't see his face. Oscar Delroy, twenty-two, said he heard the shots and saw a man in a white shirt pushing through the crowd toward him. Other students and faculty members were still being questioned by federal agents when the paper went to press. I assumed there would be more facts tomorrow. More photographs would emerge.

On page eight there was a diagram of Royce Hall. It showed the spot onstage where Seagram had been standing, and the place in the audience where people said Danny was standing. How had he gotten a gun into the auditorium? That was the question. Everyone who attended the event had passed through a metal detector. Since Phoenix, security for politicians had increased dramatically. More agents, longer advance times, no open-air appearances. And yet it wasn't enough.

Somehow the men with guns still found a way. A congressional hearing was being organized. Politicians on morning shows were demanding answers.

I read each article twice. There were facts here, but not enough. I needed to see the underlying police files, the classified reports. I needed to read the witnesses' statements, to watch every foot of film. Surely somewhere in the sea of evidence there was one detail that would prove my son was innocent.

Ellen came in. She was wearing a hooded sweatshirt, a baseball cap, and sunglasses. Diners turned to look at her, assuming she was a famous actress appearing incognito. She slid in across from me. I hadn't seen Ellen in more than five years. Her curly brown hair was long now. It looked like she'd had some work done; frown lines removed perhaps, a chin lift.

"Jesus Christ," she said, and then ordered a double espresso. "This fucking kid."

"He didn't do it," I told her.

"I know. I'm just saying. When he was small I couldn't get him to kill a fly."

"I saw him," I told her.

"Bullshit," she said. "The Secret Service won't even talk to me."

"They had him at Cedars. He had a bullet in his leg. He's okay. Banged up, but okay."

She took off the sunglasses. Her eyes were red. She had been crying. It was unlike her. When we were married I never saw her cry. She was like a Green Beret.

"He called me last week," she said. "He said he was coming to L.A. I told him to stay with me. But he said he was going to stay with a friend."

I seized on this. A clue. A name.

"What friend?"

She shrugged.

"I said, 'Call me when you get to town.' But he didn't. Is he okay? It's killing me not being able to— I'm his mother. They should . . . it should be a law. You get to see your mother."

She rubbed her eyes. I had left California when Danny was seven, moving to New York. From that moment on, Ellen had become his parent in a way that I would never again be able to claim. Yes, I visited my son and he visited me. A weekend here. A summer. Christmas vacation. We spoke on the phone every week. But Ellen took care of him. She clothed him and fed him and got him to school. She took his temperature when he was sick and kissed his bruises. I was a voice on the phone. A letter in the mail. I was "Daddy," the idea of a parent, a myth to deify or vilify.

Ellen and I had tried to keep the divorce as amicable as possible. Neither of us wanted to drag Danny through the minefield of our ruin. But it wasn't easy. Ellen felt betrayed and abandoned. In the months leading up to our separation she had become demanding and needy. She wanted me home more. She felt like a single mother, she said. And I took offense at that, felt attacked, harangued. The move to New York was as much about putting some distance between the two of us as it was about a career opportunity. I told myself it was short-term. That I would come back to California in a year or two.

"I promise," I told Danny. "I'm not going to disappear on you."

But in New York the short-term position became a long-term career. I took on more responsibility at the hospital, became a lecturing professor at Columbia. In New York I felt challenged, fulfilled. And then I met Fran, and we fell in love and got married. And suddenly the idea of moving back to California began to seem foreign and outdated. It was a resolution made by a different man in a different life.

Still, I was religious about calling Danny every week, about flying him out for long weekends and vacations. Fran treated him like a favored nephew, trying to make him feel welcome, even as our new family grew to include two more boys. When Danny was in town I would take time off work. We'd go to the park, the circus. I wanted him to want to come back. I wanted him to feel like Dad's was the place he went to get a fair deal.

Back in L.A. Ellen went through a series of bad relationships. It seemed like she was always trying some new fad diet or completing the steps of a self-help regime. She went from working for a costume designer, to working for an entertainment lawyer, then back to school for landscape design.

If I can just get organized, she would say. *If I could just catch a break. If I can just lose ten pounds, and stop dating the wrong men. But nobody wants to be with a single mother. It's easier for men. Single fathers are sexy. Single mothers are Medusa. One wrong look and you're stuck forever.*

I paid for Danny to go to private school, paid for guitar lessons and a new digital camera when he decided (for ten minutes) that he wanted to be a photographer. Because I felt guilty for leaving him, I took my son's side in every argument between him and his mother. I didn't have much love for his mother, so it was always possible to convince me that she was wrong and he was right.

And yet now I wonder: Maybe if I'd supported her none of this would have happened. Maybe if I hadn't bad-mouthed her, hadn't undermined her authority, hadn't done any of a thousand things I'd done as a father, then Danny would be a normal twenty-year-old kid finishing his sophomore year at Vassar, instead of an indicted felon coming off a yearlong road trip. So many maybes. Was this what the rest of my life would be made of? Endless nights spent building alternate histories, running simulations, looking for a way out of the maze?

The year Danny moved in with us, Fran and I worked overtime to make him feel included, make him feel part of the family. But Danny wasn't used to the formality of family life, the group dinners and weekend activities. He shared the same dynamic with Ellen that she had shared with her mother—that of inmates occupying the same cell. It was a relationship based on informality, on "friendship." Ellen wanted more than anything for Danny to be her buddy, her partner in crime. This had worked in his younger years, but as he reached adolescence Danny rebelled. His mother's funkiness began to seem like craziness, and so he fled to New York to see what being part of a real family felt like.

Inside the diner, I felt a sudden wave of exhaustion settle over me. It was just a taste of the ocean of sorrow that was waiting for me, a tidal wave of emotion rising on some dark horizon, coiling, marshaling its power, poised and ready to rumble forward, destroying everything in its path. I stirred my coffee, trying to ignore it. I needed to stay focused, to keep my mind sharp.

"We have to find out who he was staying with."

"I'm sure the FBI already knows," she said. "Isn't that what they do?"

I sipped my coffee. I had been awake for more than twenty-four hours. When I called home an hour ago, Fran said Murray was sleeping on the couch, and Ken Sunshine was in the kitchen drawing up a media strategy. I told her to keep the kids home from school.

"Let them play all the video games they want."

Ellen's espresso came. She drank it.

"He's okay?" she said, her voice small.

I nodded. She started to cry again. I considered reaching out and touching her hand to comfort her, but I didn't. This was the wife who had slept with a waiter and two surf bums while I was on my surgical rotation.

"How's Harvey?" I asked. Harvey was her boyfriend. They sent out a Christmas card together last year. He wore a red sweater with Santas on it. Ellen said he was "in the business." A producer of some kind.

"We broke up," she said. "Last night. He said this was too real for him. He has his company to think of. The film he produced is up for a DGA award. He can't afford the bad press."

"Don't you just love L.A.?" I said.

She looked out the window at the gulls.

"What are we going to do?" she asked.

"Get a lawyer," I told her. "Don't say anything that doesn't help Danny."

"I can't afford a lawyer."

"Take out a loan," I said. "The clock is ticking. They're going to ask for the death penalty. They have to. I'll sell everything I own before I see that happen."

She looked at me from under her bangs the way she used to when we first met.

"What if he did it?"

"He didn't do it. You said it yourself. He wouldn't even kill a fly."

"My friends won't talk to me," she said. "They're very political. They loved Seagram. Everybody loved him. It's like Danny shot Jesus."

"He didn't shoot anyone. Stop saying that."

"You don't understand. This is Malibu. People hug trees. They've been driving around with angry bumper stickers for years. This guy was our salvation."

"Just keep it together," I told her. "The last thing Danny needs is footage of his West Coast hippie mom flipping out."

A table of senior citizens had been eyeing us for the last few minutes. Ellen fixed them with a cold stare.

"What the fuck are you looking at?"

I shook my head.

"What did I just say?"

She shrugged. Ellen had spent her whole life claiming to be an artist. She had yet to produce a single sculpture, a single painting, a single anything.

Though I didn't know it then, in the weeks to come, she and I would revisit every year of Danny's life, looking for clues. She would call me at all hours of the night, often crying.

Remember that fever he had when he was two, she would say.

Or:

What was that fat kid's name? The bully. You know, sometimes Danny would come home from school with a black eye or a bloody nose, but he wouldn't tell me what happened. That was the thing with those Columbine kids, wasn't it? They were bullied and then they brought a duffel bag full of guns to school.

I would take the phone into the bathroom and try to talk her down. *Our son is innocent*, I would tell her. He didn't shoot anybody.

But there's something, she would say. *He's not exactly right in the head. I mean, who drops out of college and goes on the road for a year? We don't even know half the places he went, or what happened to him.*

If you love him, I would tell her, *you just have to support him. No matter what anybody says*. As if love trumped fact, trumped public opinion, trumped bloodlust.

Now, in the diner, she wiped her face, and tried to pull herself together.

"How's Fran?" she asked.

"Good. So are the twins. But I worry we'll have to move. What possible future can these kids have at that school with everyone knowing?"

"Where would you go? It's everywhere. Burma maybe."

"Myanmar."

"What?"

"It's called Myanmar now."

She had nothing to say to that. We watched the surfers rise and fall, tiny black dots bobbing in the whitecaps. As far as they were concerned it was just another perfect California day. As far as they were concerned the surf was up and everything was easy. I had always wanted to learn to surf. I had nurtured a fantasy of a middle-aged surf adventure, an escape to Mexico, a diet of fish tacos, sleeping on the beach. Now I knew it would never happen. None of these shallow balloons of idle daydreaming would ever come true. The world was a desert now, a wasteland to be survived, not enjoyed. In less than twenty-four hours all my fantasies had been destroyed.

"When he was small," she said, "he used to love to sleep on my belly. We would nap together on the sofa while you were at work. I can still feel him there, purring like a cat."

We sat in the warm California sun and watched the surfers, a doctor and his estranged first wife, stunned half to death, like a deer that's been hit by a car.

"This is all your fault," she said suddenly.

"My fault?"

"That no-good uncle of yours. These things are genetic."

I looked at her. She was talking about my father's half brother, Ellroy, who spent most of the fifties in jail for manslaughter. A convenience-store clerk killed in a botched robbery.

"First of all," I said, "our son didn't murder anyone. Second, Ellroy was a small-town boy and borderline retarded. You can't possibly connect the two. And even if you could, there is absolutely no scientific evidence that murder is hereditary."

"How else do you explain it? He's a good boy. We were good parents. We were, weren't we? I mean, not perfect . . . the divorce and . . . life. But lots of people get divorced, and their kids don't—"

She put her face in her hands. I let her be for a moment. The waitress came over and refreshed my coffee.

"I'm hiring Danny an attorney," I said, after she'd gone. "Forensic experts, whatever it takes. We are going to fight this."

"I'm afraid," she said. "This feels like one of those moments where everything falls apart. Like one of those moments you don't recover from, and five years from now there's a *where are they now* article in some local paper and it shows you drunk and living in a trailer. I can't do it. I'm allergic to wood veneer."

"Ellen," I said.

She looked at me. I had always been the sensible one. She had always been the dreamer.

"You're his mother," I said. "He needs you to be strong. We can fix this."

"No," she said. "I don't think we can."

Two

IOWA

He dropped out of school in March. He felt it was a waste of time. He had been sleeping a lot, missing classes. He wasn't depressed, he said. Just bored. When interviewed by the Secret Service, his roommate claimed he never saw Daniel spit after he brushed his teeth. He said Danny would just swirl the toothpaste and water around inside his mouth, then swallow. Was it true? Where had Danny learned this? It says right on the side of the package: *Do not swallow.*

On Thursday morning, March 12, fifteen months before Jay Seagram was gunned down in Los Angeles, Danny packed his footlocker. He drove his weathered yellow Honda up to the main entrance of his dorm. Refusing help from several boys on his hall, he dragged his footlocker to the stairs and pushed it over the landing. The long rectangular box flipped end over end, its loud crashing heard by residents throughout the building.

Daniel had made friends in school. He had dated several girls, some for several months, but he called none of them to say he was leaving. Nor did he call us, his family. Instead, at ten fifteen on a crisp March morning he levered his footlocker into the open hatchback of his Honda and drove away.

He went west, taking the Mid-Hudson Bridge to Route 9W. He drove north along the Hudson River all the way to Albany. Then he took I-90 and drove west through Syracuse. There was still snow on the ground. The sun was a hard, flat disk on the horizon. He considered heading north to Lake Ontario. He wanted to see the ice floes cracking against the shore, but instead he continued west. Around six fifteen the sun dropped behind the horizon. He drove so close to Lake Erie he could feel the arctic lake air sweeping in across the water. He slept that night at the Crown Inn, a motel in Millbury, Ohio, that had beds like hammocks. This was when he was still using credit cards.

Receipts show the gas he bought outside Buffalo, New York. They tell us about the movie he watched on pay-per-view that night, a showing of *Apocalypto* directed by Mel Gibson, purchased at 1:15 a.m. on March 13. What did he think as he lay in the flat, frozen Ohio sprawl watching a tropical tale about a dying civilization? I have watched the film myself many times since the event. I have sat in silence as disembodied heads rolled down ancient Mayan temple stairs. I have seen the panicked water birth and black panther attacks. The characters wear loincloths and speak a long-dead dialect. What does it mean? Why did he choose this movie? What must Daniel have thought as he lay half dozing, the road still rolling out before his eyes, his body still vibrating from the drive?

During his freshman year of college, Danny had developed a talent for starting things and never finishing. There was the serialized cartoon he had drawn for the school paper that petered out after three weeks, the independent study on the Outlaw Culture of the Wild West (suggested by him) that he had found increasingly inventive ways to avoid (first simply skipping his teacher conferences, then concocting elaborate excuses, even faking doctor's notes). As a handsome, underspoken boy capable of flashes of wit, he developed a mild following around the school, mostly mousy girls who knew they had no chance with jocks or frat boys. Like a hummingbird, he sparked to one girl after another, excited by the newness of their faces, the unique snowflake of their laughs, but then lost interest. Usually after he'd slept with them, but sometimes before. Once, even, during—an encounter in the middle of which he simply rolled off the poor girl, grabbed his pants, and walked out into the hall. Five minutes later he was on his bicycle, riding into town to get a gyro.

Danny was given to showing up late for class, wearing mismatched clothes, his longish hair unkempt, his sweater pockmarked with holes. This only enhanced his status with the mousy co-eds of Vassar, lending him a certain Beat poet appeal. In the cafeteria he ate mostly cereal, often without milk, picking it piece by piece from the bowl with his fingers while he read (first books about Jesse James and Billy the Kid, then futuristic tomes on the coming robot wars, then works of philosophy—Rousseau, Thomas Aquinas, Kierkegaard—books that would end up dog-eared, their spines broken in a pile by the side of the his bed).

Given his taste in literature you would imagine him to be a serious, academically ambitious young man, except for the fact that he never finished a single book. An idea would strike him, a curiosity—*I should learn Japanese*—and for two weeks or a month he would pursue it at the cost of his other studies. Then, just as quickly, the mood would pass, and a new idea would present itself—*I should learn how to fence*—and he would move on, leaving books half read, thoughts unfinished.

In this way, he realized, he was like his mother, a woman given to intense periods of manic interest, followed by long stretches of epic boredom. It wasn't a quality he liked in himself. The realization actually depressed him, giving him a few days of deep anxiety, a few days spent in bed, turned away from the clock. He did a lot of thinking in those slow, unbroken days. His mind felt fragmented. He worried that he was destined to be a hobbyist, a dreamer incapable of finishing anything. The fact that the college seemed to encourage this kind of "experimentation" made him doubt its motives as an institution of higher learning. Where was the structure? The rigid demand for attendance, for grades? He had grown up with little in the way of rules, and though it had seemed when he was applying to schools that what he needed was more of the same, what he came to realize in those three sloth-filled days was that without guidance he was becoming lost.

And then, without warning, this idea—the idea of becoming lost—took hold in him. It became his new obsession. Maybe this was the answer. To lose himself—not in a halfhearted way, like a set of car keys or a wallet, but more fundamentally, more profoundly. To become lost, literally, with no recognizable landmarks, no familiar faces to comfort him. It was a romantic idea, one relatively common for men of his age—though he didn't know it at the time.

He would lose himself completely, and in this way he would find himself. His true self. Once and for all.

After the motel, he continued west, driving just over four hours to Chicago. He had friends at DePaul University, a pair of brothers he had gone to high school with. Craig and Stephen Foreman. They were living in a house on West Haddock Place, near the Chicago River. It is the river that on St. Patrick's Day is dyed green. In 1887, in anticipation of the World's Fair, the course of the river was reversed in a heroic feat of civil engineering, mainly to keep sewage from flowing into the lake. Today it runs away from Lake Michigan into the Missouri River.

Danny spent the night drinking at the Elephant and Castle with the Foreman brothers. He bought more than two hundred dollars' worth of drinks using his Visa card. Both Craig and Stephen said Danny was in a great mood that night, elated, giddy. They say around eleven fifteen he met a girl at the bar and went home with her. A Secret Service interview of the bartender revealed that the girl's name was Samantha Houston. She was twenty-two years old, a nursing student at the University of Chicago.

Danny spent twelve days in Chicago. Of those, he spent four nights with Samantha and eight at the Foreman house. On March 17 he watched the Bulls play the Grizzlies at the United Center, sitting three rows back from courtside with Stephen and Craig, whose father had given them season tickets. I have watched the game on video. There is a shot deep in the second period in which Danny's face is visible. The Grizzlies have taken a time-out, and the camera cuts to the crowd, and there, caught in mid-laugh, is my son. He has a cup of beer in one hand, and he is bending over, his eyes crinkling in that way they do. The shot lasts 3.1 seconds. I have watched it more than a hundred times. My son looked happy, weightless. What if he'd stayed in Chicago? He could have transferred to DePaul. It is a lesser school. We would have been mad, but we would have understood. He could have moved in with the Foremans and dated Samantha. They could have married and had children. His thoughts would have become Chicago thoughts, his clothes Chicago clothes—hats and mittens, coats with big shoulders.

Instead he got up on the morning of March 28 and climbed into his Honda. The weather had turned warmer, spring creeping through the northern cold. After sitting idle for nine days Danny's car wouldn't start, and Craig had to jump-start it, stringing cables from the engine block of his Tundra.

Hauling his battered footlocker, Daniel Allen headed west on Route 80 toward Iowa City.

It was the wind that woke me. I opened my eyes and looked at the clock. It was three fifteen in the morning. My heart was beating fast. The room was silent. I had been dreaming of Danny. Fran lay beside me, sleeping. She had thrown off the covers. There was a pillow between her knees. Her naked hip was smooth and warm. How many nights had I fallen asleep with my head on her lap? The dark was a living thing, filled with her easy breathing. I checked the alarm panel on the wall. We'd installed it after Danny's arrest. There had been threatening phone calls, letters. Strange cars would drive by at all hours. But the warning light was green. We were safe for now.

I got out of bed. Momentarily dizzy, I put a hand on the wall to steady myself. It was September, three months after Jay Seagram had been killed in Los Angeles, three months after I'd sat on Danny's hospital bed and touched my son's face. Danny was being held in an unknown location. I had filed a Freedom of Information Act request, but was told the information was considered Top Secret Classified. The Justice Department had filed charges against Danny last week. They were prosecuting him for first-degree murder and twenty-two acts of terrorism. His first public hearing was Thursday in Los Angeles Federal Court. We would fly out tomorrow. Fran wanted to bring the twins. Murray said we'd be able to visit Danny before the hearing and she wanted them to see him.

What would he look like? A bearded stick figure? John Walker Lindh after thirty days in an Afghani dungeon?

Careful not to wake Fran, I went out into the hall. The children were asleep in their rooms. I watched their chests rise and fall, wanting to lie down beside them, to hold them and never let go. Instead I put my hand on the railing and slowly went downstairs. My fiftieth birthday had come and gone in the chaos of the assassination's aftermath. Fran had wanted to throw me a party, but I told her not to be absurd. Fifty years old. I had always been a fit man, strong, agile. I kept in shape, practiced my fine motor skills daily. But I had started to notice changes in the months since I sat with Danny in his hospital room. I was now a man with gray pubic hair. The skin around my jawline was starting to sag. It was perfectly natural for a man of my age, but I couldn't help but see it as a sign of defeat. As if some deep part of me had given up.

As we age, our muscles lose strength and flexibility. Our metabolic rate slows, making it hard to keep off weight. At night when I couldn't sleep, I would lie there picturing my motor nerves deteriorating. With every second that passed I was losing reaction time. My hand-eye coordination was starting to go, as was my balance. It was subtle now, but within ten years I might need help threading a needle.

I went into the kitchen, leaving the lights off, navigating by feel and memory. I opened the fridge and considered drinking some milk. My bones were losing calcium moment by moment. Every day I took vitamin supplements. I drank more dairy now than I had when I was a boy. It was a stopgap, a postponement. But then these are the things we do to put off the inevitable.

Gone were the days when I could put on a pair of jogging shorts and run through the neighborhood. In the weeks since the attack we had faced a constant barrage of press attention. We had been heckled, our mailbox destroyed. My car had been defaced with spray paint. Our phone number was unlisted, but still they called—the heavy breathers, the growlers, with their hate speech and muttered death threats. With the pretrial hearings about to start, the camera crews had doubled. They wanted to know how we felt. How were we holding up? Had we talked to our son? There was a twenty-four-hour news cycle to feed. The networks liked to play up the human-interest angle. If I peered through the curtains I was sure I would see at least one camera truck, its engine idling, bored reporters crammed inside waiting for something unexpected to occur.

Ten years after two high-school students gunned down thirty-three of their classmates at Columbine High School, Susan Klebold, the mother of one of the killers, broke her silence. She wrote, "Through all of this, I felt extreme humiliation. For months I refused to use my last name in public. I avoided eye contact when I walked. Dylan was a product of my life's work, but his final actions implied that he had never been taught the fundamentals of right and wrong."

Looking back, she wrote, "Had I been too strict? Not strict enough?" She said that every time she saw a child in a supermarket, she thought "about how my son's schoolmates spent the last moments of their lives. Dylan changed everything I believed about my self, about God, about family, and about love."

In the kitchen, I listened to the sound of the clock as it ticked off the seconds of another sleepless night. In the months since the assassination, new details had emerged—witness statements, still photos, video. I now had a clearer picture of what had happened in Royce Hall in the moments before and after the assassination. Still, there was nothing that irrevocably proved my son was the shooter. It had been dark in the theater, with spotlights shining on Seagram. The photos I had seen were murky at best. The video was clear when focused on the stage, but became grainy and hard to make out once the cameras panned to the crowd.

Ballistics results had proven that the gun my son was caught holding had been the murder weapon, but two witnesses (Alice Hader, thirty-four, and Benjamin Sayid, nineteen [*The New York Times*, page 13, June 23, 20___]) spoke of a struggle, of a man in a white shirt wrestling with another man in the moments after the gun went off. The other man wasn't described, nor did he come forward to offer his own statement.

Danny had been wearing a white shirt when he was arrested.

Who was the other man?

Six days after the shooting, *Time* magazine printed the photo that Murray's contact at the FBI had told him about. Though blurry, it clearly showed Danny holding a pistol. He is frozen in mid-recoil as a Secret Service agent grabs his wrist with both hands. They are partially hidden by the crowd. The expression on the agent's face is one of outrage, captured possibly in mid-yell. Danny has a look of fear and pain on his face, which isn't surprising. He had just been shot in the leg.

Every day I scoured the papers for more details. Who was the mystery man with whom my son fought? Was he the shooter? If not, if he was just an innocent bystander, why wasn't he coming forward?

I still did not believe my son was a murderer, but I had to admit that I had lost touch with him, that somehow after leaving home he had become isolated, troubled. And in the weeks since his arrest I found my mind returning again and again to his childhood. What had I, his father, done to make him who he was? What could I have done differently?

I sat at the kitchen table and drank a cup of tea, listening to the night sounds of the house. The forced-air system came on. The refrigerator motor idled. My knees cracked when I stood up to rinse out my mug. This is what happens when you age. Your body, which has felt for years like a safe and comfortable home, begins to turn against you. You lose the ability to maintain your core temperature. In the last six months I began to notice that I was always cold. I had become a wearer of sweaters. At home the children complained because I kept the thermostat at seventy-two degrees. I was turning into my grandfather.

The first weeks after Danny's arrest had been a blur of busywork. Fran and I had answered questions from every law enforcement agency imaginable. We had held press conferences and issued statements. We had told the world that we saw Senator Seagram's assassination as an abomination. That we grieved for his family. But, we'd said, we loved our son. And we believed he was innocent. We were positive that a jury of his peers would find him innocent, and we could only hope that Seagram's real killer was caught quickly and punished for what he'd done.

Overnight we became public figures. I turned down interview requests from every major network magazine show without hesitation. Fran supported me. We would not turn this family into a circus. There were two more children to protect, children who couldn't go to school without being pestered by reporters. So Fran took them out of school and started teaching them from home. Now they took classes with names like "Books We Have on Our Shelves" and "Math My Mom Can Do."

Fran had yet to complain about the strain our family was under, though there were times I heard her crying in the bathroom. Mostly late at night. But she kept the door closed, and I wanted to respect her privacy, so I didn't knock or ask if she was okay.

Every day, as usual, I rose and took the train into the city. I needed my work now more than ever. I did my early rounds and often late rounds, too. I listened to breath sounds and read X-rays. But I found myself distracted. My mind wasn't making the connections it used to. I found myself spending more time at the hospital talking to patients about their families. I wanted to hear happy stories, to see wallet photos: *my son the doctor, my son the lawyer.* I wanted to experience the positive, happy children who grew up to be heroes.

My patients, for the most part, were unaware of my other identity, as the father of a now world-famous criminal. They complained of spinal pain and heart murmurs without ever realizing to whom they were speaking. They complained of the tragedies of their lives without ever imagining what stories I might tell. When a patient recognized me, I tried to change the subject, to steer the conversation away from my son. It wasn't hard to do. Illness makes narcissists of us all. When we are suffering, in pain, afraid, we turn inward. Faced with our own mortality we cease to care about the daily dramas of the world.

The doctors were another matter. Colleagues of mine, men and women I had known for years, stopped talking to me. They took the stairs to avoid riding the elevator with the father of the accused. When I first returned to work, the chief of medicine stopped by my office. He wore a serious expression.

"Look," he said, "you and I both know, whatever your son did—if he's innocent, guilty, whatever—it doesn't change your standing at this hospital. But at the same time, I'd appreciate it if you'd try to keep a low profile for the next few months."

I had been drafted earlier in the year to give a talk at the hospital's annual fund-raiser. But after Seagram's death, my name was quietly taken off the program, and I was encouraged to stay home. Part of me was furious. I had given more than ten years of my life to the hospital, had saved the lives of some of the world's most important men and women, only to find myself shunned. But another part of me was grateful. Grateful to stay home, grateful to skip the knowing glances, the awkward silences, the exaggerated small talk.

On the subway one morning a woman, a stranger, grabbed my arm. When I turned to face her she hissed at me. "Shame," she said. "Shame."

A nurse at the hospital burst into tears when I spoke to her in the break room. She recoiled when I tried to console her. "Don't touch me," she said.

A surgeon I had played squash with several times approached me at a restaurant. He had been civil to me when we saw each other at the hospital. But now he had been drinking. He came up to the table where I had just been seated with the few friends Fran and I had left who would be seen with us in public.

"You should know," he said, "that nobody at the hospital can look at you without seeing what he did. I hope you're happy."

For good measure, he added "cocksucker," then stumbled off to the men's room.

My friends tried to console me after he left. To tell me that he was drunk and stupid, and not to listen to him. I told them it was fine. I said, "Everyone is entitled to their opinion." And then I stopped going out to eat.

Reporters called, their numbers blocked, and tried to get quotes. They asked provocative questions trying to get a rise.

"How does it feel to know that so many people hate your son?"

"If they execute him, will you go to the prison to watch?"

I stopped answering the phone. Its ring became a sound to fear, a mechanical scream that set my pulse racing.

I had talked to Danny only twice in the last three months, both times by telephone. As we spoke a mechanized voice kept reminding us that the call was being recorded for security purposes.

"I can't tell you where I am," said Danny, "but I will say it's hot."

"It's August," I said. "It's hot everywhere."

"I think I want to come home," he said.

"You think? You're in prison. You're supposed to want to come home. Are you okay?"

"They keep the lights on all the time. I have to sleep with my hands over my face."

"That's illegal," I said. "They can't do that."

Danny didn't say anything for a minute, then: "My lawyer says I should think about pleading not guilty on account of insanity."

"What do you think?" I asked.

"I think this call is being recorded for security purposes."

After we hung up I sat in the kitchen and watched my teacup spin around in the microwave. I no more accepted my son's guilt now than I had that day, but doubt crept in from time to time. The photograph of Danny holding the gun was a compelling argument for guilt, but I knew that just because something looked like a cancer, it didn't mean it was. I tried to quiet my anxiety with work. My son was good. He was kind. And if a person like this was capable of a crime like that, then I knew nothing about human beings.

At night when I couldn't sleep I scoured the newspapers for clues. Stories about Danny were clipped and placed into a file. I spent hours online searching for details, witness statements, anything that could shed new light on what happened that day. I was building an archive. I had become the keeper of the case. Any new detail would be cataloged. If there was something significant I would call Murray, rousing him from slumber.

"Jesus, Allen," he'd say. "It's a quarter to three. Call me tomorrow. The hooker's gotta go home in fifteen minutes."

I had sent him the *Times* article in which witnesses said they saw Danny wrestling with another man. At the top I wrote *Can we find him???* Whenever I saw an image or statement that raised questions about the official story I sent Murray a text or e-mail. At first he responded at length, but over time his responses grew sparser, eventually becoming just a single word: *Interesting*.

After I told Murray about the other man, he did some digging—calling the reporter who wrote the article, and approaching the witnesses himself—but no clear details about the wrestler emerged, other than that he had been tall and wearing a dark jacket.

The first conspiracy theories broke within days of the shooting. Seagram had been chairman of the House Appropriations Committee. He had spent the days before his death garnering votes for a bill that would have forced the administration to cut military spending by 30 percent. It also required a special prosecutor be appointed to investigate the private security firms who were getting rich off the conflict. The bill signaled the end of an era of war profiteering. But then Seagram was killed. And when the vote was finally held a week after his murder, the bill was defeated, and a new bill was introduced that earmarked an extra one trillion dollars for military spending. Clearly, wrote the bloggers, the administration had him killed to protect their war. Or the military-industrial complex had executed him to protect their boondoggle.

Then there was the army corporal who swore he'd seen Danny on a secret military base in the New Mexico desert three months before

Royce Hall. Corporal Walter Hannover said he'd been a guard at a top-secret Special Forces training facility. He said he'd seen Danny being driven onto the base last March. Once there, Hannover said, my son had been trained in small-weapons handling and infiltration techniques. Hannover claimed to have seen Danny six times in three months. The claim caught on with several national papers and was trumpeted on talk radio. The army denied that such a base even existed. Hannover took a polygraph, but the results were inconclusive. Then the army released Hannover's records and the world learned that not only had he never served on any base in New Mexico but he had been dishonorably discharged from his posting at Fort Stockton for huffing gasoline stolen from the motor pool.

Some claimed Hannover's records had been doctored by the army to protect the truth, but most legitimate news organizations closed the book at that point. Like all other data about the case, the articles were dutifully clipped and the online back-and-forth was bookmarked. I wrote *New Mexico?* on a piece of paper in my journal. I was creating a patient file. Each symptom was cataloged, each test result. In this way I was building my differential diagnosis.

In August I saw an article in *The Washington Post* that there'd been a fire in a Justice Department evidence room. Several boxes of evidence from numerous active cases had been destroyed. I became obsessed with backing up my records, pausing every thirty minutes to do both a local and online upload of my work.

Fran said she was worried about me. It wasn't healthy to fixate this way. I needed sleep. I told her he was my son. What was I supposed to do? She told me I needed to think about making peace with what had happened. It was time I accepted the fact that Danny might be guilty.

"What about the wrestler?" I asked her. "Two witnesses said they saw Danny struggle with another man right after the shooting."

"That was a Secret Service agent."

"No. These two witnesses specified it was a different man. Before the agents got there."

"Are you sure?" she said. "There was a lot of chaos. People running."

"I know what I read," I told her.

She sighed, trying to be patient. She knew that in a very real way the future of our marriage would depend on how we navigated conversations like this.

"You've seen the photograph," she said. "The Secret Service wrestled Danny to the ground. The murder weapon has his fingerprints on it."

"Photographs can be doctored," I told her. "Fingerprints aren't as conclusive as previously thought."

She put her palm on my cheek. Her eyes held nothing but sympathy.

"I think you should talk to someone," she said. "A therapist. You need to accept that this wasn't your fault."

"That what wasn't my fault?" I said. "That Danny went to a political rally? That he moved around a lot?"

"Paul," she said. "I love him, too, but you're making yourself sick over this. And your family needs you. I need you."

But I couldn't let it go.

By now I was used to seeing Danny's face in the paper. It had lost its power to shock. Two weeks after the shooting I had taken the train to Washington, D.C., to attend a congressional hearing about the assassination. I walked the ten blocks from Union Station, having Amtraked south past brick cities and factories, past rivers and streams and rusting iron mills. The sun burst like a ruby in the sky. Leaving the station, the stately wide streets of the capital stretched out before me; shaded grass lawns, monuments landscaped with bursts of floral burn, a collection of momentary parks enshrouded by northern red and scarlet oak trees. Overhead, towering American flags snapped their red, white, and blue. Each building I passed seemed to have been deliberately constructed to inspire awe or dread.

I had never visited the Capitol building before, though I had treated several congressmen and senators in my practice. I had watched hearings on TV, of course, Watergate, Iran-Contra. I knew the power of those rooms, the crush of cameras, the weight of history, the expectation of the crowd.

Behind me a man on a cell phone said, *Sterility, but they think it's treatable.*

I crossed D and C streets, noting the absence of litter and the usual entropic discoloration of cities, walked past the Russell Senate Office Building, past its members and staff entrance. Ahead of me, the floodwater expanse of Constitution Avenue was patrolled by Capitol Police in white shirts and black hats. After 9/11 the driveways to all the federal buildings had been shielded by gateposts, walled off with concrete abutments to deter terrorist attacks. The footpaths had been plugged with planters, obese, concrete weeds fisting through the pavement. *This is what fear does*, I thought. *It makes everything ugly.*

On the back lawn of the Capitol, news crews had set up their lights and cameras pointed toward the dome. Seeing them I felt a flash of panic. I wanted to remain anonymous. Murray had gotten permission for me to watch the hearings from the back of the gallery. I wore a shapeless coat and a styleless men's hat. I didn't want to sit up front, caught by the cameras, a Chiron under my face. PAUL ALLEN, FATHER OF DANIEL ALLEN, THE ACCUSED. I pulled the hat down over my ears.

Cameramen and technicians stood around drinking store-bought coffee. Anchormen in priceless blue suits sat in folding chairs, reading newspapers as they waited for some recordable action to begin. Approaching the Capitol—all steps and pillars, sharp-cornered squares and triangles—I caught a glimpse of the Washington Monument out of the corner of my right eye, a wicked sliver against a fluttering sheet of blue. At the same moment I heard the first cricket click of cameras signaling the inevitable onslaught of tourists, the elderly couples in their bright nylon running clothes, the Japanese businessmen loaded down with technology, the fat American families and glottic Germans, lining up behind velvet ropes for aseptic, guided tours.

Looking up at the Capitol steps, I had a sense of what it meant for men to rule each other. I felt a recognition of place that went beyond simple geography. This was a building whose image had been drilled deep into my consciousness by countless photographs, movies, and TV news reports. Seeing it here, muscular and broad, I endured a sensation that was not entirely human. The reverence of the elephant in its graveyard, the bear in its cave.

In my muscles and joints I felt it.

Behind me a woman said, *I'm able to compartmentalize my life more.* A man in a paint-stained denim vest made a run for the parking lot and was chased down by police. A hundred digital cameras clicked and flashed and the hair on my neck bristled. There was an aura beyond television to the agglomeration of monuments that surrounded me, beyond words or photographs. It was the difference between standing before a dynamic painting and spotting a picture of the painting in a magazine. To be here was to recognize the authority of location.

It was also to realize the full obscenity of my son's crime. After all, Jay Seagram wasn't just a man. He was a senator, a presidential candidate. Like this building he was an edifice, a symbol, as outsized as the buildings that surrounded me. An attack on a president was an attack on the presidency. An attack on a presidential candidate was an attack on democracy itself. Elections are about hope, the Secret Service agent had told me. And my son was accused of murdering hope. The hope of his country, of the world.

I showed my ID to one of the guards. His eyes widened as he realized who I was. But he didn't say anything, just wrote me out a pass and pointed me toward the steps.

Inside I stuck to the periphery, trying to go unnoticed. Men in suits stood in clusters. There were uniformed police everywhere.

The hearing room was huge. On the dais up front only a few congressmen had taken their seats. They milled around conferring with aides. I found a chair near the back.

Mark Foster was the committee chair that year. He called the hearing to order at five minutes after nine. He made an opening statement that was heavy on patriotism and outrage.

This hearing, Foster clarified, was not a trial. Daniel Allen would have his day in court. This hearing was to examine security failures in the protection of a presidential candidate. After Loughner's assassination attempt in Phoenix, he said, his committee had demanded stricter security standards. A congresswoman had been gunned down at a rally outside a supermarket. Suddenly the life of every politician was on the line. Our elected officials had become fair play, open targets for disenfranchised gunmen everywhere. Seagram's murder had only reinforced the fear that public service was now a high-risk occupation.

"To be frank," Foster said, "we want to know who screwed up, and what we can do to make sure this tragedy never happens again."

Michael Miles, the director of the Secret Service, took his place before the committee. He made an audiovisual presentation, in which he walked the committee members through a virtual re-creation of Royce Hall. He showed us the greenroom where Seagram had rested before the event. It was here he'd spoken to his children via webcam. Miles brought up a timeline on the screen.

Ever since the assassination of Robert Kennedy the Secret Service had provided security for presidential candidates. Each candidate had a team assigned. This included advance men who visited locations prior to the candidate's appearance and made sure the area was secured. In addition Seagram had two agents at his side at all times. When traveling he had an advance car and a follow car. Local police provided extra security.

At two thirty Seagram and his wife had arrived at UCLA, driving in through the main gates, past manicured lawns where students were studying. A large crowd of well-wishers was assembled to greet him. There was also a small crowd of protestors. Both groups were kept at least twenty feet from the senator as he climbed out of his town car, then turned and helped his wife. They stood for a moment and waved to the crowd, then went inside.

Royce Hall, I knew from my readings, was built in 1928, one of four original university buildings. It houses the UCLA Center for Performing Arts as well as several other departments that keep offices and classrooms upstairs. The main function of the building is to house an 1,800-seat theater. There is a large balcony in back and several rows of box seats on the sides.

At two forty-five, the doors were opened and students and faculty began to stream in. In accordance with Secret Service protocol, everyone had to pass through a metal detector. There were no exceptions. This raised the most pressing issue of the day: How had the assassin managed to smuggle a gun into the building?

"Initial test results on the firearm," said Miles, "revealed an epoxy residue, which forensic experts have matched to common duct tape. A thorough sweep of the building in the days after the attack showed similar tape residue on the rear side of a fire extinguisher found here."

He pointed to an area on the blueprint that appeared to be a hallway on the second floor.

"So," said Senator Foster, "you're saying the gun was hidden in the building before the event."

"We believe so, Senator," said Miles. "We believe the gunman, or someone known to him, gained access to the building at some point before that day and left the gun. Then, on the day, the gunman slipped upstairs and retrieved it."

He brought up a photo the Secret Service had taken of the fire extinguisher. It was a large red cylinder that sat in a recessed cubbyhole in the wall. There was a glass door with a latch in front of it.

"You said 'someone known to him,'" said Senator Foster. "Are you saying you believe there is a conspiracy at work here?"

I sat up taller in my seat.

"We are still assessing the situation, Senator. So far there is no evidence that anyone other than Daniel Allen was involved in this assassination."

Speculation. I made a note in my book: *Accomplice? Tape residue.*

"How would Daniel Allen have gained access to the building before the event?" asked a senator from South Carolina.

"Royce Hall was locked down as of three p.m. the day before the rally," said Miles. "No one came in or out without showing ID and passing through a metal detector. This means the gun would have to have entered the building before that."

The senators wanted to know how long the rally at Royce Hall had been on the books.

"As far as I know," said Miles, "the UCLA rally was set up on May 24."

"So three weeks earlier."

"Yes, Senator."

"Who would have that information?"

"Unlike a presidential visit, Senator," said Miles, "campaign rallies are public events. They are well publicized to try to gather a large crowd. Details about this rally were first announced on June 9, a week prior."

"So in the six days between the announcement of the event, and the day when the Secret Service closed the hall, the gunman—"

"Or someone known to him."

"Or someone known to him smuggled this weapon inside and taped it to the back of a fire extinguisher."

"Yes, sir."

"Am I right in believing that Daniel Allen had been a volunteer for the Seagram campaign?"

"Yes, sir. In Austin, Texas, he worked for six weeks handing out flyers and registering voters."

"And am I also right in thinking that his supervisor in Austin later went on to join the national campaign?"

"Yes, sir. His name is Walter Bagwell."

"And was Mr. Bagwell in Los Angeles on the day of the assassination?"

"Yes, sir. He was in Royce Hall at the time of the shooting."

"And is there any evidence that Daniel Allen contacted Mr. Bagwell in the days leading up to the event?"

"We have spoken to Mr. Bagwell. He claims not to have spoken to Mr. Allen for at least three months."

Senator Foster took off his glasses and rubbed his brow.

"What happened here, Mr. Miles? How could a thing like this happen?"

"There were gaps in the pre-event screening."

"Gaps."

"Errors."

"Have the agents responsible been disciplined?"

"Senator, if I may, the task of protecting a presidential candidate is substantially more complicated than protecting the president. Candidates want to maintain a Secret Service invisibility. They don't want a wall between them and the voters. In addition, events are often scheduled at the last minute, giving advance teams no time to secure the site."

"These sound like excuses."

"They're not excuses, Senator. They're facts. The agents on Senator Seagram's detail were good men. They were thorough men. The truth is, in order to ensure this tragedy never happened, we would have needed a team three times the size of the one we had. We would have needed to close off Royce Hall for three days beforehand, and perform daily sweeps of the building. And that level of security just isn't possible on a political campaign, where rallies are scheduled days, sometimes hours in advance."

"So you're saying this shooting was inevitable."

"No," said Miles. "But to stop it we would have to have been lucky. And we weren't."

My son was born at six p.m. on April 9, 19__. He weighed six pounds, ten ounces. When the nurse went to clear his airway, he grabbed her gown with an iron grip. We were in Saint John's Health Center, where I was finishing my residency. Ellen had already been in labor for nineteen hours, when the doctor performed an emergency C-section. Under bright, sterile lights my child was cut from his mother, the first incision made quickly, the first cry audible within seconds. I sat by Ellen's ear and spoke soothingly as she strained to see her son. Her arms were strapped down in a crucifixion pose. Our son was brought over and pressed to her face, and then my wife was wheeled off to recovery as I chased after the delivery nurse. I was thirty years old. I'd been on call the night before and, in the nursery, I stood over the bassinet swaying, almost asleep on my feet. But there was this energy surging through me as well. I was a father. I had a son. My own father had died when I was a boy. I had grown up, like Senator Seagram, with just a mother. Did I even know what a father did?

Daniel stared up at me with giant eyes. He was warm and dry now, mouth moving, arms and legs freed from the amniotic pool. At this moment he was a creature of pure possibility. An idea of immortality. The love I felt was uncorruptible. The things in my life that had seemed random now felt deliberate. All steps in some giant master plan. The history of the earth, with all its wars and disasters, its famines and floods, had been leading to this one moment, this one child lying on soft cotton staring up at his father.

One day he would learn how to laugh. He would drink juice from a glass. He would learn how to whistle. Everything was new. Staring up at me, hearing my tired voice, he reached out his tiny hand. He knew me, even though he had never seen me before. And I knew him. He was the love I'd been trying to express my whole life.

When Daniel was two he developed a fever that lasted for three weeks. It was a devilish foe, relentless, jawbreaking. A swollen furnace that drugs could allay but not eradicate. Every day we hoped it would end, and every day his temperature would creep impossibly high again: 104, 105, 106. I was in my residency at the time, a young doctor with an untrained mind. Danny's condition became my motivating force. I cornered colleagues and pored over medical journals. The longer the fever lasted, the worse were the scenarios I worked up in my head: leukemia, Epstein-Barr, meningitis. Ellen and I took Daniel to specialist after specialist. Doctors drew blood and looked in his ears and down his screaming throat. Danny was too young to understand what was happening, too young to accept that his parents were only trying to help, not in collusion with torturers. Thermometers were slipped into his rectum. Tongue depressors gagged him. Orderlies with clubby hands jammed him into cold imaging machines looking for shadows.

In the end, no diagnosis could be found to match the existing symptoms. One day the condition simply disappeared. The fever broke. Normalcy returned. His pediatrician chalked it up to the great mysteries of life. Ellen and I were just grateful it was over. And Daniel emerged from the experience seemingly unchanged. He ran and played and laughed as he always had. But now, in retrospect, the diagnostician in me began to wonder. Did this unexplained malady alter my son on some deeper, primal level? Did it affect some deep brain change, some chromosomal or chemical shift?

Because even as I was certain my son was innocent of murder, I could no longer avoid the conclusion that he was not what anyone would consider normal. At twenty, Daniel was a fleeting spirit, private to the point of reclusion. He was a gypsy, an escape artist who had detached himself from society, with all its rules of human contact.

If I had ever known him, truly known his hopes and dreams, his thoughts and emotions, that time had passed. His actions were now those of a stranger. They were symptoms of a larger condition—the condition of being Daniel—and I had to believe that if I could decode those symptoms, deconstruct the choices he had made, the things he'd done and said, if I could recognize the pattern, then I would understand my son.

As a scientist I knew that this thing we call "personality" is really a combination of physical and psychological factors. Hormones drive us, genetics. We are a product of our chemical wiring—too little dopamine and you get depressed, too much and you can become schizophrenic. And because of this, in order to understand Daniel's choices, I had to accept the hypothesis that some of those choices may have been made for him—that he was as much a victim of biology as an independent actor of his free will.

Modern science has yet to fully map the intricacies of the developing brain. Thinking back to that childhood malady I had to wonder: What if the fever had flipped a switch in my son that would have otherwise remained unswitched? What if that undiagnosed illness lay dormant in my son only to do some unseen damage later on? Parasites hide in intestinal linings, reemerging years later to wreak havoc. Malaria recurs long after its victims believe they are healed.

What if my son's identity, his distance and need for isolation, was a product not of personality but of disease? Would that make him capable of murder?

I was sitting in the living room looking through old photo albums when Fran came downstairs. She was wearing a T-shirt that barely reached her thighs.

"What time is it?" she said.

"Late," I told her.

She moved to the window, peered through the blinds. The shirt lifted up, revealing her rounded backside.

"They're just sitting there like vultures," she said.

"Nice ass."

She turned, pulled the shirt down. Not a single muscle moved on her face, but I could see the smile in her eyes.

"What are you doing?" she said. "Come back to bed."

I shook my head.

"We have to be up in an hour anyway," I told her.

She came over, took the photo album from me, sat on the sofa, putting a pillow in her lap to protect her modesty. She flipped the pages.

"It's always so strange to me, seeing her," she said. "Your ex-wife. She exists out there like some kind of super-villain. My nemesis. I look at you and I think, how could you ever have been married to a woman like that?"

"Like what?"

"Restless, disloyal, flaky."

"It seemed like a good idea at the time."

She put her feet on the coffee table.

"Sometimes I think we shouldn't be allowed to choose who we marry. My sister won't date a guy unless he has a police record or a victim pit in his basement. My father's on his sixth wife. Six wives. *Why do you keep getting married?* I ask him. *What can I say,* he says. *I'm an optimist.*"

I reached over and stroked her hair. My first marriage had ended thirteen years ago. It was as far from me as my medical residency, and existed less as an immediate memory than as a film I had seen several times many years ago—one I remembered well but had a hard time personalizing.

"She was a good mom," I say, then rethink it. "She did the best she could."

Fran flipped through the pages of the album. I moved closer to her and she put her head on my shoulder.

Looking at the photos of my family, fleeting emotions hit me—flashes of anger, of fear. These are the feelings that last—the extreme swings, the fights that burn themselves into your core. A decade later it is easier to remember the car crash than it is to remember the long drive leading up to it.

And yet I wanted to resist making this Ellen's fault, wanted to resist demonizing the single mother who raised my son. Though I had fundamental problems with who Ellen was and how she functioned in the world, I recognized that my opinion of her parenting was just that, an opinion. What mattered was she loved Daniel, had always loved him—fiercely, maybe too fiercely—a single woman, raising a son who is forced to become the man of the house far too young.

But that too is just a symptom, a factor in who Daniel had become. He did not drop out of college because his mother loved him too intensely, just as he did not live in his car off and on for fifteen months simply because his father moved to New York when he was seven.

Fran reached up and took my hand.

"You're a good dad," she said.

I wanted it to be true. I rested my head on the back of the sofa.

"With Alex and Wally we kept a schedule," I said. "In bed at seven thirty no matter what. A morning nap and an afternoon nap. Danny was a nomad, awake during the night, asleep during the day. There was no continuity."

"Do you think that affected him later?"

"It's hard to say. I think he learned early on that he couldn't rely on anything. Not his bedtime or when he ate. Not even his parents. Change was inevitable. When Ellen and I got divorced I think she wanted me to take Danny, to have custody. But she knew how it would look, a mother abandoning her son. I got the job at Columbia. I wanted to take him. My mom was here. I could have hired a nanny. But Ellen refused to let me win."

"Bitch."

She smiled when she said it. It confirmed for her what she needed confirmed. That she was a better wife than Ellen, a better mother. That I was happy now. That our family would survive. That this would be my real marriage. She would be the woman who slept next to me in heaven.

Alex came down the stairs, bleary-eyed and rubber-legged.

"I'm trying to sleep," he said. "Why is there talking?"

"Sorry, your majesty," said Fran, moving over so he could climb between us on the sofa. He burrowed in and pulled us closer. He had always liked the feeling of being confined; tight spaces, weight pressing down.

"Who's that?" he said pointing to a photo of Danny.

"That's your brother when he was your age," said Fran.

Alex pulled the picture closer.

"Did you always know he was broken?" he said.

"He's not broken," said Fran. "Why would you say that?"

Alex didn't answer. He studied the picture.

"Who's that?" he asked, pointing.

"You know who that is," said Fran.

"Ellen," said Alex, making a face.

"That's right."

He dropped the photo album on the floor and settled back in between us.

"Can I sit in the window when we go on the plane?"

Fran rubbed his head.

"You can take turns," she said.

He yawned, then buried his face in her side.

"Don't move," he told us.

We watched him fall asleep. His steady breathing was like that of a small animal. When he was a baby, Alex liked to sleep facedown, his mouth pressed against the mattress. We never knew how he could breathe, but if we rolled him over he would scream until we turned him back on his stomach. Outside the sky was lightening. It would be morning soon. Fran and I looked at each other. There was love in this house, unity. It had been missing from my first marriage. That sense that no matter what happened we all wanted the same thing.

"I wish Danny could have had this," I told her.

"I know," she said.

John Hinckley was born on March 29, 1955, in Ardmore, Oklahoma. His father was an oil executive. His mother was afraid to leave the house. He grew up in Texas and attended Highland Park High School in Dallas. He was the popular quarterback of his elementary-school football team. In high school, however, he became increasingly reclusive. He spent hours alone in his room, playing his guitar and listening to the Beatles. His parents thought he was just shy. His classmates described him as "a non-guy." As far as they were concerned he just wasn't there.

In April 1976, at the age of twenty-one, he moved to Los Angles hoping to become a songwriter. The number-one pop song that year was "Love Will Keep Us Together" by Captain and Tennille. Paul Simon sang "Fifty Ways to Leave Your Lover." One June night he went to a Hollywood movie theater and bought a ticket to see *Taxi Driver*. The movie starred Robert De Niro as Travis Bickle, a disgruntled Vietnam veteran who becomes obsessed with an underage prostitute named Iris, played by Jodie Foster. In the film Bickle starts collecting weapons and shaves his hair into a Mohawk.

He drives his cab through midnight streets.

"June twenty-ninth," he says. "I gotta get in shape. Too much sitting has ruined my body. Too much abuse has gone on for too long. From now on there will be fifty push-ups each morning, fifty pull-ups. There will be no more pills, no more bad food, no more destroyers of my body. From now on will be total organization. Every muscle must be tight."

Hinckley sat in the darkened movie theater, his mouth open. Every word seemed like it had been written just for him. The film ends with

De Niro lying on a brothel floor with a bullet wound to the gut, surrounded by the bodies of people he has killed. He presses a blood-soaked finger to his temple. The camera pulls up and from overhead we see policemen creeping into the apartment, their guns drawn.

Hinckley saw the film fifteen times that summer, sitting in a half-empty theater, an uneaten bag of popcorn on his lap. There was something happening. A transformation. On-screen De Niro straps spring-loaded revolvers to his forearm. He is taking control of the uncontrollable. He says, "The days go on and on. They don't end. All my life needed was a sense of someplace to go. I don't believe that one should devote his life to morbid self-attention, I believe that one should become a person like other people."

At night Hinckley went home to a roach-infested apartment, like the one from the film. He sat in the dark and strummed his guitar, trying to channel brilliance. He wrote letters to his parents describing a made-up girlfriend he called Lynn Collins, based on one of the women in the film. The next morning he would get up early, so he could be first in line for the morning show.

A month later, Hinckley left California and went home to Texas. He worked as a busboy, trying to settle into a smaller life. But Travis followed him. The dark wet road of the male mind.

Hinckley took classes at Texas Tech in Lubbock. He tried to settle into a routine. He started drinking peach brandy and wearing a green army jacket. He made no friends. Classmates stated that they rarely saw him with other people. But Hinckley had a friend, one who lived on the screen.

"Loneliness has followed me my whole life," Travis tells him, "everywhere. In bars, in cars, sidewalks, stores, everywhere. There's no escape. I'm God's lonely man."

In August 1979 Hinckley bought his first gun, a .38-caliber pistol. He started target shooting, planting his feet, right hand clutching the pistol grip, left hand pressed flat beneath the gun butt to steady the kick. He chose targets that looked like people. He always aimed for the head, trying to empty his mind and pull the trigger the way a yogi falls asleep.

In December, Hinckley took a picture of himself with a revolver pressed to his temple. Late at night he would sit at his parents' kitchen table and load a single bullet into the chamber. The lights were off, the glow of a streetlamp casting shadows on the linoleum. Hinckley clicked the cylinder shut, spun it. He tried to be quiet. He didn't want to wake his parents. When he pulled the trigger, the barrel pressed to his temple, he didn't even close his eyes.

In 1980 he bought more guns. He started getting headaches. His throat hurt all the time. He went to see a doctor who wrote prescriptions for blue pills and yellow pills. They were supposed to help him sleep, make him feel better about the world. Sometimes he dropped them into a Coke and watched them dissolve.

In May he learned that Jodie Foster, the actress who played Iris, the child prostitute Bickle fell in love with, had been accepted to Yale University. Hinckley borrowed $3,600 from his parents and drove to Connecticut. He signed up for a writing class. During the day he walked the campus filled with confidence, knowing there were guns in the trunk of his car. He found out what classes she was taking. He spied on her in the cafeteria. She was so pretty it made his teeth itch. He left love letters in her mailbox. He wrote her poetry. In his mind there was nothing more poetic than the sound the pistol's hammer makes when it collides with the flat back of a shell.

He was beginning to get a sense that history had a place for him, an elevated seat in the VIP section. A throne.

On-screen Travis goes on a date with Betsy, a campaign worker he meets in midtown, played by Cybill Shepherd. She is a nice girl, clean. He takes her to an X-rated movie. Life is beginning to feel more and more unintelligible.

On campus Hinckley got Jodie Foster's phone number. He didn't know how to talk to girls, and he stared at the phone for ninety minutes before dialing. Iris was so beautiful she made his feet feel too big for his shoes. Jodie. Her name was Jodie. Her voice when she answered was warm, open. *Did you get my letters?* he asked her. She was coy, a little flirtatious. It threw him. He told her he was not a dangerous person. Why did he say this?

It was an election year. Hinckley found he couldn't take his eyes off Jimmy Carter when he saw him on TV. The president had teeth like tombstones, oversized, important. Hinckley went to the bank and took out three hundred dollars. He bought a plane ticket to Washington, D.C. In D.C. he bought a ticket to Columbus, Ohio. He was following the president from campaign stop to campaign stop.

He wrote a poem called "Guns Are Fun!"

> *See that living legend over there?*
> *With one little squeeze of this trigger*
> *I can put that person at my feet*
> *moaning and groaning and pleading with God.*
> *This gun gives me pornographic power.*
> *If I wish, the president will fall*
> *and the world will look at me in disbelief,*
> *all because I own an inexpensive gun.*
> *Guns are lovable, Guns are fun*
> *Are you lucky enough to own one?*

In Tehran, Iran, fifty-two U.S. diplomats were being held hostage inside the American embassy. Hinckley sat in a window seat, flying from Columbus to Dayton. He composed letters to Jodie in his head. In the movie of his life he was the hero, the guy who got the girl. He had already conceived the act in his mind. He would walk up to the president and shake his hand. In the other hand would be a gun. Each shot he fired would be an angel that would sit beside him in heaven.

Later, video footage from the Dayton rally would show Hinckley standing less than twenty feet from President Carter.

On-screen Travis tells Betsy, "I should get one of those signs that says, ONE OF THESE DAYS I'M GONNA GET ORGANEZIZED."

Betsy: "You mean organized?"

Bickle: "Organezized. Organezized. It's a joke. O-R-G-A-N-E-Z-I-Z-E-D . . ."

Betsy: "Oh, you mean *organezized*. Like those little signs they have in offices that says THIMK?"

On October 6 in Nashville, Tennessee, Hinckley was detained by airport police, after baggage handlers found handguns in his luggage. The guns were confiscated and Hinckley was asked to pay a fine of $62.50. He flew to Dallas and bought more guns.

On October 20 Hinckley went home to his parents' house. He had this feeling in his belly, like the world was spinning faster than he was. He had impulses he couldn't control, and sometimes the sun was so bright he had to stay inside. One night he poured the blue pills into his hands, mixed them with the yellow ones. He woke up in the hospital. At his parents' insistence he started seeing a psychiatrist.

The psychiatrist thought Hinckley was simply emotionally immature. He urged Hinckley's parents to cut him off financially.

On November 4, 1980, Ronald Reagan was elected the fortieth president of the United States, carrying 44 states with 489 electoral college votes to Jimmy Carter's 49.

In December, Hinckley flew to New York City. It was the city of Travis Bickle, of child prostitutes and blood in the streets. On New Year's Eve he considered killing himself in front of the Dakota apartment building on the very spot where John Lennon had recently been gunned down by Mark David Chapman. They were everywhere, it seemed, these disaffected young men with their faraway eyes and their itchy trigger fingers. Hinckley stood for hours looking up at the bright white windows. Abandoned Christmas trees littered the streets. The jacket he wore was flimsy. He got cold and went back to his hotel.

That night, Hinckley spoke into his tape recorder.

"John Lennon is dead," he said. "The world is over. Forget it. It's just gonna be insanity, if I even make it through the first few days . . . I still regret having to go on with 1981 . . . I don't know why people wanna live. John Lennon is dead . . . I still think—I still think about Jodie all the time. That's all I think about really. That, and John Lennon's death. They were sorta binded together . . .

"I hate New Haven with a mortal passion. I've been up there many times, not stalking her really, but just looking after her . . . I was going to take her away for a while there, but I don't know. I am so sick I can't even do that . . . It'll be total suicide city. I mean, I couldn't care less. Jodie is the only thing that matters now. Anything I might do in 1981 would be solely for Jodie Foster's sake.

"My obsession is Jodie Foster. I've gotta, I've gotta find her and talk to her some way in person or something . . . That's all I want her to know, is that I love her. I don't want to hurt her . . . I think I'd rather just see her not, not on earth, than being with other guys. I wouldn't want to stay here on earth without her."

In Colorado Hinckley's father met him at the airport. It was March 7, 1981. He gave his son $200, which Hinckley used to pay for a motel in Denver. He sat there watching TV until the money ran out.

Later, at trial, Jack Hinckley would choke up. He'd say, "I am the cause of John's tragedy. We forced him out at a time when he just couldn't cope. I wish to God that I could trade places with him right now." He would take out a handkerchief and weep, as his wife, also crying, left the courtroom.

Fathers and sons. What we wouldn't give to trade places with our boys, to absorb their suffering and ease their pain.

The next day Hinckley's mother drove him back to the airport. They sat together in the loading zone for ten minutes, neither one of them speaking. Finally John got out of the car. He said, "I want to thank you, Mom, for everything you've ever done for me, all these years." They sounded like last words.

He flew to Hollywood for one day. The sun was too bright, and the streets were filled with freaks. On March 26 he boarded a bus for Washington, D.C. The country rolled out before him like a human tongue. Three days later he checked into the Washington Park Hotel. There were guns in his luggage. He slept with one under his pillow, another on the bedside table, hammer cocked. On March 30 he had breakfast at McDonald's. On his way back to the hotel he picked up *The Washington Star*. On page A-4 he saw that President Reagan would be speaking to a labor convention at the Washington Hilton in just a few hours. The words made colored lights dance in front of his eyes.

He showered and took a Valium, then worried it might not be enough and took another. He loaded his Rohm RG-14 with exploding Devastator bullets purchased nine months earlier at a pawnshop in Lubbock. Then he sat down and wrote one last letter to the woman of his dreams.

Dear Jodie,

There is a definite possibility that I will be killed in my attempt to get Reagan. It is for this very reason that I am writing you this letter now. As you well know by now I love you very much. Over the past seven months I've left you dozens of poems, letters and love messages in the faint hope that you could develop an interest in me. Although we talked on the phone a couple of times I never had the nerve to simply approach you and introduce myself. Besides my shyness, I honestly did not wish to bother you with my constant presence. I know the many messages left at your door and in your mailbox were a nuisance, but I felt that it was the most painless way for me to express my love for you.

I feel very good about the fact that you at least know my name and know how I feel about you. And by hanging around your dormitory, I've come to realize that I'm the topic of more than a little conversation, however full of ridicule it may be. At least you know that I'll always love you. Jodie, I would abandon this idea of getting Reagan in a second if I could only win your heart and live out the rest of my life with you, whether it be in total obscurity or whatever.

I will admit to you that the reason I'm going ahead with this attempt now is because I just cannot wait any longer to impress you. I've got to do something now to make you understand, in no uncertain terms, that I am doing all of this for your sake! By sacrificing my freedom and possibly my life, I hope to change your mind about me. This letter is being written only an hour before I leave for the Hilton Hotel. Jodie, I'm asking you to please look into your heart and at least give me the chance, with this historical deed, to gain your respect and love.

I love you forever,
John Hinckley

Later, at a pretrial hearing, Jodie Foster would sit on the witness stand. The prosecutor would stand before her.

"Now, with respect to the individual, John W. Hinckley," he would say, "looking at him today in the courtroom, do you ever recall seeing him in person before today?"

"No."

"Did you ever respond to his letters?"

"No, I did not."

"Did you ever do anything to invite his approaches?" the prosecutor would ask.

"No."

"How would you describe your relationship with John Hinckley?"

"I don't have any relationship with John Hinckley," the actress would say.

When Foster spoke those words in Hinckley's presence, he would fling a ballpoint pen at her and shriek, "I'll get you, Foster!"

Marshals would rush him out of the room.

Later, when the tape of this exchange was played at trial, an agitated Hinckley would jump to his feet and throw up his arm up as if trying to ward off blows. He would race for the door, the marshals running after him.

At one thirty he caught a cab. He told the driver, "Washington Hilton Hotel." It was a ten-minute cab ride at most. *Someday a real rain is going to come and wash away all the scum,* he thought. The revolver was in his pocket, a shining weapon of righteousness. The hand of God.

On-screen Travis Bickle says, "You're only as healthy as you feel."

He stood in the rain for thirty minutes. A crowd was gathered outside the hotel. The president's limousine stood waiting by the curb. There were cops, but not too many. Hinckley put his hand in his jacket pocket, feeling the reassuring weight of the Rohm. He worked his way slowly into the press line. At 1:45 p.m. Ronald Reagan exited the hotel with his entourage. He was smiling, waving his left hand.

On-screen Travis Bickle says, "Now I see this clearly. My whole life is pointed in one direction. There never has been a choice for me."

From the press line a reporter yelled, "President Reagan. President Reagan."

Still smiling, Reagan turned in his direction.

Hinckley pulled the revolver from his pocket. He dropped into a marksman's crouch and fired six shots as fast as he could. The first bullet tore through the brain of press secretary James Brady. The second hit policeman Thomas Delahanty in the back. The third overshot the president and hit a building. Hinckley tried to steady his breathing. He was ruining everything. He was fucking it up. The fourth shot hit Secret Service agent Timothy McCarthy in the chest. Hinckley saw the Secret Service agents start toward him, guns drawn. *Not yet.* The fifth shot hit the bulletproof glass of the president's limousine. A Secret

Service agent grabbed Reagan and shoved him into the car, just as the sixth bullet ricocheted off the door, then hit the president in the chest. It grazed a rib and lodged in his lung, just inches from his heart.

Hinckley was still clicking the trigger on the Rohm when Secret Service agents wrestled him to the ground.

We flew to Los Angeles like any other family. A mother and father taking turns ministering to the needs of their children. There was luggage to check and carry-ons to muscle through the terminal. We bought magazines for the flight, avoiding the newspapers, which all carried Danny's picture on the front page. We distracted the boys and tried to keep them from having too much sugar. They were not good fliers and sugar agitated them. It would take all Fran's energy to keep them from coming unglued.

On board the plane, I tried not to think about the flight I'd taken three months earlier, that late-night race to reach Danny before the government hid him away in whatever dark interior he'd been locked away in ever since. I looked out through the round portal window and watched the geometric grid of the Midwest passing by underneath. Danny had spent months traveling this country by car, driving its empty miles. I thought maybe if I concentrated hard enough I could see his route, a green line turning yellow, turning orange, turning red. But even though I stared, nothing came.

We checked into the Beverly Wilshire Hotel. It was cloudy in L.A., a light drizzle falling. The kids jumped on the hotel beds, bouncing back and forth like maniacs. I unpacked our suitcases while Fran took a bath, trying to wash away the stress of traveling. I had brought a briefcase full of documents. Timelines I had put together, newspaper clippings, and DVDs containing footage of the coverage from that night. I had a list of questions I wanted answered, directions I felt Danny's defense should take. Pretrial hearings in the case started the next day, and I wanted to give what I had to Danny's legal team.

As always, being in Los Angeles brought on feelings of failure. It seemed appropriate somehow that this is where everything had fallen apart for Danny, the place where his parents had met. The place where they had married. The city in which their steady slide into disappointment and rage had produced a bitter divorce, and a boy who, instead of inheriting two homes, found himself with none. This was the city to which he had gravitated in the end, like a victim returning to the scene of our earlier crime.

We had come full circle.

Two hours later we left the kids with the hotel's babysitting service and went to meet Danny's lawyer for a drink. Murray was sitting in the lounge at the Hotel L'Ermitage with Calvin Douglas, Danny's lead counsel. Douglas was a criminal law professor at Stanford who had spent his life defending capital murder cases. He had a mop of unruly, gray hair and a ziplock bag full of cut carrots in his briefcase.

"I just want to say right off the bat," he said, "that there's evidence the federal government is not letting me see."

"What kind of evidence?" I asked.

"How can I know until I see it?" said Douglas. He opened the ziplock bag and took out a carrot stick. He looked it over before taking a bite.

"I've filed motions," he said. "Given the government's claims that certain elements of the case are considered top secret, there will be a review by a separate judge to determine what we're allowed to see."

"What elements?"

"Again, I can't know for sure," said Douglas. "But the witness list feels light to me. And there are details of Seagram's itinerary that are missing. Also, when I ask for information about terrorist activity in the area at the time of the shooting I get silence."

"It seems relevant," said Murray. "What foreign cells were active? What kind of chatter was the FBI hearing? If the real shooter is still out there how are we going to find him without this information?"

I made notes on a legal pad. They would go into the file, and later I would pore over them, integrating them into the record.

"Danny said you asked him to plead not guilty," said Fran, "based on being insane."

"Temporarily insane."

"That makes no sense," I said. "My son is innocent."

Douglas looked tired.

"I'm sure he is," he said. "But his fingerprints are on the murder weapon. And a kid with a camera phone took a picture of him with the gun moments before the police grabbed him."

"I've seen the photo," I said. "It doesn't prove he shot Seagram."

"There was gunpowder residue on his hands."

"Because when he was struggling with police, the gun went off and hit him in the leg. And what about the witnesses who saw Danny struggling with another man right after the shots were fired?"

"We're now almost positive that that was the first Secret Service agent to reach the scene," said Douglas. "Look, I've watched the footage. Your son was visible on camera standing in front of the stage moments before the shooting. He was wearing a white button-down shirt. After the first shot was fired, a camera caught a man in a white shirt pushing his way toward the door. A gun was clearly visible."

"So Danny wore the same shirt as the killer," I said. "I bet there were fifty people in that hall wearing white button-down shirts."

"But only one of them had a gun," said Douglas.

"Whose side are you on?" I said. I was angry. Fran put a hand on my arm. Douglas crossed his legs, revealing a pale, hairless stretch of calf. He ate another carrot stick.

"I'm on your son's side," he said. "And that means it's my responsibility to keep him from being executed."

I put my briefcase on the table, opened it.

"I drew up a timeline," I said, pulling it out. "And I've compiled a list of conflicting witness statements. I think they raise serious questions about what happened that night."

Douglas looked through the pages I handed him.

"We have all this," he said. "It doesn't prove Danny is innocent."

Murray, who'd been silently sipping his margarita, motioned to the waitress for another.

"Tell him about the list," he said.

"What list?" I asked.

Douglas frowned.

"The Secret Service keeps a watch list," he said. "People who've threatened the president, potential crazies."

"Danny wasn't on the list," said Murray.

"Of course he wasn't," I said.

"But Carlos Peña was," said Douglas.

"Who is Carlos Peña?"

"He's an unemployed roofer who sent threatening e-mails to several members of Congress," said Douglas.

"He was also in the auditorium that afternoon," said Murray.

"Even if he was there," Douglas interjected, "it doesn't prove anything."

Fran looked at me and frowned. She could see it on my face. This was the break I needed.

"Paul," she said, "don't read too much into this."

"There is no record of Danny buying the gun that killed Seagram," I said.

"The gun was reported stolen by its owner in Sacramento three months earlier," said Douglas. "The Secret Service puts Danny in Sacramento at the same time."

"What about Peña?" I said. "Has he ever been to Sacramento?"

Douglas shrugged.

"The FBI shows Danny buying two other guns in the months leading up to the assassination," he said.

"But not this one," I said. "What if it was Carlos's gun? What if Carlos was the man my son fought with? What if *he* shot Seagram? He tried to get away. Danny grabbed him and wrestled the gun away."

"Then why hasn't Danny said anything?" asked Fran. "If he's innocent why hasn't he said anything?"

There was an uncomfortable silence. We looked at one another.

"It's possible," said Douglas, "that your son likes the attention."

"That's crazy," I said.

"You can't have it both ways," said Douglas. "Either Danny did it and he's keeping quiet so he doesn't incriminate himself, or he's innocent and he's keeping quiet for some other reason."

"He's scared," I said.

"Let's say for a moment he didn't kill Seagram," said Douglas.

"He didn't," I said.

"Here's a kid who dropped out of college, who floated around from dead-end job to dead-end job, never staying in one place for too long. He showed signs of depression, possible borderline personality ideation. We know he volunteered for Seagram in Austin. He was a lonely kid looking for connection. A kid who worried that history would forget him."

"So when Seagram was killed," said Murray, "when the gun literally fell into Danny's lap, he takes credit. He is somebody now. No one will ever be able to say Seagram's name again without mentioning Danny's."

I thought about this. Was it possible? Would my son throw his whole life away for a place in history?

"It's also possible," said Douglas, "that he feels guilty for something else he's done, and this is his way of punishing himself."

"Like what?" said Fran.

"Who knows?" said Douglas. "Maybe he broke a girl's heart. Maybe he ran over someone with his car and didn't stick around for the police. I've filed motions for a psychiatric evaluation. The prosecution opposes it, but psychiatric evaluations are pretty standard in these types of cases."

Fran sat next to me, shredding her napkin. She said, "If this Carlos Peña guy was on the Secret Service's watch list, how did he get into Royce Hall?"

"You want the conspiracy version?" said Murray.

"No."

"Human error," said Douglas. "The guest list shows Peña checked in using the name Carlos Fuentes. He had a fake ID. The hall holds eighteen hundred people. Seagram wasn't one of the politicians Carlos had threatened. He simply slipped through the cracks."

"And the Secret Service hasn't mentioned it," I said, "because it would embarrass the agency. They had the killer on their *do not admit* list and they let him in anyway."

Douglas finished his carrot sticks. He zipped the bag closed, put it away, and shut his briefcase.

"These are nice theories," he said. "But the fact remains, your son was caught with the murder weapon."

I shook my head. In my briefcase were documents ordered chronologically. There were indices and note cards, photographs and DVDs.

"Just because your EKG says you're having a heart attack," I said, "doesn't mean you have heart disease. There are half a dozen hard-to-diagnose diseases that can be misinterpreted as heart disease. I'm saying all the symptoms have to add up, not just some."

I took off my glasses, rubbed my eyes. When I opened them I could see Douglas and Fran looking at me. I'd seen looks like this in the eyes of doctors who spoke to family members who refused to believe their brothers or sisters or mothers or fathers were dead. Denial. They thought I was in denial.

"My son didn't do this," I said.

Murray stood up, threw a fifty-dollar bill on the table.

"What do you say we go for a walk?" he said.

I thought about it for a second, then closed my briefcase. Standing up I felt tired. My joints hurt. I was an old man, the father of the vilified. Would this be my life from here on out? Was I to become the argumentative man who can't control the volume of his own voice? The conspiracy nut with boxes of data who spouts dates and facts, as if coincidence alone can prove the existence of God?

We walked in silence through the lobby.

"I'm not crazy," I said.

"I never said you were."

Outside the hotel he handed the valet his ticket.

"Danny had issues," I said.

"Issues," he said, trying to sound nonjudgmental.

"Problems. He had problems. Of course. But he's not a killer. This man, this Peña, he has a history of threatening people."

"He's done time," said Murray. "Assault."

"My God," I said. "Don't you see? This is the proof we need. Why isn't the government all over this guy?"

Murray clicked his tongue against his teeth. "Douglas is right. Just because Peña was there doesn't prove he killed Seagram."

I balled my fists. The world felt like it was spinning backward. I was dizzy. For a moment I worried I might pass out. *Slow down*, I thought. *Think it through.*

"Trials are about reasonable doubt," I said. "We don't have to prove Peña did it. We just have to raise enough doubt to keep the jury from convicting Danny."

The valet pulled up. Murray walked to the driver's door. He gave the valet a twenty. I stood on the curb watching him. Overhead the sun peeked out from behind the clouds.

"Well," said Murray, "what are you waiting for? Let's go see Carlos Peña."

Ted and Bonnie Kirkland lived on Lackender Avenue just outside Iowa City. Their house was a small post-and-beam structure set a few hundred feet behind the feed store they ran. On the back forty they kept chickens and a vegetable garden and raised pigs for meat. Their daughter was away at school back east. Daniel Allen showed up at the feed store on April 1 looking for work. He blew in like a leaf on the wind. In college he had dated a girl named Cora. She told him about growing up in Iowa, about her parents, Ted and Bonnie, and what kind and gregarious people they were. She talked about cornfields as far as the eye could see, about growing her own vegetables and riding her bike through the September dusk. It was a place where people still slept with their doors unlocked, and dreamed grounded, midwestern dreams.

Danny showed up on March 28, having driven Route 88 southwest from Chicago. He drove with the windows down. It was the first real spring day. Leaving Illinois he felt himself entering a land of promise. He could smell agriculture in the air, the earthen stink of manure.

It was lunchtime when he walked into Kirkland's Feed Store. He was wearing an old T-shirt and a pair of Dr. Martens. His hair was spiky and unwashed. He looked like a lost city boy looking for directions, especially when he stood for a long moment in the center of the warehouse-size store, looking around. It was Ted who approached him, wiping his hands on a rag.

"Can I help you with something?" he said.

Ted was a tall man, broad-shouldered. He had a plate in his head where a horse had kicked him when he was a boy. When he drank at parties he would stick refrigerator magnets to his temple, much to the amusement of everyone around him. He had married Bonnie twenty-three years ago. They met when they were teenagers. He was the farm-hand and she was the farmer's daughter.

"I'm looking for a job," said Danny.

"A job," said Ted. "I thought you wanted directions."

"Don't need directions. This is the place."

Ted looked at Danny. He had just finished restocking the livestock pharmaceuticals: bags of Duramycin-10, packages of Atgard Swine Wormer, jars of Calf Bolus.

"Well," he said, "we're not really hiring right now."

Danny nodded.

"The thing is," he said, "I just drove all the way from Vassar."

"In New York?"

Danny nodded.

"And this girl I knew there, a friend of mine, she said her family had a feed store in Iowa City. She said they had a guest apartment over the garage that they rented out. Ted and Bonnie Kirkland. She said if I was ever in Iowa City I should look them up."

Ted considered the young man in front of him. Was he dangerous? A con man, maybe? The kind who sneaks into your life then tears it down brick by brick. Ted had a farmhand's stoicism. His face was unreadable.

"Well, sir," he said, "all that is true. It is. What's the name of this girl, your friend?"

"Cora Kirkland."

"And your name?"

"Daniel Allen," said Danny sticking out his hand. Ted shook it. He still didn't know what to make of the kid. He excused himself for a minute and went to call Cora. She laughed when he told her whom he'd just been talking to. She couldn't believe that Danny was in Iowa City, stand-ing in front of her father. They had dated for just a few weeks. She liked Danny, but he was always so distracted. He was a lost boy, and she was a girl with places to go, so she broke up with him one night over pizza. Danny didn't seem to mind, and they'd stayed friends. Now she asked to talk to him.

"Danny," she said, "what are you doing?"

"I dropped out of school," he said. "I needed a change of pace. I thought a few months working the land."

"My parents don't work the land," she said. "They sell horse feed and farm supplies."

"Well," he said, "that sounds good, too."

Sometimes when they made love, Danny would stop in the middle and go do something else—watch TV or make a sandwich. Cora thought of him now as a little brother.

"My parents are square," she told him. "They go to bed at eight o'clock."

"Sounds good to me," he told her. "Besides, I like it here. The air is so fresh."

"It smells like cow shit."

"Isn't that what fresh air smells like?" he asked.

He moved into the apartment over the garage. There wasn't a kitchen, but he had a hot plate and an old livestock trough to bathe in. At night he'd climb onto the roof and look at the stars. He never knew there were so many. That first night he lay on his twin bed and watched the shadows of trees flutter across the wood-slat ceiling. He listened to the wind, and for a few hours felt like somebody else.

During the days he loaded and unloaded trucks. He wore a Velcro back brace and durable canvas work gloves. He stocked shelves. He learned the names of things: the Chore Boot and the Muckmaster. Neatsfoot oil was a natural preservative and softener of leather products. Red Hot Spray was a special formula of soap, spices, and flavoring to stop animals from chewing on bandages, leg wraps, and casts.

He ate flat, fast-food hamburgers on the loading dock with the other stock boys. Mostly Mexicans. He practiced his Spanish, learning the dirty words first. *Chingar* meant "to fuck," as in *chinga tu madre*. *Manoletiando* meant "to masturbate." *Hoto* was a term for gay people. *Pendejo* meant "idiot." He liked to wait until his fries were cold to eat them. The Mexicans thought this was crazy. They called him *Cabrón*. Only later did he learn it meant "asshole."

He had dinner every night with the Kirklands. Bonnie insisted. She was a tiny brunette with a gun collection. Her father had taught her to hunt when she was a girl, and she loved the feel of oiled steel in her hands. A week earlier she'd had a long conversation with Cora about

Danny. She wanted to know if he was dangerous. Cora said, "God, no. Just a little lost." Lost was something Bonnie could handle. She was a mother, after all, and lost boys call on frequencies only mothers can hear. Danny became her mission. Bonnie would make sure he was fed, that he washed properly. She would attend to his physical and spiritual health.

They ate meat that came from the Kirklands' own pigs and corn from their neighbors' fields. It was fresher than any meal Danny had ever had. He could taste the dirt in every vegetable, the oaky compote of the soil. Eating a summer squash he felt like he could count every raindrop that went into it.

They asked him about his family. He was vague. His parents were divorced. His mother lived in Los Angeles. His father lived in Connecticut with his new family. Danny was nineteen years old. He wanted to travel, see the world.

"Well," said Ted, "I wouldn't say Iowa's the world, but we like it."

They gave him an old bike that was rusting in the barn. He cleaned it up, bought a new seat and new tires. He would ride it for an hour every morning before work, racing down dirt roads, watching the sun come up. He was getting the lay of the land, figuring out his place. On weekends he would pick a direction and bike all day, riding north until lunchtime, then turning around and heading back. The ten pounds he'd put on in college eating sugary cereals and drinking beer melted off. The muscles of his thighs and calves started pressing against the legs of his jeans. Ten-hour days hauling feed sacks was giving mass and definition to his back and arms.

One night he and the Mexicans went into town for a beer. They drove to Ugly's Saloon, a bar near the university. One of the Mexicans had landed himself a college girl, Mabel. She was fat with frizzy hair, but she had a nice laugh and Jorge said she gave great head. The four Mexicans and Danny sat in a corner booth. They ogled girls and called them names in Spanish. The Mexicans told Danny that if he was ever in Mexico and he wanted to start a fight with a Mexican he should say *Chinga tu madre*. They told him the best place to hide a knife was in your boot. The fat girl showed up with three friends. One of them looked like Olive Oyl from the old Popeye cartoons. They ordered pitchers of watery beer. Jorge put salsa music on the jukebox. Things started to get rowdy. Danny ended up sitting next to Olive Oyl. She tried to talk to him, but he couldn't hear a word she was saying.

He went to play some pool and ended up in a showdown with a blowhard from the outdoor rec program at the state college. The guy was a foot taller than Danny and he kept whacking him with his cue when he turned around. The first time he apologized. The second time he knocked the beer out of Danny's hand. Seconds later the Mexicans were surrounding the guy. Jorge was up in the blowhard's face. He called him some of the names they'd taught Danny: *maripso*, *maricón*, *mariquita*. The blowhard had friends, flat-top yokels from the rugby team. The blowhard asked Danny if he brought his wetbacks with him to the toilet, too. Danny smiled without humor. His heart was racing in a way he'd never felt before. He saw Jorge reaching down for the knife in his boot. The bouncers were almost there, hulking, farm-raised boys from Swisher and North Liberty, pushing through the late-night crowd.

"*Concha de tu madre*," Danny said, then hit the blowhard in the throat with the heel of his hand.

Later, after the melee that followed, after the bouncers charged in with their ham-hock fists and zero-tolerance policy, they sat on the curb drinking beer out of brown paper bags. Danny spit blood into the gutter. Jorge clapped him on the back. He was one of them now, an honorary Mexican. Danny told them he was probably the only white boy in America who was climbing *down* the social ladder instead of up it. The Mexicans thought that was hysterical.

That night he called Samantha Houston from a pay phone. She was the girl he'd met in Chicago. Why did he call her, a girl he barely knew? Perhaps the unfamiliarity of his surroundings and the distance from everyone he knew conspired to make Danny feel lonely. Or maybe it was the one-two punch of alcohol and violence making him horny. Whatever the reason, it was after midnight. The Mexicans had taken him to a dive bar out near the interstate where they drank cheap tequila and shouted at the soccer game on television. He stood in the back hall near the bathrooms, one finger jammed in his ear, and yelled into the phone.

"I'm in Iowa," he said.

"Why are you yelling?"

"If you'd said the word 'Iowa' to me six months ago I couldn't have even found it on a map," he said.

"Who is this again?" she asked.

"It's Danny. Or as I'm known here, *Cabrón*."

"You know that means 'asshole,' right?"

"Does it? Son of a bitch."

He put a hand on the wall to steady himself.

"Listen," she said. "I can't talk right now. My boyfriend just went out for cigarettes."

"Boyfriend," he said. She had never mentioned a boyfriend.

"I mean we had fun, don't get me wrong, but you don't even live here. And my boyfriend's in law school. A girl needs to think ahead."

"Absolutely," he said. "I couldn't agree more."

The tequila was making the room spin. He said, "Maybe when I'm in Chicago again I'll look you up."

"Do me a favor," she said. "Don't."

He went back to the bar. The Mexicans were stomping their feet and shouting. On-screen the Mexican team was running around with their arms in the air. Danny sat on a barstool and bummed a cigarette from a cowboy with one eye. He didn't even smoke.

He nursed his beer and thought about the things he'd learned in the three weeks he'd been here. He could name six brands of harvesting combines. He knew what tillage meant and how to recognize a chisel plow. He knew the difference between a rock picker and a leveler. He could identify a hoof pick by sight and tell you whether you needed that or a hoof knife, depending on the job. If your horse was agitated he could recommend Quietex paste or powder to calm him. They were real-world things, concrete. College was a place of ideas, of ephemera. Here he'd found details he could hold on to. Here the ground rose up to hit your feet when you walked.

Jorge came over and punched him in the shoulder. He had a bruise on his cheek from where one of the rugby players had elbowed him. He told Danny there was a *puticlub* nearby. For twenty-five dollars he could put his *verga* in the *culo* of a woman. Danny told him he only had eighteen dollars left. Jorge shrugged. He and the others stumbled out to the car, laughing, leaving Danny with the bar bill.

Walking home Danny felt the weight of the stars overhead. It seemed as if light was raining down on him. He stumbled along the shoulder of the road, his body rumbling from the speed of passing trucks. He could hear the cicadas in the roots of his teeth, that relentless exoskeletal scree. A Bubba in a pickup truck threw a beer can at his head. Danny left the road and navigated through the cornfields. The moon was shielded here. He followed its hazy glow through the claustrophobic press of leafy green stalks. By his calculation he had a mile, maybe two to go until he reached the Kirklands' house.

How much bigger the world felt now than it had just a few weeks ago. Wide open, like he could go anywhere, do anything.

Something hit him in the face. Something big with legs. He brushed it away, cursing, and was hit again in the belly. He spun around, waving his arms. He had always been afraid of bugs. And now they were everywhere, beating against him, getting caught in his clothes, his hair. He opened his mouth to scream and bit down on something crunchy. Panic filled him. He fell to his knees, vomited, then covered his head with his arms. Giant bugs beat against him, creatures of blind aggression the size of his fist. In the darkness he felt like he was being eaten alive, like each part of him that was hit disappeared into the corn. He rolled around like a man on fire, trying to put out flames that didn't exist. Finally, after what felt like hours, the assault stopped. He lay panting on the ground. Around him cornstalks rustled in the wind. When Danny stood up he was disoriented. He didn't know where the road was anymore. He brushed at his hair and clothes, trying to remove every last trace of the plum-size grasshoppers that had attacked him. He was dizzy from the tequila. His jaw hurt from where the blowhard had punched him. It was Saturday. The sun would be up in a few hours.

For the first time he could remember he felt truly happy.

He lay down amid the corn and went to sleep.

Carlos Peña lived in a run-down apartment complex just east of Highland Avenue. There was a soiled mattress leaning against a palm tree near the entrance. Across the street, pit bulls barked behind a chain-link fence. Murray parked his rented SUV out front. We were both in suits, and we sat for a moment looking up at the building.

"It's moments like these," said Murray, "that separate the something from the something else."

We climbed the front steps, examined the tenant list. PEÑA, C., APARTMENT 4F. Murray rang the bell. We waited. The door buzzed. Murray pushed it open. There was a kidney-shaped swimming pool in the middle of a concrete courtyard. A lawn chair floated in it.

"The thing about Los Angeles," said Murray, "is that the defining mood is desperation. It's a feeling that somewhere, someone else is getting the break you deserve."

I looked up at the windows. The place was laid out like a motel. There were bicycles chained to railings. The elevator was out, so we climbed to the fourth floor. Murray was huffing by the time we reached the top.

"I bill double for exercise," he said.

We stopped in front of 4F. Murray tried to peer through the window, but the blinds were closed.

He knocked. The door opened immediately, startling us. Carlos Peña peered out, his right hand hidden behind the door. He was a skinny man with a pockmarked face.

"You cops?" he said.

"I'm a lawyer," said Murray. "He's a doctor."

Carlos thought about this. Then he stepped back and let us in.

"Sorry about the mess," he said, "my girlfriend breaks stuff when we fight."

The living room was a wreck. There was glass in the carpet. The coffee table was busted. What looked like the handle of a steak knife was sticking out of the sofa.

"Are you really a doctor?" Carlos asked. I nodded. He lifted his shirt.

"I got this rash," he said.

The skin around his left hip was swollen and red.

"It looks like a rug burn," I told him.

He thought about this.

"Oh yeah," he said, remembering. "Never mind."

He brushed some plates and magazines off the sofa, gestured for us to sit down. The handle of the steak knife was three inches from my left shoulder. If Carlos attacked us I could grab it and stab him in the stomach.

Murray spent a few moments straightening the creases of his slacks.

"My client," he said, "is Daniel Allen's father."

Carlos looked at me.

"Who's that?"

"He also goes by the name Carter Allen Cash."

Carlos smiled.

"The guy who shot the senator."

"Allegedly," said Murray. "Allegedly shot."

"We've been informed," I said, "that you were in Royce Hall when the shooting took place."

Carlos got up suddenly and went into the bedroom. Murray and I looked at each other.

What do we do? I mouthed.

He shrugged. I reached over and touched the handle of the steak knife. It was sticky. Carlos came out of the bedroom carrying a box. I quickly lowered my hand. He sat on a gutted Barcalounger, holding the box on his lap.

"My brother had a colostomy bag," he said.

Neither Murray nor I could think of anything to say to that.

"He stepped on a land mine in Fallujah. They were able to save his legs, but his insides were all fucked up."

He put the box on the table in front of us.

"The doctors told him he might be able to crap normal again. Maybe in time. After a few surgeries. They gave him hope. So then every day he crapped in a bag he was miserable. He spends his time dreaming of the day when he can sit on the toilet like a man. When he can go back to having those miracle shits that make you feel like you just took a cruise. And he has the surgeries, and he has the therapies. And none of it works. It's two years later and he's still crapping in a bag. So one day he takes a gun and blows his brains out. My mom came home, found his skull spread all over the living room. We had him cremated, put his ashes in a box."

He reached out and taps the box he'd brought in.

"And every day I take this box out and look at it," he said. "And do you know what I think?"

Murray shook his head. I shook mine.

"Acceptance is the key to happiness," Carlos said. "If those doctors had told my brother he'd be crapping in a bag for the rest of his life, he would have accepted it. He could have found a way to be happy. But instead they gave him hope. They promised him a better life. And so he spent every day hating the life he had."

He looked at me. His face had the consistency of a pepperoni pizza.

"Do you understand what I'm telling you?" he said.

"No," I said, though even as he said it the words were resonating in my head.

"You need to surrender yourself to the truth," he said. "You won't be happy until you do."

"And what truth is that?" I said, my voice cracking.

"That your son is lost to you. *That you don't know him*. That he's going to spend the rest of his life in prison. Which might not be a long time."

"Did you wrestle with my son at Royce Hall?" I asked, my voice hard. "Did he take something from you?"

He smiled.

"Wrestle?" he said. "Did I *wrestle*?"

We looked at each other, unblinking. His smile widened, but there was no happiness in it. No life.

"Tell us about these letters you write," said Murray.

"What letters?" said Carlos, holding my eye.

"To congressmen, senators."

"I have opinions," said Carlos. "Thoughts. I express them. It's not healthy to keep that stuff inside."

"These thoughts," said Murray. "They are sometimes of a threatening nature, are they not?"

"What is that?" said Carlos. "*A threatening nature*? What does that mean?"

"Why did you go to Royce Hall?" Murray asked.

Carlos looked at him.

"There's nothing for you here," he said.

"We have a photograph that shows you wearing a white button-down shirt," I said. "You stood less than ten feet from the stage."

Carlos stood up.

"I showed you the box," he said. "Next I'm going to show you the gun."

Murray stood. He gestured to me. I stood up, too. Together we could take him, couldn't we? Two against one? A Jewish lawyer and a rheumatologist who'd never hit another person in anger.

"You own a lot of guns, Carlos?" asked Murray.

"It's not the guns that get you," said Carlos. "It's the bullets."

I looked at the steak knife. Why was it sticky? Was that blood on the handle?

"Let's go," I told Murray.

He took out his business card.

"If you change your mind and want to talk," he said, "call me."

Carlos took the card, examined it.

"I'll add it to my special-interest pile," he said.

Murray took the card back.

"On second thought," he said. "I'll call you."

We went down the stairs and past the pool. Murray had his keys out before we reached the car. We climbed inside and locked the doors. We sat there, neither of us talking, for several moments. The rain had returned, a steady drizzle that ran down the windshield in dirty rivulets.

"Well," said Murray, "that was a thing and a half."

"What should we—"

"Keep an eye on him. I'll get a PI I know to tail the guy, see where he goes."

"He did it," I said. "Don't you think?"

Murray thought about this.

"He seems capable," he said. "But there's a big difference between stabbing a sofa and shooting a presidential candidate. The world is full of crazy motherfuckers, Paul. Don't get your hopes up."

Why did everyone keep saying that? As if I had any hope left in me. I was living in a world of worst-case scenarios. Either my son was a murderer or he was innocent, and keeping his innocence a secret for reasons I could not begin to understand.

"It's not about hope," I said. "It's about facts. It's about figuring out what really happened that day, and why my son doesn't want to talk about it."

Murray looked at me for a minute, his face skeptical. I could see him form a response, then think better of it. He tapped his fingers on the steering wheel.

"You think those were really his brother's ashes in that box?" he asked.

I shook my head. All I knew was that if we didn't find some evidence of Danny's innocence soon, I would end up with a box of my own.

For his last meal Timothy McVeigh ate two pints of mint chocolate chip ice cream with chocolate sprinkles. Jimmies, some people called them. Ice-cream dirt. McVeigh had asked for them specifically. He saw ice cream as a sprinkle delivery system, nothing more. It was midafternoon, June 9, 2001. That morning he'd been transferred from his eight-by-ten cell at the federal penitentiary in Terre Haute, Indiana, to the red-brick death house five hundred feet away. It was a place few prisoners ever go. One from which none return. At 5:10 a.m. he'd stood naked in his cell. The guards had lifted his sack. They'd told him to bend over and spread his cheeks. This was a common occurrence around here. Prison is all about men in uniforms looking up your ass.

Inside the red-brick death house, McVeigh was placed in isolation, one last day in a tiny dismal cell. This one was a hundred feet from the execution chamber, a large empty room that contained the last bed on which McVeigh would ever lie. At one p.m. the guards delivered his last meal. He ate both pints of ice cream without pausing. What did he care if he felt sick later? He'd be dead. A guard watched him through a hole in the door. McVeigh sat on his cot watching television. For his last day of life the warden had allowed him to surf basic cable. McVeigh was addicted to all-news networks. He watched CNN. He watched MSNBC. He saw his own face looking back at him. He watched himself walk out of the courthouse in an orange jumpsuit six years earlier. News anchors with spray-on tans said McVeigh was scheduled to die at eight a.m. tomorrow morning New York time. They interviewed pundits who talked about closure. They talked to the family members of his victims, mothers whose children had died at day care, blown to bits by a five-thousand-pound bomb parked outside in a Ryder truck.

They didn't understand. Nobody understood. This was a war. He was a soldier. McVeigh poured the rest of the sprinkles into the bowl and licked his spoon. He had been raised Roman Catholic in Lockport, New York, though the God he had come to believe in after firing a 25-mm cannon atop a light-armor Bradley Fighting Vehicle in the first Gulf War was a God of Volume and Might.

On TV they showed footage of the siege at Waco. Had it really been eight years? The talking heads spoke of inspiration. They said Waco was where it had started for McVeigh. This is where the seed was planted. Revolution. In his cell, McVeigh remembered seeing the first reports on TV in 1993. A compound of families under siege by the federal government. Women and children being teargassed. And in that moment he saw the war to come, neighbor versus neighbor, the individual versus the state. McVeigh drove to Waco and sold bumper stickers out of the trunk of his car. He lowballed copies of William Pierce's book *The Turner Diaries*. The siege lasted fifty-one days, and then the government went in and burned those people to death. They shot them as they ran out of the flames. Women and children writhing in agony.

He joined the gun-show circuit, driving from town to town buying and selling. He stood on desert ranges with bikers and ranchers and other out-there freedom fighters. They shot bazookas into the nothing. "It's all right here," he told people, showing them a copy of Pierce's novel about the coming race war. He fired automatic weapons into the middle distance, gritting his teeth against the racket. But bullets were too small for him. A gun was a meager statement. A bomb, on the other hand—a bomb was a shout.

He made contact with an old army buddy, Terry Nichols. They sat in bars and talked about how they wanted to bring the fight to the government's doorstep. They talked about end times, about blowing shit up. They wanted to see the look on Clinton's face.

Eight years later McVeigh lay on the bed of his death-house cell. For the first time in years he was able to see the night sky. He lay under the tiny window and watched low-slung clouds glide across the dark, blacking out the moon. It felt like love.

On TV he saw his father, Bill. Dad looked old, haggard. He had retired from the radiator plant where he worked for more than a decade. There was an orange sign on his garage that read NO MEDIA ALLOWED. The reporter said Bill spent most of his time in the garden. They showed the verdant backyard where he grew strawberries, asparagus, peas, onions, corn, beans, and cabbage. Everything but cauliflower, which, he said, just wouldn't grow.

On the witness stand at McVeigh's trial, the defense lawyer had showed a photograph taken in 1992 of Bill with Timothy in the kitchen of his home in upstate New York. Father and son had their arms around each other, big smiles on their faces. The defense attorney asked Bill, "Is that Tim McVeigh in that picture the Tim you know and love?" And he said, "Yes, it is." And then he was asked, "Do you still love your son?" Bill said, "Yes, I do love my son." And then the defense attorney asked, "Do you love the Tim McVeigh who is in this courtroom?" Bill said, "I do." And then he was finally asked, "Do you want him to live?" He said, "Yes, I do."

The jury sentenced him to death anyway. His crime was too massive. What could one father do or say that would combat the misery of 168 fathers?

In the courtroom McVeigh sat stone-faced, watching his father talk. He would be strong. He would not cry. Not like yesterday when his mother had testified. Tears had leaked from his eyes, sneaking out against his will. But you can't blame a boy for that. Not when the mother sits weeping on the stand, saying how much she loves her son and how afraid she is.

Now, on TV, his father said, "I'm trying to treat it like any other day. I realize what it is, but . . ."

During McVeigh's trial, his attorney played a videotape the defense had assembled. It was made up of old home movies his grandfather had shot; Bill's voice narrated the film. Tim as a boy, the schools he went to. Images of him, his hair brushed, dressed in his Sunday suit, standing outside church.

"I think he enjoyed school," his father said. "He was a good student, although he never got the marks that he was capable of getting, I don't think. In high school he got an award when he graduated for never missing a day. In four years, he never missed a day of school. The first time Tim worked, I think, was the beginning of his senior year. He went to work at Burger King. After he was out, he got a New York State—$500 New York State Regents Scholarship. He went to Bryant & Stratton. It's a business school. And he didn't feel he was learning more than he already knew, so he decided to go back to work. And then after that, he got a job at the Burger King in Lockport. He worked for Burger King—I don't know—maybe a year—and after that he got a job for Park Security, driving an armored car. He got the job there because he had a pistol permit. Tim graduated, and he said at the graduation that quite a few of the kids were going into the military. He come home one day and said he was going in the service, and I says, 'When,' and he says, 'Tomorrow.' That's about all I can tell you about when he went in the service, or over to the Persian Gulf. He didn't seem to mind going, and he was ready to go when the time come, and they went to Kuwait. And I believe it was right around the end of '91, Christmastime in '91 or so. And he come back, he seemed to be happy when he come home."

McVeigh stood by the window and watched the clouds. He had less than twelve hours to live. On TV the news anchors talked about how McVeigh's mother has had three nervous breakdowns since the bombing. The words made McVeigh uncomfortable. There was a feeling in his stomach. A queasy expectation. Maybe it was the ice cream. Maybe it was thoughts of the needle in his arm. When they showed pictures of his mother, sad-faced and pale, with her hair falling out, he had to look away.

The death-house cell had tan walls, a bed, a sink, and a toilet. McVeigh's lawyer had visited him around three. They'd talked about last-minute appeals, but neither one of them was holding out any hope.

On August 14, 1997, McVeigh made one last statement before the judge sentenced him to death. He said, "If the Court please, I wish to use the words of Justice Brandeis dissenting in Olmstead to speak for me. He wrote, 'Our Government is the potent, the omnipresent teacher. For good or for ill, it teaches the whole people by its example.' "

McVeigh paused.

"That's all I have," he said.

With CNN on in the background, McVeigh wrote a few letters. He called the bombing a "legit tactic" in the war against an oppressive government. He said he was "sorry that people died, but that's the nature of the beast."

In an interview with *Time* magazine after his arrest he'd said, "I don't think there is any way to narrow my personality down and label me as one thing or another as many people have being trying to do. That's what they try to do with the psychological profiling, with the handwriting, etcetera, etcetera, and it's all pretty much a pseudo-science that I really laugh at when I read. I'm just like anyone else. Movies I enjoy would be action-adventure movies, comedies, sci-fi movies and shows. I can talk to almost anybody. The big misconception is that I'm a loner. Well, I believe in having my own space and being on my own sometimes. But, that in no way means that I'm a loner, which the press likes to equate with an introvert. That's a complete misconception. Women, social life. I like women [chuckle]. I don't think there is anything wrong with that."

On TV he saw his father again. This time Bill was sitting with another man, white-haired with glasses and a gentle face. McVeigh knew who the man was. His name was Bud Welch. He was the father of Julie Marie Welch, a twenty-three-year-old woman who'd been killed in the bombing. Since the trial Bill and Bud had found an uneasy friendship. They were a death's-head nickel, two-sided: the father of a murderer, and the father of his victim.

On TV Bud said, "In the months following Julie's death, I was one of many seeking vengeance for the people who took my daughter. I turned to alcohol and cigarettes to ease my pain. I was angry with God for allowing this terrible thing to happen to me. But after several months, I began to hear Julie's voice. Years before, as a child herself, I remember her telling me that she thought that executions only taught children to hate.

"With the realization that losing a child is a terrible burden, I began to understand that Tim McVeigh's dad, Bill, would soon be facing the same pain when the government executed his son. I reached out to Bill and his daughter Jennifer and that experience strengthened my conviction that we do not need to use the death penalty in this country.

"My conviction is simple: More violence is not what Julie would have wanted. More violence will not bring Julie back. More violence only makes our society more violent."

At 6:45 a.m. the guards arrived and began the final preparations. McVeigh was searched again, and then handcuffed with his hands in front of him. He took one last look at the moon, a crescent of bright salvation, then entered the hall and walked the short distance to the execution chamber unaided. There his cuffs were removed. He looked for the witness gallery, but the curtains were closed. It was important to him that they know he was not afraid. That he died not as a loser but as a martyr.

He was strapped to the gurney and covered with a gray sheet. A priest gave him the Sacrament of the Anointing of the Sick. It was meant to provide comfort and forgiveness before the crossing. Only after he had swallowed were the curtains opened and the faces of the witnesses revealed. A camera had been set up so relatives not present could watch the execution on closed-circuit TV. McVeigh raised his head and stared into the lens. He watched the curved glass, eyes unblinking. Family members at the viewing center felt as if McVeigh was looking into their souls.

Bill had not come. He couldn't bring himself to watch his son die. This was not the boy he remembered, the skinny kid who laughed too loudly. The shy kid who didn't know how to talk to girls. Last month, McVeigh had refused to hug him during their visit. In his eyes it was like he was already dead.

In the execution chamber they asked McVeigh if he had any last words. He wanted to sit up, but the straps were too tight. He quoted the British poet William Ernest Henley and said, "I am the master of my fate. I am the captain of my soul."

Next door, the executioner stepped up to the machine. He pushed a button and turned a key. Three chemicals were injected. First sodium pentothal, which causes sleep; then pancuronium bromide, which stops respiration; and finally potassium chloride, which stops the heart.

If injected improperly or in the wrong doses, a prisoner remains awake as the pancuronium bromide flows into his veins. He is paralyzed but feels an agonizing burning sensation. Is this what happened to McVeigh? Did he feel the pain his victims felt, an explosion of flames eating him alive? Or did he go peacefully, dropping off into crapulent sleep? We'll never know for sure. What we do know is that when the chemicals began to drip into the IV in his right leg around 7:10 a.m., McVeigh's skin and lips became paler. Minutes later, witnesses said McVeigh made a few spasm-like movements.

At 7:14 a.m. local time, he was declared dead.

It was Murray's idea to go to Royce Hall. I'd been afraid of it, the power it held. It was a place imbued with history, with implications I didn't know how to contemplate. We were driving away from Carlos Peña's apartment. There was a dirty unease in the car, a feeling of contamination, as if crazy were a flu you could catch from a sneeze. I thought about what he'd said. Acceptance. Was that the key? Would I never be happy again if I didn't accept that my son had murdered another human being? And yet what did my happiness matter when my son sat in a jail cell? When he would soon go on trial for his life? As his father I would gladly trade my happiness for his life.

We drove west on Sunset Boulevard through West Hollywood, crossing La Cienega and driving into Beverly Hills.

"I'll call my guy at the FBI," Murray said, "have them look at this Carlos guy again. Steak knives in the sofa. That is one creepy dude."

I watched the palm trees pass overhead through the sunroof.

"I've been reading a lot about the other assassinations," I said. "Lincoln, McKinley, Kennedy."

"Which Kennedy?" said Murray.

"Both. I've got a stack of books by the bed it'll take me months to read. I don't know why. What could it help?"

"You're a doctor," said Murray. "They're case studies. As a lawyer I find myself looking for precedents. I remember a fight with my ex because I came home late and smelled like strippers. And yet when we were dating she liked that about me. My randiness. Standing in the kitchen, pots flying past my head, I argued the case like there was a judge there who could overrule her, who could grandfather the strippers into my marriage. We can't help it. Our professions become our identities."

We drove past the Beverly Hills Hotel. The sun was out again, rainbowing the houses of the rich.

"I'm reading all their biographies," I said. "Sirhan Sirhan, Lee Harvey Oswald."

"You're looking for your son. John Hinckley watches the same movie twenty-seven times and stalks an underage actress. You think, 'Could my son do that?' Lee Harvey Oswald defects to Russia. He is America's most important Communist. He stands on a New Orleans street corner handing out 'Fair Play for Cuba' flyers. You read this and you try to picture Danny sweating in the Louisiana mug."

Case studies. Is this what I was doing? A woman presents with shortness of breath. Her pulse is weak. She has trouble lifting her right arm. Examining her, I consider these symptoms in context of all the other cases I've worked. All the other patients who've presented with one or all of these symptoms. Case studies. Inside the diagnosis of others lies the answer to every patient's problems.

"There were three shooters in Dallas," I said.

"Maybe. Or maybe that's just what we tell ourselves because Oswald is too small. How could this weakling, this sissy, have killed America's first movie-star president? Look at Reagan. He was a cowboy, John Wayne with nukes, and this fat nobody drops him like a bad penny."

"Do they do it because they're sick? I'm trying to understand."

Murray stopped at a red light. A pink Ferrari pulled up next to us, driven by a braless blonde.

"I read an article after the Giffords shooting," said Murray. "Studies show that nearly all these guys are mentally disturbed with no rational political plan. The politics are incidental. According to a recent Secret Service white paper there are four basic types of political assassins. Type Ones view their acts as a sacrifice of self for a political ideal. Type Twos are people with overwhelming and aggressive egocentric needs for acceptance, recognition, and status. Type Threes are psychopaths or sociopaths who believe that the condition of their lives is so intolerably meaningless and without purpose that the destruction of society and themselves is desirable for its own sake. Type Fours are characterized by severe emotional and cognitive distortions that are expressed in hallucinations and delusions of persecution and/or grandeur."

He turned and looked at me.

"You see your son in there anywhere?"

I shook my head. Danny wasn't a psychopath. He wasn't a radical. He didn't crave attention and he wasn't schizophrenic. If the symptoms don't match the diagnosis, the diagnosis must be wrong.

"He didn't do this, Murray," I said. "After seeing Peña I'm more convinced than ever."

"It's not what we believe," said Murray. "It's what we can prove beyond a reasonable doubt."

We arrived at UCLA just as classes were getting out. The lawns were filled with students: boys in school T-shirts, women in denim skirts and Uggs.

"I can't help it," said Murray. "I can't walk around these places without picturing the epic fucks, coed chicks with their knockout bodies. Little tits, big tits. Runner's legs. They're not tired of the whole deal yet. They still like the way a dick tastes, how it feels rubbing up against their thighs."

"You need help," I said.

A makeshift memorial lingered in front of the entrance to Royce Hall. Piles of flowers, farewell cards, testimonials. The university was considering renaming the building after Seagram. At the very least there would be a memorial. A plaque. We entered through the main doors. The building was a light-red brick edifice with porticos and archways. Two towers rose on either side of a steepled roof.

We were standing in a large entry hall. From video footage I knew that my son had entered through the middle doors. Cameras had caught him passing through the metal detectors at 2:51 p.m. I tried to picture the foyer filled with students, to imagine the energy in the air, the thrum and pulse of a crowd. Ahead of us were doors to the main theater. From my timeline I knew that these hadn't opened until just after three. There were stairways to our right and left. The one on the right led up to the hallway where the Secret Service claimed to have found a fire extinguisher still sticky with duct-tape residue. The prosecution would argue that Danny had climbed those stairs moments after entering. That he'd waited until the second-floor hallway was empty and then taken the gun from its hiding place.

I tried to picture this, my son pulling off the tape, running his hand over the sticky steel. Would he have pulled the clip and checked the chamber to make sure the gun was still loaded? Did he stuff it into the waistband of his pants like a common street thug? I couldn't picture it. But maybe this was my flaw. As a doctor I couldn't afford to rule out any diagnosis. I couldn't afford to let emotion color my judgment.

"Let's go inside," I said.

The houselights were low. We entered from the back, walking down the red-and-yellow carpet toward the stage. I tried to picture all the seats full, the restless hum of voices. Seagram's campaign manager had demanded students be allowed to stand in front of the stage. Otherwise it would look like the crowd was disinterested. They needed that rock-concert press, hundreds of fans hungry for closeness, wanting to touch their star.

The stage was five feet high. Before his speech began, Seagram had come to the front of the stage and shook the outstretched hands. The speakers were blasting the Smashing Pumpkins song "Today."

Today is the greatest
Day I've ever known.
Can't live for tomorrow.
Tomorrow's much too long.

I thought about the footage I'd seen. Seagram touches the upraised hands. He stands in the middle of the stage taking in the smiling faces, reveling in the applause. He has been campaigning for more than a year. He has won the Iowa caucus, the New Hampshire primary. He has won Super Tuesday, and now he is alone at the front of the pack. But there are still five months to go. There is the Democratic convention and then the national election, the knock-down, drag-out with his Republican opponent. He has slept maybe five hours in the last two days. There is so much to do, phone calls to be made, money to be raised.

He wants to stay close to his children. He doesn't want his wife to forget what he looks like. He stands on the stage energized by the crowd, and yet hasn't he made this same speech a hundred times? He tries to make the words fresh. He tries to give them something special. They are the future, after all. It sounds corny, but it's true. They are tomorrow's voters, tomorrow's taxpayers. He who controls the young, controls the world. He thinks about saying this, but it sounds cynical. "Controls" is the wrong word. "Commands" would be better.

Seagram takes a moment to look over at the west wing, where Rachel is standing. She smiles at him, gives him a thumbs-up. She has been so strong throughout this whole process. *First lady*. When he says these words to her she laughs. She can't believe this could be her. At the same time she says, "Couldn't they call it 'first woman'? Lady always sounds like what a cabdriver calls you when he's trying to take you for a ride."

He turns back to the crowd. The faces in front of him are white and black, Indian, Chinese. This is the America of the future, a patchwork of nations. Behind him Larry and Frank, his Secret Service detail, scan the crowd, looking for anything suspicious. Seagram soaks in the love of the crowd. It's hard to believe that anyone here would want to hurt him. He starts to talk about hope. About how the founders built hope right into the constitution. *The pursuit of happiness.*

"This is what makes our country great," he says. "We are all, each one of us, required to go out and find the things that make us happy. But that happiness comes with a price. Because isn't our neighbors' happiness just as important as our own? How can I be happy if my neighbor is suffering?"

In the balcony somebody throws a beach ball. The crowd below surges up to catch it, to bounce it around from hand to hand like they're at a baseball game or a rock concert.

"Without hope," he says, "there is no growth. Without growth there is no life."

He is in the home stretch now, climbing toward crescendo. He bounces on the balls of his feet and punches the air. When he is president he will change it all. He will drive the lobbyists out of the city. He will talk first, shoot later. He will listen to his advisers, to the people themselves.

"We were not put on this earth," he says, "to kill each other, to step over our neighbors in the streets. We were not put on this earth to get rich, or put up walls. We were put here to take care of each other, to start families and raise our children."

He steps away from the podium, walks forward. He wants to be closer to them, to feel their hands move the air in front of him.

"We were put here," he says—then suddenly he feels as if he's been kicked in the chest. The sound comes after, a metallic clap, echoing through the hall. He steps back, tries to steady himself. The second shot hits him in the neck. He drops the microphone and the world seems to tilt up around him. The stage hits him hard, breaking his wrist. He lies there bleeding. Six seconds ago he was talking. Six seconds ago he was heading toward the end. Now he is losing life, watching it spray out in a violet arc. He puts a hand on his neck, trying to stop the flow, but his arm is weak.

His wife is running now, trying to reach him. Larry and Frank stand over him, guns drawn. Frank is shouting into his wrist and searching the crowd, his head whipping left and right.

Not like this, he thinks, as Rachel drops to her knees beside him. He thinks of his children at home with their grandma. He prays they are not watching. And then he thinks of his son Nathan. Those final seconds struggling against the icy water. *Daddy's got you*, he'd said when he finally pulled the boy out of the pond. His little face was blue. His limbs limp. *Daddy's got you.*

Death comes for all of us. And now it was Jay Seagram's turn.

"Paul," said Murray.

I looked around. I was standing on the empty stage. Heavy lights hung above me, the curtains folded in the wings. Aside from Murray and me the theater was empty. I thought of John Wilkes Booth jumping from Lincoln's box inside the Ford Theatre, landing on the stage, snapping his leg. I thought of him pausing before the stunned audience, an actor savoring a moment. Though his leg was broken he stood tall and yelled, "*Sic semper tyrannis.*"

Thus ever to tyrants.

Politics had always been a kind of theater. It was the same with medicine. Surgery used to be a public affair, a man with a knife cutting open the human body in front of dozens of spectators. In the early days, the operating room was known as the operating theater.

"Paul," Murray said again. He was standing in the pit looking up at me, unconsciously occupying the very space my son had occupied, and I stood where Seagram had stood. It was the nature of the space, the way guests are drawn invariably toward the kitchen.

It's too much, I thought. *Too big.* We were standing in a place that was now a part of history, a place that housed the best and worst qualities of the human animal. Hope, and then murder. The extinction of hope. If my son had done this thing, I did not understand the world I lived in. Nor did I want to live in it.

Sic semper tyrannis.

But who is the real tyrant, if not the man with the gun?

He stayed in Iowa City for four months. The weather turned warm, then wet, then fractious. Hail fell from the sky. Tornadoes blew in like crazy drunken uncles, destroying homes and lives. Some days the heat was so bad the Mexicans would fill feeding troughs with water and take turns throwing each other in. Danny found he liked riding his bike in the rain. He liked to watch the heavy clouds roll in, to feel the static charge in the air. There was a risk to it he found he responded to, the appeal of a breathless, harebrained scheme.

He saw his first funnel cloud on July 16, God's evil finger reaching down and stirring up the American anthill. He was riding his bike north toward Cedar Rapids. Towering cumulonimbus clouds crowded the western horizon. The wind had been rising steadily for the last hour, first a steady breeze, then a thrusting gust that flapped through his hair and clothes. Rain blew sideways. Coming to a crossroad his bike tipped and bucked and he landed in a ditch. Mud soaked through his pants and into his shoes. He lay there for a moment making sure nothing was broken. In the distance he watched as massive black storm clouds squatted over the flatlands and gave birth to a twisting finger of death. The wind was roaring in his ears. He was a kid from the suburbs. What did he know about the animal threat of weather?

He watched the funnel cloud touch down and race through the farmland several miles north, swallowing cars and houses. It was an ugly black wedge. He pictured cows vaulting up in the air, circling the ground like spiders in a toilet bowl.

He got to his knees, then his feet. He started to run. The earth made a groaning sound. He looked back. The finger had become an arm, a whirling black limb battering the ground. What was he doing here? Risk is one thing. But this was insane. Around him it sounded like planes landing and taking off. He thought of another near-death experience, an airplane ride he took when he was eight. The feeling that everything was happening faster than he could control. He found a battered rock wall and hid behind it. He knew it wouldn't protect him from the twister, but there was nowhere else to go. He was soaked from the rain. Hailstones the size of baseballs pummeled his back and shoulders. It was hard not to feel hatred toward him, as if the earth, the sky, the world *hated him* in that moment.

He remembered standing on an elevated subway platform in a blizzard one night, waiting for the F train. He was fifteen years old and living with his father. Bored, he had skipped school entirely that day to explore the city. The wind was high and cold. And the snow was blowing sideways so that it came streaking, silent and hungry, right toward him. And with the darkness hanging like a shadow under every flake, and in the muffled light of the overhead fluorescents, it felt as if he was the one who was moving, blown forward by the wind into this grid work of snow that hung frozen in the air, the way snow looks when you're driving and the heavy wet flakes are leaping in through the glare of your headlights and colliding with the glass in front of you.

At some point he must have closed his eyes. The planes were landing and taking off. Freight trains hurtled past him close enough to touch. He realized he was yelling, a long, guttural keen that rose up from some deep reptilian place. It never even occurred to him to pray.

When he opened his eyes again the tornado was gone. The wind had died down and the clouds were breaking up, like a rampaging mob that has suddenly lost its outrage. He lay in the weeds, panting. His body felt electric, his brain. He started to laugh.

In Iowa they grew corn and soybeans. They grew hay and oats and strawberries. It was the home of honeybees and Christmas trees. Four million cows grazed the land, Guernseys and Holsteins and Ayrshires. Simmentals and Herefords. There were more than twenty-four million pigs, Berkshire and Chester White, Hampshire and Landrace. Blue-ribbon hogs that grew to be the size of Buicks. And there was raging, terrible dinosaur weather that could kill you. These were the facts. This was the great American farm belt.

Daniel spent forty-five minutes looking for his bike, then walked home.

That night he stood in front of Bonnie's gun case for almost an hour. Her father had been a collector, and when he died she continued his work. She had a wall of rifles, long-barreled and slim. A Winchester .30-.30, a Lee-Enfield bolt-action M10, and a Bushmaster M4 Carbine. There were pump-action and lever-action shotguns, cowboy guns resting on mahogany supports. She had tabletop cases filled with handguns on display; a Browning 9-mm, a Luger P08 Parabellum, a compact Smith & Wesson .45 ACP, and everybody's favorite, the .357 Magnum, hulking and stout.

He looked at the pistols under glass. Bonnie had taken him shooting twice since he arrived in Iowa. Once they shot cans long-distance with a .22 long gun. There was almost no recoil. He lay on his belly in the grass and watched the cans jump up in the air as Bonnie shot. When it was his turn he listened to the flat crack of each shot, but the cans stayed put. He caressed the trigger with his finger while Bonnie gave him pointers. "From this distance you have to factor in the wind," she said. "Set your sight a little to the right of the target. When you're ready to fire, hold your breath."

The first time a can jumped he felt a surge of joy. He wanted to take Bonnie out and buy her a steak dinner. The second time they shot she took him to a range. She brought four handguns in a lockbox. Before they shot she gave him a gun safety demonstration in a back room. She showed him how to disarm a semiautomatic, popping the clip and ejecting the round from the chamber. She made him practice until the moves were natural, graceful. She showed him how to load the revolvers and how to stand, legs slightly apart, left hand supporting the right. He wore goggles and a pair of bubble headphones like the ones worn by airport ramp agents as they tee their marshaling wands.

When he fired the .357 it tried to kick back over his head. Bonnie grinned at him, told him to hold his arms steady like a man. He emptied each gun at the target, hitting it every time. Bonnie said he was a natural.

He cleared the casings from the swing-out cylinder and reloaded. Compared to the Magnum, the Glock felt like shooting a potato gun. It was lightweight, with a high-capacity magazine, and the holes it punched in the target were smooth and symmetrical. He thought he would feel either horror or elation shooting such close-range weapons, but he felt neither, and later he told Bonnie that he preferred the rifles, preferred shooting outdoors, but that all in all he'd rather ride his bike.

He left Iowa on August 3. On his last night he ate dinner with Ted and Bonnie. She made pork chops and apples, and a blueberry cobbler for dessert. He ate so much he had to lie down on the floor. Who knew what his next meal would be? In the four months he had worked at the feed store he'd earned just over ten thousand dollars. He kept the cash in a shoe box, like some kind of paranoid hermit.

Bonnie told him she was worried about him. Why didn't he stay through the fall? Ted took Danny aside and said he understood a man's need to roam. Danny was a young guy. He had a lot of living to do. But he made Danny promise he'd call if he needed anything. He was the son they'd never had. Cora had been their only child. After her, Bonnie had miscarried six times, then given birth to a stillborn boy. Ted put his arms around Danny. He smelled like motor oil and cigarettes. His chest and arms were hard. It was what a father should feel like—solid, unmovable.

After dinner Danny went drinking with the Mexicans. They'd pooled their money and bought him a switchblade. Jorge told him to keep it in his boot. They told him to drive the speed limit, and if a cop pulled him over to say *yes, sir* and *no, sir*. Do not under any circumstances call him a *taconera* or a *zurramato*.

They showed him how to hold the blade in a fight. *Don't be afraid to bite*, they told him. Then they cut their palms and shook hands, their grip slippery but firm. Jorge said he had cousins in Texas and Los Angeles. If Danny needed anything he should look them up.

The next morning he took his footlocker and his shoe box full of cash and put them in the car. He put the switchblade in his boot. Ted and Bonnie stood near the car, unsure what to do with their hands. Bonnie had baked him six dozen cookies. They filled four huge ziplock bags. Danny didn't know how he could possibly eat all of them, but he would.

"Where are you headed?" Ted asked him.

Danny said he didn't know, but he thought he would drive south. He had always wanted to see the Southwest.

This time the hugs were quick, awkward. In the light of day they all realized what strangers they still were, and yet what good is a family if you can't open it up to strangers every once in a while?

He watched them recede in the rearview mirror. He felt energy in his stomach, a spinning ball of uncertainty. What was the world if not a place to explore? He put the rising sun to his left and drove south.

We ate dinner that night at Mr. Chow in Beverly Hills. The kids had moo shu and dumplings. Fran had Peking duck. I pushed around a plate of orange chicken. The kids talked baseball. I had signed them up for a fantasy league, and every morning they checked the stats. Fran watched me poke at my food.

"You're doing it," she told me.

I looked at her.

"Pushing us away. Locking me out."

I shook my head. Mostly I felt tired.

"Where did you go today?"

"We went to see Carlos Peña. And then we went to Royce Hall."

"And?"

"And there was a steak knife sticking out of his sofa. He had his brother's ashes in a box and he threatened us with a gun."

"My God. Paul."

"Well, to be fair, he threatened to threaten us with a gun. We never actually saw it."

"Did you call the police?"

"And say what? He lives in a pigsty? He has rug burns on his hips?"

"If you think he's connected to the case—"

"I'm beginning to suspect it doesn't matter what I think."

The kids ordered a caramel dessert. It arrived on fire. They played rock-paper-scissors to see who would get to blow it out, but it burned out on its own while they were playing.

Back at the hotel the boys fell asleep in their clothes. We peeled off their socks and stuffed them under the covers. Fran and I retired to the bathroom to take a bath. She unpacked the candles she had brought in her toiletry kit. Fran takes baths very seriously. She likes the water to be a temperature just south of scalding. I joke with her that she was a lobster in her last life. It was a small tub, but we made it work. I put my back to the wall, and she lay back against me, her feet pressed up against the far end of the tub. The lights were off, the candles flickering.

"I need to know," she said, "at what point do we stop fighting?"

Her hair smelled like lavender, with undertones of moo shu. I was too tired to talk.

"You tell me," I said.

"I'm serious. I feel like I'm losing you to this. To him."

"It's not a competition."

"Bullshit. You feel like you failed him as a father. You're wrong. You made the best of the situation. He knows you love him. He knows you did everything you could for him."

"Did I?"

"What I'm saying is you have to be careful. There are two boys in the other room who need you more than he does. Alex is on the edge. We've done good work this last year, but he has so much anger. And Wally is at that age where he's looking for direction, a role model. You need to be there for them."

"I am. I will be. I promise. But what if it was Alex in that cell? What if he'd been accused of a crime he didn't commit?"

Fran was silent.

"You think he did it," I said.

"I think he's a troubled kid," she said. "I think he's always been squirrelly, at least for as long as I've known him."

"Squirrelly."

"He never looked me in the eye when I talked to him. He dropped out of school without calling. He's been roaming the country."

"Not roaming. Exploring."

"This isn't the eighteenth century," she said. "He was sleeping in his car."

"He had jobs."

"Three weeks here. Six weeks there. You have to stop romanticizing it. This is not normal behavior for the twenty-first century. I've watched you since he left school. Even before the shooting you were sadder, more absentminded."

"He needs us."

"Does he? I think he's gone to great lengths to prove he doesn't need anybody."

The water was cooling around us, and I found myself shivering.

"When he was a kid," I say.

"When he was a kid he was the same way," she tells me. "I mean, don't get me wrong, I liked him. He was funny and thoughtful. And the boys loved having an older brother. He did magic tricks, for Christ's sake. But when I talked to him—even at fifteen—I always felt like he was only half listening. There was a quality he had, a transparency, like he was only ever really half there."

I thought about this, trying to picture it—the half-there boy. Fran hadn't known him as a baby, a toddler. She hadn't known the fierce, eager kid who lived for trucks, who slept with a plastic airplane the way other kids slept with teddy bears.

"All I remember is how he adopted Alex and Wally," I said. "How from the minute he arrived he became, like, their keeper. He showed them how to be big, taught them to make their beds, how to floss. And he was never too busy to play with them, to get down on the floor, and—"

"I know," she said. "He was great with them, and they love him. All I'm saying is, he wasn't that way with us. Whenever a grown-up talked to him he got a kind of, I don't know, skeptical look on his face. He was polite, but sometimes it felt like an act. Like he was giving us what we wanted so we'd leave him alone."

I watched a single drop of water form on the showerhead. It started as a pinhead, the barest hint of moisture, then grew fatter, surface tension holding it in place, until the weight of it became too great and it fell in a straight line, breaking the surface of the bathwater with an audible *plip*.

"Well," I said, "his family turned out to be a lie. The defining fact of his life, the bedrock. After that, I mean, don't you think you'd be skeptical of what grown-ups said, too?"

Fran pulled away and turned so she could look at me.

"I love you," she says. "More than I've ever loved anybody. But you need to accept the fact that no matter what you do he'll never be the son you want him to be. Even if by some miracle he's found not guilty and released, don't be surprised if he slips away again the first chance he gets. And I just don't want to see you get hurt again."

She reached out and touched my face. I closed my eyes. What kind of man would I be if I didn't take responsibility for my mistakes? If I didn't try to fix them? This was the oath I'd taken: *First, do no harm.* But doctors harmed their patients all the time. We misdiagnosed them. We mistreated them. We botched their surgeries. We didn't listen to them when they tried to tell us what was wrong. We bought malpractice insurance and hired lawyers. We hid behind our hospitals. We sat in our M&M conferences and discussed our mistakes in an effort to learn from them. But we were rarely punished. And yet if there are no consequences to our mistakes, what incentive do we really have to learn from them? In medical school we are taught professional detachment. We are told to see the illness, not the person.

But that's no way to live.

In the middle of the night the phone rang. I fumbled for it, trying to reach the receiver before the kids woke up.

"Hello," I said.

A man's voice said, "Hoboes."

"Who is this?" I asked.

"It's Murray. Listen, I don't have a lot of time. I had my guy at the FBI dig deeper into Carlos Peña, and it's a dead end."

I sat up, awake now. I looked over at Fran, but she was still sleeping.

"What?" I said.

"They've got video of him inside Royce Hall—some kid's iPhone— during the whole thing. Peña was standing center screen. Never pulled a gun. Never came anywhere near Danny. No way he was the shooter. The shots come from the other fucking side of the room."

The smothering weight of this pushed me back into my pillow. I realized how much I'd pinned my hopes to a long shot.

"You're sure?" I said.

"Totally," he said. "Carlos Peña is a no go. But check this out: I sent a PI to Sacramento. You remember the Secret Service identified Danny through an arrest report from California."

"Vagrancy," I said.

"Specifically," Murray said, "he was caught riding a freight train without permission. Common rail-hobo meshugas. A young man seeing the countryside from an open boxcar. That's the history of America. But the train companies don't like it because it fucks with their insurance."

"It's three a.m., Murray."

"Turns out, though, Danny wasn't the only guy on the train. There were two other men riding in the boxcar with him."

I felt a pulse in my stomach. The first hint of excitement. Or was it anxiety?

"What men?" I said.

"Here's where it gets interesting. Both guys are vets. One fought in Afghanistan. The other guy was in Iraq. Been out a little over two years."

"So he rode the train with some veterans. Don't you remember Vietnam? After they came home those guys lived in trains."

"Yeah, except one of these guys took a job working for KBR."

"The military contractor."

"I had to do some digging to find it. He's getting paid off the books. Checks deposited automatically every month. Hoopler. He bought a house last year, owns a fifteen-foot speedboat. And you have to ask yourself, where does a grunt get the money for that?"

I took the phone into the bathroom, trying to slow my pulse. First Peña, now this. Is it possible I'd been right all along? That my son really was innocent?

"You're sure he works for KBR?"

"I'm waiting for a couple of pieces of documentation to come in, but my guy traced the house payments to a dummy corporation that lists Duncan Brooks on its board of directors. Duncan Brooks is a VP at KBR."

I sat on the toilet and pressed my feet flat against the cold tile. I could still smell the lavender bubble bath in the air.

"What does it mean?" I said.

"Either this guy is just a train enthusiast," said Murray, "or there's a connection here. Was Danny recruited by KBR? Brainwashed? To what end?"

"This is crazy," I said. "I feel like I'm living in a spy thriller."

"Remember JFK?" said Murray. "Dealey Plaza. Police arrest three tramps they pulled off a freight train after the assassination. One of them is later identified as Charles Rogers, aka *the man on the grassy knoll*. Speculation about the other two connects them to both the Mob and the CIA."

I stood and looked at myself in the mirror. There was a line here I wasn't sure I was willing to cross. A descent into something convoluted and humorless. Fran was right. I couldn't get lost in this, couldn't disappear into obsession. Three men rode a train across the Sacramento delta. One of them was my son. The other two appeared to be war veterans, one an employee of a company that would have lost millions had the Seagram Bill passed the Senate and been signed into law. Was it true? Even if it was true, what did it mean? It was tempting to see a pattern here, a connection, but it also felt like the first step into something darker. A step down a road from which few men came back.

"I have to go," said Murray. "My guy is supposed to fax me the arrest reports."

"Listen to me," I said. "We can't sound crazy. I don't care what the evidence says. The minute people think we've become a bunch of conspiracy fanatics, we've lost."

I could hear Murray chewing on the other end of the phone.

"Ask Danny," he said. "You're seeing him tomorrow. Say Frederick Cobb to him. Say Marvin Hoopler. They may have used aliases. Tell him you know about the men on the train. See what he does."

"I should have spent more Christmases with him. I should have fought harder to get custody."

"Ask him if there are periods of time he can't remember. If sometimes he goes to sleep in one place and wakes up someplace else."

"I should have known he was going to be troubled. He never liked to be hugged. His entire adolescence he wouldn't take off his headphones."

"That's every teenager. I'm talking about mind control. Brainwashing. We need to figure out where Danny was for those days we can't reconstruct. November 14 through December 1. February 2 through 8. There are holes in the FBI's records. Was this when KBR had him?"

"I appreciate the work," I said. "Don't get me wrong. But none of this has anything to do with my son. He was just in the wrong place at the wrong time."

"Doc," said Murray. "I love you like an Indian gaming casino, but you need to accept that this thing is going to get a lot worse before it gets better."

He arrived in Austin on August 15, having meandered through Kansas and Missouri. He drove the NAFTA highway dodging eighteen-wheelers driven by men hopped up on chemically altered cold medications. When he got bored he lost himself on back roads and city streets. In Oklahoma he slept in a motel next to a truck stop. He found a bullet behind the toilet and what looked like the outline of a body shadowing the carpet. In the dappled light of the August dawn he decided that sex with truck-stop prostitutes was just another form of prayer, if the cries coming through the wall were any indication.

In Austin he sat inside the Whip In and looked for a place to live. He went on Craigslist and found a room in a house full of frat boys near the university. Someone had painted the Texas Longhorn logo on the lawn. There were beer cans in the trees. Inside, the place looked like a museum of trash. The house had been handed down from class to class over the years, never really changing hands completely. Students moved into rooms for a semester, stacking beer cans on windowsills, failing to wash the toilet, and adding to the ever-growing Honorary UT Underwear Pile that someone had started in the living room. Then they moved out. The lease was still in the name of a guy who'd graduated when Reagan was president. It was like a time-lapse photograph of a river making a canyon out of a mountain. The mess was archaeological. Dig deep enough you might find a half-eaten sandwich from when Elvis was king.

Danny's room was on the second floor facing Rio Grande Street. Across the street there was a house full of sorority girls, and the frat boys would take turns lying on the roof with binoculars hoping to catch sight of some premium Texas snatch. Danny sat in his room and listened to the radio with the windows open. It was muggy in Austin, a hot, lazy climate of ceiling fans and afternoon thunderstorms.

The frat boys called him *Sport* and *Chief*. They called him *Broheme* and *Jefe*. One guy called him *Albert*. It was easier than learning his name. Like the others, Danny would do his time at number 1614 then fade away, leaving only a false memory and a pair of stretched-out underwear on a pile. He was just another guy pissing in the toilet and dunking his toothbrush in a dirty mug.

Around him things went on as usual. Austin was a city of growth. It had a population of less than a million people, many of them musicians. This made it a landscape with a soundtrack, bands playing in the supermarket, at the airport. Pecan trees lined the streets, live oaks and Texas sycamores. The city had been built on a slow bend in the Colorado River, and much of its activity had to do with water. There was canoeing on Town Lake and swimming in Barton Springs. It was a city of parks and creeks and young men in baseball caps playing frolf. If you didn't bike or swim or run or hike in this town, he was told, there was something wrong with you.

Riding his cheap, secondhand bike around town, Danny realized that everything in Texas either said Texas on it or was in the shape of Texas. Place mats, road signs, security gates. It was as if residents were worried they might wake up in New Jersey if they didn't surround themselves with reminders.

It was in Austin that Jay Seagram first entered Danny's consciousness. It was Thursday, August 20. The first Democratic primary wasn't for five months, but already politicians were touring the country, doing the morning shows, making stump speeches, and forming exploratory committees. Danny was riding his bike on the Lady Bird Lake Trail when he saw the first banner. He settled into a coast and wiped his brow. He could hear the sound of a crowd up ahead. Riding past the First Street Bridge he saw them, a throng of registered voters crowding the great lawn of Auditorium Shores. Onstage a man in a suit told them it was time for a change. The sun sparkled on the river. A light breeze blew in from the west. Last night the humidity had finally broken, and today it felt like anything was possible.

He left his bike by the gate and wandered through the crowd. Young women in bikini tops sat on towels, squinting toward the stage. Dogs ran off leash, kids played with Frisbees.

"I'm tired," said Senator Jay Seagram, holding the microphone casually, speaking without notes. "Tired of making excuses for why bankers get rich while the rest of us get screwed. Tired of hearing stories about families being evicted from their homes. Tired of children going to bed with empty bellies. I'm tired of being told I should be afraid of people I've never met. I'm tired of fighting a war based on a lie. I'm tired of living in a country where people can't get help when they're sick, and I'm sick of multinational corporations getting away with murder at our expense. I'm sick and I'm tired, and looking out at you, I can see from your faces that you too are sick and tired."

The crowd cheered.

"You're sick of feeling like your voices aren't heard. You're tired of paying taxes that go to buy bullets that kill people just because they speak a different language than you do. You're sick and tired of spending half your paycheck on gas, when car companies have the technology to make cars ten times as fuel efficient. Today. They could do this today, but they don't. Why not? Aren't you sick and tired of asking 'Why not?'"

People were standing now. Danny walked among them, his fingers brushing their arms. There was electricity in the air around him, like the static before a storm.

"It's time to stop asking," said Seagram. "It's time to start doing. To make demands. We *demand* universal health care. We *demand* a living wage. We *demand* our politicians stop raising our taxes while cutting taxes for corporations. We're tired of asking. We have been patient and we have been polite. But we're not going to be polite anymore."

Danny stood next to the stage and watched as Senator Seagram raised his arms over his head. The crowd roared. Seagram looked down and his eyes met Danny's and he winked.

The next day Danny went to Seagram Campaign Headquarters. It was on Guadalupe, near the Co-op. He talked to a man in blue jeans and a white button-down shirt, Walter Bagwell.

"What can I do?" Danny asked.

Bagwell gave him a clipboard and some flyers and sent him out to raise candidate awareness. Daniel stood on the corner of Twenty-second and Guadalupe and handed flyers to students. The flyer asked the same questions Seagram had asked at the rally. It listed a website you could visit and a phone number you could call. Danny handed out five hundred flyers his first day. Walking home he saw them discarded, stuffed into trash cans and stuck to the windshields of cars. This seemed to him like a metaphor for politics itself. One man's outrage was another man's trash.

At the UT library he read everything he could find about the senator. Seagram had grown up poor. His father walked out on the family when Jay was three. Seagram had put himself through college, and then through law school by starting his own college prep course for high-school students. By the time he graduated from Stanford Law, Seagram had more than eleven hundred employees, and branches of his course existed in eighteen states. He sold the company to the Princeton Review for six million dollars.

Danny sat in the library looking at pictures of Seagram and his wife, Rachel. She was a pretty brunette with laugh lines around her eyes. She looked like a good wife, like the kind of wife who never said anything mean, who played with her children and cooked complicated meals, and liked to give head. The children were bright-eyed, pink-cheeked. They looked like kids who got good grades and played team sports. Happy children from an intact home whose parents loved them. Children who weren't shuffled back and forth between their mom and dad for the holidays. Children who never had to listen to their mothers screaming at their fathers how they "fucking hated" them. How they "wished they would die in a fiery car crash." Children who never had to watch their fathers slam doors and kick holes in the wall.

It was clear. Not only did they have good parents, these children; they had each other. Someone to play with, someone to lean on. They weren't like Danny, an only child who, when he was six, snuck out of his house one night and slept in the car just to see if his parents would notice. They didn't. Here they were on vacation, a happy family smiling beside a lake. Here they were on a sailboat, floating on Caribbean waters. Here they were at Christmas standing next to a giant tree, bright lights flashing like smiles.

He e-mailed himself the pictures, the articles. He wanted to look at them later in his room. To make some notes.

He first noticed *the girl* in Russian History. She was reshelving books about the civil war. She had light brown hair and a pointy nose. Her ears stuck out a little but not too much. Something about her face made his chest contract. Something about her light summer sweater and the swell of her buttocks against her slacks. He hid in Current Events and spied on her as she made her way through the stacks. She had a bright white smile and an easy laugh. Everyone around seemed to know her. Danny couldn't turn his eyes away. She was the kind of girl, he thought, who gets up early to swim laps, then delivers Meals on Wheels after work. The kind of girl who doesn't just drop off the meal but stays to hear stories, to look at pictures of grandchildren.

He lay in bed that night and thought about her. He pictured them sailing on Caribbean waters. The thought of her in a bathing suit made his skin tighten. Downstairs the frat boys shouted at the TV and ate pizza they'd found in a box under a towel. He could hear the baseball announcer calling the game, that clipped rapid tone, the flat vowel sounds of an eastern industrial city.

In September he registered people to vote. The Seagram campaign coordinator said she'd never seen so many signatures collected in one day. He was good with people. He saw things about them. He chatted up housewives in supermarket parking lots. He talked sports with jocks. He stood on street corners with the illegals waiting for work and learned what the slang words were for *pussy* in Ecuador and Brazil.

After his shift ended he would go to the library and read about Texas. He felt it was important to know everything he could about the place where he was living. The girl didn't work every day. She did the afternoon shift Monday through Wednesday, and morning on Thursday and Friday. Her name was Natalie. Danny got to the point where he could recognize her silhouette from a distance. He became familiar with her clothes, her outfits: the jean jackets and the long skirts. She wore an anklet on her right leg. It was something a boyfriend might have given her. He wondered if she wore it to bed. If she showered with it on.

He thought about talking to her many times, but he never did. She was so clearly the perfect girl, and he worried that if he spoke to her she would say something or do something that would ruin it, and then she'd be just another pretty girl with a great ass he had slept with.

He was happy in Austin. He liked the weather and the people. He liked riding his bike beside the water. He even liked the frat boys with their beer bellies and affectionate head butts. There was a girl he couldn't stop thinking about, and a job that felt right to him. He had found a purpose. A cause.

And then he saw the tower. And everything changed.

The University of Texas clock tower was built in 1937. It stands just over three hundred feet tall on the west end of the campus. It is the tallest building for blocks in each direction. The first time Danny noticed it he was standing on the corner of Twenty-first and Guadalupe handing out flyers. He had worked the area for two weeks, but this was the first time he could remember looking up. The time on the giant clock read 3:15 p.m., gold hands crossing over brass roman numerals.

He left the flyers on top of a garbage can and walked toward the main concourse. Entering from Twenty-first Street he passed a monument to student soldiers killed in World War I. He climbed the steps toward the main administration building, past Benedict Hall and Mezes Hall, past statues of George Washington and Jefferson Davis, president of the Confederacy. He stood on the wide concourse staring up at the tower. It held a strange hypnotic power over him. For some reason he thought of the funnel cloud that nearly killed him back in Iowa. This, too, felt like the arm of God somehow.

As he was standing there a girl came up beside him. She was someone he'd registered to vote two days earlier. They'd talked about school and the weather. It was clear she was attracted to him, but he wasn't interested. Susan something. Now she slid up beside him and said, "Can you believe he killed all those people here? It still gives me the willies."

He looked at her. He had no idea what she was talking about.

"The marine," she said. "Charles something or other. Whitman. It was back in the seventies or something. He went up there with a rifle and just started shooting."

She asked him if he had time for a cup of coffee. Danny made an excuse. He hurried to the library. The tower was looming in his head.

Natalie wasn't working that day. Yesterday he'd overheard her ask for the day off. It was for the best. He had to be back at work in an hour and didn't have time to pine for her today. He went straight to the computer lab and typed in *Austin, UT clock tower, Charles Whitman.*

The facts were these. Just after midnight on August 1, 1966, Charles Whitman, twenty-five, had strangled his mother with a rubber hose, then bashed the back of her head in. He then stabbed his sleeping wife, Kathy, five times with a hunting knife. The next morning he drove to the University of Texas, climbed to the top of the clock tower, and shot forty-six people with a sniper rifle, killing sixteen and wounding thirty, before he was shot and killed by police.

Danny read the reports. He found old TV footage, news reports from the day. He saw still photographs of victims on gurneys, of police hunkered down behind squad cars.

In the months leading up to the massacre, he read, Whitman had remarked to various people that a sniper could do a lot of damage from that tower. Cultural theorists called it history's first modern crime, and said Whitman's random shooting spree had given birth to the twentieth century.

Charles Whitman was born in Lake Worth, Florida, the son of a wealthy family. He was a gifted student, an accomplished pianist, and an Eagle Scout. But he had a violent father, who would later admit, "I did on many occasions beat my wife. But I loved her. I did and do have an awful temper, but my wife was awful stubborn. Because of my temper, I knocked her around."

He also beat his sons, using belts, paddles, and, when nothing else was around, his fists to discipline them. In June 1959, shortly before his eighteenth birthday, Charles came home drunk and his father beat him badly and threw him into the swimming pool where he almost drowned. A few days later Whitman joined the Marine Corps. He was determined to get out.

In the marines he earned a sharpshooter badge, scoring 215 out of a possible 250. He excelled at rapid fire from long distances and seemed to be more accurate when shooting at moving targets.

The marines saw officer potential in Whitman, so they sent him to

Austin, Texas, to attend the university. In Austin he married his girl-friend, Kathy Leissner. He also started gambling and was arrested for poaching. His grades were average. The marines decided they'd made a mistake and called Whitman back to active duty. He was posted at Camp Lejeune in North Carolina. He resented the Marine Corps and it showed in his behavior. In November 1963 he was court-martialed for gambling, usury, and unauthorized possession of a nonmilitary pistol. He did thirty days in confinement and ninety days of hard labor.

Back in Austin, he returned to school. He was determined to make up for lost time. Then, out of the blue, he was struck by fits of blind-ing rage. His wife convinced him to see a therapist. Whitman sat in his office and told him he had fantasies of going up into the clock tower and shooting people with a deer rifle. The therapist told Whitman they'd made progress and asked him to come back in a week.

Whitman started self-medicating with Dexedrine. He thought it made him a better worker, but in truth it made him sloppier. He went days without sleeping, sitting at the kitchen table trying to get orga-nized.

On July 31 he bought a Bowie knife and binoculars at a surplus store and canned meat at the 7-Eleven. He picked up Kathy from work and took her to dinner. Back at home he sat down and wrote the following letter.

> Sunday, July 31, 1966, 6:45 p.m.
>
> I don't quite understand what it is that compels me to type this letter. Perhaps it is to leave some vague reason for the actions I have recently performed. I don't really understand myself these days. I am supposed to be an average reasonable and intelligent young man. However, lately (I can't recall when it started) I have been a victim of many unusual and irrational thoughts. These thoughts constantly recur and it requires a tremendous mental effort to concentrate on useful and progressive tasks. In March when my parents made a physical break I noticed a great deal of stress. I consulted a Dr. Cochrum at the University Health Center and asked him to recommend someone that I could consult with about some psychiatric disorders I felt I had. I talked with a Doc-tor once for about two hours and tried to convey to him my fears

that I felt some overwhelming violent impulses. After one session
I never saw the Doctor again, and since then I have been fighting
my mental turmoil alone, and seemingly to no avail. After my
death I wish that an autopsy would be performed on me to see
if there is any visible physical disorder. I have had some tremen-
dous headaches in the past and have consumed two large bottles
of Excedrin in the past three months.

Leaving Kathy at home, Whitman drove to his mother's apartment.
Inside apartment 505 he choked her with a length of hose until she
passed out, then stabbed her with the hunting knife. In this way a boy
surpasses his father. He placed her body in her bed and pulled up the
covers. He left a note on the door for the super, asking not to be disturbed.

At home he went to the bedroom where Kathy was sleeping. He pulled
back the sheet and stabbed her five times. Then he sat down to finish the
letter he'd started earlier.

He wrote, "3:00 a.m."

Both dead. It was after much thought that I decided to kill my
wife, Kathy, tonight after I pick her up from work at the telephone company. I love her dearly, and she has been as fine a wife
to me as any man could ever hope to have. I cannot rationally
pinpoint any specific reason for doing this. I don't know whether
it is selfishness, or if I don't want her to have to face the embarrassment my actions would surely cause her. At this time, though,
the prominent reason in my mind is that I truly do not consider
this world worth living in, and am prepared to die, and I do not
want to leave her to suffer alone in it. I intend to kill her as pain-
lessly as possible.

Similar reasons provoked me to take my mother's life also. I
don't think the poor woman has ever enjoyed life as she is entitled
to. She was a simple young woman who married a very possessive
and dominating man. I was a witness to her being beaten at least
one [*sic*] a month. Then when she took enough, my father wanted
to fight to keep her below her usual standard of living.

I imagine it appears that I bruttaly [*sic*] kill [*sic*] both of my loved ones. I was only trying to do a quick thorough job. If my life insurance policy is valid, please see that all the worthless checks I wrote this weekend are made good. Please pay off my debts. I am 25 years old and have been financially independent. Donate the rest anonymously to a mental health foundation. Maybe research can prevent further tragedies of this type.

As the sun came up, Whitman placed the following items in a green footlocker: *One (1) Channel Master 14 AM/FM transistor radio, one (1) blank Robinson Reminder notebook, one (1) 3 1/2 gallon water jug, one (1) 3 1/2 gallon plastic gas jug, four (4) "C-"cell flashlight batteries, several lengths of cotton and nylon ropes, one (1) plastic Wonda-scope compass, Paper Mate black ballpoint pen, one (1) Gun Tector, one (1) green rifle scabbard hatchet, one (1) Nesco machete with green scabbard, one (1) Hercules hammer, one (1) green ammunition box with gun-cleaning equipment, one (1) Gene alarm clock, cigarette lighter, one (1) canteen filled with water, binoculars, one (1) green Sears rifle scabbard, one (1) Camillus hunting knife with brown scabbard and whetstone, one (1) large Randall bone-handle knife (with "Charles J. Whitman" inscribed on the blade) with brown scabbard and whetstone, large lock-blade pocket knife, one (1) ten-inch pipe wrench, one (1) pair of eyeglasses in a brown case, one (1) box of kitchen matches, twelve (12) assorted cans of food and a jar of honey, two (2) cans of Sego, one (1) can of charcoal starter, one (1) white-and-green six-volt flashlight, one (1) set of earplugs, two (2) rolls of white adhesive tape, one (1) solid steel one-foot bar, one (1) green rubber army duffel bag, one (1) green extension cord, several lengths of clothesline wire and yellow electric wire, one (1) pair of gray gloves, one (1) deer bag, one (1) loaf of bread, sweet rolls, Spam, Planters Peanuts, sandwiches, a box of raisins, one (1) plastic bottle of Mennen spray deodorant, three (3) rolls of toilet paper.*

At 5:45 a.m. he called Kathy's supervisor at the phone company and told her his wife was sick and wouldn't be in today. He spent the morning accumulating supplies. At around 7:15, he went to Austin Rental Company and rented a two-wheeled dolly to help him transport the heavy footlocker. He cashed $250 in checks at the Austin National

Bank, and bought guns and ammunition at Davis Hardware, Chuck's Gun Shop, and Sears.

He packed the guns (a .357 Magnum Smith & Wesson revolver, a Galesi-Brescia pistol, a .35 Remington, a sawed-off Sears 12-gauge shotgun, a 6-mm Remington bolt-action rifle with a 4-power Leupold scope, and a .30 caliber M-1 Carbine) into the footlocker, along with the receipt from Davis Hardware. He also had more than seven hundred rounds of ammunition.

It was time to get moving.

At home he called his mother's employer and said she was ill and wouldn't be coming to work. It was ten thirty in the morning. He needed to hurry if he was going to get this done before lunch. Then he took his new shotgun out to the garage and sawed off part of the barrel and the stock. At eleven he pulled a set of blue coveralls on over his clothes, trundled his footlocker to the car, and headed for campus.

Whitman arrived at a security checkpoint on the edge of campus at eleven thirty. He showed Jack Rodman, the guard at the checkpoint, his Carrier Identification Card, and told him that he would be unloading equipment at the Experimental Science Building. He asked for a loading zone permit. Five minutes later Whitman unloaded his gear and entered the tower. With his coveralls and dolly he looked like a janitor or maintenance man. Once in the elevator, he asked for help from an attendant, who informed him how to turn it on. "Thank you, ma'am," Whitman said. "You don't know how happy that makes me."

There was a receptionist on duty on the twenty-eighth floor. Whitman brained her with his rifle butt, then dragged her across the room behind a couch. Moments later a man and a woman entered the reception area from the observation deck and found Whitman leaning over the couch, holding two guns. They saw blood on the floor. There was an uncomfortable silence. Then the elevator doors opened and the couple climbed on board. Whitman watched them disappear. Then he dragged a desk in front of the stairway door.

He was reaching for his footlocker when he heard the scraping sound of the moving desk. Someone was trying to force the door open from inside the stairwell. Whitman grabbed a shotgun and moved toward the stairs. Tourists stared up at him, four adults and two children. He leveled the sawed-off and started shooting. Each shot felt like a chain snapping.

On the roof he wedged the door shut behind him. The time was 11:48.

It was a hot day, muggy, and the noon sun felt like a blanket smothering him. He took a minute to calm himself. There was a tingling in his groin that was almost sexual. He took the Remington bolt-action and leaned it against the stone balustrade, facing south. He bent his eye to the scope. The South Mall was a sea of teen motion. *This is what the Lord must feel*, he thought, as he moved the sight of his rifle from bystander to bystander.

The first shot hit a pregnant woman, killing her unborn baby. The second killed the man next to her. A visiting physics professor took a bullet in the lower back. Whitman saw each shot before he made it. He anticipated the hit and was already on to his next victim before the bullet struck.

The first squad car arrived just after noon. Whitman had already turned his attention to Guadalupe Street. He shot a newsboy off a bicycle. The way the kid went flying made him burst out laughing. He shot a seventeen-year-old girl, but at the last second the wind picked up and he could tell he'd only wounded her.

Police officers crouched behind cover and tried to eyeball the shooter's location. Bodies lay where they had fallen, shimmering in the hundred-degree heat. Whitman shot a kid through a six-inch space between two balusters. *Was there no one he couldn't hit?* he thought. He was a prizefighter in his prime, the heavyweight champion of the world. Each shot made him taller, stronger. Each life he took added a hundred years to his own. He crossed the roof and shot a doctoral student coming out of a newsstand. Whitman saw two kids jump behind a barricade. When one of them peered out to see what was happening, Whitman shot him through the mouth.

He heard gunshots. The police had started shooting back. Austinites had gone home to get their guns, and they, too, were trying to pick him off, raining bullets up at him from the street. It was Texas after all, the land of the cowboy vigilante. Whitman listened to the bullets ricocheting off the stone walls around him. It was only right. What fun would it be if they didn't fight back? He started shooting through the rainspouts on each side of the building, making himself almost impossible to hit. He'd been up there for half an hour already. In thirty minutes he had brought an entire city to its knees. The sun was beginning to make him feel like a marshmallow over a campfire.

Fifteen hundred feet to the south, a man standing next to a pickup truck took a bullet in the stomach. Whitman was a killing machine. He was the wrath of God, as unrelenting and imminent as death itself. He could shoot the man in the moon if he wanted to. He could shoot people in the future. He could execute the past.

Whitman never heard the roof door being kicked open. He was in the zone, bullets from the ground peppering the walls above him. As he took aim on a half inch of bare skull, two police officers came around the corner of the roof. They opened fire. Whitman turned, bringing his rifle around, but he was too slow. A shotgun blast caught him in the side of the head, knocking him to the ground. It was 1:24 p.m. He had been on the roof for ninety minutes. He had been God for ninety minutes. It was more power than most people ever felt in a lifetime.

Officer Ramiro Martinez stepped up to Whitman's still-twitching body and fired his shotgun point-blank, nearly severing Whitman's left arm and killing him instantly.

Danny sat back from the computer. He was surprised to find that it was dark out. Had he really been here for more than five hours? He couldn't describe the feelings he was having. But then he'd never been good at that, turning hurt into words. The hunger he felt for the details of what had happened that day in 1966 unnerved him. It was an unhinged sensation. A moment of terrifying sobriety, where the driver realizes he is drunk and speeding down a crowded highway with his lights off. What scared him was not the recklessness of Whitman's crimes, the randomness of his victims. It was the recognition of justice. An acknowledgment he felt in parts of him that he wouldn't even admit existed, that a man who had been so wronged by the world, by his friends and family, could exact revenge. And that that revenge, though terrible, would be justified.

There is a moment for each and every one of us in this life where we discover, often to our great surprise, whether we are wolves or sheep. To be a sheep is to surrender to fear. But there is fear, too, for the wolf. Fear when we realize that the rules of society do not apply to us. Rules are for sheep. And this moment of realization is terrifying in its liberation.

What resonated for Danny was not Whitman's violence. It was his transgression. He had renounced every convention of civilized life. He had rejected hundreds of years of evolution. By standing atop that tower and leveling his rifle at the world below, Charles Whitman had declared his independence from the society he lived in.

And it was this idea that made Daniel Allen feel faint.

My father, who died when I was eleven, grew up in southern Michigan. There was automobile money in his family. His father, Darryl Allen, was a senior executive at General Motors. Darryl's wife, Francine, died giving birth to my father. A few years later Darryl fell in love with the receptionist at his local auto mechanic's garage, a woman named Margie Brubaker. They dated and married quickly. Margie soon became pregnant, and nine months later another boy was born. A half brother. They named the boy Ellroy Buck Allen.

Ellroy was a troubled child from the start. He suffered from dyslexia and what was most likely attention deficit disorder. Ellroy was hyperactive as a child, quick to anger, always lashing out. Unlike my father, who would go on to get his engineering degree from MIT, Ellroy dropped out of high school. He felt uncomfortable around members of my father's family, many of them wealthy, preferring to spend time with his mother's blue-collar relations. One of these relations was a no-good cousin named Busby Hix who had been arrested several times, starting in elementary school, for crimes as varied as petty larceny, public drunkenness, and assault.

It was with Busby on a chilly night in November that Ellroy walked into a convenience store and ordered the clerk to empty the cash register. They had been drinking and had recently taken speed. Busby was carrying a .38 Special with four bullets. Just before entering the shop he had given Ellroy a .22-caliber revolver. The wooden grip of the .22 was held together with electrical tape. It held a single shot. While Ellroy aimed his pathetic gun at the clerk, Busby went to the refrigerator to get a six-pack of beer. Coming back, he attempted to open one of the bottles with his key chain but dropped it. The bottle smashed on the floor. Ellroy turned at the sound. The clerk reached for a pistol hidden under the counter. Busby yelled "Look out," and Ellroy fired the only shot in his gun, striking the clerk in the temple. There was sixty-five dollars in the cash register.

Ellroy was sentenced to twenty-five years to life. He served eighteen, and died three years later, after passing out drunk in a snowbank.

A hapless armed robber and a political assassin. Was there a genetic connection? It is not an easy mystery to solve. Because Ellroy was my father's half brother the lineage is not pure. It's easy to postulate that it was Margie's genes, her blue-collar blood that infected Ellroy, not my father's.

And yet there is another symptom to factor into the diagnosis: my grandfather, Darryl Allen, was said to have been abusive. A staunch conservative, he believed in corporal punishment, administered at the end of his belt. Most of his "corrections" were aimed at Ellroy, the black sheep. But my father also saw his share of beatings—when he brought home a low grade or snuck in past curfew. Were these beatings the sign of an inherently violent nature or simply a philosophy of child rearing? If it was inherent, if my grandfather was a violent man, is it possible his aggression was the source of Ellroy's aggression? And yet, if this is the case, then that aggression was just as likely a product of environment and not genetics. Aggression as learned behavior.

For the last several years, researchers have been experimenting on mice to try to ascertain whether aggression is hereditary. Through select breeding they have tried to identify genes that lead to increased aggressive behavior. Most studies have focused on polymorphisms of serotonin receptors, dopamine receptors, and neurotransmitter-metabolizing enzymes. In particular, the serotonin 5-HT seems to be an influence in intermale aggression either directly or through other molecules that use the 5-HT pathway. Aggression in animals and humans is normally dampened by 5-HT. Mice missing specific genes for 5-HT were observed to be more aggressive than normal mice and were more rapid and violent in their attacks.

Other studies have been focused on neurotransmitters. Studies of a mutation in the neurotransmitter-metabolizing enzyme monoamine oxidase A have been shown to cause a syndrome that includes violence and impulsivity in humans.

So aggression can be caused by genetics. But were genetics responsible here? Let's answer this by asking another question. If we look at history's most violent men, do we find violence perpetuated in their lineage? Take Charles Manson, perhaps the country's most notorious murderer. In the late sixties, Manson was responsible for the brutal murder of at least six people, including the actress Sharon Tate, wife of director Roman Polanski. Tate was eight months pregnant when she was stabbed multiple times. Manson, the leader of a self-proclaimed "family," had surrounded himself with drug-crazed followers eager to help him start a race war. After his arrest, he sat in the courtroom with a swastika carved into his forehead. Over the previous ten years, Manson had fathered several sons with different women. Forty years later, not one of those men has ever committed a single violent crime.

Then there was Gary Gilmore, who, seven years after the Manson murders, became the most famous criminal in America. In the summer of 1976, Gilmore murdered two men in Utah, gunning them down in cold blood after successive robberies. Like Manson, Gilmore had been in and out of prison since he was a boy. His father routinely beat him and his brothers, often for no reason. Gilmore came from a long line of hucksters and religious zealots. He had become the most famous criminal in America, because when sentenced to death he chose to be executed by a firing squad. As the son of a Mormon mother, Gilmore was drawn to the concept of blood atonement, which states that the only way to atone for spilling blood was to have your own blood spilled. And so when given the choice Gilmore chose to be executed by firing squad, and on January 17, 1977, he was shot to death by five men. His last words were: "There will always be a father."

There will always be a father. What did it mean? Was he blaming his crimes on his father? Was he talking about God? Gilmore was the product of a long line of criminals. He was beaten regularly by an angry father and raised by the prison system. Whether violence was in his genes or his blood, he was in many ways a product of his environment.

This was not my son. None of these killers were anything like my son. Not just because aggression is different from premeditation. One could argue that what my son was accused of doing to Senator Jay Seagram was the opposite of aggression. There was a cold calculation to the act. Premeditated crimes, by definition, are not crimes of passion. The assassination of Seagram was planned and executed meticulously.

But if murder is not an act of aggression, what is it? And where does it come from? If it is not an act of passion, at a time in a young man's life when he is consumed by passions, then what is it? My son was a boy with no history of aggression, a peaceful child, a pacifist.

When I made this argument to Ellen, she reminded me of the Spider Incident. It happened when Danny was thirteen and still living with her, two years before he came to live with me. One day Ellen called to say she had found a jar full of dead spiders in Danny's room.

"What kind of spiders?" I asked.

"I don't know the kind," she said, "but there are a lot of them, and, honestly, I almost threw up when I saw it. You know how I feel about spiders."

I told her she was being dramatic. Maybe it was a science project for school.

"Then why hide them in the closet?" she asked.

I told her I'd been to her house. She lived near the state park and there were a lot of spiders. Maybe Danny had developed a fear of them as a child, and this was his way of conquering that fear. Besides, I said, we didn't know that he'd killed the spiders. Maybe he collected dead ones.

"Because there are tons of dead spiders just lying around," she said.

Ellen told me that when she'd asked Danny about it he'd gotten angry. He accused her of spying on him, of going through his things. I told her it all sounded like perfectly normal teenage behavior.

We hung up the phone and I promptly forgot that the whole conversation had taken place. The following year when Danny came to stay with us, I remember Alex found a spider in his room. He wanted to kill it, but Danny stopped him. He trapped the spider in a glass and brought it outside and set it free.

Thinking about both incidents now I wondered—what did it mean? I had spent the last three months trying to compile the evidence, to add up all the moments from Danny's childhood that could provide a diagnosis, a definitive answer as to who he was and why he did the things he did, and yet in life everything is open to interpretation. We see the past through the prism of our perception. When a man is indicted for a crime you review his life looking for patterns. Incidents that may have been meaningless before suddenly loom large. *Look. He killed spiders. That must have been an early-warning sign.* But at the end of the day, isn't a story about a boy who kills spiders balanced out by a story about the same boy saving spiders?

I tried to picture my son at thirteen systematically exterminating insects, tracking them to their webs and capturing them in a jar. I tried to imagine him watching as the oxygen in the jar slowly ran out. What thoughts would go through his head in that moment, watching the spider's hunt for an exit become increasingly frantic, then slow, then stop altogether?

The scene felt invented when I imagined it, like something out of a movie, the junior serial killer with his starter prey. Ultimately, it was a pill my body just wouldn't take.

I have looked into my son's eyes throughout the course of his life and never once have I seen a freak, a sociopath, or a murderer.

No. I was convinced that the answer to this mystery did not lie in Danny's lineage or his childhood. It was out there on the open road. Somewhere between New York and Los Angeles. Somewhere in the cornfields and mountain ranges of the middle of the country.

Murray found a last known address for Frederick Cobb that put him in Eagle Rock, twenty minutes north of Los Angeles. The address turned out to be a homeless shelter. Since riding that westbound freight train with my son a year ago, Cobb had popped up sporadically in various parts of the state. He sought medical care from a veterans' hospital in Santa Rosa. He applied for unemployment benefits in Riverside. There was a second citation for vagrancy in Santa Monica, followed by an arrest for public drunkenness. Cobb appeared, for all intents and purposes, to be the classic homeless veteran, unable to form real relationships or put down roots.

Murray drove city streets to Glendale Boulevard, then jumped on Route 2 heading east. It was just after morning rush hour and the roads heading away from the city were mostly empty. Daniel's arraignment hearing was scheduled for four o'clock that afternoon, so whatever investigation we conducted would have to be quick. When I woke Fran that morning to tell her I was going she just shook her head. It was clear now that nothing she'd said to me the night before had sunk in. I was Don Quixote chasing windmills. Trying not to wake the kids, I promised I'd be back in a few hours, but I could tell she wouldn't be holding her breath.

"I'm a little worried about my marriage," I told Murray as he drove.

"I'm a little worried about your marriage, too," he said.

"Thanks. That's sweet."

"No, seriously. I've seen a lot of unhappy women in my life, and she has the look."

We sat in silence, watching the road for a minute. I worried that events were conspiring, forcing me to make a choice between my first-born son and my new family. It was a choice I couldn't begin to fathom how to make. Where was the middle ground? Was it really true that to be a good father to Danny I had to abandon Alex and Wally as I had abandoned Daniel? And yet didn't I owe it to my firstborn son to see this through? And shouldn't my new family understand and support that choice? Didn't being a good parent to Danny make me a better man, and thus a better husband and father to my other boys?

"My second wife," said Murray, "used to text the word 'disappointed' to me so often, that if you typed the letter 'D' into her phone the word would automatically fill itself in."

I rolled down my window to let in the wind. Somewhere a fire was burning, and the smell of smoke filled the car. Fran would wait a few weeks, wouldn't she? She would grumble. She might even threaten to leave me, but she wouldn't really go. Would she?

I looked at the stack of paper Murray had handed me this morning when he picked me up. A private investigator he used on divorce cases had run the standard document check on Frederick Cobb—credit report, military records, various state and federal databases—and, as we drove, I studied the facts of Cobb's life. Born in Lexington, Kentucky, in 1985. A high-school graduate who went to state college on a football scholarship, until his knee blew out and he was cut from the team. Three months later he dropped out. The file said Cobb had floated for a year, working minimum-wage jobs around Lexington. There was an arrest for marijuana possession and another for driving under the influence, but both were dismissed. In the file was an application for a marriage license filed at the Lexington Civil Court by Frederick Cobb and Marilyn Duncan. But though the application had been filed, it appeared that no formal license was ever recorded. So the ceremony either never took place or went unrecorded. But the certificate remained, evidence of at least a fleeting desire on Cobb's part to grow up and settle down, and at the same time proof that he hadn't. What happened? Who was this Marilyn Duncan and what had kept her from landing her man?

Maybe the engagement was the by-product of an unwanted pregnancy, a pregnancy that either terminated itself or was terminated in a moment of teenage clarity or lover's revenge. Or maybe Cobb had simply gotten cold feet and left his bride-to-be standing at the altar.

What was clear was that six weeks after applying for a marriage license, Cobb joined the army. Elements of his service record were classified, but it looked like he had gone through Special Forces training at Fort Hood. His record showed that he was sharpshooter qualified, scoring thirty-five on his marksmanship exam, and that he was deployed to Afghanistan in early 2003. There, Cobb served as a sniper for eight years, rising from private first class to a staff sergeant.

Those were the facts, and there were three that struck me as critically important. First, that Cobb had Special Forces training. Second, that he had served as a sniper. And third, that parts of his service record were classified.

Could it really be a coincidence that this man happened to find himself riding the same freight train as my son?

In 2008, halfway through his third tour of duty, Cobb's Humvee hit a roadside bomb. Everyone in the vehicle was killed except Cobb, who lost three fingers and the hearing in his left ear. He also suffered damage to his peripheral vestibular system that resulted in recurring feelings of vertigo. It was this chronic dizziness that ultimately forced Cobb out of the military.

"So what do we know?" said Murray, after I filled him in. "We know Danny was arrested on May 20 of this year outside Sacramento, California, when he was discovered inside a boxcar on a freight train at a switching station. We know that there were two other men in the car with him. Both were army vets, Hoopler and Cobb. Cobb has Special Forces training. Hoopler—we're pulling his service records. We should know more by the end of the week. One fact that stands out, though, is that Marvin Hoopler has connections to KBR, the arms manufacturer. The guy owns a speedboat. What's a guy like that doing stowing away on a freight train with a homeless vet and a twenty-year-old kid from Connecticut? Speaking of which, our records of Danny's activity in the week prior to the arrest are fuzzy. We know he spent time in Sacramento and would end up in Los Angeles a week later, but the fact that we're missing information about that particular week seems suspect. Did Danny meet Cobb and Hoopler on the train? Or did they get on that train together?"

"And," I said, "what connection, if any, did they have after the arrest? Can we find any evidence that puts Hoopler or Cobb in Los Angeles the week of Seagram's murder?"

Murray changed lanes to get around a pickup truck that appeared to be carrying half a house.

"Are you—we should be writing this down," he said.

I found a pen, made some notes. The file noted that Cobb had returned to the States in 2011 with an honorable discharge. He spent six weeks at home in Lexington, probably hoping to pick up his life where he left off. But apparently that proved to be impossible, and in February 2012, he hit the road. Information became sparse after that, but Murray's private investigator turned up the address for a homeless shelter where it appeared Cobb had been living for the last few weeks.

We found the shelter on a quiet tree-lined street next to an Episcopal church. Men with blank-eyed stares huddled by the door. They wore the standard uniform of the homeless—layers of baggy clothing weighed down with dirt. To a man, they looked away when we got out of the car, some shuffling into the street in a "casual" attempt to evade the two men who might be cops. Instead of a badge, however, Murray held up a hundred-dollar bill.

"Frederick Cobb?" he said. Silence. The desire for money apparently was no match for the impulse to remain uninvolved in the affairs of others.

Inside, we found a social worker behind a cloudy sheet of Plexiglas. Murray introduced himself and said he was looking for one of her customers.

"We call them clients," she said.

Murray told her he was a class action attorney who represented Cobb in a civil suit. The suit had settled recently and Cobb was owed a large sum of money. The lie came out easily, casually, his eyes never leaving hers. The social worker shrugged, neither impressed nor suspicious, and consulted an invisible list somewhere below the lip of the Plexiglas.

"Not here," she said. When pressed if Cobb had left any kind of forwarding address, the social worker turned to an old desktop computer. She hunted and pecked, as if the whole idea of technology was inconvenient to her. Minutes passed. Murray and I exchanged a look. We had three hours before we had to get back in the car and drive south. Two if we wanted to get to the courthouse with any kind of breathing room.

"Section 8 housing," she said. "Over on Powell."

She wrote an address on a piece of paper, slipped it through a slot in the plastic. Murray thanked her and we hurried out to the car.

It cost us a hundred dollars to get the manager of Cobb's apartment complex to confirm that Cobb lived there, and another two hundred to have him let us into Cobb's place. He was the kind of skinny man who spied on women in the next apartment through a peephole.

"He's five days late on the rent," the manager told us. "Two more days I'm putting his crap in the trash."

"Does he work?" asked Murray. "Cobb? Does he go out a lot?"

"Do I look like his social secretary? Most of these douche bags, you know, the state puts 'em up, but they get used to living on the street. They don't know what to do with a home, where they don't have to shit in a bush with one eye on their stuff."

The building was about ten years old, built to convey a sense of optimism in the face of poverty. This meant that despite its location and hangdog infrastructure, the building had been painted with bright primary colors. Colors that had faded down to a ghostly hue, like a Donald Duck costume left too long in the sun.

Cobb's apartment was small and nondescript. There was a mattress on the floor and three hard-back chairs, but no table. Boxes of junk lined the walls, clothes stuffed in trash bags. It smelled like the trunk of a serial killer's car.

"If he comes home while you're in here," said the manager, "I'd think about going out a window."

"Thank you," said Murray. "We'll keep that in mind."

The manager closed the door behind him when he left. Murray and I studied the decor. It was a studio apartment with a small kitchenette. There were piles of newspapers lying around, and, strangely, several copies of *Parenting* magazine. I knelt and started sorting through the boxes and trash bags. Murray went into the kitchenette.

"I dated a schizophrenic girl once," he said. "Her place looked a lot like this. The bathroom was full of crosses. She even had one hidden in the toilet tank. And there were like a hundred stuffed animals on the windowsill that used to watch us fuck."

"How long did you date?"

"About three weeks," he said. "She seemed nice, a little nutty. She was a philosophy major at NYU. Then one night I come to pick her up and she'd cut all her hair off, and was calling herself Sally. Her name was Jean. She'd eaten a bowl of pills with milk, like cereal. So I drove her to the emergency room where they sedated her. Locked her in the mental ward. I visited a couple of times, then changed my phone number. I mean, what's the etiquette on a thing like that? We weren't married. She was just a girl I banged sometimes who kept crosses in the toilet."

There was nothing noteworthy in the cardboard boxes. Stolen library books, a few pots and pans. Inside a trash bag full of clothes I found a bullet.

"Look at this," I said.

Murray came in. "Take it. We'll run some ballistics."

I looked around for something to put it in, then realized how stupid that was. What was I worried about? Contaminating evidence? I wasn't a cop. Would anyone believe that I, the accused's father, had miraculously found the exonerating bullet in another man's home, even if I produced it in a plastic bag? I slipped the bullet into my jacket pocket. Murray returned to the kitchen. Outside, we could hear kids playing basketball, the scuffling of their shoes, the sound of the ball caroming off the rim.

"Bingo," Murray shouted.

I got up and went in the kitchen. Inside a drawer there was a newspaper article that had been cut out of the paper. There was a picture of Danny. The headline read ASSASSINATION SUSPECT TO BE ARRAIGNED NEXT WEEK.

I stared at the picture of my son. What did it mean? Did Cobb clip the article because he was connected to the murder, or simply because he recognized my son as a man he'd ridden a train with six months earlier?

Murray grabbed his phone and took a picture of the article in the drawer. Then he walked around the apartment photographing every bag and box. He knelt and shot the mattress, one corner propped up awkwardly against the wall, then went into the bathroom and looked inside the toilet tank. I put my hand in my pocket and felt the smooth weight of the bullet. There was something about being in this dark space that made the hair stand up on my arms.

"What now?" I asked.

Murray came out of the bathroom.

"How long until Danny's hearing?"

I checked my watch.

"We've got ninety minutes," I said.

Murray sat in one of the three chairs and thought about this.

"The guy clipped an article about the case," he said.

"That doesn't mean he's connected," I said, but even as I said it my mind was racing.

"I'll send the bullet to a guy I know," Murray said, "see if we can link it to the murder weapon."

I sat in the chair next to Murray's. We made a strange sight, two men in suits sitting in the middle of a hobo's flat. I thought about how the clues in a human mystery are nothing like the clues in a medical mystery. With medicine you are dealing with scientific facts. Tissue samples, blood tests. The human body is a finite entity, with a finite number of systems. There are external factors—environmental issues, exposure to chemicals, drug use, alcohol, questions of diet, and the introduction of outside pathogens—but the answers ultimately lie within the body. At worst—if the malady proves undiagnosable and thus untreatable—an autopsy can be done after death to determine the cause. And from this one learns the answer to the mystery.

But with a human mystery, it is difficult even to decide what constitutes a fact. A man rides a train. He is familiar with weapons of all kinds. In his home is a newspaper article that would appear to connect him to the mystery. That is a fact, but is it relevant? Is the symptom connected to the underlying malady?

And facts are only a piece of the puzzle. There are also issues of psychology and emotion. Cancer is cancer, no matter what you think about it or how you feel. It has no motive, no alibi. It operates according to a prescribed set of factors and is either treatable or not. But people are more complicated. Their actions are harder to understand, and even harder to predict. My son had been accused of a crime and was refusing to acknowledge his guilt or proclaim his innocence. That in itself was a fact, but a fact that proved what?

We sat in those chairs for forty minutes waiting for Cobb to come home. The sun threw shadows on the floor that crept slowly toward our feet. At 2:55 we stood and took one last look at the sum total of Cobb's life, then ran to the car and drove to the courthouse.

We hit traffic on the highway, a wall of red brake lights stretching as far as the eye could see. A four-car pileup in the center lane at a downtown interchange. I searched the radio for news. Murray tried to switch lanes, but we were boxed in. For twenty-six minutes nothing moved. It was 3:25. Daniel's arraignment started at four. I called Fran.

"At least half an hour," I told her. "Whatever you can do to stall them."

"I'm a housewife from Connecticut," she said. "How exactly am I supposed to stall them?"

"I'm just saying," I said. "If there's anything—"

Her voice was tight. "It's a zoo right now. The kids don't understand why you're not here."

"I told you, Murray found Frederick Cobb, the veteran who was on the freight train with Danny."

She sighed. I could almost hear her trying to decide how much of this conversation to have with me.

"They let us see Danny for five minutes," she said. "He asked for you. Where you were. I told him you were following a lead, like we're all characters in some hard-boiled detective novel now."

My pulse quickened.

"What did he say?"

"He said they don't feed him that much. He said that what they don't tell you about prison is that you're hungry all the time."

I felt worry settle into my hands. I said, "Is he—can you get a message to him? Mention the names Frederick Cobb and Marvin Hoopler, see what he—"

"Paul," she said.

I stopped. Silence built between us. She exhaled softly.

"I say this with all love, and I want you to listen to me very carefully. If you want to be here for Danny because you feel like you were never there for him when he was a kid, well then *you have to be here*—physically. You have to sit in that waiting room for hours at a time, and then take the five minutes they give you without complaining. And in the five minutes they give you, you have to hug your son, sit with him and hold his hand, and tell him you love him. Not talk strategy or pick his brain for details. You just have to hold him. Because that's what he needs now. He has lawyers. He needs his father."

Murray finally managed to nudge the nose of his car into the right-hand lane. The exit was a thousand yards ahead.

"Fuck it," he said, and pulled onto the shoulder, gunning the SUV to fifty, racing past the frozen traffic.

"Okay," I told Fran. "We're moving. I'll see you in twenty."

"Paul," she said. "Did you hear what I said?"

I rubbed my face with my free hand.

"I heard it," I said, "and I'm—you're not wrong. But I think what Danny needs more than anything right now is his freedom, and I'm—"

"No," she said, "you're not listening. You're running around, chasing smoke, and doing everything you can to stay basically a thousand miles from all the emotions you don't want to feel. Baby, I love you, but that's what you're doing, and I just—I worry that when this is over, you're going to feel like you missed the chance to spend time with him."

When this is over. What she meant was, after the trial, after his time on death row. What she meant was after they executed my son.

"We're taking city streets now," I said. "Murray will drop me out front. Just don't let them arraign him before I get there."

I hung up. Murray blew through a yellow light, took a left turn too fast. The back of the car threatened to go into a skid but Murray corrected, as if he did this for a living.

"She's pissed," he said.

"No. Not pissed. Just . . . worried. She thinks I should be there, holding his hand instead of . . . what I'm doing."

Murray pulled around a city bus, the SUV floating briefly into oncoming traffic. Ahead of us, cars flashed their lights. Murray made a hum-ming sound in his throat, corrected his course.

"Not to be, you know, a dick," he said, "but that's her job. Or Ellen's. The mothers. You and I—we're men. We act. That's what we do. Their job is to nurture or whatever, and we—we protect our families. We provide for them. We fight. And anybody who tells you different—well, don't even worry about that."

He leaned on the horn, scaring half a dozen pedestrians out of the crosswalk.

"I'm beginning to understand why you've been divorced three times," I said.

He smiled. I looked at the clock on the dashboard: 3:55.

"We're not going to make it," I said.

"Yes, we are," he told me. "But you might want to close your eyes. It's gonna get intense."

At 4:07, Murray skidded to a stop outside the courthouse. There was a fist-size dent in the front right wheel well that hadn't been there when we left Eagle Rock, and the inside of the car smelled of burning brake pads, but we were there. The area was choked with cars and pedestrians. Police barricades had been set up, the crowd pushed to either side of the courthouse steps. News vans were parked in the shade, dishes raised, cameras deployed, their feed sent in real time into the homes of millions of Americans.

"I'll park the car and meet you inside," Murray yelled to my back, and I slammed the door in his face.

I lost six minutes getting into the building, flashing my ID, waiting in line, another nine going through the metal detectors, first unloading my pockets, then taking off my jacket, finally my shoes. I'd had the sense—just barely—to leave the bullet we'd taken from Cobb's apartment in the car.

I tried Fran's phone over and over, but she wouldn't answer. I had to assume that she was in court, that the proceedings had already begun.

The clock on the wall read 4:30 as I stumbled down the hall, trying to get my shoes and jacket back on without losing any more time. For the first time in weeks I felt like we had a chance, like all the digging and arguing and the dogged refusal to lose hope was about to pay off.

My cell phone rang. The caller ID showed Murray's name.

"I can't talk," I said. "I'm trying to get in there."

"They found Cobb," he told me.

"Who?"

"It was the fingers. Remember I said he lost three fingers in Afghanistan? Well, I had my guy comb hospitals and morgues. He just called. Cobb's body is in Riverside."

"His body?"

"He's been there about three days. Cause of death looks like stabbing."

I stopped walking. "He's dead?"

On the other end of the phone I could hear Murray leaning on his horn.

"My guy's getting the autopsy report," he said, "but I'd say sometime Monday night our boy Cobb ran into the wrong end of a knife something like sixteen times."

As the gist of what he was saying caught up with me, time seemed to stop. I felt myself going into a kind of shock. The sensation was physical, the flight response of an animal in the moment it realizes it has become prey.

"Murray."

"Hold on," he said. "I just found parking. I'll be there in five minutes."

He hung up. I held the silent phone to my ear. Cobb was dead. What did it mean? Was this proof of something or just another detail? I felt the predator on my heels, its measured breathing getting closer, the thunder of heavy feet.

Up ahead I saw the courtroom doors fly open. Men and women poured out, walking quickly, some yelling into cell phones. I saw Fran emerge, pushing herself through the bodies. She looked around, saw me.

"Paul," she said.

"There's no time," I told her. "Cobb's dead. The vet. Somebody stabbed him on Monday. This is—we have to find Douglas. Danny's lawyers need to get on this right away."

"Paul," she said again, more forcefully this time, worry on her face. "Danny pleaded guilty," she said.

I stared, trying to understand. She held my eyes.

"The prosecutor presented the charges and the judge asked him how he pleaded, and Danny stood up and said, *Guilty.* And his lawyers started shouting. They asked for a recess. The judge said no. He asked Danny if he knew what it meant to plead guilty and did he need a moment to consult with his lawyers, and Danny said no. He understood. He said, 'I killed him, and I don't want to waste any more of anybody's time talking about it.' "

A tunnel of darkness surrounded me.

"That's . . ." I said. "No. He's protecting them. It's—don't you see? He's not . . ."

The thoughts were coming too fast to articulate. I felt the panic of the animal in the moment of capture, the mouth of the trap closing down.

"He pleaded guilty?" I said. None of it made any sense.

Fran grabbed me, pulling me to her, as if worried I might fall. Her hair smelled like apples. Behind her I could see Murray pushing his way through the crowd.

"Murray," I said.

"I know," he said. "I just heard. We'll get a psych evaluation for Danny. Sane people don't confess to things like this."

I pulled myself free from Fran's grip.

"Unless he was—what if he was covering for them? Hoopler and—I don't know. I don't know."

I made fists of my hands, punched myself in the legs, trying to think.

"Paul, please," said Fran. "You're starting to scare me."

Murray took my elbow, pulled me to an empty corner.

"Look," he told me. "This is bad, but it's not the end of the world. The judge is going to order a psychiatric evaluation. He has to. If Danny's unbalanced, or if he has another agenda here, we'll know. And if he is, then we may have to have Danny declared mentally incompetent. Meanwhile we push Douglas to dig into Cobb and Hoopler."

He kept hold of my arm, using himself as a ground, trying to keep me from floating off into the void. At the end of the hall I saw movement. A crowd of men in uniforms emerged from a doorway, escorting a shackled prisoner.

"Danny," I called. I pulled away from Murray and pushed my way through the crowd. "Danny!"

At the end of the hall, my son turned. Our eyes met.

"It's okay," he called.

"Wait."

"It's okay."

A man in a suit broke off from the pack and moved to intercept me.

"Sir," he said. "You need to stop."

"Please," I said. "I just want to talk to him. Danny!"

"Sir, our transfer protocols are very specific."

I felt like a man standing on a riverbank, watching his son wash away.

"Fuck that," I said. "Danny!"

The agents tightened their grips and dragged my son toward the exit.

In five seconds he would be gone. Who knew when I would see him again. If he could be pushed to confess to a crime he didn't commit, what else could he be pushed to do?

Or worse. What if he'd confessed because he truly was guilty?

I had to talk to him, had to know once and for all. What was the truth? How could I save my son if I didn't know what I was saving him from? Half mad, I tried to push through the agent, to chase my son down. He grabbed me by the neck, his hand closing down like a vice. We wrestled.

"I know about the vets," I yelled. "Danny! On the train. I know!"

And then the floor disappeared. I felt myself moving in space, revolving. The next thing I knew, I was lying on my face, my right arm jacked up behind me. There was a knee in my back, knocking the wind out of me.

"Stop fighting," the agent told me. I tried to breathe, tried to call out.

"I'm going to get you out of this," I said, or tried to say. It came out as half squeak, half grunt. I struggled to get to my knees, but Danny was already gone, washed away, lost to the river of history. And as the agent moved to put me in handcuffs I finally surrendered to him, the way the rabbit goes limp in the jaws of the wolf.

The moment where he finally accepts that death is inevitable.

Three

CARTER ALLEN CASH

PSYCHIATRIC EVALUATION OF DANIEL ALLEN
Conducted by Dr. Arthur Fielding, MBBS, MD
Dated: October 11, 20___

This psychiatric evaluation was prepared for the U.S. District Court, Western Division, by Dr. Arthur Fielding. It draws information from two three-hour interviews with subject, and a review of 147 pages of subject Daniel Allen's writings.

EXECUTIVE SUMMARY

Subject is accused of murdering Senator Jay Seagram on June 16, 20___ in Los Angeles. The court has asked that subject be evaluated to determine if he is mentally capable at this time of entering a plea of guilty.

Though subject shows several signs of dissociation and has suffered at least one serious bout of clinical depression in the last twelve months, he does not, in this evaluator's opinion, suffer from a mental illness, as defined by the *Diagnostic and Statistical Manual of Mental Disorders*. Therefore, it is the conclusion of this evaluator that Daniel Allen, sometimes known as "Carter Allen Cash," is legally competent to enter a guilty plea in this matter.

It is also the conclusion of this evaluator that, at the time of the assassination, subject was able to distinguish fantasy from reality. Based on in-depth interviews and a review of subject's own writings, it is clear that he knew the difference between right and wrong, as defined by the M'Naghten Rule and the Durham Standard.

PHYSICAL DESCRIPTION

Subject is twenty years old. He is 5' 10", and weighs 150 pounds. At the time of his interview, he was dressed in an orange prison jumpsuit. He was well groomed, and, though underweight, seemed healthy and alert. Subject appears to be a young man of above-average intelligence, who spoke articulately about many subjects, though he was reluctant to delve too deeply into matters of his own emotional state.

HISTORY

Subject Daniel Allen was born April 9, 19__ in Santa Monica, California, to Ellen Shapiro, mother, and Paul Allen, father. Subject reports his early life was basically happy, though he says his parents divorced when he was seven years old. His father, a doctor, moved to New York City that same year. The mother retained primary custody, and subject traveled to New York to visit his father for summers and holidays. When asked, subject reports that he was "fine" with this arrangement, though he says his mother was "a little scattered" and "used to cry all the time." A review of subject's school records shows he did well in primary and elementary school, displaying no signs of a PTSD adjustment disorder, such as bed-wetting or the development of a stutter or other speech impediment.

Subject reports one incident from this period that is worth further consideration. He states that in his eighth year, he was "almost killed in a plane crash." The details are as follows: Subject had been in New York City visiting his father for Christmas. Subject was to fly alone back to Los Angeles, which, he says, was standard. While over the Midwest, his plane developed "an electrical problem" and fell into a steep dive. "Everybody thought they were going to die," subject reported. The pilot subsequently fixed the malfunction and righted the plane.

When asked how he felt during the free fall, subject reported, "I felt . . . it's hard to say. I was scared, but I didn't think I was going to die." When asked why, he said, "Just a feeling. It wasn't my time." When asked how he believed the incident had affected him, subject stated, "It must have affected me, but . . . I'm not sure exactly how." When asked whether the incident changed the way he felt about his parents, subject said, "Yes. It made them seem smaller." When pressed to expand his answer, subject stated, "I didn't feel like I had to listen to them anymore. Almost like they weren't my parents anymore." When asked why, subject stated, "Parents are supposed to protect you from things like that, aren't they? Mine just didn't seem that interested in me."

HIGH SCHOOL

When subject was fifteen he asked to live with his father. When asked why he said, "I just wanted a change. My mom was a little clingy, you know? She'd had a number of bad boyfriends and was sad a lot. I think she wanted me to fill that hole for her." Subject stated that his father had remarried several years earlier and had two young sons. "They were like a real family," subject told me, "and I guess I wanted to see what that was like."

After the move, subject continued to do well academically. His teacher evaluations focused on his attentiveness and creativity, and stated he was most always prepared. But subject stated the change in custody did not bring the feelings he'd hoped it would. He told this evaluator that instead of feeling like he was part of his father's new family, he felt outside of it. An intruder. When asked how this made him feel, subject stated, "It didn't bother me too much. I wasn't that surprised, actually. I mean, my dad never really felt like a huge part of my life. And now, I don't know, I guess I felt like one of those exchange students, you know? When you go to France or something, and they put you with a French family. That's how it felt."

Subject applied to and was accepted by several colleges. He chose to attend Vassar in New York State, though he only stayed for one and a half semesters. He stated that he had a "hard time focusing" on his curriculum at college. "It just didn't feel that important, you know?" he said. When asked if he had made friends, subject stated that he'd made a few, but "no one I felt really close to." He stated that he "hadn't had many friends in high school, either." When asked why he thought that was, subject stated, "I don't really like to talk about myself. I guess that's a big part of friendship, but I just don't like telling people how I feel about something, or what I think. I think most of the time people say stuff just to hear themselves talk." When asked if he felt his opinions were less valid than others, subject stated, "No. I just think you learn more by listening than you do by talking."

Subject stated he left college because he felt he could learn more "out there, on the road. You know, where life really happens."

THE ROAD

Subject spent the next fifteen months traveling. According to him, "I went all over—the Midwest, Texas, Portland." Federal records show that in the aforementioned fifteen-month period, subject spent time in Chicago, Iowa City, Austin, Helena, Portland, San Francisco, and Sacramento, before driving to Los Angeles, where the incident occurred. Subject stated that he never stayed in one place longer than four months. When asked, he said this wasn't a rule, but "I just felt antsy if I did."

In the course of our interview, subject became increasingly uncomfortable as he discussed his time on the road. He said, "I don't like talking about this stuff. I went where I went. I did what I did. Who cares why?" While he spoke with genuine enthusiasm about the time he spent in Iowa, working for Ted and Bonnie Kirkland, he refused to talk at all about the three months he spent in Montana during the winter of 20__.

When presented with pages from his own journal detailing his thoughts and feelings from his time on the road, subject stated he didn't want to talk anymore. Our first interview ended on this note. It is worth noting that several dozen pages outlining his time in Montana have been torn from his journal.

In our second session, subject apologized for his "attitude" in our previous session. But, he stressed, "I don't really want to talk about what I went through last year. It's not relevant, you know? I mean, all you care about is why I did it, right? Why I shot the guy? And, you know, we can talk about that, I guess, but I just don't see the point. All this why, why, why. My reasons are my own, you know? All that matters is that I did it, and I'm, you know, sorry about it."

Subject's own writings from his journal are more insightful into his mental state over the fifteen months between his decision to drop out of college and the day he claims he shot Senator Seagram. A more in-depth analysis can be found in Addendum #1 to this report. But as the purpose of this examination is to determine subject's capacity to enter a plea, not to conduct a full analysis of his overall mental state, the evaluator will move on to other matters.

CARTER ALLEN CASH

One of the more interesting factors in this case was subject's decision to "change his name" from Daniel Allen to Carter Allen Cash. Starting in September 20__, subject began to refer to himself as Carter Allen Cash in his own writings. We also know he began to introduce himself to others as Cash starting around the same time. This continued until the time of his arrest. The name itself does not appear to be symbolic of anything.[1]

When asked about the name, subject stated that "It just felt right." When asked about the origins of the name, subject said, "I'm not sure. I was at the library one day and I was just doodling, you know, just writing in my notebook, and I put those three words side by side. And when I looked at them, something clicked."

Subject says he does not believe that the words themselves contain any deeper meaning. He stated, "It's not something I was looking for, a new name. I feel like it just found me, and I accepted it."

After careful evaluation, this expert does not believe that the person known as "Carter Allen Cash" is a distinct personality from the person known as "Daniel Allen." There are no signs of the dissociative identity disorder, most commonly known as "multiple personality disorder." Instead, the name change seems to relate to a desire by subject to disown his given name, to renounce the identity his parents gave him, in

---

[1]Though it is interesting to note the reference to former president Jimmy Carter (whom John Hinckley is known to have stalked, before he attempted to assassinate Ronald Reagan). Also, the last name "Cash" could be seen as a reference to country music singer Johnny Cash, who was known throughout his career as "the Man in Black" and was viewed by many to be a rebel or an outsider. It is also possible that the name "Cash" is a reference to money, and that the combination of the word for money with the name of an American president in the name of a political assassin could be a statement of cynicism about the American political process.

exchange for an identity of his own choosing. When asked what qualities Carter Allen Cash personifies that are different than those of Daniel
Allen, subject stated, "It's hard to say. [long pause] It's about choice. I
didn't choose to be this person, *Danny*. It's a child's name, kind of. The
name you give a child. And I wasn't a child anymore. But sometimes, I
think, to be a grown-up you have to take control, you have to separate
yourself from your past. To say, 'I am not that person. I am a new person.'
So I guess that's what the name was for me. A way of growing up."

It is interesting to note that when the evaluator first introduced himself to subject, and asked how subject would like the evaluator to refer to
him, subject said he would like to be called "Daniel." When asked about
this later, subject stated, "Well, it feels a little silly now, you know? I've
had time to think about it, and I don't really think we can change who
we are. Not really. So, you know, I can call myself Carter or Maestro or,
like, Sam, but it's just a disguise, you know? Well, not a disguise, but an
affectation. And I always used to hate that, people who were affected,
like the girl in high school who started talking with this fake British
accent. But, I don't know, on the road, you know, it just felt right. To
change my name. To think about myself differently."

Subject was asked by this evaluator if he had ever thought about
killing himself or attempted suicide. Subjected stated that for a time
in Montana during the winter of 20__ he had "lost the will to live." He
stated that it was his "low point," and he had thought about killing himself at least twice but never made a serious attempt. When asked what
pulled him out of these feelings, he stated, "I'm not sure. There was a
lot of darkness around me. Some days it seemed like I never saw the
sun. And the cold, well, if you're not prepared for it, it can really get you
down." When asked why he didn't just leave the area and drive south,
subject paused, as if the idea had never occurred to him. "I don't know,"
he said. "I felt like I couldn't leave until it was time."

When asked what he meant by that, subject stated, "I felt like what I
was going through was part of the journey. That clearly I was meant to
go through this . . . sadness. That if I could just hold on it would help me
somehow, I don't know, *figure out what I had to do* [emphasis added]."

At this time the evaluator asked if subject felt he'd figured out what
he had to do. Subject nodded and stated, "Obviously." When asked what
the words "had to do" meant to him, and why he used them instead of

"wanted to do," subject stated that he believed that the things that happen in life are "meant to happen." He continued that though his journey may have seemed random, "looking back I can see that it was all adding up to what happened. What I did."

The evaluator asked whether this meant subject felt that these things had happened *to* him, as opposed to being choices he'd made. Subject stated, "No. I think I made the choice, but it was also fate. Does that make sense? Like it was my choice, but there were no other good options."

When asked whether he believed it was acceptable human behavior to kill someone, subject stated, "We're not all put on this Earth to do what's right. In order for there to be good, there has to be bad, and that bad has to come from somewhere. I've been thinking lately about Judas, about how he betrayed Christ, and Christ forgave him. But it's interesting, because both Jesus and Judas had to do what they did. You could argue that there would be no Jesus without Judas. Without darkness there's no light, right? This is what I think about when people say God has a plan. Maybe what I did will motivate other people to do good. Maybe what I did was give them a push. Or maybe I'm just trying to rationalize it. But I wonder sometimes. You know, Hitler was a monster, but by being a monster he gave the world the opportunity to do enormous good. Good they might not have done otherwise. There'd be no Israel without Hitler, right? Not that I'm Hitler. But, I don't know, I do wish it hadn't happened. I wish I hadn't done it."

When asked why he thought he had killed Senator Seagram, subject paused for more than a minute. He said, "When Charles Whitman killed all those people in Texas, they found out he had a brain tumor in his head. You kind of feel sorry for him, knowing that. Knowing that he didn't want to kill those people. It was the tumor forcing him to do it. But then you think maybe that's just a cop-out. Maybe the tumor had nothing to do with what happened. Maybe it was a coincidence. I could tell you a lot of things about how my daddy didn't love me or how some girl broke my heart, but the truth is, I have no idea why I did it. It seemed like the right thing to do at the time."

He went to the library every day for three weeks, wandering the stacks, waiting in computer lines behind the fetid homeless. He liked the way the spines of books felt when he ran his hands along the shelves, the rounded ridges, like spokes on a bicycle. There was a pleasure in finding an unused chair in a hidden corner, the feeling of a small animal nestling peacefully into its burrow. He was a nineteen-year-old man-child who had dropped out of Vassar. A kid who had surrendered his education to the road. Now, in the Hill Country of Texas, he was designing his own curriculum, an independent study of young men and their guns. Whitman, Oswald, Hinckley. He would work for Senator Seagram in the morning, handing out flyers on Guadalupe or registering voters on MLK, then walk down to the main library, passing the chain stores on the campus drag. The girl was part of it, his attraction to the place. Natalie, the librarian. She of the nose freckles and pouty lips. On September 14, he finally worked up the courage to talk to her. At three fifteen he approached the main desk and asked her for directions to the bathroom. He knew, of course, where the bathroom was, but when he'd stopped before the information desk, when he'd seen her long brown hair and slanted eyebrows, this was all he could think to say. She was wearing the blue dress that day, the one that gave her eyes that glacial shimmer. Natalie smiled and pointed. Daniel mumbled a thank-you and followed her finger, though he did not have to go. In the bathroom he splashed water on his face. Every day he spent in the West felt like a step away from himself.

He bought a notebook, started writing things down: notes, observations, theories. He had never felt that his thoughts were worth writing down before. They had seemed so ordinary. Rudimentary. The predictable, pedestrian ruminations of a typical American teenager. But now he felt inspired. There was something important floating around in his mind, something just outside his reach. Each word he wrote was like a shovelful of dirt taken off the top of a buried treasure. He uncovered many things under that dark earth, connections, theorems, a slowly revealed map of the world. One of the things he discovered in the midnight loam was a name. It came to him one day, an amalgam of his own and someone else's. *Carter Allen Cash*. He stared at it, those three words, the heavy crescent of each "C." He liked the way the first letter of the first two names were the same as the first two letters of the last. Carter Allen CAsh. But whose name was it? Was this someone he was going to meet? Someone he should look for? And then one day it occurred to him. It was his own name. The name he was supposed to have.

He gave the girl this name when he finally worked up the courage to talk to her again. Natalie. She of the white pants and blue tank top. The frat boys at the house talked about how wearing white pants meant a girl liked it in the ass, but Daniel couldn't imagine this girl enjoying anything so coarse. The truth was, if he thought about it too much, he felt light-headed. He could hardly even believe she had a hole back there. He pictured Natalie like a Barbie doll—smooth, tan, devoid of animal orifices, just a tiny ridge running between her legs where the plastic molding had been set.

She was reshelving books when he approached her the second time. This time Daniel had written down what he wanted to say, sketched it out on the back of the notebook he held in his hands. She was wearing sandals today. He noticed her toes were perfectly tan, and, where most people's were of different length, hers were all the same, as if each one of her toes had been forged from the same mold.

"Excuse me," he said. "Where do you keep the Russians?"

That wasn't right. He glanced at the notebook. He had forgotten a word.

"Novelists," he said. "The Russian novelists."

He had noticed that Natalie liked to eat her lunch among the foreign classics—Pushkin, Tolstoy, Solzhenitsyn. She seemed to gravitate to these shelves several times a day, touching the spines of each book, as if for luck.

She smiled at him, and again it made his tongue feel watery.

"Are you looking for someone in particular?" she asked.

"Dostoyevsky," he said. "*Notes from the Underground.* Oh, and, uh, Gogol."

He could see she was—not impressed but intrigued. He was a good-looking boy, with an open face and a body hardened by months working outdoors. He was also the progeny of East Coast intellectualism and West Coast freethinking. A catch, in other words.

"Is this for a class?" she said.

"No," he told her. "Just for me."

She chewed her lip for a moment. It was one of those gestures that may have started as unconscious but had become something she did, an advertisement.

"Follow me," she said, and led him through the stacks. His chest felt tight, and he couldn't figure out what to do with his hands. His fingers kept curling into fists. The way she moved in those white pants was nothing short of a miracle. At night, when there wasn't a game to watch, the frat boys would put on porn. They kept a library in the bathroom, the boxes stacked chest high. Someone said the collection had been around since the eighties, with each successive generation adding a few classics. The titles lined the walls, so that when you were sitting on the bowl you could read the names—*Beaver Tales*, *Breast Man*, *Asspounders XII*. As Daniel lay on his bed in his room and read his library books, the sound of women being violated clawed through the walls.

White pants, he thought now. *White pants.* Why did they have to tell him that? Now it was all he could think about—this beautiful, innocent girl and the frat boys who wanted to sodomize her.

"*Notes from the Underground*," she said, stopping in front of a set of worn hardcovers. She pulled a book off the shelves and handed it to him. "Gogol is in the next aisle."

He could see her excitement to share these books with him. It was a pleasure she took in her job—to help others discover the words that mattered so much to her.

He looked at the cover, a bearded young man, formally dressed but disheveled, an unbalanced look in his eye. It was the kind of book he normally shied away from, one that felt old, outdated, irrelevant. He could feel her looking at him expectantly. He didn't know what to say next, so he flipped to a random page and found himself reading aloud.

"'I invented adventures for myself and made up a life, so as at least to live in some way. I tried hard to be in love. I suffered, too, gentlemen, I assure you. In the depth of my heart there was no faith in my suffering, only a faint stir of mockery.'"

"It's one of the earliest *psychological* novels," she told him. "One of the first books that tried to look at what people think, not just what they do."

He slid the book on top of his notebook to indicate he would take it.

"I could use help with that," he said. "Understanding why people do what they do."

"And by people you mean 'girls,' right?" she said with a little laugh.

He knew he should laugh, but the weight of the moment kept him quiet, its import to his future. Instead he said, "Does Gogol do that also? People's minds?"

"No," she says. "He was more of a satirist."

"How do you know so much about this stuff?" he asked.

"I'm a literature major," she told him. "I like the Russians best. Their passion."

He thought about saying something clever, something the frat boys might say, like *I bet you do*, or *Well, if you like passion* . . . but it didn't feel real. It felt like a movie thing to say. So many moments in life felt this way, and he wondered when the world had stopped being a real place and had started being an opportunity for rehashing movie moments— the *meet cute*, the *race against time*, the *big confrontation*. It had gotten so you felt driven to satisfy the conceits of the moment as imagined by screenwriters, instead of saying what you really meant. He was sure the Russians of Dostoyevsky didn't live like this, nor did Brits in the age of Dickens. When had it started? The fifties maybe. Everyone trying to be Humphrey Bogart or Gary Cooper. Real people aspiring to be fake.

Six days earlier he had walked into a gun shop on South Congress. There was a buzzing in his fingertips, a kinetic thrum. A tiny silver bell rang as he entered, the harsh sunlight behind him turning the store into a dark cave. The chime of the bell triggered something in him, an antici- pation, and it took his eyes a moment to adjust, to identify the shapes hanging on the walls as what they were: rifles and shotguns. There was a bearded man and a middle-aged woman behind the counter. Faded paper targets hung on the wall behind them. The bearded man had a submarine sandwich on the glass counter in front of him, wrapping paper splayed out in a star pattern, crumbs falling across the glass display. The woman watched a melodrama on a small black-and-white TV.

The floor was linoleum. The walls were a faded wood veneer. He had grown up in coastal cities where guns were taboo. What struck him most about the shop now was how ordinary it felt, how pedestrian, as if buying a gun were like buying chains for your tires or spackle for your walls. There wasn't even the artificial embellishment that surrounds buying a new television—the myriad displays blaring hallucinogenic action sequences from summer blockbusters. *Get excited!* Standing there, he realized that there are places in this country where a gun is just another tool, like a rake or a shovel, a few ounces of oil and metal— dangerous, certainly, but so is a chain saw. So is the lye you buy to clean your drain—with none of the mythos assigned to guns at cocktail parties on the Upper West Side or celebrity fund-raisers in Beverly Hills. This was where he stood now, inside a nine-hundred-square-foot yawn, searching for a tool he wasn't sure he needed, in order to carry out a job he had yet to define.

The woman turned from her program when he came in. She greeted him cheerfully and asked if there was something she could help him with. He said he was thinking of getting a gun, his first. She asked if he was thinking of a handgun or rifle. He said a handgun. A gun you hold in your hand. He tried to be nonchalant about it. He was a carpenter buying a hammer, a housewife loading up on dishwashing detergent.

It turned out that the bearded man's name was Jerry. He learned this when the woman told Jerry to *move his damn sandwich so she could help this young fella.*

Jerry gathered his food and went into a back room.

"We've got a special on nine-millimeters," she said. "Glocks. You pay full price up front, but there's a mail-in rebate."

He looked down at the rows of revolvers—snub-nosed, long-barreled. Shiny metal instruments with hard wooden handles. He thought about what he wanted, the fantasy of the gun. It wasn't weight or size that interested him. He didn't want a gun that made a statement, a .357 with a titanic barrel. This wasn't an exercise in bravado. He was looking for a secret.

His eyes moved over the case, taking in the geometry of cylinders and trigger guards. They were hard objects, machine-tooled and hand-finished. The guns in front of him existed outside the automation of modern technology. They were stubborn Luddites, easy to dissect, easy to take apart and reassemble. Easy to clean and oil. Easy to load. Easy to shoot.

"Could I see that one?" he asked, pointing to a Smith & Wesson semi-automatic. It was compact and matte black.

The woman opened the case with a key and slid the gun off its pedestal. She put a gray chamois on the glass counter and laid the pistol on top of it.

"Compact forty caliber," she said. "Very reliable. Good stopping power. It's a polymer frame with a stainless barrel."

He touched it with his fingers, slid his thumb under the body, and then the gun was in his hand. It felt light, the polymer just rough enough to give the gun a feeling of grip.

"How many bullets in the clip?" he asked.

"Eleven," she said.

Standing there, holding the Smith & Wesson, he thought of Bonnie Kirkland. He thought of the Mexicans and the knife in his boot. Iowa seemed like a movie he had watched on a plane. He lifted the pistol and aimed down the sight at one of the targets. He tried to figure out what it meant that every time he had held a gun it had been handed to him by a woman. Could that be just coincidence?

"I also have a Glock compact and a Ruger," she said. "Like I said, there's a special on the Glocks right now."

He stared down the barrel of the gun. The target he was aiming at contained two figures, the silhouette of a man hiding behind the cartoon outline of a woman. The man was a criminal. The woman was his hostage. He stared down the barrel, moving the gun back and forth imperceptibly between the two figures. Criminal, victim. Criminal, victim. He thought about what the cartoon woman had done in her life to bring her here, to this place, to this endless crisis.

"Looks like love," the woman said.

It was meant to be a joke, but he didn't so much catch the words as hear her tone. It implied that another few moments without responding and she would begin to wonder about him. He turned to face her, lowering the gun toward the floor.

"Do you think I could shoot it?" he asked.

The woman smiled, sensing a sale. She asked him which target he wanted. He pointed to the hostage crisis, and she unfolded a stepladder and took it down.

Now, in the library, he thought of the gun in its hiding place in his room at the frat house. He wasn't brave enough yet to carry it around with him, to walk the streets with a .40-caliber pistol pressed into his spine, but he was getting there. He had taken it to the park the other day, a short walk, fifteen minutes tops, feeling the polymer grip rub against his skin. It felt like an erection, the fevered, insistent wood of a thirteen-year-old boy who has just discovered the meat between his legs, but doesn't know how to use it yet.

Holding the Russian novelists, talking to the girl in the white pants, he smiled. He had a secret, and the secret was power. Wolf or sheep? The answer was becoming clear. The girl smiled, brushed the hair from her face.

"I've seen you in here," she said. "The last few weeks. Except you're usually in American History."

He felt a great heat run through him. She had noticed him.

"I'm taking a trip," he told her. "I started in New York."

"Wow. I always wanted to go to New York. I'm from San Antonio."

"I spent some time in Iowa," he said. "I like Texas, though. It seems important somehow. Like a place where big things happen."

"That's what we like to think," she said. "But personally, I wish I'd lived in Moscow at the turn of the century. The twentieth century. Or St. Petersburg. Before the Revolution. All those passionate Russians, the long winters, the big hats."

"You have big hats here, too," he said.

She laughed. "It's true."

"I think it's normal," he said, "to want to be from someplace else. To glamorize another time. I think everybody feels like their lives would be better if they were someone else."

She studied him.

"What kind of trip?" she said.

"What do you mean?"

"Are you in school? Did you run away from home?"

He didn't know how to describe it, what to say. When she looked at him, he felt like a tape measure respooling back into its case, disappearing by inches.

"I find it interesting," he said, "that the word for journey is the same word you use to describe a fall."

He smiled to show her it was a joke. She smiled back. In her eyes he could see something click.

"I'm Natalie," she said, holding out her hand.

"Carter," he told her. "Carter Allen Cash."

Spring came early to the American West. That's what the locals said anyway, in the streets and shops of Colorado Springs. They clucked their tongues and talked about global warming. Some nodded their heads in a southerly direction and talked about how it was all "their" doing. The "them" in this case being the military men of NORAD, whose bunker lurked deep in the heart of Cheyenne Mountain just outside town. The Allen family had become residents of Colorado Springs in January, blowing into town with the brunt of winter. We had left the East Coast in the dark of the night just after New Year's, detaching like an iceberg and drifting west. After the privileged, urbane lives we'd enjoyed in the wealthy suburbs of New York City, it was strange to find ourselves in the tumbleweed sprawl of the work-boot West, surrounded by cowboy iconography and strip malls.

Gone were the local bagel shops with their overstuffed Sunday papers and house-smoked fish. Gone were the hole-in-the-wall ethnic restaurants with their thin-crust pizza, Thai noodles, and Szechuan takeout. We said goodbye to sophisticated French cuisine and the regional menus of southern Italy. Now we lived in a region of chain restaurants and barbecue huts, where Italian food meant a fried, breaded chop smothered in cheese, and Chinese food was served with frozen peas and carrots. Ordering "a large" here meant something different than it did back east, as was evidenced by the bucket of ice tea the waitress brought me that first day at Applebee's. These details were startling, not just because it felt as if we had moved to a different region of the country but because it felt as if we had relocated to another country entirely.

A country of obese women and men with mustaches. A country of cheap cars, snowmobiles, and Jet Skis. In short, Walmart country. For the first few weeks the boys mocked everyone they saw, mimicking their accents in low-slung *Sling Blade* voices. Their mother and I scolded them for it. In the past I might have shown similar prejudice, but my experiences of the last year had humbled me. As backward as I may have thought some of the characters we encountered, none of them were parent to an infamous murderer.

We tried to settle in, getting used to a new house, a new climate, a new life. The kids started public school, climbing onto a bright yellow school bus, book bags stuffed with oversized geometry and history text-books. Three days a week I drove a used Jeep Cherokee an hour north to the University of Colorado Medical School in Denver, where I had accepted a position as a guest lecturer. Despite my recent notoriety, the president of the medical school jumped at the opportunity to bring me on staff. We agreed it would be part-time at first, but with an eye toward making me a full professor and head of the rheumatology department by the end of the year.

The drive to school took me from the rust-colored flatland of south-ern Colorado, through the foothills of the Rockies, and into the smoggy valley surrounding Denver. It was my first real experience with the emptiness of western states. To harbor this much land undeveloped—miles of scrub grass and rolling hillocks stretched out as far as the eye could see—seemed criminal. Every day I thought of the hungry millions crammed into third world cities. We had more space in this country than we could ever use; deep canyons and impossible mountain ranges, remote riverside acreage and volcanic lake beds. I was used to the nar-row, cluttered highways of the East, where in the span of eight hours you could drive from New York to Maine, passing through four states. But here, in the massive sprawl of the West, eight hours wouldn't even get you across the state.

Of us all, Fran seemed the least affected by the move. She contin-ued her virtual assistant work, uninterrupted. That was the benefit of being virtual. To her clients she was just a voice on the phone, an e-mail address. It mattered not whether she was in Connecticut or Calcutta.

We had moved to Colorado Springs two months to the day after Danny was sentenced to death in a Los Angeles courtroom. In the weeks before, his attorneys had fought to get his guilty plea thrown out. They'd filed motions and briefs, had appealed all the way to the Supreme Court, but in the end, the judges were unmoved.

It didn't seem to matter that Frederick Cobb's autopsy had shown fourteen separate stab wounds, that a former Special Forces operative who'd been arrested riding a freight train with my son a month before the assassination had been murdered in cold blood just weeks after. The details of Cobb's last day were sketchy at best. He may or may not have bought a lottery ticket from a 7-Eleven in Glendale. We know that, at some point, in the early evening he had eaten a Happy Meal at McDonald's. His stomach was full of half-digested French fries. Somewhere around ten that night, Cobb found himself in a culvert under an overpass, where he was stabbed repeatedly, with defensive wounds to both hands. The police quickly assessed it as a transient murder, possibly drug related, and made little effort to solve the case, despite a considerable amount of pressure from Daniel's legal team. To the police, Cobb was just another army vet who had come back from the war and fallen on hard times.

Murray and I had taken what we knew to every newspaper and magazine we could think of, but other than a small article in *The Sacramento Bee* about Cobb's "coincidental connection" to Daniel, the press was unresponsive.

Marvin Hoopler, the other veteran from the train, proved impossible to locate. After he was arrested with Daniel and Cobb last May, Hoopler seemed to have disappeared without a trace. His past turned out to be just as hard to analyze. The government rejected numerous Freedom of Information Act requests for Hoopler's service record, saying it was classified. I took their letters and put them in the file. No detail was too small, no idea too preposterous not to catalog. A presidential candidate had been assassinated. We had a dead veteran who'd been a sniper in Special Forces, and another, service record unknown, who had vanished into the abyss, and my son, a college dropout with no history of violence.

When I wrote the facts on a piece of paper I found I couldn't make them fit together. They were like a man with a limp stumbling into an emergency room. The initial exam reveals a deep gash in the calf that requires seventeen stitches, but rather than treat the wound, the doctor on call diagnoses the problem as neurological. Looking at Cobb's autopsy photos and the letters from the army denying our requests for Hoopler's service record, I couldn't help but see the truth as a wound no one wanted to acknowledge.

My son had confessed to murder, and there were three possible explanations. The first was that he was, in fact, guilty. That he had, of his own free will, smuggled a handgun into Royce Hall and, standing a few feet from the stage, fired two bullets into another human being. The second was that he had shot Seagram as part of a larger conspiracy, in which Cobb and Hoopler were involved. And the third, which I had to admit seemed far less likely, was that he truly was a patsy, that he had been a bystander to the assassination, that Cobb or Hoopler had been the trigger man and had somehow planted the gun on Daniel after the shots were fired.

So putting aside the third option for the moment, the question became either (1) why had my son allowed himself to become involved in a conspiracy to assassinate Senator Seagram, or (2) why had he, of his own free will, pulled the trigger, a lone gunman standing in a crowd, expressing his dysfunction with a gun?

On November 6, three days after Daniel's guilty plea was formally accepted, the Republicans won the presidential election by a narrow but decisive margin. Seagram's death had left a void in the Democratic leadership that a dozen candidates had rushed to fill. They had succeeded only in cluttering the landscape. Meanwhile, the Republicans had used the assassination as a wedge, calling for tougher antiterrorism laws. They had spun themselves as the party that would stop at nothing to protect the country, and though they did not win by a landslide, they had received enough electoral votes to announce that they'd been given a mandate by the American people.

Two weeks later, on November 17, after a short sentencing phase, my son Daniel Allen was sentenced to death. Both his mother and I had testified on his behalf, taking the stand to beg for his life. It was a moment beyond description. We had done everything in our power to prove to the jury that Danny was a warm and thoughtful human being. We had shown pictures and told stories, had shared our brightest memories, our hearts sickened by love and regret. Ellen wept so much during the hearing that the court had to break three times so she could finish her statement. There are no words to convey the feeling you have as a parent as you plead for the life of your child. No words to describe the unmoved expressions of the jury, the judgment and cold detachment in the eyes of the prosecutor. There are no words to describe the feeling that comes over you when the judge announces his verdict, when he tells a crowded courtroom, and a national audience, that he is ordering the death of your son. It is a deep, sucking blackness. Another form of death. And that is all I'm going to say about that.

The next day Daniel was shipped to the country's only supermax federal penitentiary, in Florence, Colorado, known as ADX Florence, or ADMAX. There my son was placed in solitary confinement twenty-three hours a day, locked in a seven by twelve cell, behind a steel door with a grate. His furniture was made out of poured concrete, his desk, his stool, his bed. There was a toilet on one wall that shut off if plugged, a shower that ran on a timer to prevent flooding, and a sink without a drain trap. Some prisoners had polished-steel mirrors bolted to the wall, but not my son. Nor was he allowed a radio or television. Instead he had a long narrow window, just four inches high, through which he could see only the sky. This was to prevent him from knowing his specific location within the complex. Communication with the outside world was strictly forbidden. The single hour per day he was allowed out of his cell was spent wandering by himself in a secure outdoor yard, under the watchful eye of armed guards.

ADMAX had opened in 1994 on the outskirts of Florence, Colorado. It was two hours north of the New Mexico border, two hours south of Denver. The prison covers thirty-seven acres and has four hundred and ninety beds. Its inhabitants are considered to be the worst of the worst— terrorists, rapists, murderers. Many had killed fellow prisoners in other correctional facilities. Others had murdered or attempted to murder prison personnel in other prisons. Many, like my son, were famous. Theodore Kaczynski, the Unabomber, was housed at ADMAX. As was Terry Nichols, the surviving Oklahoma City bomber. Zacarias Moussaoui, the alleged "twentieth hijacker" on 9/11, was there, as was "shoe bomber" Richard Colvin Reid. Andrew Fastow, former CFO of Enron, was serving time at ADMAX, as was Robert Hanssen, the FBI's most famous double agent. It was a prison full of legendary men, which was the kind of creature the world believed my son to be, a Cyclops, a Minotaur, a monster of mythic proportions.

In the months since his sentencing, I had taken my investigation underground. Daniel's arrest and trial had devoured our lives. My family was exhausted, my wife's patience at an end. Daniel had confessed, Fran told me in no uncertain terms. It was time to move on. So two weeks after Daniel's sentencing, I went to the box store and bought two dozen cardboard boxes. As the kids watched, I emptied our lives of every trace of the investigation. In the past year I'd amassed an exhaustive collection of biographies of men who had assassinated other men— Oswald, Booth, Burr—their histories imagined from every angle. The pages were dog-eared, text highlighted and underlined, the margins filled with handwritten notes.

I had collected stacks of research on the places my son had visited— geographical data, climate charts, anything that might contextualize his crime. In ten minutes I could find you a list of Iowa City mayors stretching back to the city's inception. I could hand you a highlighted map of California rail travel, including timetables and discontinued routes. My file cabinet was filled with newspaper and magazine articles, computer printouts, blogs, and transcripts of telephone conversations. There were blueprints of Royce Hall and lists of gun dealerships in the greater Los Angeles area. Based on witness lists I had compiled biographical data on more than two hundred people who had stood in Royce Hall the day Senator Seagram was assassinated: pictures, résumés, educational histories.

I packed this material away, even as I found myself unable to move on. The case had become my obsession, my addiction, and like a drug or gambling habit I knew it must now be hidden from the people around me. So I filled a banker's box with documents about Hoopler and Cobb: birth certificates, military and work histories.

I took the case I had built and boxed it up. My family watched as I carried the boxes to my car. I told them I was taking it all to the dump, but instead I drove to a storage facility and rented a locker. I would lead two lives now. On the surface I would be Paul Allen, the man who had surrendered to the inevitable, who was trying to put the past behind him. But underneath, I would continue to dig, reasoning that if I succeeded in proving Danny's innocence, if I could manage to commute his sentence and save his life, then my family would forgive me. Even Daniel.

In this way I became two people.

At Fran's urging we put the Connecticut house on the market. It was time to accept that our old lives, the community we had built, the schools our children went to, the neighbors, the friends were gone. We were pariahs now, shunned in supermarkets, heckled at PTA meetings. The community that had once embraced us now went out of its way to show us we were not wanted.

Last summer I had taken a leave of absence from Columbia to concentrate on Daniel's case. This January, when I called Alvin Heidecker, the school's president, to say I wouldn't be returning, he seemed relieved. Alvin and I had been friends for years, but he was a practical man, who understood that my presence on the faculty was a detriment, not just academically but also in terms of fund-raising. Many of the school's biggest donors were staunch Democrats, who could not be expected to bequeath millions to the school that employed the father of the man who had murdered their hero.

So we began to plot our escape. We fantasized about where we might go—London, Paris, Rome. I'd had invitations to work abroad in the past, and we believed, rightly or wrongly, that Europe would offer us our only real opportunity for anonymity and rebirth. But when push came to shove we found ourselves unable to abandon the country in which we had lived our lives, even though it had abandoned us. Fran grew up in Denver. Her family still lived there. A move to Colorado made sense. When the idea first came up, I nodded soberly, trying not to betray the surge of excitement that went through me. Danny's prison was in Florence, just an hour drive. But I didn't say that. Instead, I let Fran bring it up, holding the fact out like a carrot, as she tried to convince me that a move to rural Colorado was truly the best thing for both of us.

So we boxed the dishes and filled cardboard wardrobes with our East Coast fashions. We packed our books and sporting equipment. We took our paintings off the wall, our framed photographs (art and family), and wrapped them in plastic. We paid for insurance. We counted our boxes. Fran and I took a trip to Colorado in late November and found a house— a two-story craftsman on a quiet hillside with a view of the Rockies. All that was left was to move.

A strange thing happened to me, however, as we boxed up our past. The more of our things we packed, the less of them I wanted. Fran came into the bedroom one evening and found me stuffing my clothes into trash bags.

"What are you doing?" she said.

"I don't want it," I said. "Any of it. Out with the old."

I told her that if we were going to be moving, changing our lives, then I wanted to change, too. Reinvent myself. So into black, triple-strength leaf bags went my Connecticut doctor's suits, my chinos and linen shirts, my docksides and John Varvatos T-shirts. When they were full, I put the trash bags in the car and drove them to Goodwill. Let someone else wear them. Let someone else walk around disguised as me. I would give the world the slip. Into trash bags went my aftershave, my designer skin lotions. Anything with a scent. Anything that had defined me, the old me, the me I had decided to leave behind.

The next day I went down to the barbershop and told them to cut my hair short. I watched as the barber ran his clippers over my head, watched my hundred-dollar, salon-cut hair fall to the floor in clumps. With it went my identity. Looking in the mirror afterward I did not see the prosperous New York doctor, that leader of men. I saw a chastened man, vulnerable, exposed. The hair that remained was mostly gray. The lines around my eyes had deepened, a newfound weight pulling at my face. It was disturbing for me to see the years of life that defeat had added to my face, but it was the truth. And I needed the truth right now. It felt important somehow to understand just where I stood.

I had been an overconfident man, smug even, and because of this I had overestimated the control I had over the world. The man who stared back at me now did not look smug. He looked scared. He was fifty years old. He had suffered a stunning, last-minute reversal.

He was running out of time.

And so, seven months after two shots rang out in a packed California theater, my family became a Colorado family, mountain people, nature lovers hungry to start again. The week we arrived, Alex and Wally celebrated their eleventh birthdays. Fran and I bought them snowboards, with the hope that this would help them assimilate. In our minds, we saw our sons becoming mountain rats, suntanned mini-jocks, trailing their fingertips in fresh white powder, as they crisscrossed the slopes in a lazy S. Colorado would be a return to a life of innocence, healthy and carefree.

Children. My sons would be children again.

The day after their birthdays, they started at a new school. Aside from an early rough patch, they fit in quickly. I think they appreciated the return to normalcy. It was a relief to have homework to complete and tests to study for. They liked the grounding nature of soccer practices and Little League tryouts. They made friends. Wally quickly fell for a Mexican American girl two grades ahead, and suffered the inevitable psychic pain of unrequited love.

Fran made a good show of meeting the neighbors, of bulk-store shopping and planning weekend discovery excursions into the Rockies and down to Santa Fe and Albuquerque. We spent time with her family, aunts and cousins, who embraced us openly, despite the obvious taint we carried. This was our de facto witness-protection program. With people we met, we adopted a friendly but subtle distance. We built a social life of barbecues and card nights, PTA meetings and bake sales.

In public I refrained from mentioning my previous marriage. I glossed over where we had come from, saying we had lived all over the East Coast. To new friends, we embraced the lie that our family was no bigger than what they could see. The trips we took to ADMAX were done in secret, the family rising before dawn and piling into the Jeep. If asked, we lied and said we were taking advantage of the early spring, using day trips to familiarize ourselves with our new terrain. In truth, we snuck forty miles south, through increasingly desolate country. In silence, mostly, but sometimes listening to classic rock on the radio. Daniel had become our secret weight, the pariah we carried in our hearts.

We adapted wordlessly to the prison rituals, the metal detectors and redundant security checks, the waiting area filled with men, women, and children of all races. We endured the judgmental stares of the guards, looks that implied *we* were responsible for the crimes of our loved ones. And if not responsible, then at least contaminated by them. The stares suggested that we, too, should be incarcerated. None of this surprised me. America was a country that believed that crime was who a person was, not just what they did. In this light there could be no such thing as rehabilitation, only punishment. And part of that punishment was, inevitably, the ostracism and conviction of a convict's family.

So we waited in the lines, and endured invasive searches. We accepted the insults and withering looks. We did this so we could sit in a narrow cubicle facing five inches of tempered Plexiglas. We did it so we could pick up a germ-ridden telephone handset and talk to our kin.

Ironically, ADMAX had been good for Daniel. He had gained fifteen pounds. The color had returned to his cheeks. He told us he had been reading a lot, classics mostly, Tolstoy, Pushkin. He said a girl he knew in Austin had turned him on to Russian novelists. He liked their scope and emotionality. Though we asked repeatedly, he never talked about what it was like to be locked up in a seven by twelve room twenty-three hours a day after having spent so much time on the road. He never complained about the epic awfulness of the food or the disdainful treatment he received from the guards. In fact, he never complained at all. He said he had discovered that he liked the solitude. It was what had attracted him to life on the road in the first place.

Transience had given my son a necessary level of separation from the world, knowing he was only in a place for a short time, that he could only ever get so close to someone. He told us that he had enjoyed the endless hours spent alone in his yellow Honda. He said he liked walking the streets of a town he did not know, filled with people he would never meet. He saw the human need to socialize as a weakness. It was a moment of rare confession, and when pressed to explain, he changed the subject.

During the week, we were a normal nuclear family with after-school activities to organize and dinner parties to plan. We talked about replacing screen doors and having the HVAC serviced. During the week we watched prime-time television and tried to keep up with our reading. We separated our household trash from our recyclables and packed lawn clippings into biodegradable paper sacks. On Thursdays I dragged the Toters to the bottom of the driveway and left energy drinks for the garbagemen. I had become a friend to workingmen everywhere, the kind of person who chatted about hardware to men in Velcroed weight belts at Home Depot or talked sports with auto mechanics. It was my disguise. During the week my family was invisible in our normalcy. It was on those weekends that our true identities came out.

We visited Daniel twice a month, making the hour drive early Saturday morning. Round-trip, the whole excursion took five hours, door to door. We always stopped at the same Starbucks for coffee, the same Shell station to use the restrooms. We made sure we were home by two in time for soccer practice.

On these visits I stuck to safe topics—the new house, how the kids were doing in school. Danny seemed relieved. Each visit lasted no more than twenty minutes, just enough time for small talk. Danny showed us a joke book he'd found in the prison library. Every time he tried out new material on the kids. The jokes were mostly groaners—off-color tales of farmers and their daughters—but the kids loved them and would deconstruct each joke in the car on the ride home.

I watched my family during these visits and wondered: Is this really our lives now? I was amazed that the human animal could, over time, come to define any situation, no matter how unnatural, as normal.

I watched them and I worried. I looked at my two young sons. How would this experience affect them? I looked for signs of permanent scarring, of behavior that might give an early warning of long-term damage. Looking at my boys through the prism of Daniel's life, I could not help but analyze every word they said in anger, every sullen mood, every negative action. I was desperate to protect them, desperate not to miss any warning signs, the way I had missed them with Danny.

I spent hours talking to Fran about things we might do to minimize the damage. I suggested the boys stay home. I thought we should avoid exposing them to a prison environment.

But Fran said no. She thought the boys should see their brother. She thought they should understand that actions had consequences. That bad behavior was punished. So we continued to make the drive together as a family, listening to talk radio but rarely speaking ourselves.

Those afternoons Fran allowed me to take a few hours by myself, I would go to the golf course and spend two hours hitting balls at the driving range. I found the emptiness of the experience, the smooth, mechanical repetition, soothing. It felt good to escape into something physical, a thing that required no thought but real focus. When the first bucket of balls was empty I would buy a second. Around me, men in baseball caps used hybrid clubs for extra distance. Coeds took lessons from pros, giggling at double entendres. I set my feet, shifted my hips, settled in. Each ball I hit was a regret cast into the brush. I teed up, leveled my clubhead. I tried to stay loose, to empty my mind. I tried to let the club lift itself, to keep my left arm straight without thinking about keeping my left arm straight.

Afterward, I would drive into the mountains until I found a vista spot. I would park the car and stand among tourists looking into the far distance. I never got used to the overblown majesty of the mountains or to driving the curvy, narrow roads guarded by thin metal barriers. At first these sojourns were just a form of self-preservation, a way to satisfy my panicked need to keep moving, but I came to enjoy the drives. I came to enjoy pulling my car onto the rough, sloped shoulder and pissing into the dirt.

On weekdays I stood in front of a lecture hall filled with medical students. I talked about diseases of the nervous system. I explored the interconnectedness of things. I wore short-sleeve button-down shirts and Western-style slacks. My waist size had shrunk from thirty-six inches to the thirty-two I had been in med school. I kept my hair short. Every morning I did a hundred sit-ups, a dozen pull-ups. I started trail running, rising before dawn, driving to a nearby state park. I liked the feel of my pounding heart, the thrush of my heavy breath. Some days I came home red-faced, cheeks scratched by brush.

"There are no small details," I told my students, "only small doctors."

I could not watch movies or television shows where soldiers faced certain death to save their fallen brother without a lump forming in my throat. I could not watch buddy pictures or dramas where beloved characters died of slow wasting diseases. Themes of forgiveness and loyalty made me weep privately in the downstairs bathroom. The same was true of films where the hero keeps his word at any price or where the weak were protected and the frail rescued. My son was imprisoned in a federal prison, waiting to be executed. He was beyond my reach, and I was trying to figure out how to live with that.

So I set my feet and tested my iron. I practiced my short game, chopping down at the ball. I ran through browning bramble, jumped over tree roots and fallen branches. I drove the green-brown back roads of Colorado, past ranches and farms, past Holsteins and men on horseback. I cooked steaks on the backyard grill and made small talk with the neighbors. I took the kids to water parks and helped them build boxcars. I showed Alex how to throw a curveball. I took Wally to a florist so he could buy flowers for the girl he'd never have. Inside, I made him put back the roses and pick out something less obvious. I went on date nights with my wife. We ate at mediocre restaurants and saw blockbusters at the cineplex. I drove her to the impossible vistas I had discovered, and we leaned against the warm hood of the car, gazing out at the moon.

"I think we're doing okay," she said. And I nodded because that's what I wanted her to believe. That was my job now, to protect my family from the truth, which was that I might never again be whole. This change of character had unexpected side effects. Out of the blue, our sex life reignited. The routine we had settled into in Connecticut, a brief foreplay of kissing and manual stimulation, leading quickly to the missionary position, was thrown out. We attacked each other now with recklessness. Before, sex had been a means to an end. Now it became a destination. Passion is, in many ways, a kind of violence—the only sanctioned means by which one spouse can attack the other—and, in this spirit, Fran and I found ourselves grappling with an often frightening ferocity. She clawed at me, bit my neck and shoulders. It was as if she had decided to use sex as a form of punishment. She would pin my arms to the bed and grind against me the way the ocean wears at the shoreline. In the depths of the night she expressed a newfound desire to penetrate me. For my part, I had lost the will to come. It was not that I was withholding my reward. It's that I was often unable to climax. I felt nothing. As a result our sessions sprawled into the later hours. We would wrestle each other into exhaustion, collapsing winded and sore onto the bed.

"That was incredible," she would say. And I would agree because it was. Incredible that life had brought us to this place. Incredible that pleasure could feel so much like pain.

I was beginning to understand what my son meant when he talked about levels of detachment. I felt, at once, of a thing and outside it. Was this how Daniel felt as he traveled the country? Was this who Carter Allen Cash was? The unnameable other inside each one of us? The part of my son that felt alone? Unconnected?

I went in for my annual physical. The doctor was Indian, an internist who was recommended by the head of the university. Dr. Patel. He took my pulse, my blood pressure. A nurse drew blood. They ran an EKG and took a chest X-ray. When it was time I bent over and allowed him to check my prostate, grimacing at the cold intrusion of his finger. Afterward, in his office, he asked how I was feeling.

"Fine," I told him.

"No aches or pains? Headaches?"

"No," I told him.

"How about your digestion? Any heartburn or diarrhea?"

"Occasionally."

"How's your mood?"

"My mood?"

"Yes. Your outlook. Would you say you are feeling well?"

I looked at him, a young man with his whole life ahead of him. There was a photo on his desk, Patel with a smiling wife, a baby in her arms. Was I feeling well? The question was absurd, and what's more, I knew this man was incapable of understanding the answer. What did he know about anything?

"I feel fine," I told him.

He nodded. This was good news.

"Okay," he said. "We should get the test results back in a few days, but your EKG was good, prostate was normal."

I stood and offered him my hand. He rose and shook.

"Thank you for your time," I said.

The next morning I told Fran I was going to run some errands. I drove to a gun range outside town, parked the Jeep in the shade. I told the clerk I wanted to rent a gun and buy a target. He showed me three shelves of revolvers and semiautomatics. I chose a 9-mm Smith & Wesson, then demonstrated that I knew how to disarm the weapon, ejecting a round and removing the clip. The clerk handed me a pair of headphones and some plastic goggles, then led me into the back. I followed him, carrying my pistol in a tray, clip out, along with a box of shells. The paper target, a simple bull's-eye, I had rolled up under my arm. Inside the range, the clerk placed the tray on the narrow shelf and told me to return the weapon as it was, with the clip out.

There were three other men on the range, shooting targets. Through the headphones the sound of their shots was muffled but by no means quiet. I unrolled my paper target and clipped it to the line, then pressed a button near the shelf, sending the target gliding down the range. Next I opened the box of ammunition and slid eleven cold brass bullets into the clip, feeling a metallic click as they settled into place. My breathing was steady. My hands did not shake. I inserted the clip into the gun and chambered a round. My goggles were scratched but functional. I took a deep breath, let it out, then raised the gun and pointed it at the target.

My uncle had taken me shooting once when I was a boy. I remember the blood thrill of it, the way the pistol jumped in my hand like a living thing. It was that memory that sent me to the range several times during my college years, usually with one or two boys from my dorm. Once I started medical school, though, the allure of shooting wore off. During my surgical rotation I saw the damage a bullet could do to human tissue, witnessed the destructive mayhem of multiple gunshot wounds during a spin in the emergency room. After that there was no romance in guns anymore, no mystery. It had been three decades since I'd held one in my hand. It was heavy but balanced. I felt the wood of the grip against my palm. The air smelled of cordite and gunpowder. I thought of my son standing on a hilltop shooting cans. I pictured him on a motel-room floor, oiling the barrel of a store-bought weapon. I remembered the photo of Daniel that had been taken at Royce Hall, wild-eyed, gun in hand, a Secret Service agent squeezing his arm.

I looked down the barrel at the paper bull's-eye. My finger rested on the trigger. How was this different than hitting golf balls? How was it different than running through the Colorado greenbelt? I tried to imagine how I looked, an older man with a military haircut, his knees slightly bent, pointing a handgun down a narrow range. My son had confessed to murdering a man with a gun, much like this one. He had spent time in gun ranges all over the country. Could I know what he knew just by doing what he did? Could I understand the things that only he understood?

I was Dr. Paul Allen, son of Rhoda, father of Alex and Wally. Or was I? Was this man pointing a weapon at a paper target the same man who diagnosed illnesses, who treated the sick? Something was happening to me. I had lost direction. I didn't know what I was meant to do anymore. My son was going to be executed. Why was I playing golf and hosting dinner parties? Why was I jogging and recycling? And yet, what else could I do? I owed it to my wife, my other children. I had to let my boy go. Around me the sound of gunshots was like a metronome ticking off the seconds of my life.

I squinted at the target. It was a man, a woman, a child. It was everyone I had ever hated, everyone I had ever loved. I put the gun back on the tray and took off my goggles. There were no answers here, only noise and violence.

For the first time in my adult life, I began to pray.

At night, when everyone was asleep, I wandered the house like a ghost. I watched my sons sleep in their beds. They were like windmills stopped in mid-turn. Wally had already forgotten about Maribel, the Mexican siren. He was in love now with a blond twelve-year-old with breasts, as I suspected were all the other boys at school. Alex had discovered football, and he spent hours in the yard throwing spirals at a plastic target.

They had been babies once, chubby and small. I used to change their diapers in the depths of the night. We would give them a bottle and read them to sleep. There was one book I think of now as I watch them sleep, a board book called *I Love You, Stinky Face*. In it a mother tells her son she loves him, and the boy says, *But Mamma, what if I were a big scary ape?* The mother says, *If you were a giant ape, I would bake you a cake of bananas and say, I love you my big scary ape.*

But Mamma, the boy says, *what if I was a one-eyed monster?*

During our visits to the prison, we were prohibited from touching Danny. At the end of each conversation—when the guard came to collect him—he would blow us a kiss, and we would reply in kind, standing to watch as he passed through the iron door and disappeared.

Wally seemed unaffected by these visits, but Alex developed night terrors. He took to sleeping in bed with us, the way he used to when he was three.

"Maybe you shouldn't visit Danny for a while," I told him one morning. We were the first ones up, and as he sat at the kitchen island eating cereal, I stood across from him stirring milk into my coffee.

"No," he said. "I want to."

"Maybe just for a little while," I said, "you should stay home when we go see Danny. Or maybe we'll all take a break. It's been a really hard year. This is a lot to handle even for a grown-up. I think we all need a rest."

He thought about this.

"But what if they kill him?"

My heart skipped a beat. He was talking about the execution. I thought about the things I'd had to deal with as a child, my father's death and the hole it created in my heart. I had gone to his funeral, had stood by the graveside and watched as his family and friends dropped dirt into the grave. None of it seemed real to me at the time. The grief came later, the true understanding of death, its finality. Standing in the kitchen, I thought about Alex and Wally, their awareness that Daniel had been sentenced to death, that he was stuck in prison waiting to die. By taking them to visit their brother hadn't I really been bringing them to his funeral not once but week after week? My father's death had been sudden. But Daniel's was an event to be calendared, a landmark visible on the horizon, growing closer every day.

The horror of this thought made me sick to my stomach.

I put my hand on Alex's back, still so small, so delicate.

"They can't just execute him," I said. "They have to set a date, and then there are appeals. Okay? We have time. It's okay to take a break, to rest."

He nodded. I put my arms around him, feeling trapped. His hair smelled of sweat and children's shampoo. The love I felt in that moment was savage and dizzying.

That night, when everyone was asleep, I sat on the back patio, restless, agitated. It had been ten months since Daniel's arrest. I'd uprooted my family, given away my clothes, cut off my hair, and started a new life in a new town, believing I could still save him. But at what cost?

I sat in the backyard, shivering in the chill. The truth was, though I'd changed my life tectonically, nothing had really changed. The differences were merely cosmetic. It was foolish to think otherwise. Though I had packed away all evidence of my obsession with my son's case, it was still defining our lives. Knowing this I felt both dirty and trapped.

I was on a path, and I could no more change direction than I could turn back time and start again. That was clear to me now. A man was dead and my son was in prison. One death was pulling all of us inevitably toward another, like a whirlpool.

What choice did I have but to fight?

I called Murray twice a week from a pay phone at the driving range, piling my change on the metal shelf, listening to the snick of each quarter as it dropped into the coin slot. I was covering my tracks.

"I've got a lead on a guy at the DOD who may be able to get us a look at Hoopler's file," Murray might say. Or "My guy thinks Hoopler may have visited his parents in New Hampshire last month. He's trying to figure out what alias he traveled under."

I had stopped writing things down. I couldn't afford to leave a paper trail. The truth was, everything that mattered, all the relevant details of Danny's life, was already stored in my head.

"I'll call you in two days," I told him.

Afterward, I set my ball on the tee, shifted my weight. I ran up hills, my arms chugging. I took my kids for ice cream and showed them how to throw a perfect spiral. I made dirty martinis for the neighbors, and chimed in good-naturedly as we complained about our wives. I recycled, separating bottles from cans. My resting heart rate dropped from 102 to 74. My face was tan. My stomach was flat for the first time in decades. I was, for all appearances, a man in the prime of his life. And yet I felt nothing. I was a recording of a human voice, lifelike but artificial.

When I'd packed up my son's case files, there was one document I kept: Daniel's psychiatric evaluation. I hid it in a folder filled with old tax returns. It was a document I had read only once, in the middle of a sleepless night, while my children slept in their beds. Earlier that day, on the phone, I had begged Danny to appeal, to push for a new trial, but he said no. He just wanted to be left alone. I told him I would appeal it myself. But Danny was adamant. He said if I filed an appeal without his approval, he would never speak to me again. What a thing for a son to say to his father. What a choice for a father to have to make. In the end I had agreed. What good was a live son if I couldn't talk to him? I reasoned that the execution itself would take years to carry out, and during that time I could convince Danny to file his own appeal. I could fix the things between us that had been broken.

We're not all put on this Earth to do what's right.

I pictured my son, underweight, his body bruised, sitting across from a bearded psychiatrist. He'd recently pleaded guilty to murder in the first degree. The motions for and against his psychiatric evaluation had taken weeks to ready and debate. So he'd had time to think about what he wanted to convey. He'd had time to consider his crimes. Now he was being given the opportunity to explain, and this is what he offered: *We're not all put on this Earth to do what's right.* What did it mean? Did my son really believe he had been destined to kill another human being?

I bent my knees and tried to empty my mind. In my hands the driver felt like a surgical instrument, a scalpel meant to excise thoughts from my head.

You know, Hitler was a monster, but by being a monster he gave the world the opportunity to do enormous good.

Hitler? Why would Daniel invoke the name of the greatest monster in the history of the modern world? Did he want to be seen as a defender of the Holocaust? A Nazi? He had also mentioned Charles Whitman. Was there a strategy at work here? Was the boy trying to find his place in the history of violence? To rank himself on a chart of evil?

And what had he meant when he said his parents *just didn't seem that interested in me*? Is that what he really believed? That he had been a bore to us, an afterthought? Didn't he know how much we'd agonized about his custody? How we'd watched his moods and debated his progress? Didn't he know his mother and I used to speak several times a week, unraveling every childhood funk, every incident at home or school?

I mean, my dad never really felt like a huge part of my life. And now, I don't know, I guess I felt like one of those exchange students, you know? When you go to France or something, and they put you with a French family. That's how it felt.

I thought about my own memories of this period. Danny was fifteen when he'd come to live with us. Fran and I had done everything we could to make him feel at home. We'd put the boys in a single room and given Danny his own bedroom. We'd planned extra outings and designed family activities to include him. Every night we sat together at the dinner table and shared stories of our day. We allowed Danny to babysit the boys. We gave him responsibilities. We gave him praise.

And yet, if I am being truthful, though I remember this as a happy time for us, it was also an especially busy time for me at work. I had just been made chief of my department at the hospital. I worked late almost every night. So there was no way I could have had dinner with my family every night. Strange how that idea had cemented itself in my mind—of the Allens as a happy, intact family. The truth was, I saw Danny mostly on the weekends. It was Fran who fed him, who took him to school and picked him up. She'd had more of a relationship with Danny than I'd had. This wasn't something she ever chastised me for—Fran wasn't the type to scold—but in the months after Danny arrived she had encouraged me to make more time for him. And that summer I had, turning down a lucrative lecture tour in order to take Danny camping in the Adirondacks.

Early one Friday afternoon in June, I packed up the Range Rover—tent, sleeping bags, folding chairs—and Danny and I set off for the wilderness. My father had been a lifelong camper and had, in the years before his death, taken us camping numerous times. There was something about the chill of the midnight tent and the smoky taste of a campfire that made me feel closer to him. It was a memory I cherished, and one I hoped to impart to my own son—believing foolishly that a few great experiences could outweigh the paucity of time we had spent in each other's company over the last seven years.

In the car on the way up I did most of the talking. I began by telling Danny about my day, the patients I had seen that morning. That led to a larger discussion of my role as a doctor and how I had come to choose the field when I was Danny's age. I talked about the setbacks I had suffered early on—a psychology-rotation fiasco that taught me I had no business analyzing the personalities of others, a long year I spent fulfilling an ob-gyn internship—and how the subsequent crisis of faith (did I even want to be a doctor?) led me to the study of rheumatology.

Somewhere around Albany I realized that rather than simply making conversation with my son I was trying to teach him who I was. As if I were a job applicant and he the employer. As if we were on a blind date, and I was determined, even desperate, that he like me.

But, of course, this is not what family is. Familial bonds are not created through the transfer of information. They are forged through experience over time. They are the sum of Potty Training times Sick Days, of Nights Spent Sleeping in the Same Bed times Knee Scrapes Kissed in Playgrounds. The intimacy of parents and children is not based on data as much as it is on proximity. Case in point: I was probably ten before it even occurred to me ask where my father went when he left the house in the morning other than "to go to work."

Instead, my father was a voice (low and resonant), a smell (woody and earthen). My father was a feeling, a sense of security transferred from his body to mine when I put my arms around his neck. The details of his life were irrelevant. He was an extension of my body, as I was of his.

I felt this intimacy with Wally and Alex. Their runny noses were my runny noses. I felt no more compunction wiping their asses than I did wiping my own. Through years of interdependence I had become attuned to the rhythms of their breathing, the movement of their limbs. Because of this I could easily tell when something was wrong.

The truth is, a fifteen-year-old boy whom you spend less than thirty days a year with is not your son. Not in the same way as a boy you have tucked in every single night of his life. You share none of the inherent intimacy, the ability to inhabit the same space thoughtlessly, to drape an arm or leg over him as you watch TV together on the couch, to literally take food that has fallen from his mouth and eat it yourself.

Instead what you have is an awkward synergy. The expectation of a familial bond without the actual bond. This had never been more clear to me than it was on that trip.

"It seems like you're doing well in school," I said, trying to change the subject, "settling in. Are you liking it here okay? With us?"

He shrugged. Danny had never been the most talkative kid, and now he was fifteen, the official age of sullen silence. Perhaps he saved all his expressiveness for others, I thought. But who? Kids his own age? Teachers?

"Are you talking to your mom?" I asked. "Calling her?"

Another shrug.

"She's not thrilled I'm here," he said, something I knew to be true. Danny and my ex-wife had had a series of fallings out in the last year— about skipping school, lying, staying out late, the classic teenage triumvirate—after the last of which Ellen had screamed something along the lines of "You hate it here so much, try living with your father." And much to her surprise, Danny picked up the phone and called me. Two weeks later he was moving in with us.

"This is the closet," I said, showing him around his room, as if he were a visiting space alien who had never used a closet before. "You can hang your clothes in here."

I was nervous. The night Danny had called Fran made lasagna, and after dinner we played Rock Band on the kids' Wii. Sitting there, holding hands with my wife, watching my sons jump around in front of the TV, I'd had one of those rare "life is good" moments. I was forty-five years old. It had taken me all that time to find the perfect balance between work and family, between ambition and relaxation, but it felt like I'd finally reached it. And then the phone rang.

"It's Danny," Fran told me, coming back from the kitchen, the receiver in her hand.

"Hey, buddy," I said. "What's up?"

He told me he'd had it with his mom. That he wanted to come live with me for a while. I looked at Fran and the kids, our sacred family unit, at home, at peace. Did I have a moment of doubt? A flash of reluctance? I would be lying if I said I didn't. Balance had been achieved, and with Danny moving in would come a new dynamic, a different equation. And yet hearing his voice on the phone I also felt sadness, guilt. He was my son. The boy I'd left behind. I wanted him to feel what it had taken me forty-five years to find—a sense of contentment.

"Absolutely," I said. "We want you here. I'll buy you a ticket in the morning."

Now, setting up our tent in the woods of upstate New York, I watched my firstborn son. He had been a late bloomer, waiting to break five feet until he was thirteen. His hair was marine short and called attention to his ears. He had deep-set eyes and elegant long lashes. Left to his own devices, Danny read books about explorers and other survival tales. He couldn't do his math homework, but he could tell you just how many of Ernest Shackleton's men had survived their eighteen-month odyssey after their ship, the *Endurance*, was frozen in an ice floe (all twenty-eight).

Danny liked tales of men climbing mountains, of lone explorers setting off into jungles on trips from which they'd never return. He was, it seemed, a collector of outcast narratives. Looking back it seems clear that even in youth he saw something in the lives of these men that he identified with—an impulse to go it alone, to strike out for undiscovered lands. What strikes you when you read about the lives of explorers is that they were often literally strangers to their children, their wives. They would set off for years at a time, coming home only to raise money for another mission. They chose the camaraderie of the journey over the bond of a family.

Daniel, too, it seemed, was uninterested in traditional family life. We had instituted a nightly dinner rule when Alex and Wally were two, believing it was important for the entire family to sit down at least once a day and share a meal. But in the year he lived with us, Danny missed at least three dinners a week. There was always an excuse. He signed up for after-school activities. He joined a band. And sometimes he was home but simply chose not to come downstairs.

This was one of the things I tried to address with him as we prepared our evening meal. It was late June, and the last of the sun's light was beginning to fade just after eight. The night before I had marinated lamb chops in rosemary and lime. We cooked them with kidney beans from a can over the roaring campfire.

"This is nice," I said.

He nodded.

"I used to go camping with my dad a lot before he died," I told him.

He thought about this.

"My teacher died last year," he told me. "People said he had AIDS, but I think it was just pneumonia. He was pretty old."

"How'd that make you feel?" I asked.

He shrugged. "He was nice. But it didn't feel real. One day he was there, and the next there was a lady with one big shoe who took over the class. So it just felt like maybe they fired him."

"One big shoe?" I asked.

"You know," he said, "because she had, like, one leg longer than the other."

I considered explaining to him the biological realities of death, what happens to the body, the way it looks, the way it smells, but decided against it. Let him go on believing his teacher had been fired. The knowledge of death can consume you if you let it, the inevitableness of it, and I wanted to protect him from that for as long as possible.

I asked him if he remembered the things we had done together when he was young and his mother and I were still married.

"Like, do you remember going to Venice Beach, to the promenade?" I asked.

He shook his head.

"We would take you there every Saturday morning and have breakfast on the beach. You used to love to run in the sand. You were three, maybe four."

"Really?" he said. He told me he hated beaches now. "I don't like the ocean," he said. "The way it never stops, the sound of it."

"What else?" I asked him.

He thought about it.

"Blenders," he said, "and horses. Horses creep me out. And flowers. The way cut flowers smell, the water, when you leave them in the house for too long."

"That's decay," I said.

"Yeah. Also people's teeth, when they're bad. Like witches in movies. I have to turn it off. It makes me want to knock out my own teeth. Just the feeling of all those tombstones on my tongue."

I turned the lamb chops on the fire. Fat dripped down into the flames, making them dance.

"So what do you like?" I asked.

"I like it when it snows," he said, "and everything gets muffled. And then when you walk there's a crunch. I like the way it feels, and how you can tell where people have been."

"I like the feeling I get when I jump into water," I told him. "How for a second when I first submerge it's like I'm in and out of the water at the same time."

"Movie-theater seats," he said. "All that red velvet."

We ate everything in sight that night, two men by a fire, licking our plates clean.

Later, I lay in the tent listening to the sound of his breathing. It was a sound I hadn't really listened to in years, the rhythmic sighs of my eldest son as he slept. He had been a baby once, needy and small, but that time had passed. Where had it gone? How can life move so quickly? Now he was a fifteen-year-old boy with a teenager's mustache. Now he was a book with a torn cover. I had known him once, his tiny body, the energy of his smile, the smell of his breath, but he slipped away from me.

The next day we hiked two miles to the lake, stopping to hydrate along the way. It was partly cloudy, but there was rain in the forecast. We reached the water around eleven, passing through rows of narrow pines, last year's needles still thick underfoot. Daniel seemed friendlier after our night together. He told me stories of his classmates, who was an idiot and what girls were cute.

I asked him if he had ever had a drink or experimented with drugs.

He told me he'd been high a few times, that he had friends back in L.A. who smoked, but he didn't like the feeling very much.

"I don't like feeling muddy or, like, out of touch," he said. "I was reading about how we have so many chemicals going into our bodies, like, all the time and we don't even know it. I think it's important to be pure, you know? To try and stay clear."

I told him that I thought that sounded right. I told him people usually turned to drugs and alcohol as an escape. I said I wish I'd had that kind of perspective when I was fifteen.

Walking back, I let Danny get ahead of me. I was enjoying the air, the sound of the leaves shivering in the wind, and the way the morning light filtered through the trees. When I looked down again, I saw Danny standing still on the path ahead. I was about to call out to him, but something about his body language made the words catch in my throat.

When I reached his side I saw that he was staring down at the body of a dead deer. It was a doe and small, maybe a year old. Scavengers had gotten to it, and some parts were just bone. But the face was relatively untouched.

Danny didn't say anything. I glanced at his face, not wanting to make him self-conscious but trying to gauge his reaction.

"He's really dead, isn't he?" he said.

"Who?" I said.

"Mr. Santiago. My teacher. He's really dead. He didn't just quit."

I reached over and put my hand on his head, pulling him to me. After a minute he put his arms around me, and we stood there together, listening to the sound of the wind in the trees.

The next day, when we got home, Fran asked me how it had gone. I told her it was a great trip. I said I felt like I'd made a breakthrough with Danny, that we'd reestablished our bond. I felt high from the experience—the woods and the fresh air, the time spent with my son in the kind of environment I had shared with my own father—but the next day I went back to work, disappearing into my busy schedule, and three months later Danny packed his things and moved back to California, to his mom's house.

That camping trip turned out to be the last time Danny and I ever spent more than a few hours together. The brief glimpse of his true self I felt I had seen, the insight I had gained, grew murkier as the next few years passed, until finally, when he'd dropped out of college, he had become only slightly more than a stranger.

But at that moment, standing in the kitchen with Fran, my arms still vibrating from the steering wheel, I felt triumphant, as if I had just erased eight years of casual parenting in a single weekend.

Isn't it interesting how we rewrite the past in our minds, how we paint our memories in the most flattering light? With patients I am always aware not only of the things they tell me but of the things they leave out.

It's not just that people don't like to share information that embarrasses them. It's that they often block out their most painful memories. They create a subjective history, different from the truth. Was this what I had done with Danny's childhood? Taken an absent father and rewritten him to be loving and warm and omnipresent?

And yet how many children grow up in broken homes? How many suffer through divorce and neglect, and don't grow up to be assassins? These truths, though painful for me, were not explanations. They did not answer the deeper question of motive. They did not tell me what I most needed to know. Why did my son feel he "had to" kill another human being? What fate or destiny did he believe in that had pushed him to join in the murder of an American hero?

The psychiatrist who interviewed Daniel had written about a journal he had kept. I needed to see that journal. I needed to read my son's words, to understand his journey, his process. What insights were hidden inside those pages? Truths that might be meaningless to a stranger but would not be meaningless to me. When I finished reading the psychiatric report the first time, I'd called Murray.

"We have to get it," I told him.

"I'm working on it," he said. "The problem is, he pleaded guilty, and the judge accepted it. So there's no trial. They're arguing that the journal falls into the trial discovery phase, and we don't need it now. I told them if they didn't turn it over the discovery phase would involve me discovering what it felt like to shove my fist up the guy's ass. Mostly he stopped returning my calls after that."

"Murray," I said.

"I know. Don't worry. We've filed a motion to get it before the sentencing hearing. We'll appeal it all the way to the Supreme Court if we have to."

But the prosecution hadn't turned over the journal, and the courts didn't force them to. And now my son was on death row. He had refused to appeal his conviction or petition to have his sentence commuted. It was accepted that he'd killed Seagram. The more time that passed, the less anybody cared about why.

Except me. I was still fighting, still struggling to understand. I was the lone voice in the dark, the fringe dissenter, still asking questions.

I would get that journal, if it was the last thing I did.

The next time he saw her, he invited her to a rally. It was October, eight months before the event. The presidential election was just starting to heat up. Senator Seagram was coming to town to drum up support. There would be fund-raising dinners and photo opportunities. At head-quarters a fresh sense of urgency filled the air. They had registered more than thirty thousand new voters in six months. Seagram was going to come by the office and personally thank the staff for their hard work. Walter Bagwell, who managed personnel in the Austin office, called the staff together and said it was "a historic moment." Seagram was poised to become the Democratic front-runner, and Texas had played a big part in his ascension.

Near the back, someone asked if Seagram's family would be with him. Bagwell said his wife would be joining him, but the kids were in school. Carter Allen Cash thought about the boy in the lake, Seagram's frozen son. He wondered if he would ever know that kind of sorrow. Even as he stood there he was imagining himself asking her to be with him when he met Seagram. Natalie. It had been almost a week since he last talked to her. She had missed a few days of work. Sick, the temp had said. Carter had left the library early that day, riding his bike along Mopac all the way to north Austin and back. He spent the night lying in bed reading old Russian novels.

He went to Barton Springs every night at nine to swim. It was Indian summer, sweat running down the small of his back and trickling down his sides. He rode his bike without a helmet, without lights or even reflec-tors. He liked the feeling of invisibility. Hot wind blew past him, like a convection oven, cooking him evenly on all sides. Pulling into the park-ing lot he would ditch his bike in the bushes and dive straight into the water, still in his clothes. He liked to lie on his back in the cold water and watch the stars flicker overhead. The wavy sound of the divers found his ears through the ripple of water. He swam laps across the deep end, feel-ing the vegetation caress his hands and feet. He liked that there were fish navigating somewhere beneath him, lurking in the dark. He lay on the grass listening to the wind in the trees. He studied the girls in their bikinis. The fullness of their breasts made him self-conscious. He won-dered how they could walk around on display like that, wondered what it took to be a woman who markets her sex.

Did Natalie come here? Did she wear a bikini like these girls, the wet fabric hugging every curve, broadcasting her sexuality like some girl in a men's magazine? The thought was too much. He dove deep and let the silent pressure calm his nerves. There was something about this false summer that made him restless.

He rode to a Tex-Mex joint and smoked cigarettes out back with the busboys. He missed the camaraderie of Latin men. The joking insults, different somehow than the macho cocksmanship of the frat boys. He liked the way they drank beer from the bottle and smiled through their teeth like sharks. The busboys were from southern Mexico. They talked trash about northern Mexicans, how their *chiles* were smaller and their women took it in the ear.

His clothes dried quickly in the convection-oven heat. He liked buying drinks with wet money, handing over the soggy bills, taking the cold, hard change in return. After-hours he sat on the curb out-side Schlotzsky's drinking beer out of a paper bag. One of the busboys said he knew a girl who would fuck three guys at one time. The dish-washer passed around photos of his girl back home. They had three kids together. He was going to bring them all to Texas as soon as he could put together enough money to pay the coyote.

Lying on your back in the water of Barton Springs there was nothing to do but breathe. You felt the water cupping your face, tracing the out-line of your body. His wet clothes clung to him, pockets full of water. His flip-flops threatened to float away and sink down into the pitch black below. He could feel his imminent departure, like a head cold coming on. He gave himself two more weeks, three at the most. The girl was the wild card. The possibility that she might fall in love with him, that they would date and she would be able to see who he was. To see the reason for him, the point. If she did, would she tell him? Is that what he was waiting for? Someone to explain himself to him?

He was ready when he saw her the next day. He had spent all morning thinking of the right words, practicing his offhanded tone. At the library he lurked beside the Russian classics, waiting for her to walk by, the girl in the white pants, a girl he thought he could love.

"Hey," she said, when she saw him and smiled.

The smile made him feel liquid in the middle, like a cookie fresh from the oven.

He said, "There's a rally tomorrow. Seagram's in town—the presidential candidate—and, you know, I volunteer for the campaign. Anyway, he's coming by the office afterward to say thanks. I thought maybe you might want to go—with me. Meet him."

She flushed and nodded. Her smile was like that moment where a rainbow forms, a great arc of color, brightening the storm-dark skies.

The next night he picked her up in a cab. They went to Shady Grove on Barton Springs Road. He was wearing a white button-down shirt and slacks he had spent twenty minutes steaming flat in the shower. They sat out under the trees and ate burgers and onion rings. She had a whiskey. He drank water without ice.

Natalie was too pretty to look at directly. When he did, he felt like a man falling down a circular staircase or water spiraling down a drain. This was the way it worked. Men are a brick wall. Women are a doorway. Sitting across from her, he felt a great need to *explain* himself, and the stronger the need became, the less he knew how to satisfy it. Trying to put who he was into words was like trying to say how many marbles were in a giant jar. The best he could do was guess.

She laughed a lot and told him about her hometown, the way her parents raised her to be a *yes person*, not a *no person*. He listened to stories of her buddy-buddy nuclear family as if they were tales of the outrageous.

He told her that his own father had moved out when he was seven. The muscles of her face formed a frown.

"That must have been hard," she said.

He shrugged. He wanted her beauty to be a calming thing, but instead it agitated him. He could not think about her lips without picturing them on the head of his penis. He wanted her to be a nun, but he knew that under the right conditions she would yield to heat and pressure. Why, he wondered, did everything have to be so base and predictable? When it came right down to it, no one ever asked you if you wanted to be an animal. You just were one.

Wolf or sheep?

That was the question.

They took another cab to campaign headquarters. There was a line outside, security doing pat downs and checking purses. Waiting to be screened, Natalie took his hand and squeezed it. He could see the excitement in her face, a certain redness in the cheeks. Her breathing was shallow and fast. As they approached the front door, she leaned over quickly and kissed him on the cheek. He recoiled as if slapped, then tried to cover.

He had never had a problem being with women before, the intimacy of words and bodies, but something had shifted in him on the road, the part of him that was open to connection. It was like a gear that had broken off in transit and was rattling around somewhere inside the engine, just out of sight.

He squeezed her hand in apology and managed a smile. She smiled back questioningly, eyes hopeful. The spot where she'd kissed him was itchy, like a bug bite.

Inside, they found their place in the crowd. The room was packed with well-wishers, Austinites of all ages, shaking with liberal Pentecostalism. Carter positioned himself and Natalie so that they were near the door. Beside him, Natalie was literally vibrating with excitement. This was the effect Seagram had on people. They smiled when he walked into a room. Their core temperature rose. Carter had observed it before on TV, but now he was experiencing it firsthand. Around him everyone grinned and rocked up on their toes. Natalie put her hand on his arm and squeezed. He glanced over at her, and she said, "Thanks again for bringing me."

He didn't reply. Seagram was almost to them now. There were two Secret Service agents in the lead, checking the room. Two more followed closely behind. Carter felt like a surfer waiting for a wave. He took a deep breath and made his face friendly and open. As Seagram got closer, he stuck out his hand. Seagram grabbed it firmly with both hands, and squeezed, but his eyes were elsewhere, lighting up with something like recognition.

Charged by the power of the handshake—the dominating pressure the Great Man exerted, like the stranglehold of a python—Carter turned to see what Seagram was looking at and found Natalie, blushing. She was wearing something new tonight, something she had bought just for the event. It was a blue dress, sleeveless, mid-length, low cut. Her hair was down. Her eyes were sparkling. Her lips resembled fruit that would go bad by tomorrow, collapsing into soft, blackening pulp.

Carter turned back in time to see Seagram's eyes drop to Natalie's cleavage. It was a fast glance, almost imperceptible, the candidate's eyes already moving on, but Carter saw it, saw this so-called "great man" check out his date's rack. He felt dizzy, like a balloon that had sprung a slow leak. It was the vertigo of crushed expectations, the disorienting feeling that a landmark he had steered by these last few months had turned out to be a mirage.

The Great Man was not a great man. He was a regular man pretending to be a great man. He was a false diamond, a common body that shits and fucks and lusts, just like everyone else.

By the time Carter had processed this, Seagram had an older woman's hand clasped in his. He was posing for a photo, his smile perfunctory once more. How many hands had the candidate shaken in the last three years? How many wives or girlfriends had he ogled? As Carter watched, Seagram made his way to the center of the room, where he took his place in preparation for a speech.

"That was amazing," Natalie said.

Carter looked at her, his face closing down, like a door that slams shut in the wind. Whatever magic he had felt with her was gone now, extinguished like a cigarette beneath his shoe. She was no longer the muse of famous Russian novelists, no longer the bright beacon he would steer toward on dark and treacherous nights. Now she was just another witless country girl, seduced by power.

Men were predators.

Women were prey.

He watched Seagram take the podium in that packed office in Austin, grinning through the applause. Carter saw how the candidate's wife looked at her husband, with hope and love in her eye. It was a look he had seen her give him many times on TV, and it had always made him feel warm—to know that a woman could feel such love for her husband (and he for her), that a family could exist where trust and faith was just a normal part of life.

But now, watching Seagram take his wife's hand, watching him kiss her on the cheek, Carter saw that love for what it was. Another lie. Not only was Seagram not a great man (because he was victim to gross and petty lusts, like some kind of degenerate trucker); he was also not the devoted husband and reliable father he made himself out to be. He was false, the way a marketing campaign is false, just another American hypocrite, a clandestine seducer of women, a wolf in sheep's clothing.

And it was at that moment that Carter had the first awakening as to what he would have to do. He saw it in a flash, the vision like a gunshot with a massive recoil. The power of it rocked him back on his heels.

Afterward, on the street, when Natalie asked if he wanted to get a drink someplace, he told her he was sorry, but he had to get up early. He was leaving tomorrow and had packing to do. He needed supplies. He could see the hurt and surprise on her face, but he didn't stay to explain. He simply left her there on the sidewalk, protesting to the moon.

When he got home the frat boys were bumping bellies. It had been a long night of Jell-O shots and Indian burns, and they were feeling rowdy. He tried to squeeze through the crowded hall and slip into his room, but one of them grabbed him, folded him into a headlock. He dug his knuckles into Carter's skull.

"This guy," he said. "This fucking guy."

There was porn playing in the living room. Black women with enormous asses in spandex walked slowly away from the camera. He set his heels into the floor, tried to pry himself loose. Below him, the carpet smelled of cigarettes and vomit. The frat boy hung on. Whatever playfulness he'd had in mind when he started this maneuver was now replaced by a drunken need to humiliate.

"Where you going, Nancy?" he said.

On-screen, a black woman poured milk onto her naked buttocks.

Carter struggled to break free, but the frat boy had him tight. The guy started walking him around the apartment, dragging him by the neck, making jokes.

"You guys have met Nancy, right? Anybody wanna see what color her thong is?"

The frat boys laughed and slapped him on the ass. He could feel his face burning, something ugly filling his mouth with the taste of metal.

"See if he's got any money on him," somebody said. "We're out of booze."

He felt hands going through his pocket. The frat boy's armpit smelled like beef and cheese. They found a fifty in his back pocket. Carter threw a horse kick, connecting with something soft. Somebody punched him in the spine.

"Calm yourself, Susan," the frat boy told him, increasing the pressure on Carter's neck until he thought he might black out. Together the frat boys bum-rushed their hostage to the bathroom, tossed him inside. He heard them lock the door. His face was red, temples throbbing with trapped blood. They laughed and grunted. He banged on the door, but they just turned up the music. Carter looked around for another means of escape. The clear, plastic shower curtain was caked with so many years of mildew it looked, for all intents and purposes, like a green shower curtain. He tried the small window over the toilet. Its swollen frame creaked but yielded. He put his head out and studied the two-story drop.

The frat boys were huddled around a bong when he came out of his room with the gun. They thought it was a joke at first, but then he slid the action back, priming the Smith & Wesson, and suddenly they were all on their feet, hands up, telling him to "calm the fuck down." But he was calm. The fury that had filled him in the bathroom was gone, replaced by a flat certainty. He could see the fear on their faces, except for the fat guy passed out on the sofa, who slept through the shouting and the thunder of feet, as he had through the riot that preceded it.

Carter showed them the gun, forcing them backward. There were six boys, big and dumb and drunk. Five were residents. They were the ones who called him *Chief* and *Sport*. They were the lummoxes who broke the toilet with their beer-soaked logs, who grilled cheese sandwiches directly on the burners of the stove, until the stovetop itself had become a Tolkienesque mountain range of fly-encrusted dairy. They were the ham-fisted troglodytes who butt-fucked wasted coeds on the wall-to-wall carpeting of their rooms, and then chased them out with rug burns on their knees.

He told them his name wasn't Susan. It wasn't Nancy. He didn't go by *Chief* or *Sport* or *Jefe* or *Jeeves*. The gun was his name. They should remember that. When they talked to him they were talking to the gun. On-screen, a white woman with hard round boobs flinched when some faceless fat man's money shot nailed her in the eye.

The frat boys told him to put the gun down. They said they were just kidding around. He told them they needed to understand that there were consequences to their actions. He said their daddies should have taught them that, but clearly their daddies were assholes, so he was going to teach them. He said their mommies should have taught them not to rape women, not to spit on their drunken, roofied bodies, but clearly their mothers were whores, so he was going to teach them. He asked how many of them had a sister. Half of them raised their hands. He wanted to know how they would like it if he slipped a pill into their sister's drink and then took pictures of her unconscious body with his dick in her mouth. They intimated that they wouldn't like that very much, but he suspected that it was the gun that was making them so compliant. Without the gun they wouldn't be so agreeable. Without the gun he would in the middle of a foot-storm.

He put the gun up to the frat boy's forehead, the one who'd noogied him.

"From now on you are going to flush the toilet," he told him. "You are not gonna knock on my door at two in the morning and ask if I want to see the biggest shit you ever took. I don't. Nobody does. And you are going to stop puking in the shower and peeing on the wall. We are human beings. This isn't a barn."

"Sure thing, Sport," the guy said, going cross-eyed trying to keep sight of the gun.

Carter stepped back, keeping them all in sight.

"Now I'm going in my room and going to bed," he told them, "and anyone who wakes me up is going to talk to the gun again. Understand?"

They all nodded. Sobriety comes quickly when weapons are pulled. Carter backed into his room and closed the door. He could hear them outside whispering furiously, trying to figure out what to do. He went over to the window and out onto the lip of the roof and slid down a drainpipe. He walked three blocks to the park and hid the gun in a culvert, then walked back through the lamplight and climbed up to his room.

He thought about how it had felt to point the gun at those frat boys. The power of it, like a potion you drink that makes you fifty feet tall. He imagined that he'd had the gun with him earlier, when he'd taken Natalie to the rally. He pictured the feel of it, hidden in the small of his back, then imagined himself pulling it, imagined showing it to Seagram, the change in the man's expression—from lechery to fear, respect, awe.

Who was the great man now?

In his mind certain ideas had solidified into fact: The candidate was a hypocrite, a liar. The gun was the truth. The gun could not lie. It said what it meant, every time. Using the gun, Carter would show the candidate how to be truthful. He would teach him about honesty, the way falling from a great height teaches a man about gravity.

As quietly as he could, Carter closed his bedroom window, picturing the look on Natalie's face when she saw him with the gun. When she saw that he, too, was a powerful man, not just another sucker pawn. He pictured the arousal in her eyes, the blue dress falling from her shoulders. She would be naked underneath, but where her dark triangle had been there would now be a blinding yellow sun.

He was lying in bed reading Gogol when the cops came in, kicking the door open, guns drawn. He sat up slowly, showing them he wasn't armed. A black police officer grabbed him by the wrist and maneuvered him onto the floor, putting a knee in the small of his back. He asked them what the problem was, and they wanted to know where he'd put the gun. He said, *What gun?* He didn't own a gun.

The cops pulled him out into the living room while they tore apart his room. He could hear things breaking in there, the rip of sheets, clothes being pulled from their hangers. When it became clear there was no gun in his room, the cops mellowed slightly. They offered him the opportunity to tell his side of the story. He affected an irate but civilized tone, and explained that he had come home, yet again, to find his roommates drunk and loud and watching porn. He explained how, unlike them and their rich daddies who paid tens of thousands of dollars so their pampered children could sleep it off in class, he was a workingman who needed his sleep. But when he'd asked them to turn it down they'd gotten aggressive. One of them had put him in a headlock and another had punched him in the back. He lifted his shirt to show them. The area had already started to bruise. He told the cops that he had threatened to call the landlord in the morning and have them thrown out. And then he'd gone to bed. And the frat boys must have decided to teach him a lesson. So they called the cops and said he'd threatened them with a gun. But he didn't own a gun. He was a doctor's son working on the presidential campaign of a man who had sponsored six gun-control bills. He hated guns. And if they didn't take these fucking cuffs off him right now he was going to sue them for wrongful arrest.

The cuffs came off in a hurry. Worried he'd gone too far, Carter assured them that he understood they were only doing their jobs. He asked them if they would wait while he packed up his things. He said he didn't feel safe sleeping under the same roof with those guys, not after this. They gave him fifteen minutes to throw his stuff in a suitcase. He didn't have much. Just some clothes and books. The frat boys were outside, smoking cigarettes on the curb, casting nervous glances at the windows. They started yelling when they saw the cops lead him out, not in cuffs but a free man, carrying all his worldly goods.

One of the officers took the frat boys aside and gave them a talking to. He could see them protesting, pointing. There was a heated conversation, which ended with a cop putting a finger in one frat boy's face and telling him to *shut the fuck up*. The frat boys stood stunned in the middle of the street and watched as the cops put Carter's suitcase and book box in the trunk of a prowler, followed by his bike. A uniform asked him where he wanted to go, and he said it would be dawn in an hour. Maybe they could just take him over to the Seagram campaign headquarters. He'd get some coffee at Austin Java and wait for the doors to open. And by the way, did the officer know of any available apartments?

And it was in this way that Carter Allen Cash came to relocate, waving from the back of the police car as the frat boys stood openmouthed on the curb.

That April, Ellen Shapiro called me from the parking lot of ADMAX. It had been five months since Danny was sentenced to death, ten months since the assassination. For Ellen, this worked out to eight haircuts, three hundred and six showers, eleven hundred daydreams, sixteen thousand waves of remorse and regret. This is how she saw it, she told me, the way your nails and hair continue to grow after death. As if each commute, each meal and troubled night's sleep added bricks to the one-way street of her life.

"I'm here," she said. "I came to see Danny. He looks awful. I told him I'd come back tomorrow, but I don't even know where this is. I don't have a motel. I'm driving a rental car."

I gave her directions and told her I'd meet her halfway. An hour later I found my ex-wife sitting in a landlocked country diner, staring at a cup of coffee. Her hair had turned entirely gray in the months since Danny's conviction. She wore it up now, loosely fitted with a clip. Her lips, which had always been thin, were pursed to the point of near invisibility.

"He looks bad," she said.

"He doesn't look that bad."

"He seems vague to me now, like he's already fading away."

I unzipped my windbreaker. Ellen and I hadn't spoken since Danny's sentencing. Seeing her now brought back feelings from that day, an unwanted glimpse of all the hysteria and fatigue, like the view of the abyss from space.

"Did you talk to him about appealing?" I asked.

"He won't have it," she said. "I begged him, but he says no. I told him I was going to hire a lawyer. He said if I did he'd never talk to me again."

I nodded. It was the same conversation I'd had with him.

"Don't give up," I told her. But I could see that she already had. It seemed I was the only one crazy enough to hold out hope for my son's salvation in the face of all that had happened.

"I'm forty-eight years old," she said. "And I never got a handle on things. I never figured out how to have a career. I never figured out how to make a relationship work. I never got my body back after the birth or learned to multitask. And now it's too late. Danny was the only thing I ever did that I was proud of. And then he did this."

"He didn't do it," I said.

"How can you say that?" she asked. "He confessed. They sentenced him."

I considered telling her what I knew—Cobb and Hoopler on the train, the possibility that our son hadn't been the trigger man at all, or that he had been brainwashed into doing it—but the leap was too great. I could see from her face that what she was looking for was forgiveness, not information. She needed to know that she was not the cause of Danny's destruction. That giving birth to a murderer would not be the only lasting mark she would leave on the world.

"I think he's covering for someone," I said.

She gave me a look, exasperated, pissed, like I was a con man who had fleeced her once then come back for more.

"But how do you prove that?" she wanted to know.

I shrugged. Ellen stared out the window for a long moment. A lock of hair fell across her face. I found myself feeling a tenderness toward her I hadn't felt in more than a decade. We had loved each other once, had walked down the aisle, had made promises about forever, in sickness and health. We'd had a child together, had raised him in tandem for years, rising in shifts to handle his late-night needs. And then, when the fighting became too much, we split and started new lives.

"We were so young when we met," I said. "It's hard to believe."

It had started to rain, and streaks of water ran through her reflection in the glass.

"You were a cute doctor at a party," she said. "I was in town ten minutes. I thought everybody I met was going to be a movie star."

"I was wearing scrubs and you asked if it was a costume."

She smiled wistfully.

"I'm dingy. My brain gets things wrong. Danny would ask me to help him with his homework and I would tell him *that is not a good idea*."

After a pause, I said, "I know we've been through it and over it a hundred times, but was there anything? When you think back, was there anything that we could have done? Anything we missed? A warning sign?"

She thought about it.

"He never really seemed that into girls," she said. "I mean he had girlfriends, but he never seemed invested."

I thought about this.

"What else?"

"I caught him a few times," she said, "smoking pot with his friends. He was thirteen, fourteen. I picked up the phone to call you, but then I stopped because I knew you'd blame me. You'd make it my fault somehow."

"Was I really that awful?" I asked her, strangely hurt that that was what she thought, the impression she had of me, her ex-husband, as some kind of punitive ogre.

"You judged people," she said. "Me especially. I think you were embarrassed by me. You were this successful doctor and I was the ditz who didn't graduate from college. And then we had a kid and you thought you knew better. All your complex theories about child rearing. But do you know what the most important part of being a parent is, Mr. Fancy Pants Doctor? Showing up. And I was there for that kid every day. So say what you want, but I did it. It's not my fault."

I reached out and took her hand. She pulled back instinctively, but I didn't let go.

"I know you did," I said. "And I want to thank you for doing that, for being there. I left. I admit it. I moved away and left you. I left him. And it is my one great regret."

She looked away.

"Who's going to take care of me when I'm old?" she said. "That's what I keep thinking. I should have had another. I should have had girls."

Not for the first time I wished that I could go back in time, make different choices. I wish that I could have helped her more with the transition. That I'd stayed in L.A., helped her raise our son. I wish I could have found a way to share the burden, to free Ellen somehow so she could find some kind of happiness. But what would my life have been like if I'd done that? Would I be married now? Would I have children? At the end of the day was I really ready to sacrifice my other children so that my firstborn son could be whole?

And even if I'd stayed, there's no way of knowing if Danny would be a substantially different person as a result, that events would have unfolded differently. Because it was equally possible that his inability to have meaningful relationships was chemical, not experiential, his impulse to buy weapons at gun shows and drive for weeks on end, talking only to his car.

The problem with alternate histories is that they provide no real insight into the lives we live today.

"Come on," I said, trying to be playful, "you and me? We're never gonna get old."

She smiled sadly.

"We already are," she said.

On June 16, a year to the day after the assassination, Murray surprised me by showing up in Colorado on his motorcycle. It was time to take the great American road trip, he said. The idea had come to him like a stroke in the night. His face was sunburned in a goggle pattern. There was a skinny blonde with him.

I was standing in the kitchen, eating a sandwich, when he knocked. For a moment, seeing his grinning face I had a complete sense of displacement. Who was I? Where was I? What day was it? I opened the door. Murray—in leathers—handed me a large manila envelope.

"Merry Christmas," he said. He was wearing jeans and a bomber jacket.

"What are you—" I said.

"I like the haircut," he said. "And the new wardrobe. You look very rural, very ex-military, middle America."

I touched my head. I had gotten used to the new sparser me, with my crew cut and my dress-for-less wardrobe. But now I realized how strange I must look to someone seeing it for the first time.

"This is Nadia," Murray announced, moving past me to get to the fridge. "Nadia this is Paul."

Nadia smiled. She gave a little wave. Murray told me she was a Russian immigrant who spoke very little English.

"She's got her green card," he told me. "Although there's a good chance it's fake. She hangs around with some pretty skeevy guys."

As he spoke I became aware of the package he had handed me. It was a nine by fourteen envelope. It weighed about a pound.

"What's this?" I said, holding it up.

Murray was rooting around in the fridge for something to eat. He looked over.

"That's the journal," he said. "Danny's journal."

I felt all the blood leave my face. I stared at the envelope he had given me. It was as thick as a paperback book. I reached inside and pulled out a hundred loose pages. The top sheet was a photocopy of a notebook cover. Written on it were three letters: *CAC*. Carter Allen Cash.

Seeing the name, I felt the room start to spin. I took a shaky step backward. Nadia put a hand on my arm to steady me.

"Where did you get this?" I said.

"Guy I know at Justice," he said, putting a bowl of pasta salad on the counter. "I hit them with an FOIA and threatened to sue. It showed up out of the blue last week."

He peeled back the plastic wrap and started eating from the bowl with his fingers. I thumbed through the pages. My son's handwriting stared back at me. Seeing it made me light-headed.

"Did you read it?" I asked.

"I looked through it. There's no smoking gun. He doesn't write *Must kill Senator Seagram* a thousand times. Or *Rode train with black ops conspirators*. There are no drawings of decapitated men or oversized animal penises."

"So what is it?"

"A journal. He started it in Austin, but he goes back and writes about his time in Iowa, too. The stuff on Montana is pretty hard to take, the time he spent digging into Seagram's life, visiting his childhood home. Reading it now, in context, knowing what he did. Honestly, some of it made the hair on the back of my neck stand up."

I stared at the pages. I had gone to see Danny by myself for the first time three weeks ago. After Alex developed night terrors, we had decided to stop the family visits and give the kids time to get settled. I promised Fran that I, too, would take a break, but I hadn't. At the prison, I'd passed through the metal detectors, raised my arms for the wand, emptied my pockets, and took off my shoes. I'd stepped through iron gates and thick metal doors until I was in the waiting area. It was about half full.

I found a plastic chair, sat, aware that people in prison waiting rooms don't like to look each other in the eye. The truth is, we don't want to acknowledge why we're there, the crimes of which our loved ones are capable. It's not embarrassment. It's shame, deep and biblical. So we keep our eyes on the floor. We listen with envy to the careless laughter of children, who have not yet learned to feel the way we do.

When it was my turn, I took my seat in the narrow visitation cubicle. The Plexiglas in front of me was crisscrossed with metal wire. When I'd first started coming here with the family I carried hand sanitizer in my pocket. But one day I realized that there was nothing I could catch in prison that was worse than what I already had, which was a convicted murderer for a son. So now I didn't bother.

After a few moments, a guard led Daniel in. He sat across from me. He was pale, and he had spent the last six weeks growing a beard. It was a young man's beard, patchy in places. He did not have the capacity to grow a great beard. He was a fair-haired kid with a young face. The beard gave him the appearance of a small-town meth addict.

"It's time," I told him.

"Time for what?"

"I need to hear you say it."

He stared at me dead-eyed.

"If you did it," I said. "If you killed him, I need to hear it from you."

He stared at me. I realized I was sweating. There were men with truncheons guarding the exits.

"I don't have any answers for you," he told me after a long silence.

"Danny."

He rubbed his nose angrily.

"You know, it's okay if you want to come here, if you want to see me, but I'm not going to talk to you about those things. I'm not going to explain myself."

"Daniel."

He looked at me. What could I say to cross this gap between us? To convince him I was on his side?

"I know about Hoopler and Cobb," I said. "The men on the train. If they were involved . . . if they made you do this . . ."

He closed his eyes.

"We're done here."

Without opening his eyes, he signaled for the guard to come get him.

"Wait," I said, panic in my voice.

He stood, eyes still closed.

"What did they promise you?" I said. "Why are you doing this?"

He opened his eyes and looked at me. "Don't come here again."

The guard approached. Daniel turned to leave.

"Daniel, please," I said. "Daniel."

I watched him disappear through the metal door. I sat there as long as they let me, hoping he would come back. But he didn't.

The next day I called in sick. I sat in the waiting room for an hour before a guard told me that Daniel wasn't coming out. The day after that the guard at the gate told me that my son had asked that I not be allowed to visit him. I didn't care. I drove to the prison every day for two weeks just to be turned away. I sat in traffic. I braved inclement weather. I listened to hate radio, to classic rock, to NPR. I drove to ADMAX so often I saw yellow lines in my sleep. But Daniel refused to come out of his cell. Every day I told the guards to tell him that I'd come. I did it so that he would know—I was his father. I wasn't going to give up on him. I had made so many mistakes. I had let him ruin everything, but I was still his father.

The clandestine nature of these visits, their increased frequency, began to feel like an affair. For the first time in my life I understood how it was that a man could take a mistress. It wasn't the sex. It was the transgression, the act of doing something you knew was wrong. By doing so, in many ways you cease to be yourself. A man builds a life. He starts a family. He loves his children. He likes his job. But one day he meets a woman, and despite all common sense, he begins to pull his life down brick by brick. Who is that man? Is he the same man who built that life? Or is he another man? An imposter?

Is he Carter Allen Cash?

Leaving ADMAX, I drove north in my used Jeep. I stood on the driving range and tried to drop my ball on the 150-foot tee, the 200, the 60. I interlocked my pinkies. I slid the covers from my drivers. I picked dirt from the heads of my irons.

I called Murray from the pay phone.

"We have to find Hoopler," I said. "He's the key."

"Short of joining the CIA," he said, "I'm not sure what else I can do. The guy's a ghost. Literally. Meaning he may not even be alive. Cobb's body was dumped in a culvert. Hoopler could be at the bottom of the ocean."

I ran uphill in the heat of the day, breathing through my mouth. At school I kept sporadic office hours. I encouraged my students to e-mail their questions to me. I would answer their e-mails at two or three in the morning, explaining the holes in their diagnostic philosophies, encouraging them to rethink a particular set of symptoms. Insomnia had become just another word for bedtime. After everyone else had gone to sleep, I sat on the back patio and watched the moon shift slowly across the sky.

If my son wasn't going to give me answers, I thought, I would have to find them for myself.

And now they were here.

In the kitchen, Nadia stood smiling at us, uncertainly. She had yet to fully enter the room.

"Soda?" she said hopefully.

I thought about the word for a moment, how it could possibly be relevant to the conversation, and then snapped back to reality.

"Of course," I said, moving to the fridge. "I'm so sorry."

She took the soda and smiled again.

"*Spasiba*," she said.

"Isn't she great?" Murray said, his mouth full of pasta. "I met her at a nightclub. She's from Minsk. She's studying cosmetology in Queens. I asked her if she wanted to go to California. I'm not sure she understood we'd be driving."

The journal felt like an anchor pulling me down. I laid it on the counter.

"I don't think I can handle this," I said.

"Put it in a drawer," he told me. "Burn it. I just wanted you to see it. To know it's there. For peace of mind, but also, it could help with the appeal, if you decide to go that way."

He bit down on a cherry tomato and a stream of seeds squirted onto his jacket.

"You ever ride a motorcycle, Paul?" he asked, wiping at the stain. "Scares the shit out of me, but I do it anyway. Why? Because I'm a man. Or at least that's what I need women like Nadia to think. God bless those girls. I'd forgotten how easy it is to get a twenty-six-year-old to take off her clothes. You don't even have to ask. It's like a sport to them. What do they care about commitment? Marriage? Last night this chick rode my dick so hard I think she snapped it off."

I looked over at Nadia, embarrassed, but if she understood what he was saying she gave no sign.

"Should I read it now?" I asked, after a moment.

"Not my call," he said. "I just wanted you to have the option."

CAC. Looking at the initials, I realized that this was not my son's journal. Daniel Allen. It was *his*, the other man, Carter Allen Cash, the man my son had become. If I read it would I understand any better the journey that my boy had taken? Would I understand the moment he disappeared? The reason?

"What's going on in here?" Fran asked, entering through the kitchen door. Her cheeks were flushed from the outdoors. Instinctively, I opened a drawer and stuffed the pages inside. Murray saw me do it but betrayed nothing. Fran threw her car keys on the counter, gave Murray a quick kiss on the cheek.

"We have silverware, you know."

He shrugged, mouth full.

"I'm eco-friendly," he managed. "Think of the kilowatts saved, the water conserved."

Fran studied Nadia, who smiled winningly, and made a small *cheers* motion with her soda can.

"Who's this?" Fran wanted to know.

"That's Nadia," I said, helpfully. "She's Russian."

"Did you offer her a chair?" Fran asked.

I stared at my wife, flummoxed by the question. She smiled patiently at me, but I could see worry in her eyes. Murray had long ago stopped being a source of good tidings in our house. He opened the fridge, shoved the nearly empty bowl of pasta salad back inside.

"Like I told Paul," Murray said, "I just decided one night. The great trek. New York to California. I'm doing it. Tennessee was beautiful. Who knew? Next it's the Southwest. Utah, the Grand Canyon. I showed Nadia our route, but all she knows is that we're going someplace hot to stare into a giant hole."

Fran considered a retort, but instead she reached up, touched her ear. The Bluetooth activated.

"I'm working on those reservations now, Mr. Colby," she said, exiting into the dining room.

Murray wiped his hands on a dishrag.

"She seems happy," he said.

"I'm trying."

He took two sodas from the fridge, put them in his jacket pockets.

"Well, we should hit the road. I told the Russian we'd eat at this sushi place in Vail tonight."

I nodded. "You're more than welcome to . . . to stay," I said. "A few days. Whatever you want."

He put a hand on my shoulder.

"No," he said. "This is your new life. You look good. Fit. I'm glad to see it. But I've got no place here. I'm just a bad memory. But I wanted you to have, you know, the thing."

I felt panicked that he was leaving me here with the journal.

"I may come to New York next month," I said.

"Cool. Call me. We'll go out. Nadia's friends with everybody south of Fourteenth Street."

I showed them to the door. Nadia handed me back the soda can.

"Bye bye," she said, and gave me a wave.

At the door, Murray hugged me. His body felt lean and strong, like a wire.

"My suggestion?" he said, quietly. "Put it on the barbecue and spray it with lighter fluid. There's nothing in there you don't know already."

"But that's the problem," I said. "I don't know anything."

I stood by the open door long after they were gone. I could hear the sound of dogs barking somewhere in the distance. A wind struck up, making the grass shiver.

Fran came up and put her arms around me.

"Did you know he was coming?" she asked.

I shook my head.

"They didn't want to stay, at least for dinner?"

"No. He said they were gonna have sushi in Vail."

She smiled and shook her head, then kissed me on the cheek.

"I'm going to go for a run," she said.

It took me a long time after she was gone to work up the courage to open the drawer that held my son's journal. I had to sidle up to it, moving sideways across the kitchen under the auspices of getting a glass for water. The onus of the journal was too great. Its power to destroy my life. I stood for a while with my hand on the drawer pull. There was an invisible line in front of me. I couldn't see it, but I knew it was there. If I opened the drawer, if I read the journal, I would have to abandon all pretenses that I had moved on with my life.

Inside that drawer, quite possibly, was the end of my family. The end of everything.

But it also held the truth.

I opened the drawer.

The name stared up at me. Carter Allen Cash.

I closed the drawer. I wasn't ready. But I couldn't leave it there. It felt wrong, obscene to even keep the document in the house. I opened the drawer again, and grabbed the papers. I hurried out to the car and hid them in back, slamming the hatch quickly, as if to keep something from escaping.

For the next few days, wherever I went, whatever I was doing, I felt the journal in there, calling to me. I thought about driving somewhere and reading it, but the truth was, even that felt too close to home. I was like a man planning an affair, looking to cover his tracks—except in this case rather than cheating with another woman, I felt that by reading the journal I would be cheating on my new family with my old one.

I tried to ignore it, to forget it, but I couldn't.

So I invented a reason to leave.

A few months earlier, I had been asked to present a lecture on Kawasaki disease at a medical conference in Austin. I'd declined, but now I decided to attend the conference anyway. It felt like fate. Austin was a place my son had spent time. A place that was, arguably, pivotal in his transformation. I would go and read the journal there. I would take one last trip and try to exorcise the obsession, to satiate it, and then cut it off like a limb that has turned black and begun to stink.

And so, ten days after Murray's visit, I stood in the bedroom and packed a suitcase. Early the next morning, Fran drove me to the airport. We talked about how the rain gutters needed cleaning. She asked if I would be back in time for Alex's soccer game on Friday. I assured her I would. I said it was only two days. She said she hated it when I was gone. She never knew when to go to bed. I told her to go to bed at eleven. We kissed in the drop-off zone and she half jokingly suggested a quickie in the parking structure. I told her I didn't want to miss my flight and opened the door, retrieving my suitcase from the back.

The flight was quick, just over an hour. I could have driven, but Fran said she didn't want me on the road for that long. At the Austin airport I sniffed the air. I was looking for subtle changes, an indication that this place was different somehow from all the other places I had ever been. My driver met me at baggage claim. He took Highway 71 to South Congress and headed north. We crossed over Lady Bird Lake, and he pointed out how every night at dusk from May to September millions of fruit bats emerged from under the Congress Street Bridge, billowing like a cloud of smoke into the sky. He dropped me at the InterContinental Hotel. A bellboy took my suitcase.

In my room, I lay on top of the bedspread and stared at the ceiling. It felt dangerous being here. I had been doing so well. I had been keeping it under control, keeping my two halves separate. By coming here, by bringing the journal, I had broken my promise. To Fran, my kids, myself. I was a liar now, a keeper of black secrets.

The room was dark, blinds drawn. My suitcase sat on the floor like a corpse, watching me. I felt nervous in my hands, and as I stared at the suitcase, a great weight settled over me, a heavy blanket of exhaustion. Was it self-preservation that caused me to fall asleep then? An anvil of depression dragging me down? Whatever the cause, I slept like a dead man, waking hours later in a panic, unsure of where I was. Outside the sun was setting.

The suitcase hadn't moved.

In my socks, I walked over to it and cracked open the lid. I dug down through suit jackets and toiletries and took the photocopied pages from their envelope. They still had a slight chemical smell, a residue of ink and heat.

And then, before I could chicken out, I turned on the lamp by the bed and settled in to read.

EXCERPTS FROM THE JOURNAL OF CARTER ALLEN CASH, AKA DANIEL ALLEN.

[Editor's note: What follows are the only surviving entries in the Montana Section of Daniel Allen's personal journal. They begin seven months prior to the assassination of Senator Jay Seagram.]

To whom it may concern: This is a private journal! If you are
reading this without permission you must stop! These words are
not for you. You cannot understand their full meaning.
All you can do is get it wrong.

November 5, 20___

Snow. Light to moderate. Driving north on 287 I realized I could
see my breath <u>inside the car</u>. Need to get the heater fixed. Near Ennis
I had to pull over. Found a sweater in the trunk. I did some jumping
jacks to get the blood moving. It's hard to resist the idea that the drop
in temperature isn't a signal of something bigger. Winter as a symbol.
The end of the year. The death of it.

Fact: This far north the sun sets around six. Today the cloud cover
made nightfall seem earlier. The northern woods feel gloomy. There's
no other word for it. The trees are thicker here, and I go miles without
seeing a town. Montana is the triumph of nature. It is survival.

This morning I found myself thinking about Austin. Fact: It's been a month since I left. I did the math while I was driving. A month. The word used to mean something, a measure of time made up of weekdays and weekends, but now there is just the road. There is sunrise and sunset. There are gas stations and rest stops, mile markers and two-lane blacktop. Sometimes I go so long without seeing another car I worry I have driven off the edge of the earth.

To occupy my mind, I make up my own books on tape. I tell myself the story of the Explorer, a man who first discovered this endless stretch of woods. He is bearded and rides a heavy packhorse, but the horse breaks its leg in a hidden gully after the first snowfall, and he's forced to shoot it.

That winter is the hardest. The Explorer loses thirty pounds and has to eat the shoe leather from his boots. At night he hears wolves circling his tiny camp, scheming, howling. There is a wife somewhere waiting, a son who has forgotten his father's face. When he feels lowest, the Explorer reminds himself that he is doing this so that others will have light where he had darkness. They will have the Map. They will be able to avoid the hidden gullies, the dead-end trails. There will be no more secrets. He will expose them, every one.

Some days the sun doesn't rise at all.

November 17, 20__

The mechanic wanted three hundred dollars to fix the car. I thanked him and drove to an army surplus store. For one hundred dollars I bought gloves, a warmer coat, and a pair of used boots that looked pretty waterproof. I forgot a hat though, and spent the next few hours in the car covering my ears with my hands, one at a time.

I've been collecting change, building a lump of loose coins in my pocket like a tumor. I like the weight of it. Paper money feels increasingly meaningless to me, a scrap of nothing, an IOU. Every time I saw a pay phone I thought about calling her, but I never did. What would I say? Not that it matters. Soon enough she will know everything. She will think back on that night and swoon.

At a rest stop I purged myself of anything that tied me to Austin, the Longhorns T-shirt, the campaign flyers. I dumped the library books she had given me in the trash, all the mad Russians with their bloated words of sadness.

Tomorrow I will be there. HIS town. HIS home. I picture a mansion on a hill, fires burning in the fireplace, a Christmas tree in the hall. But what if it's a lie, like everything else? A set on a soundstage, filled with actors. A false home for a false man.

Fact: There are no speed limits in Montana. The state is so big and the population is so small I sometimes go hours without seeing another car.

November 19, 20__

I arrived in Helena on Tuesday, and have been exploring it as the weather permits. Fact: It is the state capital, founded in 1864 by the "Four Georgians."

My plan was to sleep in the car outside town. The backseat is plenty comfortable, and I would spend the money I saved on food. But the cold made that plan untenable. So I've found a motel—the Derbyshire. It satisfied two of my conditions for lodging. First, it is not a chain. Second, the rooms are nonsmoking and cheerful.

After checking in yesterday, I visited the capitol building. They offer a guided tour, which is where I learned about the Georgians. They were gold prospectors, apparently, though some say only one of them was actually from Georgia.

The capitol building is built of limestone and granite. The people waiting in line for the tour were obese and dressed in bright, puffy down coats that made them look like grapefruits. Like most state capitols, the Montana state capitol has a huge rotunda with an impressive dome. Montana was founded by gold miners, and everything inside is painted gold, with big murals of Indians, miners, and cowboys.

HIS office was on the tour. There wasn't much in the way of security. I spoke to Xxxx [Editor's note: name redacted] who is a staffer for the senator. She told me that HE had been in the office last week, but with the campaign they don't see HIM that much.

I asked about HIS family, if they traveled with HIM, and she said they did, but that the senator doesn't want HIS kids to miss too much school, so they only go on certain trips.

I smiled at the perfection of the lie. You tell the child you are leaving, but say it's for their own good. They will be safer here without you, better off. When what the father really means is, you are a burden and I have more important things to do.

I told Xxxx I had volunteered at the campaign headquarters in Austin. She said she loved Austin. We talked about Town Lake and barbecue. Xxxx said she was born in Bozeman and that she came home to be close to her parents, but that she hates the winters.

I said that I'd be in town for a few weeks. I told her that I'd been traveling the country this semester, getting to know "the real America," and that I hoped to see it all before I had to be back at school in the spring. Xxxx said that sounded really fun. She told me if I had time I should try the pie over at a place called Doreen's. She said the apple was her favorite.

I guess I was feeling lonely or I don't know what, because before I could stop myself I asked her if she might want to have some pie with me sometime—not as a date but just for companionship—and she got kind of a weird look on her face, and said she had a boyfriend. I told her I didn't mean it like that. I just meant that I was new in town and didn't know anybody.

Behind me the docent said that the tour was moving on. He had a beard like a pirate and wore a checkered shirt and bolo tie. He was <u>authentically Western</u>, with zero irony.

Xxxx told me she had to get back to work. She said, "Thanks for coming by." I offered her my hand, but she pretended not to see it, and I went back to the tour, my face burning, embarrassed. I spent the rest of the tour thinking of what I could have said differently. It was stupid to suggest we see each other socially. Xxxx could have been a good resource, someone in HIS office, who knows HIS schedule.

Then, on the way out, I saw my reflection in the glass of the door. My face was unshaven. It had been close to three months since my last haircut, and though I was wearing my new coat and boots, they were scruffy and cheap. All in all I looked grungy and (to my eye) untrustworthy. No wonder she hadn't wanted to be seen with me.

I drove back to the motel, angry at myself for letting things go. At the gas station next to the motel, I bought a razor and some scissors. I took a hot shower as soon as I got back to the room—very hot, my skin turned bright red under the water—then put a towel on the bathroom floor and cut my hair, careful to keep it even on both sides. Then I lathered my face with soap and shaved. I couldn't afford to spiral too far, looks-wise. You forget when you spend enough time alone that you have an outside image, a public face for others to see. The last thing I wanted was to become some kind of fringer, a loony with Jesus hair, who people cross the street to avoid.

December 6, 20___

Tonight was one of the loneliest nights I can remember. Weather has been a real factor this week in limiting my ability to move freely around town. It snowed so hard today that I left the room only to get food from the vending machine in the lobby. I feel bloated on junk food and TV. After the sun went down I lay on the bed, my face stinging from the cheap gas-station aftershave. I tried to remember the faces of people I knew.

Something's happening to me. But what?

I thought about the office, HIS office, with its high ceilings and stained-glass windows, like it was a church. Like they were saying that somehow HE was more than just a man. HE is a senator from a golden state. A Golden Boy from a Golden State.

Last night I ate pretzels and peanut butter packets for dinner. I lay on the lumpy bed, bathed in the light of the television, a lump myself. My thoughts felt too big for my head.

Why did I come here? Why do I do anything I do? A person, alone in the dark, disappears little by little, piece by piece . . .

[Editor's Note: Here several pages have been torn out of the journal.]

December 15, 20___

It's been a hard week. A second blizzard followed the first, and I found myself snowed in at the motel for several more days. Honestly, I lost count of how many. On Thursday I borrowed a shovel from the clerk and dug out my car, but when I turned the key in the ignition it refused to start, refused to even turn over. The mechanic tells me it's the battery and that a new one will cost me two hundred dollars. He smiled when he said it, like I was a big meal and he hadn't eaten in days.

As soon as the roads were clear I hitched a ride into town. My new boots proved themselves to be not as waterproof as I had thought, and by noon there was bright pain in the toes of my right foot.

In Austin, through cleverness, I had found HIS home address in a correspondence file on Walter's desk. There was a bus that stopped a few blocks away, and I took it after eating some chili at a diner. When the bowl came, I realized that it was the first real meal I'd eaten in close to two weeks. The smell of the meat and tomatoes made my head swim.

I ate it fast, almost without stopping, then went into the bathroom and threw it all up, the tomato sauce burning my nose and throat. Back at the table I felt shaky. The waitress asked if I wanted anything else. I said no, and while she was getting the check I ate three packets of saltines that had been left on an adjacent table by another diner.

There is not a lot of foot traffic in Helena, Montana, during the winter months. Getting off the bus in the upscale residential neighborhood where HE lived, I tried to think of excuses I could make if the police stopped me or a neighbor became curious.

Car trouble was good. Or maybe that I had gone home with a girl the night before, and now I was walking back to the bar to reclaim my ride. That sounded good. I was a clean-cut young man with all his teeth, and though I had cut my own hair a few weeks ago, I'd kept it even, and it had grown in nicely. I would smile when I told my lie, as if to say to the cop: <u>You know how it is. The girl was hot and we'd been drinking and I didn't think</u>. Then, with a wink: <u>But I guess it's a small price to pay for a night in Heaven, to have to walk a mile or so in the cold.</u>

HE lives on Xxxxx Street [Editor's note: The address has been redacted]. Luck—or fate—was with me, as HIS wife, Rachel, and kids, Neal and Nora, were coming out of the house just as I walked past! A Secret Service agent escorted them to a big black SUV.

Rachel was wearing a long black jacket and jeans. She had a wool cap on her head. Neal wore a backpack and carried an action figure. It was the sound of a little girl laughing that first drew my attention to the house as I rounded the corner. Ahead, I saw Nora pack a snowball and throw it at her brother, who ducked and bent to pack his own.

Rachel scolded the girl, but halfheartedly. They were too far away to make out the words, but you can tell a lot from someone's body language.

As I approached, the Secret Service agent looked over at me. I could see him assessing the threat level I presented, comparing his own instinctual assessment against a well-worn checklist (probably engrained in him at the academy). At that moment, Rachel looked up as well and saw me, and I raised my hand and waved.

But now I was smiling. The sun on my face—while not warm—was still a welcome relief from the endless gray of the last few days. It rang off the bright white snow, like the pure, open tone of a bell. Walking through this upscale neighborhood, stretching my legs, filling my lungs with cold air, I felt good. I felt right again, whole, like the sun and the air and the ground under my feet were pieces of me that had gone missing.

It's hard to find the right words (how do you describe the indescribable?), but seeing her, Rachel, the luck of it, the impossible chance of it—combined with the heat and the air, and the light of the sun—made me happy, and so I raised my hand and waved, and Rachel smiled and waved back, the wave of a friendly neighbor.

And though it was fleeting, this brief wave connected us, brought us together, joining us in a gesture of friendship.

And then, behind her, Senator Seagram emerged from the house! HE was flanked by two Secret Service agents.

Too many things happened in that instant to recount here. I was at once stunned by HIS appearance, and aware that I must not falter or show any chink in my disguise—as that of the friendly local.

I forced myself to finish the wave, and to turn my eyes back to the street. I thought of the gun hidden inside the toilet tank in my room, the bullets stored in the bottom of my duffel. Was this it? The moment? Had I misread the day? From my peripheral vision I saw HIM and the family climb into the SUV. I noticed for the first time the advance car in the driveway, and also—looking ahead—a third car, this an unmarked sedan, inside of which sat two more Secret Service agents in long black coats—also looking at me.

I nodded to them in a way I hoped was casual, as behind me the two
SUVs pulled out of the driveway and sped away. Now the forgotten gun
felt like luck.

After a moment, the third car started its engine, executed a U-turn,
and sped off in pursuit.

I stood there in the silence afterward, half bent at the knees, trying
to catch my breath. I was dizzy over what had just happened. I had
gone to HIS house and HE had appeared. It couldn't be simple
coincidence. In my memory, the blinding warmth of the sun blended
with HIS appearance. It was as if HE had been conjured up by the sun
itself.

Overhead, the sun went behind a cloud, and I saw spots, floating
bubbles of cloudy gray, gliding across the snow.

The Great Man was home, perpetuating the lie, reinforcing it like
a stack of sandbags by a river. But where were the camera crews? The
photo ops staged to sell the lie? Or was this lie personal this time? Told
just for the benefit of the family?

I pictured them now in my memory. The father and mother, and
their two children. How happy they seemed—I thought of Rachel's
friendly wave. How happy to be whole, complete. And yet in that
moment, as the sun reemerged from behind the clouds, I realized that
there was an even bigger lie at work here.

Because they weren't a complete family. There was a crack, a
missing piece. There had been a First Son, had there not? The
Drowned Boy. He was a ghost, a shadow that followed them. He was
gone, physically absent, but his shadow haunted them.

And then I saw my own shadow on the ground. It stretched out
toward HIS house, an elongated silhouette cast by the morning
sun. Seeing it, I felt dizzy and had to sit down, right there on the icy
concrete. The shadow was that of the missing boy. I was sure of it. But
at the same time, I could see that it was my own shadow. Somehow
it belonged to both of us. The shadow stretching toward HIS house
connected me to HIM, to HIS family.

I was overwhelmed momentarily by a landslide of thoughts.
Coincidences? Synchronicities? Wasn't I, too, a missing son? A lie?
My own father had left, had moved to New York and remarried, had
fathered two children. He had his own complete family now, his own

happy family to stand in the driveway and wave to the neighbors. And yet they also had a ghost (me) that haunted them, a shadow son.

Ahead, a dog trotted across the quiet street. (A wolf?) I was the link. THE LINK. That was clear to me all of a sudden. HIS lie was my lie. Picture three numbers side by side: 2 2 4. They are just a series of numbers until you add a + and an =.

Suddenly, they become an equation, a conclusion (2+2=4), irrefutable.

This is how these realizations felt to me. Like the final piece of a jigsaw puzzle.

I am the shadow son.

Son/Sun??

Alpha/Omega

Wolf/Sheep

[Editor's Note: The remaining pages of this section have been torn out.]

I finished reading, and lay back on the bed. The pages of Danny's journal were arranged in a neat pile on the bedspread next to me. After Montana, the entries had gotten sparser, the details more mundane—miles driven, meals eaten, as if Danny had started keeping secrets from himself. There was barely any mention of Senator Seagram. No more talk of shadow sons, of the revelations that had come to him on a sunny street in Helena.

Why? What did it mean?

Maybe the thoughts in his head had frightened him too much. Maybe after Montana, the journal started to feel like a nosy traveling companion, someone from whom he needed privacy. Or maybe what happened in Montana had humbled him, had driven the thoughts of Seagram from his head. Maybe that dark moment in the snowbound north had shocked Danny, put him back on a saner path.

And yet the words haunted me.

I am the shadow son.

Looking over the pages, it was hard to argue that Danny hadn't had some kind of break with reality. The logic of his thoughts, especially those revolving around his time in Montana and his run-in with Seagram, was misshapen and troubling.

Did my son really see himself as a ghost who haunted his own family? Or was this just a symptom of some kind of depression? Had he, in a moment of delusional clarity, connected himself to Seagram through a series of warped insights, like a man who handcuffs himself to a corpse?

I went into the bathroom and splashed water on my face, careful not to look myself in the eye. Though I knew that Danny had gotten lost during his time on the road—physically, spiritually, emotionally—it still hurt to read the words. Why hadn't he called? Why hadn't he asked for help? And why hadn't I, his father, known in some unnameable part of my heart that he'd needed it?

The room felt claustrophobic to me now. Not knowing what else to do, I changed my clothes and went downstairs to join the opening-night cocktail party, pasting the label with my name on it onto the breast of my suit jacket. I needed to be with people, to talk about the weather. I needed to feel grounded.

Men in suits held champagne flutes and made small talk with women in sensible dresses. Their voices were a senseless buzz, punctured by the occasional shriek of laughter.

Murray was right. There had been no murder confession in the journal. No smoking gun. This was not the journal of Sirhan Sirhan, who wrote *R.F.K. must die. R.F.K. must be killed*. It was something harder, more mysterious. Though Danny wrote about his time in Sacramento, there was no mention of his arrest, no mention of two men in a boxcar, the things they may have said.

Where the journal answered certain questions, it left others maddeningly open. Would I ever know for sure the real truth, step by step, fact by fact? Or was it a fool's exercise to even try? Were the factors involved—physical, psychological—too complex? At the end of the day, if a man chooses to lose himself in a wormhole of his own making, how can any of us reconstruct his path? The actions he took? The thoughts in his head?

Wandering through the crowd, the world seemed surreal to me now, as if Danny's mental unbalance had been contagious. I felt like I was having my own break with reality. I had traveled hundreds of miles from home to read his journal, and now I too was alone, reeling from the flashlight I'd just shined into the dark recesses of his brain.

I struck up a conversation with doctors from Portland and Nebraska. We made small talk about new technology. An anesthesiologist from Providence told me I should really get out and hear some music while I was here. She said Austin was her favorite city. They even had live music at the supermarket. I told her I would be sure to do that, and excused myself to get another drink.

I looked at the faces of strangers, and thought about the people in my son's life: Ted and Bonnie Kirkland, the Mexicans who got him drunk and gave him a knife for his boot, the beautiful librarian. He had described them all in the journal. Good people, kind and smart. Why hadn't he grabbed on to them? Why hadn't he asked for help? And why hadn't they volunteered it?

I went into the hall and called Fran, needing to hear her voice and talk to the kids.

"Are you okay?" she said. "You sound weird."

"I'm fine," I told her. "I've just had a few drinks."

"Good," she said. "You need to unwind. I want you to get shitfaced. Go to a strip club or, I don't know, go streaking. Have some fun."

"I miss you," I said.

"We miss you, too," she said. "We had spaghetti and meatballs and watched some movie with superheroes. The kids are brushing their teeth now. I didn't even have to ask."

After we hung up, I walked through the lobby and out onto the street. I needed air. The temperature was around eighty degrees. I took off my tie and put it in my pocket. It was eight o'clock and only a glimmer of daylight remained. A man peddling a rickshaw approached me. Did I need a ride? I thought about it. Where would I go? And then it hit me. I gave him an address in the university district, just off Guadalupe. He quoted me a price, and I stepped into the back of his cart.

We must have made a strange sight, an older man in a suit being peddled through the streets of the city by a hippie in flip-flops. We rode up Congress toward the capitol and turned left on Eleventh Street. I pictured my son on his bicycle, dressed all in black, riding through the moonless night. What made a person want to be invisible?

I am the shadow son.

I thought about what a shadow was, a trail of darkness left by an object in bright light. In Daniel's mind was I the object or the light? Had I overshadowed him, my success? Had I somehow, in my drive for accomplishment, pushed him to fail?

I wracked my brain looking for the truth, but deep down I worried that the answer, when I found it, would make little sense. If Danny had set off on his journey because of an underlying mental illness, or if somewhere in the wilds of this sprawling, friendless nation, he had suffered a break from reality, how was I to understand the ideas and motives that drove him?

The frat house was on Rio Grande Street three blocks west of Guadalupe. It was a two-story structure of indiscernible style, with a white picket fence and large bay window in the front, in which what looked like a bedsheet had been hung for privacy. The orange-and-white Longhorn logo my son had written about had faded to a barely visible smear on the otherwise brown grass. I paid the rickshaw driver and stood looking up at the house. The low bass krump of a nearby party rumbled through the trees. The house was dark except for one window. I could see no movement inside. The rickshaw driver asked if I would need a ride back. I told him I would be fine, and he rode off, jingling his bell. It had been nearly two years since my son had lived at this address. Would any of the boys he wrote about still be here? I tried to imagine what their faces must have looked like when they saw those first images of my son on TV after Seagram's assassination. Did they remember the gun in their faces? Did they think about how close they themselves had come to death? Did they understand that they had become a part of history?

My mouth was dry but so were my palms. It had always been a strength of mine, this grace under pressure. A pickup truck cruised by, local boys looking for the party. I crossed to the door and rang the bell. Silence. I rang again.

A young man answered, maybe nineteen. He was slim, with sandy brown hair.

"I don't mean to bother you," I said.

"Am I in trouble?" he wanted to know.

It was the suit. Boys his age did not talk to men in suits, except under exigent circumstance.

"You're not in trouble," I told him.

"Everyone else is at a party."

"That's okay," I said. "I just—I have a favor to ask. I'm a doctor. I'm in town for a conference, and my son—he used to live here."

"Your son."

"He died last year, and I thought I would be able to come back here without doing this, but I'm afraid I need to see his room."

The boy studied me. His parents had taught him to be skeptical of strangers who come to the house at night.

"Your son," he said.

"He drowned," I said, "in a boating accident on Lake Travis. There was alcohol involved. His mother and I, we're from Michigan, and we buried him there, but, well, I'm in town for a conference and—"

"What was his name?"

"Jeremy," I said. "But we used to call him Jerry."

"Do you know which room was his?" he asked.

I took a step forward, using my momentum to move him back out of the doorway. Rather than let me bump into him, he stepped aside. I walked through the front door. The place was as my son had described it, a sty. I smelled stale beer and moldy wall-to-wall carpeting. Empty beer cans lay crushed on the floor.

"Upstairs," I said. "Next to the bathroom."

"That's my room now," he said. "I moved in last month."

He lowered his voice, as if to convey confidentiality.

"I don't really like it. It's kind of gross."

The wallpaper was discolored, peeling. What had my son felt, living in a place like this? He had always been a neat boy, orderly.

"Do you mind if I . . ."

I pointed to the stairs. He led me upstairs to his room, then offered to wait outside.

"I just need a minute," I said. "I promise I won't cry or do anything embarrassing."

He shook his head.

"My mom died when I was seven," he said. "My dad's new wife is a total bitch. You take your time. I'm gonna go downstairs and watch TV. Just come down when you're done."

"Thank you . . ."

"Robert. But around here they call me *Chief* or *Sport*." He turned and descended the stairs. I stood in the hall for a moment, trying to picture my son here, in this context. His dorm room at Vassar had been in a stately brick building, imbued with a century of dignity. This house was rotting from the inside, like a melon. The ceilings were low. There were stains on the carpet and a smell coming from the bathroom that could only be described as bovine. I toed open the door to Daniel's old room. It was small, somewhere between square and rectangular.

On the walls were posters for rock bands and maps from various foreign destinations—Germany, Vietnam, Australia. Unlike the clutter of the rest of the house, the room was neat, with no clothing or trash visible. A computer sat on the desk. The room was only big enough for a twin-size bed, which had been set on the one wall without a door or window. It was there that my son would have set his bed. I tried to imagine him on it, not yet a murderer but instead just a boy on the road. I tried to picture him reading Russian novelists to impress a girl. But the picture would not come. Instead I pictured him at the desk reading computer printouts about famous lunatics. I pictured him opening the closet door and pulling a handgun from the bottom of a laundry hamper. I saw him check the chamber to make sure it was loaded and stride purposefully to the door, intent on showing these oversized Texas boys that they couldn't bully Daniel Allen. Or should I say Carter Allen Cash. He was the man with the gun. But the room was just a room. There were no ghosts to capture, no shadows to mine. I had come looking for answers but had found only furniture. I turned off the light and went downstairs.

Robert was on the sofa in the living room, sitting on a protective layer of newspaper. He was watching *Ice Road Truckers* and eating a bowl of cereal.

"All done," I said. "Thank you."

He nodded.

"It'll get easier," he said. "You don't want it to. It just does."

Outside I felt the need to walk. I went east to Guadalupe. Across the avenue stood the orange-roofed buildings of UT. I was a bloodhound on a trail. Seeing the frat house had only whetted my appetite. I had to find the storefront that had housed Seagram's campaign headquarters, the place where my son had worked. I walked south a few blocks, then turned back and headed north. I found it next to the Church of Scientology, half a block from the Co-op bookstore. It was a tattoo parlor now, its window filled with sketches and designs. This is the history of cities. What was once one thing is now something else.

I pictured my son standing in this spot, a clipboard in one hand, registering students to vote. He was Oswald in New Orleans handing out flyers. A man with a terrible destiny. Could he imagine at that moment, tying string around a ballpoint pen, that he would one day stare down at the body of the very candidate he was promoting? Can any of us see our future, catch a glimpse of it in the dazzle and sparkle of whitecaps?

Or does it lurk deeper, hiding in black holes under gnarled tree stumps in a boggy swamp?

What were the symptoms? What was the disease?

As I was standing there, my cell phone rang, startling me. I fumbled it out of my pocket, expecting to see Fran's number come up. Instead the LCD readout read "Blocked." I pushed Answer, heard a prerecorded message, a woman's voice telling me I was receiving a call from an inmate at a federal penitentiary. My heart rate tripled. Was something wrong?

"Daniel," I said.

"Hey, Dad."

"What's going on? It's late there."

"Yeah, they don't usually let us use the phone after eight."

"Are you okay?"

An ambulance drove by, siren screaming. I plugged my ear with my finger to hear his answer.

"I'm okay," he said. "Where are you?"

"At a medical conference," I said. "In . . . Houston."

Why did I lie? What would my son say if he knew I was retracing his steps?

"Are you sleeping okay?" I asked him.

"Couple hours at a time," he told me. "I read a lot. They let me have some watercolors. So I try to paint what I remember. The great outdoors. It helps to have a vanishing point to look at."

I thought of my younger sons asleep in their beds.

"Listen, Pop," said Daniel. "I just wanted to let you know. They set a date."

"A date?"

"For the execution. December 14."

December 14. Six months. I was an astronaut lost in the weightlessness of space.

"December 14 of this year?"

"Yes."

"But that's so soon."

"Yeah."

He let me absorb it. A recorded voice came on the line to remind me that I was talking to a prisoner at a federal penitentiary. It was a woman's voice, and I tried to picture her face. It was a harsh, Nurse Ratched face, a taskmaster's scowl, a dirty-bitch glare.

"Danny," I said. "Please. I don't want to fight, but you have to let us appeal this."

"No," he said. "It's better this way. I can't do this much longer, live in a box with a toilet, looking at a watercolor horizon."

"Maybe we could have you transferred."

"No, Dad. This is where I belong, with the worst of the worst."

We're not all put on this Earth to do what's right.

"Bullshit," I said. "Bullshit. You're a good kid. You made a mistake."

"Dad," he said, his voice calm, "we both know the truth."

"What truth?"

"I should have died in a plane crash," he said.

A stunned silence. I had no thoughts. No words.

"Well, I just thought you should know," he said. "Have a good night."

"No. Daniel. Wait."

But he was gone. I stood there for a long time holding the phone to my ear, willing him to come back. December 14. Six months. My son had six months to live. The knowledge was a fist squeezing me, a choke hold.

I stood there for a long time, watching the traffic with unseeing eyes. I felt like I was trapped at the bottom of a dry well, dying of thirst in a hole meant to water a village. A teenage girl approached me. She was leading a puppy on a frayed rope leash. Her hair was stringy. She asked if I could spare some change. I took out my wallet and handed her a hundred-dollar bill.

"I'm not gonna blow you, dude," she said.

"No," I told her. "I'm a father. Please. Get yourself a meal."

I asked her if she was in school. She told me she was working on it, but right now she just needed something to eat.

"You have someplace to sleep tonight?"

She shrugged. Without hesitation I handed her the key card to my hotel room.

"This is to a room at the InterContinental. The room is paid up through Thursday. Take a bath, order room service. No one will bother you."

She looked dubious.

"I came in for a conference," I told her, "but I'm not staying. I can't. I have someplace else I have to be."

"Where?" she asked.

I thought of all the clothes I had shed in the move, the hair I'd cut, the weight I'd lost. I thought of my three sons, the wife who loved me, the ex-wife who only loved herself. I thought of the chemicals they would inject in my boy, the toxins that would paralyze his muscles and stop his heart. The man I'd been for fifty years had ceased to exist. This was something new.

"Iowa," I said. "I'm going to Iowa."

He decided to ride the trains for a while. It was May 20, 20__, three months after his exodus from Montana, his epic escape from winter. The journey between there and here was a study in rootlessness. He drove quickly from town to town, never staying anywhere for more than a few days. Yakima, Seattle, Portland, Eugene, Klamath, Eureka, Ukiah, San Francisco, Berkeley, Davis. He had seen enough redwood trees to last a lifetime, had slept on the beaches of Northern California and woken with his feet in the ocean. After the year he'd spent inland, the endless waves felt like a relief. Along the way, rain forests had given way to Pacific cliffs, then arid hills and vineyards. The men were shaggy, then clean-cut, then fat. Women of indeterminate age eyeballed him from trailers and campsites. They winked at him in diners and gave him the finger from the backs of their daddy's motorcycles.

He spoke to no one, except to put twenty dollars in pump six or order a hamburger. He was warier now, suspicious of strangers and more furtive. His smile had been lost somewhere in the snowdrifts of the northern plains. He laughed now only in anger.

He had stayed too long in Montana. He knew that. Trapped in the suicide funk of a rural motel. It was the fault of the weather and his broken car. After the incident at the senator's house, the revelation, he had spent six more weeks holed up at the Derbyshire, socked in by storms that barreled through the great north like freight trains. The sun was only out for a few hours a day, and under it everything looked cold, sterile. In daylight everything turned blue. His own skin looked mottled and deathly, as if he was a zombie in a town full of the undead.

Things that had seemed clear to him that day on the senator's street became murky in the moldy coffin of his room. Whiteness surrounded him, and yet everything he touched was gray. He found himself sleeping for hours at a time, entire days. His thoughts darkened. It felt as if he were being punished for his Moment of Understanding, like a man who has flown too close to the sun. The energy that had coursed through his veins in the days directly after seeing the senator turned to sludge, suddenly and inexplicably. He couldn't remember the last time he had heard a woman laugh. His muscles were lead. He no longer felt worthy of love. All he wanted to do was sleep. With the TV on he became familiar with the oily metallic taste of his gun barrel. Death, in those moments, felt welcoming. He could not, for the life of him, figure out how he had fallen so low. Was this who Carter Allen Cash was? A burrowing animal? Gollum in his cave?

On TV he watched Senator Seagram ascend the stage. He listened to him speak, sitting across from Leno, from Letterman, from Conan. He watched the smile. They had been so close, he and the senator—words away, a smile, a friendly wave—and yet now there was this gash between them. A sprawling, wounded nation of other people's need. They had been so close. He had seen himself in the bright sunlight—a part of something bigger, a being of love connected to other beings of love—and yet here he was, alone. He felt abandoned. This was nothing new. He had been there before, unwanted, the boy you left behind. The recognition of this—the coldness that came from having felt the warmth of connection and then lost it to solitude—turned him first on himself in that musty roadside grave, and then on the world.

Who was HE to say the boy was unworthy? To exclude him from the fold? The boy would prove his worthiness. He would show the world he mattered, that he was not just trash to be discarded. The feeling, the bright hot lightning of it, shot him out of bed. It opened the curtains and forced him out of his stupor. He started showering again, started exercising, eating right. He had a mission now, a cause. He had come to the wilderness to get lost so that he could find himself, could figure out his purpose, and here it was.

Wolf or sheep?

The answer was clear.

It had been good to get back to the car, to climb inside its protective shell. He had been on the road for almost a year now since leaving school. In that time the Honda had molded to him, like a pair of shoes breaking in. He knew every nuance of its handling, how it listed slightly to the left on straightaways, the way the tires would spin without gripping for a moment after he drove through a puddle. He knew every sound intimately, the rattle of the air conditioner as it struggled to cool the interior, the hard clunk of the transmission slipping into reverse. He knew that after it rained the car smelled like an old gym bag, that the passenger window didn't shut squarely and as a result there was always a thin whistle of wind pestering the cabin.

He considered the car a friend. Maybe his only true friend. They had been through a lot together. Sometimes, when he was on the road for more than two weeks at a time, he found himself talking to the car. At least he supposed he was talking to the car. He wasn't talking to himself, he didn't think, not that he ever addressed the car by name or title. He just needed to hear his voice from time to time to remind himself that he was real. Besides, he found the car worked better when he spoke to it. He could coax the radio to find an electrical connection and turn on. He could coach the starter to ignite. On cold nights, lying in the backseat in the empty parking lots of chain stores, he would find himself humming, a low, melodic tone, like a piece of industrial machinery warming up.

Now he stood in a park in Sacramento and stared up at the capitol dome. Spring was everywhere, a warm breeze, a burst of color. Life. Shadows from the palm trees fell across the capitol steps. He had read that rats liked to live in palm trees, and he was careful not to walk beneath them in case one fell.

He thought about Lynette "Squeaky" Fromme, who on September 5, 1975, in this very park, had pointed a gun at President Gerald Ford. The gun was a .45 Colt semiautomatic, which had only been loaded with four rounds. Later Fromme would tell reporters that she had deliberately ejected a bullet from the chamber before leaving her hotel room. Investigators would find it in the bathroom, lying next to the tub. At the time of the assassination attempt, Squeaky was dressed in red robes that witnesses described as "nun-like." She was already a famous woman in this country, given her ties to the man who was arguably the most famous murderer of the modern age—Charles Manson.

Two weeks later, in San Francisco, another woman, Sara J. Moore, would fire a single shot at Ford outside the Post Street door of the St. Francis Hotel. She would be wrestled to the ground by the man next to her, and arrested. Which raises the question, what was it about President Ford that made women want to kill him?

At her trial, the U.S. attorney recommended Fromme receive the maximum possible sentence. He said she was "full of hate and violence." Fromme threw an apple at him, hitting him in the face and knocking off his glasses.

The next day, Fromme stood before the judge. She said, "Am I sorry I tried? Yes and no. Yes, because it accomplished little except to throw away the rest of my life. And, no, I'm not sorry I tried, because at the time it seemed a correct expression of my anger."

Carter Allen Cash stood under ancient oak trees and tried to picture her face as she'd lifted the gun. It had started to rain, and the sound of raindrops on the leaves around him was like a mother saying *Shush*. He thought about calling home. It had been a long time since he had spoken to anyone who knew him. A long time since someone had spoken to him with love in their voice. When you are a stranger in the world, the voices become impersonal, detached. People say things like *Don't forget your change*. Or *Do you want cheese on that?* Nobody ever says your name with affection.

The event was close now. The distance could be measured in terms of weeks. He couldn't see it yet, not entirely. It loomed at the edge of his vision like an iceberg. He'd had a glimpse the other day when he'd purchased the gun at a gun show out in Woodland. The show was held in the gymnasium of the high school. Dealers had trucked in folding tables and covered them with lethal black steel. A once-famous wrestler signed autographs, and surgically altered women posed in swimsuits holding semiautomatic weapons like action stars. He wandered the aisles, looking at cases of pistols and shotguns and rifles. Men with mustaches asked him what he was looking for. They demonstrated the action on weapons with names like *The Bulldog* and *The Street Sweeper*. They talked about recoil ratios and magazine capacity.

He asked to see a German 9-mm, tested the hand feel of a Smith & Wesson .38. If he paid cash, the dealer said he'd throw in a carton of armor-piercing rounds.

"They'll stop an intruder," the man said. "I don't care if he's wearing a Kevlar vest or what."

Austin seemed like a hundred years ago, another life. The time he had spent there felt like the memories of another person. He could no longer remember what Natalie looked like, other than the general details. He remembered the way her hair had fallen across her shoulders. He remembered the white pants.

Every place he visited disappeared as soon as he left. He had a hard time believing there was still a place called Austin in a state called Texas, where women in bikinis swam year-round in water that was always sixty-eight degrees. To that end, was there still a place called New York or Connecticut? He read about them in the paper, when he read the paper, which was almost never. They must still exist, but he couldn't really picture that world anymore. Not here, standing in a high-school auditorium handing a man in camouflage pants three hundred-dollar bills in exchange for a Walther P99 and a box of bullets.

Three weeks later, as he sat in the boxcar of a speeding train, he would remember this moment—the dealer had put the Walther bullets in a used plastic bag from Popeyes—and it too would seem like a dream. It was becoming harder for him to stay focused. At the same time, he felt the world was becoming simpler. Sleep, eat, shit. Sleep, eat, shit. And though he could no longer see the society around him, he knew where he was going. He had the foresight of the arrowhead, which knows its destination long before the crest or the fletching. He was a race-car driver, smashing through the peripheral blur, eyes focused on the vanishing point.

A girl he met in Portland last month had turned him on to riding the trains. He had stayed in a flophouse downtown for three days on his way to California. The girl had been sitting on a blanket in the park, holding a puppy on a leash. She gave him a lollipop and told him her dad used to drive her family to the terminal and tell them to pick a platform at random. She said wherever the train went is where they'd go. Riding in a vacant boxcar now, he realized she meant he should buy a ticket and travel in a seat. But he had taken her literally. Hop on a train, she'd said. Go where it goes.

And so one night he ducked low as the caboose rode past, and took off through the weeds, arms outstretched, reaching for a thin metal bar. It was a foggy night. The bar was slicker than he thought, and his hand slipped. For a moment he saw himself falling under the wheels of the train. He saw his death, and it was a lonely death, a hobo's death. Kids would find his body a few days from now. The sheriff would be called, and his body taken to the morgue, where he would be listed as John Doe and given a number. In a few weeks his unclaimed body would be cremated or interred in an unmarked grave. The thought of it made him sad, though maybe it was the right death. After all, wasn't that what he was doing out here? Trying to disappear without a trace? He heard the screech of the brakes, as the train settled into a turn, and felt the world tumble away from him, and then he was rolling on the hard ground, the breath knocked out of him.

He lay under the stars for a long time listening to his own blood. It struck him then that he wasn't done yet. He thought of the snow. He thought of Natalie in her white pants. It was May and the spring rains had turned the rivers fat and angry. He wiggled his fingers, his toes, then climbed to his feet. The freight train was pulling away, almost out of sight. He was going to California now, the promised land, and he knew what he was going to do, and it no longer felt ugly. It was an ice sculpture shaped by a chain saw.

Sometimes, he thought, *it takes a weapon to make something beautiful.*

When he walked into the diner later that night, he knew what song was going to be playing on the jukebox before he heard it. It was "Today" by the Smashing Pumpkins. And the next train he chased, he caught.

The last plane to Iowa left at 12:35. I missed it by fifteen minutes. The clerk at the information desk told me the first plane out in the morning would depart at 5:30. I had given away my hotel room, and it seemed pointless to ride all the way back to the city just to turn around and come back, so I decided to spend the night in the airport. Wandering the empty concourse, I fought the urge to count the days until my son's execution. To add up the weekends and national holidays, to multiply days times hours times minutes, to work it out down to the second how much time my boy had left to live.

Outside the runways were silent and dark. The empty airport embodied a kind of bloodless limbo. The word "terminal" is not used by accident. The darkness made mirrors of the windows, reflecting everything exactly backward. These were the ghost hours of the night. The hazy cataract dream of time, where we come unmoored from our lives, floating in non-space, in non-time, divorced from the context that makes us who we are. Two a.m. Three a.m. I watched the clock. I rode across treadmill floors. I pissed in bathrooms with a hundred self-flushing urinals. How different this airport was than the one I had scrambled through in New York, trying to reach Los Angeles that first night. The battle was over. The war was lost. Eight hundred miles from here, my son slept in a concrete coffin, locked inside the last home he would ever know.

I was running out of time. A familiar panic came over me. How naïve I was to think my son had been safe on death row these last few months. That just because he was somewhere that I could see him, visit him, he would stay put. He had always been an escape artist, after all. When he was an infant we had to dress him in two onesies when he slept, the top layer zipped in the back, to keep him from slipping out of his clothes in the night like Houdini escaping from a straitjacket. As soon as he was old enough to walk he would disappear in supermarkets and clothing stores, vanishing somehow the minute your back was turned. During high school in L.A., he would go out the window after midnight, shimmying down drainpipes and clinging to the teardrop siding like Spider-Man. He had always found a way to slip from my grip, like a wounded animal I had tried to save and failed. One that would not listen to reason.

Death would be his final escape.

As I wandered the empty concourse I told myself I would call Murray in the morning. We would appeal the sentence. It was the only thing I could do. I was his father. If Daniel chose never to speak to me again because of it, I would accept that silence as the price for his life. I would do what I had to do to make sure he didn't leave me again, this time for good.

At three forty-five I stood before a urinal, half asleep, swaying on my feet. The fluorescents overhead flickered at a frequency that seemed to mimic the exact rhythm of REM sleep. Behind me I heard a few soft footsteps, then a man's voice, soft and low.

"I hear you been looking for me."

I half turned. A stocky man in his fifties stood six inches behind my right shoulder. He wore a janitor's uniform.

"I'm sorry?" I said.

Instead of speaking, the man walked over to the stalls, and one by one pushed open the doors to make sure they were unoccupied.

"They put up rope lines and metal detectors and tell you you're safe," he said. "But the truth is, anybody can bypass airport security if they know where the gaps are."

Nervously, I zipped up my pants and stepped away from the urinal. If I called out for help would anyone hear me? The urinal flushed automatically, startling me, the boom of it echoing in the empty bathroom.

"Is the bathroom closed?" I asked, confused. "Did I miss a sign?"

The janitor checked the stalls, keeping an eye on me in the mirror.

I thought about the words in my son's journal.

Wolf or *Sheep*?

"Do you know who I am?" the janitor asked.

I looked at him, clueless. The sum of all time collapsed into that moment. This was a dream, a dream about a janitor. He was a symbol of something. But what? Then, out of the blue, it hit me. A black hole opened up beneath my feet.

I said, "You're Marvin Hoopler."

He nodded.

"Captain Marvin Hoopler," I said. "Special Forces, retired."

"And you're Paul Allen," he said. "A doctor who lives in Colorado, via Connecticut, via New York. I hear you've been looking for me."

My mouth was dry. "From who?"

Hoopler finished his tour of the stalls. He stood for a moment, listening, a faraway look on his face, then, satisfied we were alone, he turned to face me.

"From people."

I was sweating in the small of my back.

"I need your help," I said. "My son."

He nodded.

"I met your son once," he said. "On a train."

My heart beat faster.

"A freight train," I said.

"He said his name was Carter, but it's not."

"No, it's Danny. Daniel."

Hoopler turned from me to wash his hands at the sink, the soap and water dispensed automatically onto his hands.

"You have questions," he said. "Your life took a turn and you can't make sense of it."

I nodded.

"These things happen," he said. "Events. They blindside you. They're like those asteroids—what do they call them?—global killers. They knock you out of your life and into something else."

"I need to know what happened," I said. "What really happened."

He studied me, assessing something—my level of desperation, my ability to hear hard truths, how far I'd gone off the rails.

"I had a son," he said. "Maxwell. He choked on a carrot in preschool. I was in Yemen, fighting. His mother packed his snack—apples and carrots. Not cookies or candy. A healthy snack. She used the baby carrots. The ones that come prepackaged. He was three."

"I'm sorry," I told him.

"They make coffins for babies," he said. "I didn't know that. I mean, it only makes sense, but you don't think about it, you know? And then you see them and they're like . . . jewelry boxes for children."

"It's not fair," I said. "The things we live through."

He dried his hands with a paper towel, slowly, meticulously.

"You want to know, did I tell your son to kill a senator? Did I plant the seed, the idea? Or more. Did I meet him outside Royce Hall and slip him an unregistered handgun? Was I his handler, his controller? You want your son to be a vessel, a tool."

I nodded.

"But it's not true," he said. "I can give you eight witnesses who'll say I was in Dallas that day."

"An alibi isn't always the truth," I said.

He thought about this.

"I don't know where he got the gun," he said.

"But you told him to use it," I said.

"Why would I do that?"

"Because you work for KBR," I said. "Because they wanted Seagram dead. You found him on the train and you—pushed him into being a part of this."

Absently, he took the wet paper towel and used it to wipe down the sink basin.

"After my boy died," he said, "I asked to be sent to the front. In front of the front. As dark and as deep as they could jam me. The day they buried my son I was a hundred miles behind enemy lines, crawling in the dirt. Me and six guys. We grew beards and wore traditional clothing. We carried knives and had to drink our own piss. Not all the time, but enough."

"Why were you on that train?" I said. "You and Cobb."

I used Cobb's name like a weapon. I wanted him to know that I knew the details. I wasn't an amateur. This wasn't a hobby. I would save my son. I would pry the truth from his lips, no matter what.

"My wife sent me letters," he said, "but I didn't answer. I was afraid of what I'd write."

He used the wet paper towel to erase a smudge from the mirror, rubbing at a spot directly in front of his face, as if trying to erase all evidence of himself.

"I mean, how long does it take to cut up half a dozen carrots?" he said. "Slice them lengthwise or chop them into tiny pieces? What did she want me to tell her? He was a little boy who loved carrots. She was his mother. She was supposed to protect him."

"My son has an execution date," I said. "They're gonna kill him."

"In country," he said, "we communicated primarily with hand signals. English was off-limits. Somebody might hear. We lived in the mountains, places I'm not allowed to name. Six guys with knives looking for trouble. Cobb was one of them. He used to chew all the skin off his lips. He had nervous hands, but he could shoot the eye out of a potato from a mile away."

There it was. The connection. Overhead the lights flickered, stuttered.

Hoopler balled the wet towels in his hand.

He said, "These arc guys you would die for, guys you would swallow a grenade to protect, but that doesn't mean you like them. Cobb was squirrelly. He used to polish his shoelaces. I think the altitude made him partially insane. But the guy shot an RPG out of the sky with a handgun, so you learned to ignore the batshit behavior."

"Somebody stabbed him," I said. "A few months ago. Sixteen times under a freeway."

He nodded. If he was surprised by the news he didn't show it. As I watched, he dropped the used paper towel in the trash, careful not to touch the metal with his skin.

"A few missions later he catches some shrapnel, ends up with a discharge. And you think, no way is that guy gonna make it back in the real world, where you gotta get a job and pay the gas bill and remember how to turn the other cheek. It's just not gonna happen. And meanwhile, I'm in the process of joining a certain private enterprise."

"KBR."

He shrugs.

"Why fight for free?" he said. "I had skills, assets. These things have value."

I didn't respond. What did I know about it?

"It took my wife two years to divorce me," he told me. "I didn't call. I didn't write. What do you think she was waiting for?"

I felt dizzy.

"Can you—please—talk about my son?" I said. "Tell me what happened."

He stood without moving, leaning against the sink. He was a man who had learned how to be still in a place where any movement got you killed.

"You're wasting your time," he said. "This is what matters: He did it. Your son. He bought the gun. He hid it, and on the day in question, he retrieved the weapon and used it. That is what matters. That is all that matters."

"Did you tell him to do it?" I asked. "Somehow plant the idea in his head?"

"You're asking if I—what—brainwashed your kid? Planted, like, subliminal commands in his medulla oblongata? He was twenty, and aimless and—honestly?—a little fucked in the head. I joined the army when I was twenty. I was a wrecking ball in combat boots, ready to kill and die for the United States of America. The world is full of twenty-year-olds with too much in the way of balls and not enough sense. This is what young men are good for. Revolution and murder. You can't let them wander. For your kid, dropping out of school, that was a big mistake. You should have stopped that. He needed structure. He needed something concrete to believe in. Terrorist training camps are full of twenty-year-old boys with no job, no direction, no positive role models. I'm saying—living free-range, your son was a guided missile. He just needed a target."

"And you gave him one?"

He didn't smile as much as smirk, as if the breadth of my naïveté was somehow ridiculous to him.

"So now it's two years ago," he said. "Cobb goes to Germany. And they cut the shrapnel out of him and send him home. And he malfunctions big-time. The whole classic mess—drinking, drugs, large-scale mayhem. And his mother gets worried and she's looking for a way to help him, anything. And she finds some phone numbers in his book—old army buddies—and she starts calling. And like I said, even though you don't necessarily like a guy like that, he's your guy. So I talk to his mother and I say, *I'll see what I can do.* Maybe talk old Freddy into committing himself voluntarily. At least talk to a shrink.

"And so I track him down in California. He's been couch surfing, sometimes sleeping in his car. I talk to people, follow the clues, and then somebody says he's riding the trains. That maybe they heard him talking about hopping a freight train to L.A. So I climb aboard."

I felt a click in my stomach, like a bomb had just been armed.

"You're saying you were on that train looking for Cobb," I said.

"A guy's mother calls," he said. "Even if you don't want to, you beat the bushes. Because what if it was your mom, right?"

"And my son just happened to be riding the same train."

"You want it to mean something," he said. "I understand. My son choked on a carrot. The truth is, none of it means anything. It's just noise."

I felt myself losing control. I was too tired, too strung out, had been chasing this truth for too long, desperate for a miracle reprieve.

"So it's, what?" I said. "A coincidence that you just happened to work for a military contractor who would have lost a billion dollars in contracts because of Seagram's bill?"

He shrugged.

It was a fast gesture, an exaggerated feint of indifference. Looking at this anonymous man in his coveralls, I wondered if he had come here to hurt me. A former Special Forces operative, a man trained in the dark arts of human erasure. Were these the words before the bullet? The shrug before the knife? Was there a fast-acting poison, undetectable, that would soon find its way into my system? Newspapers would report that I'd died in my sleep, sitting up at the Austin airport. They would describe me as *father of convicted assassin Daniel Allen.* Or would he take me in his arms and squeeze the life from my lungs, two strangers wrestling like lovers in an empty washroom?

Even as the thought occurred to me I pushed it aside.

I said, "You want me to believe that it's a coincidence that Cobb had sniper training and you were special ops? You want me to believe that you and my son talked about the weather, or maybe if the Mets were gonna go all the way this year, and then he got off the train and assassinated a presidential candidate? I just—I want to be clear."

I saw something like sympathy in his eyes for a second.

"I get it," he said. "The truth is too hard. It's a jewelry box for children. So you want to believe that we were sent there looking for your boy. That somehow we'd been tracking him for months—a lone nut job lost in the West. Maybe we got wind of him at Vassar, watched him drop out, added his name to a list of potential patsies. And then somehow we—what? Read his mind? Saw that he was programmable? Capable of violence under the right conditions? And so the company deployed two former secret agents to brainwash him, arm the missile? And in the span of ninety minutes on a freight train we turned your son—your sweet, misguided, never-hurt-a-fly son—into something sinister, something you don't recognize anymore. Is that your theory?"

I chewed my lip. It sounded crazy but that was exactly what I was saying. I needed it to be true for my own sanity.

"They're going to execute him," I said.

He thought about it.

"Let me say this," he said. "Even if it were true, even if I said something to him on that train, gave him a push—I didn't, but I'm saying, even if I did—so what? Even if he was a pawn, a pawn is still playing the game. I'm saying even the best scenario is still bad. You can't make a good person do bad things. You can't change who they are fundamentally in the time it takes to eat a sandwich. That's science fiction. The only thing that can change who we are is life."

"What are you saying?"

"I'm saying, once you realize that there was no second shooter, that nobody else pulled the trigger, you're stuck with the truth. Which is that your son is a murderer."

I stood swaying on the white tiles, punch-drunk on rubbery legs.

"No," I said, "that's—"

"You have to stop now," he said. "You have the truth. Your son is guilty. That's all you need to know."

"No. I need more."

"What? You want to know the reason he pulled the trigger? To understand it? What made him do it? Who is he really, deep down inside? But don't you see? Understanding the reason makes killing *reasonable*. You're looking for justification that somehow, some way, your son did something noble. Or if not noble, at least relatable. But he didn't. And you have to accept that. You will never understand him."

I thought about this. My pulse was booming in my ears. Was that what I was trying to do, explain my son's actions so I could excuse them? So that I could make him the hero in a story where he was really the villain?

A man stands in a crowd listening to a speech about hope. He raises a handgun and pulls the trigger, and, in that moment, extinguishes hope for everyone. Who is that man, if not a monster? Do we really need to know his reasons? Read his manifesto? If understanding him makes what he did seem right, justifies it, even for a moment, then doesn't that make the very act of understanding obscene?

"Why did you come here?" I asked.

"Because I had a son," he said, "and he choked on a carrot. And it's time to let it go."

My knees felt weak. I felt a sudden urge to grab him, hold on to him, like a boxer who is tired of being hit, who is suddenly too tired to stand. But I didn't. The gulf between us was too great.

"Good luck to you," he said.

And with that he walked out of the bathroom. I felt a cold panic tightening in my throat. He was lying. He had to be. There had to be more to it than coincidence. Three men on a train, thrown together by fate. I hurried out after him and caught a glimpse of his back as he headed toward the exit. I looked around, desperately. A man in a TSA uniform was leaning against a wall, talking on his cell phone. I hurried over.

"Hey," I said. "I just—in the bathroom—there was—I saw a man in a janitor's uniform carrying a gun."

The guard hung up the phone. I pointed toward the exit. Hoopler had reached the top of the stairs. He was heading toward baggage claim.

The guard took out his walkie-talkie. He started after Hoopler. I followed. I was sweating, my breath coming in gasps. *To explain is to excuse*. We reached the stairs just as Hoopler reached the bottom.

To understand the murderer makes murder reasonable.

Hoopler was ten steps from freedom when three TSA agents converged on him, guns drawn. They shouted at him to get down on the ground. Hoopler stopped, raised his hands, and turned.

And it wasn't Hoopler. It was another middle-aged man with a hangdog face wearing gray coveralls, his face frozen with fear. A janitor. It was just a janitor.

Hoopler was gone.

And in that moment I finally accepted it.

Daniel was guilty.

Hoopler was right. Murray was right. Fran was right.

The diagnosis was clear, had always been clear.

A man smuggles a gun into an auditorium and uses it to kill another man. There are witnesses, photographs. The man even confesses to the crime.

The symptoms were irrefutable. The conclusion was clear.

He was guilty, and so was I.

I had been a bad father, selfish, neglectful. I had sacrificed my son for my career. I had abandoned him and moved across the country. I had put my needs ahead of his, and he had suffered because of it.

It was time to stop fighting, to stop looking for loopholes.

The only thing left was to find a way to live with myself.

June 16, 20___. The event was very close now, only hours away. He had been in Los Angeles for eight days. Jorge's cousin, Mexican Bob, got him a job smoothing tar on a hot roof. For the better part of a week Carter got up before dawn and tied a handkerchief around his mouth like a Wild West train robber. He waited on the curbside in East L.A. with all the other migrant workers. At 5:45 a.m. a purple pickup truck pulled up, and Carter and the others climbed into the back. If you listened closely you could hear coyotes howling in the hills, stirring up the dogs. He felt very close to the end now, the way you feel when the word you have been searching for finally finds your tongue. On his first day tarring roofs, he bought a pair of gloves from another man in the truck, trading his watch for them.

It was on this corner in the predawn that he had first learned that Senator Jay Seagram, the Democratic presidential front-runner, was coming to Los Angeles. A newspaper headline peeked up from the gutter. SEAGRAM TO VISIT UCLA. Carter grabbed the paper off the street. He read the article under the yellow streetlight. Seagram would lead a rally at Royce Hall on June 16. Carter asked one of the Mexicans where UCLA was.

"West side," the guy said. "Just look for all the *aguayon torneados* driving BMWs."

That afternoon after work he took the bus to Westwood, riding along congested city streets with the blacks, the Chinese, and the Mexicans. He watched the city pass in measurements of blocks. Unlike the rest of the country, every car he saw was European, and the drivers, well, as far as he could tell, they were all *testículos* in their fancy cars, yelling into their hands-free phones. Somewhere around Beverly Hills he began to feel nauseous, but he couldn't tell if this was from the ride or the view. After the emptiness of the West, the snarled streets of L.A. were like a machine that dispenses medicine. Each car was a pill, an ampoule, passing through sickened blood.

The bus dropped him at the corner of Wilshire and Westwood. He walked north past Peet's Coffee and Urban Outfitters. The streets were filled with students searching for cheap meals. Carter was still in his work clothes, tar-stained jeans and a sweaty brown T-shirt. His sneakers had warped in the heat of the black sludge he'd laid down, their soles melting into gaps and nodules that gave his gait a rolling, unpracticed quality. He smelled like the inside of a smoker's lung.

North of Le Conte, he left the city streets and entered the tree-lined roads of the campus, passing pink-hued stone buildings. A couple of coeds pointed him toward Royce Hall. They called him *Pigpen* in a way that made him think that one or both of them would have slept with him if he had applied a little pressure, the way you bear down to open a jar. He thanked them and left them unsatisfied, flirting with his back. He saw the Romanesque towers of Royce Hall before he found the building, built in 1929. Students lay on the lawn out front, girls in bikinis, boys in surfer shorts throwing Frisbees. The sound of the fountain reached him before he saw the water, that irregular splatter of liquid. The sun was falling behind the trees to his right. Looking up at the towers, he thought of another tower, this one in Austin, from which one man had taken the lives of sixteen men, women, and children, dropping them one by one by one. He felt a synchronicity from this that went beyond architecture, the way a puzzle piece feels when it clicks into place.

He found flyers for Seagram's visit posted on a bulletin board in the lobby. There was a picture of the man with his arms up in the air, a sign of triumph, victory. Standing there, Carter could feel the pulse in his throat. He had to get out of the building before what he was thinking climbed up his throat and out of his mouth. But when he tried to move, he discovered that his melted shoes were stuck to the floor.

The next day he stood on the roof with the Mexicans and poured cold water over his head. It was ninety-five degrees in the shade. The Mexicans were used to the sun, but Carter felt dizzy standing three stories above the ground, cooked from below by the molten sludge. Around him the skyline was wavy from the heat, making the city itself appear to be a mirage. Not for the first time he wished he was back in Iowa, sitting in a watering trough, the smell of fertilizer stinging his eyes.

He considered what he had to do. It was a simple thing, really. Point, aim, shoot. Last month he had spent a few hours at the shooting range. He knew he could hit the target. Last night he'd chosen the gun. An STI Trojan 9-mm he'd bought at a pawnshop in Long Beach. Lucky's. This, too, was a sign. He was bunking with Mexican Bob at this point, sleeping on a cot in the laundry room of a two-bedroom house the Mexicans had tricked out to sleep twelve. After everyone went to bed Carter took out the gun and cleaned it, checking the firing pin. He loaded it with 147-grade Winchester Silvertips. The gun had a thinner grip than he liked, but it was said to be pinpoint accurate up to fifteen yards, and he'd had good luck with it at the range. Holding it in his right hand he thought about Bonnie Kirkland, and how she'd told him to steady his hand when firing, to bend his knees and hold his breath. He thought about John Hinckley dropping into a shooter's crouch on Connecticut Avenue. He figured it wouldn't be hard to hit a man on a stage, especially if he was standing in a spotlight, as he assumed Seagram would be. Two shots, three to be safe, then . . . what? Surrender? Drop the gun and run?

If he had emotions about the idea, he didn't show them. The time for emotions had passed. They were a sinkhole, if the time he'd spent in Montana was any indication, a feedback loop, growing stronger with each regeneration. Sitting on the cot he thought about something his father had told him once, how a doctor has to put aside his emotions when trying to diagnose a patient. The only thing he should consider are the facts. This is what Carter tried to focus on now, the facts.

Fact #1—Carter Allen Cash was a wolf, not a sheep. This meant he could act when others hesitated. It was his nature.

Fact #2—The candidate was a fraud. He presented himself as a hero, but in truth he was a liar.

Fact #3—Ordinary people had been fooled by the candidate.

Fact #4—If the candidate was allowed to win the election, then ordinary people would suffer.

Fact #5—Carter Allen Cash had to stop the candidate.

Fact #6—The only way to stop the candidate was to kill him.

He sat on his cot and loaded the gun, bullet by bullet, pushing them into the cartridge with his thumb. The next day he brought a change of clothes to work. The gun was rolled up in a T-shirt at the bottom of his duffel. At four o'clock he stripped off his top and washed himself with a hose, changing in the Porta-Potty. Before he left the orange plastic shitter, he ran his hand over the reassuring bulk of the T-shirt-wrapped gun at the bottom of his duffel. When he came out, Mexican Bob said he and the other *cabróns* were going for some *cervezas* and *putas* on Whittier. Did Carter feel like getting wicked *borracho*? He shook his head, saying he had plans with a girl lined up already, over at the college.

On the bus, he held the duffel bag with both hands. He watched an Asian woman scold her daughter, the girl's head bowed submissively, accepting the mother's rebuke. In addition to the gun, he had a roll of duct tape he had stolen from the job site that afternoon.

Back on campus he walked the tree-lined streets, looking like every other student. He wore a burnt-orange-and-white baseball cap, the Longhorn symbol prominently displayed over the bill. He accepted the jeers of the frat boys without reaction. *Go back to Texas, pussy.* Inside Royce Hall he looked for a place to hide the gun. He knew from working the campaign that Secret Service agents would seal off the building at least two days before the speech. If he didn't plant the gun ahead of time, the metal detectors would catch it. He'd never make it inside the hall.

He considered taping the gun under a seat in the main auditorium, but figured the agents would look there. Plus there was no guarantee he would be able to sit in the seat he'd chosen when the day came. Trying not to look suspicious, he examined the air vents and molding but found nothing. The auditorium itself was a bust. He walked up the carpeted aisle and back into the main hall. It was there he noticed the fire extinguishers set inside recessed boxes in the wall. This struck him as the perfect place to hide a weapon. But he would need to choose a box that was out of the way. He surveyed the first floor before climbing the stairs to the second. There, he found a box near the men's room, at the end of a dead-end hallway. It was perfect. He looked around to make sure no one was coming, then unlatched the glass door. He bent quickly, unzipped the duffel. He pulled out the T-shirt and the duct tape. Another quick look around, and then he was unfolding the T-shirt, unwrapping the gun.

It lay there on the blue T-shirt, vivid and oiled. The feeling it brought him was elemental. He pulled a length of tape off the roll, bit the end, tasting the bitter adhesive. He lay three strips across the right side of the gun, stood. Still nobody in sight. He reached inside the box and turned the heavy red extinguisher, then placed the gun in the center of its hard, rounded back. He added another strip of tape to be sure, then carefully rotated the fire extinguisher until the gun and tape were invisible to the naked eye. Finished, he carefully closed the glass door, bent and zipped the duffel. Straightening he saw a teenage girl at the top of the stairs. She was pasty and nondescript. He smiled at her.

"How you doing?" he said.

She smiled.

"Fine," she said. "Do you know where . . . I thought the ladies' room was up here."

His heartbeat was steady, calm.

"Other side," he told her.

Outside the sky was bluer. The grass was greener. He felt like a cook setting a timer, waiting for a roast to be done. Seeing the girl had only confirmed for him that he was on the right path. A few seconds earlier she would have seen him place the gun. A few seconds earlier she would have run back downstairs and found a guard. But instead she had arrived after he was done, and now the gun was safe, an egg waiting to hatch.

He decided to walk home. It was an eight-mile walk, down the Wilshire corridor, through Westwood, Century City, and Beverly Hills. He was a young man with nowhere to be now for four more days. He threw the duffel bag in a garbage can and started walking east, past doorman apartment buildings, past the long green curve of the Los Angeles Country Club, past the Beverly Hilton with its Oscar parties and power lunches, past the office towers of Beverly Hills, crossing the clotted artery of La Cienega. He began to feel like a dog at the airport. The rumble of cars assaulted him, jarring sounds of road rage. He entered Miracle Mile, passing the tar pits, passing Highland Avenue, zeroing in on Koreatown. In four hours he saw three pedestrians. He was a refugee, a camel in the desert. The gun kept him going. The gray tape arranged in a crisscross pattern. The thought of it hidden in plain sight. He was a spider and the tape was his web.

The sun went down—golden, rosy, then surrendering to navy—and still he walked. He was beyond hunger, beyond thirst. A month ago he had slept on the ground next to his car in the foothills of the Sierras. He had woken to the taste of dew. Now he was a wolf in the city, a forest creature in a factory of noise and steel.

The next three days were a blur of heat and tar. He woke early to do his push-ups, his sit-ups. He sat in the back of the purple pickup and felt the wind on his face, watching the sun rise between a canyon of tall buildings. This time the boss drove them to the valley, a new job site. Here it was a hundred and five degrees in the shade. The Mexicans wore long sleeves and long pants. Carter took off his shirt and stirred the pots. He climbed the ladders and spread the foul muck. He didn't feel the heat anymore. It was a test, he knew, the way the steel of a sword is tested in the forge. He drank water from plastic bottles. It didn't matter if he got burned. All that mattered was that the web stayed where he'd left it. The impulse to return to Royce Hall and make sure was like a scab he couldn't stop picking, but he restrained himself. They would be there now, the men in black suits. He had to have faith. His plan was sound. His destiny was secure. Otherwise the girl would have seen him. Otherwise she would have called for help.

Instead he stirred the hot black fudge, breathing its toxic fumes. Sometimes the poison went so deep he had to go behind a Dumpster and throw up. All that came out of him was water.

He watched the news, making sure Seagram didn't cancel. He saw footage of rallies in Michigan and Miami. A man at a podium, smiling, cheering, goading a nation to change. The act of waiting made his insides feel like they were twisted, the way laundry is wrung to dry. He couldn't stop clenching his jaw. But he did not falter. Deep down he believed in the passing of time. He had been a baby, then a boy, and now a man. He knew that tomorrow was inevitable, and yet waiting for his destiny required the patience of the sea.

Sometimes he thought about death, but not often. He knew that a gunman firing from the crowd could easily become a target himself. With this in mind, he got his affairs in order. The night before the event he laid out his clothes. He packed his few remaining possessions into a blue backpack, laying his journal on top. The Honda was parked in a lot near the Staples Center. There were two handguns in the trunk, six boxes of ammunition. If he were a religious man he would have gone to church, confessed his sins to cleanse his soul, but he wasn't, so he didn't.

Instead he woke early, after only an hour of sleep. He rose quietly and showered, stepping over sleeping Mexicans. He stood under the paltry trickle of tarnished water and made sure his armpits were clean, his groin and crack. He shaved in front of the mirror, careful not to cut himself. His hair was short, and his face and body were tan from weeks spent outdoors. He was twenty years old, with the rangy musculature of a runner.

He missed the gun, wished he had it now so he could conduct the ritual of stripping, cleaning, and loading it. He thought it might relax him. Instead he stepped over the Mexicans and got dressed, putting on jeans and a white button-down shirt. He had bought a pair of black dress shoes in Sacramento, and he put them on now, lacing them tight. Then he dropped and did a hundred push-ups, trying to burn off some of this crazy energy. He didn't even break a sweat. When he left the house, the sky was just beginning to lighten.

He walked the trash-lined streets, hands in his pockets. He stopped at the Gaylord for breakfast, sliding into a dark-red booth. The place was half empty, cabdrivers and delivery men fueling up. A few tables down sat several bleary-eyed hipsters, desperately hanging on to the last traces of night. Looking at the menu, Carter realized he couldn't remember the last meal he'd eaten. He thought of Timothy McVeigh eating two bowls of ice cream before his execution. When the waitress with the neck tattoo came over, he ordered pancakes and eggs, hash browns, and orange juice. He had five hundred dollars in his wallet. It was all the money he had left in the world. He would need three dollars to get across town on the bus. The rest he would leave as a tip, hidden under his empty plate.

Afterward, he felt drunk on calories. His belly was like that of a pregnant woman. The sun was up now, and leaving the dark restaurant he shielded his eyes from the light like a vampire. It was six thirty in the morning. He had eight hours before he needed to be at UCLA. He got on the bus, heading west, and rode it to the ocean. Along the way he got used to the rhythm of traffic and may have dozed. It had been weeks since he'd slept through the night.

Stepping off the bus, he could smell the ocean breeze. The Santa Monica pier stood in the distance, Ferris wheel bald against the skyline. He walked down Ocean Avenue past the pier and angled onto the beach, past the dapper white awnings of Shutters. When the police searched him later they would find sand in his shoes. He stood in the shade and watched the volleyball players, boys in knee-length trunks and women in jogging bras, spiking the bone-white ball into the sand.

There was something about the blue relief of water stretching into forever that relaxed him for the first time in days. He took off his shoes and walked down to the water's edge. There was a gun waiting for him in Westwood, a twenty-four-ounce hammer of metal, mechanized and deadly. Standing there, feeling the foam bubble around his toes, he realized that this was his prayer. The ocean. He was a man in a mosque, bowing toward Mecca, readying himself for the mission to come.

As soon as it had come, the relaxation he had felt disappeared under a wave of intestinal urgency. His system, unused to food in such quantities, had decided to rebel. He hurried back to the street, ducked into a taco restaurant, locking the bathroom door behind him. He voided his breakfast in seven great surges, enduring the pounding of other patrons. Outside he felt light-headed. The sand in his shoes shifted and bunched. He walked east into Santa Monica, passing the promenade. He had grown up near here. The woman he sometimes referred to as his mother lived on Twelfth Street, just north of Montana. He pictured her home now, sitting with her coffee and *The New York Times*. He had promised to call when he got to town, but he hadn't. He felt as much allegiance to her now as he did to the homeless in their bumzebos. The son she knew had vanished somewhere in the Texas Hill Country.

He kept walking. It was what he was now, a pilgrim. He reached the campus around one. A crowd was already gathering, police barricades set up outside the hall to direct the flow of traffic. He saw the girls who had called him Pigpen standing near the front of the line. He worked his way toward them.

"I clean up okay, right?" he asked them.

They were happy to see him. It was one of those callback moments that young people mistake for fate. He was a handsome, clean-shaven young man with a rich tan wearing a clean white shirt. He introduced himself as Carter. The blonde said her name was Cindy. The brunette was Abbey. He asked them where they were from.

"I'm from Albuquerque," said Cindy.

"Montana," said Abbey.

Carter told them he had just come from Montana. He said he'd spent the winter up there.

"Doing what?" they wanted to know.

He told them he'd been studying wildlife. He was going to be a naturalist. The girls thought that sounded cool. Carter told them that before that he'd worked for Seagram in Austin. The girls wanted to know if he'd met the man.

"A few times," he told them.

Cindy suggested that Carter go in with them. They were supposed to meet some friends, but maybe they could all hang together. Did Carter think the senator would remember him? Carter said he did, suggesting that the three of them might even get backstage to say hello. This seemed to animate them, and they squealed and chattered rapidly. Carter checked out security at the main entrance. He saw six campus security guards and five Los Angeles police officers in uniform. Looking deeper, he saw two men in black suits standing near a metal detector at the front door.

At two forty-five, a guard removed the barrier and the crowd surged forward. Carter stuck close to the girls. They showed their IDs at the door, emptied their pockets, and stepped through the metal detector one at a time. Inside the girls tried to remember where they were supposed to meet their friends. Cindy decided they should head in and grab seats before the good ones were all gone. Carter told them to save him one. He had to go to the men's room. He climbed the stairs, hand on the railing, feeling electricity shoot up his arm, as if the banister were the third rail in a subway tunnel. On the second floor he saw more guards standing at the balcony doors. He walked past them, heading for the restrooms, then stopped. There was a police officer standing near the bathroom. The gun was in a box three feet behind him. Carter considered turning back but didn't. He walked past the cop, entered the men's room. It was empty. He felt the urge to urinate but didn't. Instead he washed his hands, dried them, then washed them again, trying to figure out what to do. He settled on a lie about overhearing some students plotting to sneak in through a side entrance. He would approach the officer and try to manipulate him into leaving his post. It felt wrong. Too ambitious. There was fear in his belly.

But the cop was gone when he left the bathroom. The feeling he had on discovering this was that of a man who realizes that God is his accomplice. For a brief moment the hall was empty. He took six fast steps to the extinguisher and opened the door. He reached behind the extinguisher. The gun was still there. He fumbled at the tape, knowing that at any minute the cop would return or a dozen students would pour into the hall.

He was sweating by the time he freed the pistol. He tore off the tape, balling it and dropping it back into the well behind the extinguisher. The gun was sticky with adhesive residue, but he didn't care. He slipped it into the small of his back, feeling it tug at the hairs there. Then he closed the glass door and started for the stairs. He was just starting to descend when he saw the officer heading up toward him. Carter smiled and nodded, feeling the stairs rise to meet him.

He entered the auditorium through the center doors. It was already half full. He could see security guards manning the exits and lining the stage. Music was playing over the PA system. The song was "What Light" by Wilco. Carter blended into the crowd. The gun in his back was like a power source feeding his heart. He had heard this song before, in Austin, the day Seagram had addressed the crowd at Auditorium Shores. The synchronicity of this was another green light. Amazing. It was clear to him now. He was born to do this.

He thought about the day he had left Vassar, the unnameable pull that had woken him from his slumber, the certainty that he needed to be lost to find himself. He had followed the feeling. He had seen the country. He had driven its febrile core. He had seen the hand of God as it tore asunder Iowa farmland, had lain in the spring-fed pools of Texas. He had waded through the waist-deep snows of Montana, ridden the steel-brown rails. All of the things he had done were training. He could see that now. He had had to get away, to truly lose himself in the silence of wild isolation in order to find clarity. How else was he supposed to hear anything in the clutter of everyday life?

The hall was full. The Wilco song ended and the familiar opening of the Smashing Pumpkins song "Today" kicked in. The lights dropped. The crowd surged to its feet.

Today is the greatest
Day I've ever known.
Can't wait for tomorrow.
Tomorrow's much too long.

As a child, he had fallen from the sky. He had that same feeling now in his belly. He worked his way into the pit. They were elbow to elbow, the youth of America, its future, standing on their feet, hands in the air, letting the moment overtake them. The stage lights came up. The heavy guitars pounded the balcony. Senator Jay Seagram walked onto the stage.

And though he could not see the future, Carter Allen Cash knew exactly what would happen next.

BOY

Bonnie Kirkland was bald. It was the chemotherapy, she told me. Her hair had fallen out last month and she was losing weight. Her skin was papery, tinged yellow. There was a blue kerchief around her head. We were sitting in her kitchen. Her husband, Ted, was at the store, closing up. It was late afternoon. I had rung the bell fifteen minutes earlier. Bonnie had answered, wiping her hands on a dish towel. Her condition took me off guard. I could see it immediately in the sallowness of her cheeks, the way the skin clung to her skull. It was a clear day, the kind you should spend lying in the grass and breaking clouds apart with your mind. I had landed in Des Moines that morning and rented a two-door Ford. The tan passenger-seat fabric was torn and patched. Despite a sign that read NO SMOKING, the car stank of cigarettes. I unfolded the map the clerk had sold me and headed east. The state was astonishingly flat, and voluptuously green. Cows and cornfields lined the interstate.

I called Fran from the road. I told her I was sorry. That I'd lied to her. I explained where I was, what I'd done. I said I knew I'd been a bad husband. I'd kept secrets. I'd been selfish. But I was finally ready to accept the truth, which was that Daniel was guilty. That somewhere, somehow he'd fallen apart and no one had been there to fix him, and now it was too late. I told her that I knew I had to accept it, to accept that I'd been a bad father to him, but that I had a new family now, a wife I loved and two beautiful boys, and I wasn't going to make the same mistake twice.

I told her I was coming home. That I just had one more stop, and then I would put it all away. I would come back to them, and be the kind of husband and father they deserved.

After I finished there was a long silence. I stood in a gas-station parking lot watching a cornfield shiver in the wind. It was noon exactly. I was a man who wanted nothing more than to make amends, to fix what he had broken, and to learn to live with the things that were beyond repair.

And then, after an endless silence, she said one word:

"Okay."

And in that moment I knew we would survive.

"I love you," I said.

"Yeah," she said. "I know you do. We love you, too. Come home soon."

I climbed back into my rental car and started the engine. On the radio, the DJ said, "This one goes out to everyone who's ever missed someone."

He played "Gimme Shelter" by the Rolling Stones. I rolled the windows down and let the warm air rush over me.

The Kirklands lived on Lackender Avenue, at the end of a long gravel driveway. I climbed from the Ford, stepping out into the midday sun, my back protesting after hours of sitting. After spending the night at the airport I needed to go for a run, to stretch. Instead I walked to the front door and climbed the creaky wooden steps. And then Bonnie Kirkland was standing in front of me in her blue kerchief. I told her who I was, the father of the boy who had lived over their garage for three months. She told me she knew just by looking at me.

"You have his face," she told me, and invited me in.

We drank sweet tea at a small wooden table between two doors. A ceiling fan spun lazily overhead. The sky outside was cornflower blue. The kitchen windows were open and a light breeze blew in through the screens. I was still wearing my gray suit. It was all I had. My suitcase was at the hotel in Austin, abandoned. There was nothing in there I would ever need again. I asked Bonnie how long ago she'd been diagnosed with cancer.

"Last fall," she said. "Around the time your boy pleaded guilty."

It was pancreatic cancer, she said. The doctors were not optimistic. They had removed a tumor and given her two courses of chemo and radiation, but pancreatic cancer is notoriously fatal. Only 5 percent of patients live for five years. Most die in months. I told her I knew a world-renowned oncologist who'd had success with focused radiation.

"I'd be happy to call him," I told her.

She shook her head. "It is what it is," she said. "Going to New York isn't going to change that."

"No," I said, "but there are new treatments being developed all the time. Clinical trials."

She thanked me, but insisted she had made her peace with it.

"It's a funny thing. I think Ted is scareder than me. I'm determined to embrace it. I'd like to have a May death. May's a good month for those kinds of things—weddings, babies, funerals."

"People are always more optimistic in the spring," I said.

"I find I'm seeing things differently now, patterns in the corn. The ground smells sweeter. I'm noticing textures, the way the shower curtain feels on my fingertips, the way a raisin feels on my tongue."

We heard footsteps on the stairs and looked over. A girl of about twenty appeared.

"Dr. Allen," said Bonnie, "this is my daughter, Cora. She dated your boy for a bit at school."

Cora was a pretty girl with broad shoulders. What they used to call a farm girl. It was a strange thing to watch Cora realize who I was, to do the math: Dr. Allen plus father of a boy she used to date. When she added it up, her normally open face shut down quickly, anger coming into her eyes.

"You can't be here," she said. "We don't want you here."

I stood.

"I'm sorry," I said.

"Cora," Bonnie snapped. "Don't be rude. We don't treat people that way in this family."

"But, Mom," she said.

"No," said Bonnie. "That boy was a good boy. I don't care what they say he did. And his father has shown us the kindness of a visit. If you can't be civil, then please go back upstairs."

Cora kept her eyes on me, the way you watch a snake so it won't slip into the shadows and come at you from a different angle.

"The doctor said my mother needs to rest," she said.

"I won't stay long," I told her. "I just needed to see this place, to meet your family. I have a family, too, a wife and two young boys. Separate from Daniel. I didn't want to leave them to come here, but I had to. The not knowing is worse. I had to see the place, to meet the people who took my son in. But I promise, I'm only going to stay as long as it takes me to drink this tea."

I touched my glass, holding her eye. I could see fear in there but also great sadness.

"You stay as long as you like," Bonnie said. "Cora, why don't you get some tea, and join us?"

For the first time Cora looked away. Her mouth was a straight line.

"No," she said. "I'm going out."

She grabbed her car keys off the counter, took two steps toward the door, then stopped, turned.

"He was a lie," she told me. "You thought he was just lost, but he was a lie. And we believed him."

"I know," I said. "But he's sorry. He doesn't say it, but I can see it in him. He didn't do this to hurt the people he loves."

"Why else would he do it?" she said, as if I was stupid, and left.

I stood in silence for a moment, listening to the whir of the fan.

"She's wrong," Bonnie said. "He was a sweet boy."

I looked at her. The thing about chemotherapy most people don't realize is it's not losing the hair on your head that makes you an alien, it's the eyebrows, the lashes. Without these markers, the face becomes something other than human. Some people, women mostly, choose to draw their brows back on with a makeup pencil, but Bonnie had left her face raw. It was the sign of someone who had surrendered her vanity, who had come to accept the direction her life had taken.

"Thank you," I told her, sitting. "No one has said anything nice about my son in a long time."

She stirred her tea.

"Cora feels responsible for Daniel coming here," she said. "She says she *exposed* us to him, like the boy was some kind of flu."

"You said he just showed up one day," I said.

Bonnie nodded.

"We thought he was lost, a city kid looking for directions. But he told Ted he wanted a job, and then he said he knew Cora. Looking back, I guess it wasn't that smart to take him in, a strange kid from another part of the world, but back then it seemed only Christian."

"I didn't even know he'd dropped out," I told her. "For maybe three weeks, until the dean called to ask why Daniel hadn't been in class."

"With Cora we prayed she wouldn't turn into one of those terrible teenagers they warn you about. We were lucky."

"No," I said. "You raised her right. Daniel's mother and I, we got divorced when he was young. He spent his childhood flying back and forth between us, like a tennis ball. I didn't think it bothered him that much, but clearly . . ."

She coughed into a napkin. With each cough color came back to her face, but it was only temporary.

"You never know with kids," she said. "My daddy used to hit me and my brother. It was expected back then. Normal. You spoke out of turn, you got the belt. You broke curfew, you got the belt. I never felt damaged by it."

"He was a good worker?" I asked. "My son."

"He was. Conscientious, reliable. And he got along real good with the Mexicans, which surprised us. Well, not surprised, but they're a pretty close-knit group. Sometimes I'd look out the window and they'd all be out back horsing around. It made me feel good, to think he was fitting in, that maybe he'd finally found a place. It was so obvious he was looking for that."

The kitchen door opened and Ted Kirkland entered, kicking his work boots off on the rough rope mat.

"Hello," he said, surprised to see a stranger at his table.

"Honey, this is Daniel's father."

The smile died on Ted's face, but he recovered quickly.

"Well, think of that," he said.

He wiped his hand on his jeans and stuck it out.

"Ted Kirkland," he said.

We shook. His hands were rough, notched like old wood. I wondered what he thought of mine.

Bonnie got up to get Ted a glass of tea.

"You don't have to do that," he said.

"Hush now," she told him. "How was work?"

"They sent us the wrong boots again," he said, washing his hands at the sink. "Third time this month. I'm beginning to suspect that Lambry hired that girl for her looks, not her brains."

Bonnie put another glass of tea on the table, sat heavily. Ted dried his hands on a towel and sat next to his wife, putting a protective hand on her arm. I watched them for a moment, a man who had loved his wife for forty years, a wife who would be dead in months. I could see from his face that he didn't know how to let her go, and it was destroying him.

"Listen," I said, "I wanted to apologize."

"For what?" Ted asked.

"For my son. For that moment when you turned on the TV and saw his face. For realizing the kind of boy you'd invited into your house. It's taken me a long time to come to terms with what he did. If I have. And I wanted you to know that his mother and I, we never suspected he was capable of that kind of . . . violence. If we had, we would have kept him home. We would have watched him closely, instead of losing track of him, which is what happened."

I found I couldn't look at them. I wanted it to be true, what I said, but I wasn't sure. After all, hadn't we known, deep down, that any child left unsupervised was going to get into trouble? Isn't that the point of parenting, to watch them closely, if only to ensure the child knows they are loved?

"Mr. Allen," said Ted, "I appreciate your coming here. I can only imagine the kind of burden you've been carrying around, but you don't have to apologize to me or anyone. Your son did what he did. Him and only him. People blame their parents for everything anymore, but it's just an excuse. Your son was a grown man, not experienced, but old enough to know better. This was not a schoolyard lesson you forgot to teach him, unless you never told him 'Thou shalt not kill.' "

"No," I said. "We told him that."

"Well then, there you have it. He was a smart kid. He had a good handshake and a ready smile, and he was strong where it mattered. I've known a lot of men in my life, and your son struck me as one of the better ones."

Next to him Bonnie had started to cry, not dramatically, but with quiet sadness. She may not even have realized she was doing it.

"We begged him to stay," she said. "At least until Christmas. He seemed happy here, and I didn't understand why he would want to leave. Why he'd want to go someplace he didn't know anyone, where nobody cared about him."

"I think that was where he was from," I said. "He grew up on airplanes.

I don't think he ever felt settled or safe. We tried, but divorce is a kind of hypocrisy, and kids are smart. They know the difference between the life you promise them and the life they have."

We thought about that for a minute. I thought about my son in his cell. Why didn't he ever complain about the food, or the treatment, or the fact that he was trapped now, waiting for the footsteps that would walk him to his death? Unless he felt he deserved these things. Unless he believed he was exactly where he was supposed to be.

"Well, if you won't let me apologize," I said, "at least let me thank you. You took my son in. You were good to him, and he loved you for it. Maybe more than he loved his actual parents. And I'm glad for that, glad that he found two people he knew he could rely on."

Bonnie looked at Ted. She had an expression on her face, a pleading look. Ted nodded, *go ahead.*

"He called us," she said. "The week it happened. Maybe two days before."

I tried to process this. My son, who, at that point in his journey, I hadn't spoken to in weeks, had called Ted and Bonnie Kirkland two days before he murdered a man.

"What did he say?" I managed.

"He said he was in California. He'd been all over, Texas, Montana. He told us he'd seen the spot where that lady tried to shoot President Ford in Sacramento, which I thought was weird. He said he was good, except sometimes he forgot to eat. I told him we all missed him. I said Cora would be home in a few days and maybe he should come back for a visit. I told him the Mexicans asked about him. He thought that was great. He asked me to tell them *Me cago en la leche* from him."

"What does it mean?"

"I told Jorge that Daniel had said it, and he started laughing. He said it meant something like 'I've had bad luck,' except not as polite."

I've had bad luck. Was there meaning there? Or just a joke?

"I told Daniel he had to remember to eat. Did he need me to send him some more cookies? He said no. He'd be okay. He said he was in Los Angeles. I knew his mother was there, so I made him promise he'd call her. I told him that all mothers worried about their children. He didn't want to be a bad son. He said he would. I told him a little bit about how things were here, which was the same. Ted was working too much. Cora was doing good in school."

"Did he say anything else? Anything about . . ."

I couldn't finish, but I didn't have to. Bonnie shook her head.

"No. He said he'd been doing some roofing, that he was bunking with some Mexicans from the job site. And then I heard him cover the mouthpiece and talk to somebody else. Just a few words, and then he came back on to tell me he had to go."

"Do you know what he said?"

"No. It was something like *Just a minute.* I told him to call me next week when Cora was home. I said she'd get a kick out of talking to him. He promised he would. And that was it."

"Nothing else?"

She shook her head. Her eyes were droopy. It was clear the conversation had taken a lot out of her. Ted noticed.

"Why don't you go into the living room and lie down?" he told her.

She nodded.

"I'm sorry," she said. "I don't think I knew what tired was until this."

I watched her look over at her husband. It wouldn't be long before she stopped getting out of bed. Her strength was leaving her day by day, her will.

"You should eat more ice cream," I told her.

"Will that help?"

"No, but it's time to do the things you love. Do you understand?"

A beat. She nodded. I could tell from her expression that she did. Death. I was talking about death.

"I don't," said Ted. "What does he mean?"

She patted her husband's cheek. Her look said it all, and I could see him swallow hard.

"I'm going to go and let you rest," I said, standing.

Bonnie took my hand.

"It was good meeting you," she said.

"I'm glad. Please tell your daughter that I said goodbye."

I pulled my hand back, but she held on.

"Tell your boy," she said, "tell him I'll be waiting. Tell him not to be afraid. We are all of us going someplace wonderful, and he won't be alone much longer."

I nodded. There were tears running down my face.

Walking me to the front door, Ted said, "You know, she sold all her guns after it happened."

"Her guns."

"She collected them. Bonnie took Daniel shooting a few times, out in the country. She believes everyone should know how to handle a firearm. After he killed that man she said she couldn't look at them anymore. She wanted them out of our house. So I packed them up and took them to a gun show, made almost ten thousand dollars. I wanted to use the money to buy a new front loader for the store, but Bonnie said no. She said we had to give the money away. So we gave it to Greenpeace."

He opened the door. The bright Iowa sun blinded me for a moment. Ted put his hand out.

"Get home safe," he said.

I nodded. There was so much I wanted to say, but he was not a man who wanted to talk about these things with strangers.

"Make her comfortable," I said. "And then, afterward, change everything. You won't be the same once she's gone."

He nodded.

"She's the best person I ever knew," he said.

Outside, I climbed into my rental car, with its bitter cigarette stink, and fumbled for the keys. Tears were pouring down my face, and it was all I could do to put the car in gear and drive away, wheels spinning gravel. I drove until I couldn't see anymore through the tears, and then pulled over to the side of the road and wept for the first time in years, truly wept, a man in a car that was not his own, in a state to which he had never been, parked on an anonymous stretch of road, weeping, trying to catch his breath, making animal sounds, beating the hard plastic of the steering wheel.

When it passed, when I became aware of other sounds, of a world outside my own grief, I found I had parked beside a willow tree, next to a long stone wall. I got out of the car. The sun was hanging on the edge of the horizon. My legs felt weak. My arms were heavy. I had a jagged, swollen feeling in my throat. The willow stood beside a small cemetery. Grave markers stretched out in a lazy rectangle below a gently sloping hillside. The afternoon sun threw long shadows against the thick green grass. Looking at the gravestones, I knew that this was where Bonnie

Kirkland would be buried, in the cemetery that had stood near her house for a hundred years. For her, death wouldn't be that long a journey after all. A mile, maybe, a short walk down a gentle road.

I thought of my son on his bicycle riding past this place, the wind in his hair, his face tan, his body lean, his soul fat with the loam of good work. I pictured a smile on his face, a smile he didn't even know he was wearing. They would execute him soon, six months from now, December 14, a week before Christmas. A Wednesday. He would be led down a long hallway in an orange jumpsuit. Prison guards would lay him on a table and slip a needle into his arm. I would be watching through glass from the next room. I would stand as he entered so he could see me, so he would know that I was there, that now, in this final moment, I was where I should have been all along. By his side.

I would watch as they strapped him down, knowing that never again after I witnessed his death would I ever smile with real joy or laugh with true humor. I would watch as they asked if he had any last words and see him shake his head. There had been too many words already. He had said all he wanted. His eyes would be clear, his body relaxed. I would want to break through the glass and fight them all, to pull the needle from his arm, but I wouldn't. We had come to this place, he and I, and there was nothing we could do about it. It was the last stop on the journey.

Once he had been a newborn boy who drank from his mother's breast. He had learned to speak, to say *Dada* and *Mama*. They were the first words he spoke every morning, calling to us from his crib. He was a child who could not wait to see what the new day would bring, what new wonders. A boy who smiled with pure and unmitigated happiness every time he saw my face, who charged me, hands outstretched, diving into my arms. He was the reason I had been born, my mission. But soon he would be lying on a table surrounded by men in uniforms. And I, his father, would be watching from the next room as they stepped away, as they manned their machines, as they tilted the table back to flat.

There are things in this world that no human being should be able to endure. We should die of heartbreak, but we do not. Instead, we are forced to survive, to bear witness.

They would tilt the table back and press a button, and the chemicals would begin to flow, death in liquid form. I had seen it as a doctor a thousand times, the way the breathing slows and the color disappears from the skin. You start to count. Each breath is farther apart, each pause that much longer than the last. The body becomes still. That person you knew, his expressions, his gestures, the sound of his voice, that person whose identity was imbedded in every cell and follicle, dissipates. He takes a breath and you wait, but this time the pause is eternal. Life vanishes.

After he died we would bury him here, in a tiny graveyard in the last place on earth he had ever been happy. We would fly his body to Iowa, and stand around it on a dapper winter day. There would be no songs, no psalms, no sermons. The sun would hide its face behind the clouds.

I stood beside a cemetery in Iowa. In my bones was the ache of unrelenting burden. A wind kicked up, blowing through the willow tree with a shimmer that sounded like rain on the water. It was time to stop fighting. There would be no appeal, no last-minute stay. I would finally do what my son had asked, what he had been asking me to do all along.

I would let him go.

Acknowledgments

For their faith, passion, and guidance I would like to thank my agent, Susan Golomb, and my editor, Alison Callahan. To my father, Thomas Hawley, who taught me what it means to be a good father, all I can say is you are missed every day. And to my bonus father and mother, Mike and Trudy, I want to say thank you for taking me in and showing me that we are stronger with families than we are without. To Kyle, my wife, who supports me and gives my life meaning, thank you. You have made me a better man.

And to Guinevere, my Guinevere, for whom anything that happened in the past happened "last weekend," and who insists on growing up no matter how hard we try to stop her—thanks for letting me be your dad.

You make me want to live forever.

About the Author

Noah Hawley is the author of three previous novels, including *The Punch* and *A Conspiracy of Tall Men*. He created and ran the ABC television shows *The Unusuals* and *My Generation* and wrote the film *Lies & Alibis*. Hawley's short fiction has appeared in *The Paris Review*. He currently splits his time between Los Angeles and Austin, Texas, where he lives with his wife and daughter.